KOLBY RAE

Kolby Rae
Author: F.R."Fritz" Nordengren

Published in the United States by Two Mile Ranch
ISBN-13: 978-0990324102
ISBN-10: 0990324109

Dedicated to the music maker, writer, and lover in all of us.

PART ONE
CARAVAN TO CROSSINGS

CHAPTER ONE

ANOTHER DRIVE CHASING STARS

"ARE WE THERE YET?"

The question came from the backseat of the black SUV as it cruised up and down the hills that led out of town, past the only gas station and convenience store any of the passengers had seen since crossing the county line. The voice was punctuated with a comic lilt and accented with enough of his native Norwegian to make the others laugh out loud as their headlights lit up the road.

"He's touching me," replied a melodic, Cuban-accented voice from the other side of the backseat. The driver and front-seat passenger looked at each other with tired but appreciative glances. When he returned his eyes to the rearview mirror, the driver challenged the men behind him. "If you don't cut that out"—he paused for dramatic effect—"right now"—a second dramatic pause brought smirks from the backseat—"I'm turning this car around, and we're all going back to Nashville."

"Promise?" asked the Cuban voice.

The driver was the only one who looked like he belonged in this backwoods hill country. His grey hair was pulled back into a loose ponytail, and his Rip-Van-Winkle-length beard was peppered with enough black to suggest at one time both the beard and hair were as black as the SUV he was driving. The tattoos on both his forearms were older, the ink faded. The woman in the passenger seat had been dominating the conversation most of the trip and turned to the pair in the backseat.

"What was the name of that place?" she asked, "You know, the one with the fish in the fountain in the lobby?"

"The casino?" both men in the backseat answered in unison.

"Yeah, the casino—with the guy—and the mustache?"

"Something Isle," answered the Norwegian.

"Something Isle something something," the Cuban answered.

"Yeah, yeah, yeah, and that one room service guy kept knocking on Kolby's door, yeah. That's the place. Do you remember? I remember we had to drive down that dark, twisty road, just like this one, to get there."

"I don't think we had to. I think we were lost."

"God help us if we're lost again," the ponytailed driver said to himself, loud enough that the others nodded in agreement.

"Where was that? Illinois?"

Before she heard their answer, the brake lights on the car leading them brightened, and the three-vehicle convoy came to a rapid stop. At the roadside, a pair of deer eyes glowed. In the lead car, the newcomer and the fat man watched out the windows as the deer crossed the asphalt and vanished into the trees on the driver's side of the road.

They drove on, and the caravan returned to road speed. The Norwegian began to drum his fingers on the passenger seat headrest. He worked through eight bars of a sixteen-bar riff when the talkative woman, Kim Hartunian, turned and glared at him.

"Honest to God, Nils, you're worse than a child. Stop it."

The driver rolled his eyes. "Okay, here we go. Someone needs a cigarette."

Nils protested, "I can't help it. I miss the bus, and I hate being cramped up in here." His rapid finger drumming continued on the back of Kim's headrest.

"Cut it out."

The Norwegian mocked her command in his native language. *"Mor di svetter lite til å være så feit."*

The three men chuckled, and the woman shouted above them, "Dammit, Nils, when I find out what that means..."

On the radio, a song interrupted Kim's tirade. She reached and turned the volume up before she settled back into her seat and listened. She began to hum during the main verse and then sang along at the beginning of the chorus:

:: Dance with me, Daddy, let me dance on your shoes ::

:: Twirl me around and chase away my blues ::

From the backseat, the two men began singing with her. The three voices had both perfect pitch and rhythm as they echoed the lyrics louder:

:: I'm your angel, your princess, your daughter, your light ::

:: Dance with me, Daddy...dance with me tonight ::

The last vehicle in the caravan was a twin to the other SUV carrying the singers. The only way to tell them apart was their personalized license plates. KRAEZY held the four singers. SMILES brought up the rear and was driven by its owner, Sarah Miles. Her black, wavy hair was cinched by a leather barrette as tightly as her hands clenched the truck's steering wheel.

Behind her, with her body twisted against the door and resting one leg on the leather bench seat, her older sister was sprawled out in the glow of the overhead light, signing postcards. She finished the short note on the postcard in her lap and signed it, "Love, Kolby Rae."

Their radio played "Dance on Your Shoes," too, and at the beginning of the final verse, the postcard signer sang along:

:: You stand there so proud, about to walk me down the aisle ::

:: I saw that tear, you tried to hide it with your smile ::

:: He's a good man, Daddy, his love is so true ::

:: And I hope God forgives me when I compare him to you ::

To Sarah, the song and her sister's voice were reminders of why they were taking this remote two-lane excursion into the night. Sarah gently rocked her head with the song; Kolby Rae sounded as perfect singing the song as she had the first time she sang it on her demo disc. That was a dozen years ago, before her name change from Kolby Ruth to Kolby Rae. She wrote the song and sang it flawlessly, and the record label told her to let the woman on the radio, Sherrie Elliot, sing it. Sherrie made it a classic beyond what an unknown could ever hope to do. Nine million sales later, Sherrie, the singer, was singing in stadiums while Kolby Rae, the singer-songwriter, was in the backseat of an SUV chasing Nashville stardom following a long string of near misses with success.

"Looks like we're turning in up here," Sarah said to Kolby and pointed to a pair of reflectors marking the edges of a lane that curved around a horse pasture. They turned in and followed the others until the lane ended at a sprawling one-story house.

The SMILES SUV hung back a few car lengths in the lane as they circled in a loop in front of the entrance, and all three came to a stop. Sarah and Kolby stepped out and approached the lead car.

"Sean, this is all yours?" Sarah asked with a bit of doubt in her voice.

The newcomer, a thin man in his twenties with waist-length hair and an enthusiastic grin, was walking back from the lead car to welcome them all. "It belongs to my family. My parents live in another town where my dad works. The studio is in the basement here in the big house. There's no one to bother us, so we can work any time we want, play as loud as we like, and at night, you won't believe how close we are to the stars."

They all looked skyward.

The passenger from the lead car walked up to them. He was a round, overweight man, slightly short of breath. "C'mon kid, show me the studio. We can chitchat later."

The younger man answered, "Yes sir, Frankie," and the two men began to turn away.

Sarah was the first to see the outline of the small cabin in the dark. "What's that?"

Sean turned back to the women. "There?" He pointed at the shape in the dark. "It's a cabin. My dad built it the year I was born. One of his friends is retired and is staying there now. He's a writer. Real quiet. Maybe you can meet him tomorrow."

Inside the cabin, waking from the dark of sleep, a German shepherd growled and moved to the window to look. The dog's growl woke the retired friend of the family. The man's first thought was about the opossum scrounging for grubs in the grass he and the dog had seen the last three nights. But as he opened his eyes, the ceiling reflected three sets of headlights moving in an arc. The man knew that meant they were turning in the circle drive at the big house. He got up and stood next to the dog. Before he looked out into the night, he glanced over at his pistol safe. The man watched the outside activity from the cabin window as Sean Adams stepped out of the driver's seat of the lead car.

The man said to himself, "Long time no see, Sean. Welcome home." He scratched the dog's ear as he shook his head. The dog looked up and then back out the window. The pair watched a moment longer, hearing both men and women talking in jaunty voices.

"Have a nice party, kids." And with that, he returned to bed.

The riders were rummaging through the backs of both SUVs. They began unloading bags and musical instruments, hooting and laughing as they followed the tall Sean Adams and the rotund Frankie up the covered entrance of the big house.

The single door, flanked by wide sidelights, was at the end of the covered, brick-stepped portico. Above the entry were three evenly spaced decorative dormers with eyebrow arches. In front of the portico, lush green plants camouflaged the four columns supporting the portico's roof. The outside of the house was a preview of the furnishings and showcase style inside.

Kolby Rae and Sarah Miles looked over the house and surrounding grounds from the edge of the drive.

"Well, here we are," said Sarah.

"I have a good feeling about this kid, and everything he's told us has been true. We need this, Sarah. We need this time. We need to get back to what we do best. Besides, Frankie will give us the thumbs up or down. If there's anything weird here, we're out of here tomorrow."

"Pinkie swear?" asked Sarah.

Kolby Rae looked back at Sarah in agreement, holding up her right hand with an extended pinkie finger. "Pinkie swear." They interlocked pinkies and then both dropped their hands.

"The house looks nice," Kolby offered, looking at the columns, the grand entry, and architectural details of the one-story mini mansion. "You don't suppose there's a moonshine still in some backwoods clearing?"

"We're so far in the sticks. Nashville is a long way from here, nothing but a memory."

Sarah was holding her smartphone, first at her waist, then up to her face, and then up in the air with the screen pointed down as she slowly turned her body in a circle.

"Where are we?" she asked, glaring at the screen. "I've got maybe one bar?"

Kolby began to sing an imaginary melody.

:: Forgettin' your memory… one bar at a time ::

Sarah looked at and encouraged her. "Write that down. That's a good one."

That's why we're here, Kolby Rae thought to herself. *One more chance to find a good one*. And lately, she hadn't been able to get it right.

CHAPTER TWO

I GUESS YOU'RE THE SINGER?

THE NEXT MORNING, KOLBY RAE walked out the front door of the big house with guitar in hand and a pink cowboy hat on her head. She sat on the brick steps at the edge of the covered portico and felt the warmth of the rising sun against her skin before she began strumming the chords to the new melody.

She turned toward the other building on the farm, the small cabin, and heard and saw an older Range Rover turn toward the big house. She looked up, ready to wave at the driver sitting on the right-hand side of the Rover, when he stopped the truck and turned it off.

He had dark hair, just over his collar. Kolby kept playing the guitar and nodded as he spoke. "I saw you come in last night, I guess you're the singer?" he said to her.

"I guess you're the writer?" she answered. "So how goes the writing? You working on a project?"

"Yeah, I've been working on it for over year, and"—he laughed— "can I be honest? It's just not going very well. How's the singing?"

"Well, can I be honest? It's just not going very well, either." She stopped strumming her guitar and looked up at him. "I'm Kolby."

He opened the door of the truck, stepped toward her, and extended his right hand, which she shook firmly. "I'm Joshua. Joshua Stone."

"Pleasure to meet you, Joshua Stone. Who's your friend?" She pointed the guitar at the German shepherd sitting in the backseat of the Range Rover.

"Her name is Fylgja. It means—"

"A spirit guide, a protector. Are you Norske?"

Joshua looked at her, rolled his eyes, and shook his head.

Kolby looked at him from toe to head and then stated, "No, I guess you're not. Not with that hair. So what brings you to Tennessee?"

"I'm a friend of Sean's. Well, actually Sean's parents. I used to work with his dad. Don't tell Sean, but they asked me to come down here and keep an eye on him."

"Oh, really? Okay, so how's that working out?"

"Well, until you guys rolled in last night, I hadn't seen him in two weeks."

Kolby made her face into a crooked smile. "So let me get this straight; you're a writer who can't write and a babysitter who lost the baby?"

Joshua shrugged with a smirk. "You're perceptive."

"What else can't you do?" She grinned back at him.

"The truth?"

"Yes, I always expect the truth," she told him.

"Okay then, I'm awkward with women." He smiled again as she rolled her eyes and looked back at her guitar strings.

Joshua stood there looking at the woman and the guitar and then looked around over his shoulder. Kolby could tell he was trying to decide if he should continue or finish the conversation. He surprised her by continuing. "So what do you sing? Anything I would know?"

Kolby listed some song titles. "'Kissed with a Lie'? 'Candlelight and Chaos'?" Joshua's face lacked recognition as she ticked off the titles. She continued, slightly less enthusiastically. "'Tequila Temptress'? 'Looking Glass Memories'? 'Next of Ken'? It was kind of a pun with a man's name?"

"Sorry, no. I guess I don't know much about your music."

"What about 'Dance on Your Shoes'?" She offered the biggest hit she had ever written.

He shook his head. "No, sorry."

She sighed a dejected sigh, but not loud enough for him to hear.

"Okay then, how 'bout you? What have you written?"

Joshua hesitated a bit. "*Bottle Rocket*? *The Fistfight*?" Kolby shook her head. "Um, how about *Hoop*?" She looked back at him blankly. He continued, "Surely you've heard of *One Good Bread Pudding*? Or *Our Final Days*?"

She shook her head. "Sorry, haven't heard of any of them."

They looked at each other. Joshua pushed his left hand a few inches deeper into his pocket to hide the scar on the back of his hand.

"So, Joshua Stone, what is there to do for fun around here?"

"Well, uh, let's see." He pretended to think. "There's always…or no, wait, you can…Oh, I know, there's…" His voice trailed off.

"Okay, okay, I get the picture." She laughed as she discovered his sense of humor.

"Seriously?" He began again. "There's a restaurant in town. Most of the locals go there Friday night. They do a big dinner buffet. I think they have a dance floor. On Saturdays, some of the locals play cards. Most of the big lakes nearby have fishing lodges and marinas, but that's mostly for tourists."

Kolby folded both arms across the body of her guitar and looked at him. "I'm gonna guess that Joshua Stone doesn't dance, play cards, or fish?"

"Um, well, not a lot. Lately."

"Well, that pretty much sums up why you're awkward around women. Good luck with that." She stood up, gave a polite wave goodbye, and walked to the house.

Kolby lingered in the doorway, thinking about his scar on his left cheek, then thought of a musical hook: does that scar point to your heart?

As she stood there, Joshua Stone noticed how short her dress was. It had been a very long time since he had seen that much of a woman's leg. He looked higher and took in her whole body as she crossed the threshold and closed the door behind her. Fylgja whined twice.

As she closed the door, both Kolby Rae and Joshua Stone had the same, silent thought, *Wow, someone is a long way from home.*

PART TWO
NASHVILLE

CHAPTER THREE

COVER GIRL

FOUR DAYS EARLIER, KOLBY RAE'S phone display lit up with a text message:

<Sarah> Hey, when you get here, go around to the side. Road construction out front.

Kolby Rae glanced over at the phone and then her speedometer: 55 mph. She looked ahead several blocks, and with no cars as far as she could see, she picked up the phone. She peeked down as she typed, then ahead and to the side at the parked cars as they zipped through her peripheral vision.

<Kolby Rae> Running late.

Kolby Rae looked ahead far enough to see the light turn green. She was about to give her truck more gas when instinct kicked in, and she stomped the brake pedal, sending the bags from the backseat onto the floor and spinning the cell phone off the shotgun seat and onto the floor mat. She cringed in the mirror at herself as she stopped and then watched as the car coming from the left ran the red light, blasted through the intersection, and sped on its way.

"God bless," she said in a voice more like a snide church lady than a country music artist headed to the recording studio. She moved her boot to the accelerator and drove a more controlled forty-five mph the rest of the way to her session.

Sibilance Studios was a small studio about as far from music row as a studio could be and still claim to be in Nashville. It was like every studio in any medium-sized market in America. Its reputation—and its payroll—were built producing radio commercials for car dealers and mixing audio for the occasional independent film director. The cash flow came from an endless stream of Nashville hopefuls who paid $995 for a three-song demo session and a master audio file.

Ordinarily, neither Kolby Rae nor her sister, Sarah Miles, would have given the studio a second look, but it had two things going for it. Room C, a stylish recording room, had some of the best acoustics in town. Stars and studio musicians both said it had a vibe and a sound that were ideal for an intimate recording. Second, it had that sound because Earnest "Frankie" Ryder designed it. Frankie had come to Nashville in the early eighties when country music was enjoying a new mainstream market following the success of John Travolta and *Urban Cowboy*. Frankie signed on as a recording engineer at Sibilance and, over the next decade, became a well-known face and popular producer on projects all over the city.

Frankie and Sibilance owner Ross Epoch built out Room C with a dream of attracting Nashville's biggest stars. It didn't work out that way. When big labels hired Frankie, they loved his ways but wanted his ears and hands in their favorite studios.

The three of them—Kolby, Sarah, and Frankie—had worked together briefly in the very beginning. Sarah worked for Kolby's label, Pier Records, as a modestly paid assistant when the label brought Frankie into one of their favored recording studios to mix Kolby's self-titled debut album. Frankie mixed "Landslide," the Stevie Nicks classic, covered by Kolby Rae on the disc. Frankie called Kolby's version "the only Grammy I deserved and never won." That was twelve years and two hundred pounds ago. To call Frankie a heavyweight in the business had dual meaning. "Landslide" was a bittersweet memory for them all. Now that they were free of Pier, Kolby and Sarah sought a creative reunion with Frankie.

Kolby Rae pulled onto the street in front of Sibilance and stopped, surveying the traffic barricades and construction crews. She switched off the truck, reached over onto the floor mat, and retrieved the cell phone. She typed, looking up and then back at the phone:

<Kolby Rae> How do I get in?

Sarah looked up from her phone and out the window of the small studio control room at both the construction and Kolby's SUV in the road.

<Sarah> Go back and around the block, come in from the back.

With the seat pushed all the way forward, Kolby stretched to look over the steering wheel and the dashboard and then over both shoulders, put the truck in reverse, backed up, and then headed around the block to the studio back parking lot. She parked next to the matching black SUV with the SMILES personalized plates and got out. From the backseat, she retrieved her bag and an express envelope that had spilled out when she jumped on the brakes to prevent the near collision. She walked inside the chilly studio and waved to the young girl at the front desk. "Hey, Lila, how did your finals go?"

"Kolby, I did it! I got a B-minus," the high schooler replied.

"Way to go, girlfriend!" Kolby moved down the hall and into the control room where Sarah was sitting, holding her phone to her ear. Sarah held up her hand like a traffic cop, and Kolby listened to one side of the conversation.

"Tommy, look, I know we booked the bus for the whole summer, but we had a last-minute change in our tour schedule. So I bet you have someone who's desperate for a bus, and now. I'm doing you a favor by releasing it. This is a big win for you. And it's not just any bus; this is Captain Malcolm's bus. You know how well liked he is."

Kolby rolled her eyes. Little sister Sarah knew how to work it. Kolby had a downtown Nashville lawyer minding her contracts, music licensing, and money. Sarah had stepped in to help her sister as tour manager for a few weeks. The weeks became months, and now, two years in, it was her full-time job.

"Sure, I know. This is a bum deal, but you'll get a premium from your new lease. So I'm saying we skip this month's payment, you make it up, and we all win."

Kolby heard Tommy's agitated voice over the cell phone. Sarah held the phone out away from her ear, nodded in mock agreement, and winked at Kolby. "Okay, okay, Tommy, you win. We'll pay this month's lease, and we'll call it even."

Sarah listened as Tommy finished talking and then pulled the phone away and disconnected.

"So we're set then? The bus went back?" asked Kolby Rae.

Sarah nodded. "We've got enough in the cash account to ride out the summer and into early fall."

The two women looked at each other with stoic, trusting expressions.

"Where are we with the crowdfunding?" asked Kolby.

"We're at five percent funded. You need to do an update video today for the pledgers," replied Sarah.

"How many more days left in the campaign?"

"We set it for sixty days, and we have fifty-two left. If we don't make it, we can extend it, but they say that usually doesn't help much."

"We're gonna make this album the one. I feel it. The band has never been stronger," Kolby said.

Sarah looked down at the bag and express envelope in Kolby's hand. "Is that it?" she asked, pointing to the envelope.

"Yes. I wanted you to read it to me. I want to hear the words. I don't want to read them."

Sarah took the package and ripped the pull tape on the edge and retrieved a magazine from the inside.

The magazine, *Garden Party*, featured a July cover story about Kolby Rae written by Jeffrey Toomey. They had tolerated Toomey for weeks of interviews. They'd hoped to tie it into their summer tour and crowdfunding campaign for the studio album, but now, with a major show canceled, the tour and timing were all off. The best they could hope for was a bounce in sales and downloads as a warm-up to the new album. And what was left of a fall tour.

The relationship with Toomey was strained. He was both journalist and microcelebrity, dominating social media and blending gossip and enough truth to be taken seriously by close to a million followers.

Sarah looked at the cover. "Oh my God, you look so-o-o-o-o cute." She turned the cover around and there was Kolby Rae, wearing her pink cowboy hat with turquoise hatband and a very coy expression. Her butterscotch hair was styled in big curls.

Both women, in their thirties, shrieked like high school cheerleaders. Sarah, still wide-eyed and giggling, turned the cover around and then stopped. Her face fell. She looked back at Kolby and gave her a look. Kolby caught her breath, blew out, and then sank into a chair at the mixing board.

Sarah read the headline: "Why Kolby Rae Can't Get it Right."

Sarah began turning pages as Kolby twirled her hair with the fingers of her left hand. Sarah read from the article, "'Kolby Rae is Nashville's nameless household name. Unless you've been living in Guantanamo, you know her biggest hit: "Dance on Your Shoes." It's the best-selling and most downloaded song of the last twenty years. Except like everyone else, you never knew it was Kolby Rae's song. She was the song writer, but the hit, the recording, and the accolades all belong to Sherrie Elliot, the multiplatinum, Grammy- and CMA-award-winning artist who recorded it. To understand "Dance on Your Shoes" is to understand the whole of Kolby Rae's career: never a one-hit wonder and never big enough to be a has-been.'"

Sarah lowered the magazine. Kolby looked up, frowned, formed her right finger and thumb into the shape of an *L*, and smacked it against the center of her forehead.

"It's not that bad. The pictures are great," Sarah said.

"It's not that great, but it's a cover. And it's Jeffrey Toomey," said Kolby.

Sarah skimmed ahead. "Wait, listen to this: 'But there is no denying that Kolby Rae is a show-stopping *tour de force*. A night with Kolby Rae in concert will leave you convinced she performed a private show just for you. Once your ears taste the Kolby Rae whisper live, you're ruined for every other female voice in country music. If she can ever find that mojo in the studio, she might actually break the top ten on her own. The reality is, she's forever competing with her own invisible success with "Dance on Your Shoes."'"

Kolby expressed some optimism. "This album is all me and the band, Sarah; no producer egos, no labels to get in the way. We've got Frankie, and now we've got the whole summer."

Sarah's phone beeped, and a text blinked across her screen.

<Nils> WTF? Where's the road?

Sarah grinned. "Nils is here." She replied to Nils with quick taps on her phone.

<Sarah> Road closed, drive around the block.

They looked up to see Nils's truck and Skeeter's motorcycle side by side doing a U-turn and then easing down the side street.

"Everybody's gonna be here. What do you think about the article? Do you want to show this to them now?" asked Sarah.

Kolby looked around at the control room and through the glass divider into Room C. Seated on a stool was a young musician with waist-length hair and a Slipknot T-shirt, surrounded by a pile of energy drink and beer cans on the floor and open guitar cases on the edge of the wall opposite the control room glass window.

"Sure, let's talk. I'll show them."

Sarah nodded at Kolby and then rolled her head toward the glass window. "I think junior wannabe in there is cleaning up from his session. Looks like he's gonna be awhile."

With those words, the studio monitor began sounding a funky bass lick, a little Motown and a lot seventies groove. Kolby looked up into Room C to see the wannabe playing his bass, and then she moved over to the mixing console. She reached for and pressed the record button, and the monitors started displaying a waveform with each note played by the musician. The bass was raw, thumping, crisp. This was retro, with a very fresh edge.

Sarah cocked her head to one side with a raised eyebrow. "Our bassist?"

"Shh-h-h-h-h-h," Kolby interrupted as she listened carefully to the groove laid down by the heavy-metal-influenced rocker in the studio. Nodding her head, she twisted a knob, adjusting the midtone of the inputs to the recording track.

Nils and Skeeter barged into the room. Both Sarah and Kolby moved their fingers to their lips and gestured with their heads toward the player in Room C. The men, at first confused, started hearing the same gritty beat that caught Kolby's attention. After about sixteen bars, almost as quickly as it had started, it stopped.

Kolby listened a moment or two more, then pressed the keyboard and stopped recording. Her hand moved over to the intercom button marked *I/C*. She pressed it and began speaking. "Nice groove. I like the sound. What's your name?"

The player looked up and around and then into the glass partition to the control room. He heard a woman's voice but could only make out figures behind the glass.

"Sean Adams."

"Well, Sean Adams, that's a great sound. So what's your story? Are you a studio musician?"

"No, I'm in a band. Well, I was until we broke up about twenty minutes ago. I hate egos."

In the control room, everyone chuckled.

Sean Adams added, "Drummers are the worst." Skeeter punched Nils in the shoulder. "Except for maybe guitar players." And with that, Nils punched Skeeter back.

"And how do you feel about singers?"

Sean Adams didn't know it at the time, but his answer was a career-defining moment.

"Singers are great. If I could sing, I'd be one."

Kolby looked at Sarah. "We have a winner." She pressed the I/C button. "Right answer, Sean Adams. We need a bass player for one of our tracks. Come in. Let's talk about it."

CHAPTER FOUR

START A BAND

THE TALL, TWENTY-YEAR-OLD SEAN ADAMS was mature for his age, but his maturity was obscured by his musician's impulsiveness. For a bass player whose natural sense of tempo held bands together musically since junior high school, his respect for both clocks and calendars was truant. He didn't own a wristwatch. If his cell phone display time wasn't automatically set by the network phone service, he wouldn't know the time. Not that it mattered to Sean.

As the son of a college professor and a real estate agent, Sean had a clear future, at least as his parents had mapped it out. He was college-bound to a good music school, and maybe he would follow in his father's steps and teach. But at the end of his first freshman semester, with a 1.76 GPA, Sean approached his parents with a well-thought-out plan for a new life direction. He laid the brochures in front of them, talked about being a recording engineer, and persuaded them to redirect his college tuition dollars into a recording studio.

"We can turn the big house into a studio getaway for bands, and I can run the show," he told them, then added, "with Mom's business help."

Both parents were impressed and, with only slight hesitation, agreed. Sean went to a Nashville school and studied recording engineering. And on breaks and over the summer, Sean, his father, David, and some local men finished construction.

But impulse control is hard to learn, and in Sean's case, it was completely lacking when he read a late-night text two weeks ago:

<Jimmy> Dude, come be in our band.

Sean was standing in front of the open side-by-side refrigerator, staring at frozen pizzas, boxes of frozen egg rolls, and a frost-crusted, torn package that read *Lean* something. He looked at the pizza box and then juggled the phone and the box, alternately typing on the screen and tearing at the cardboard.

<Sean> Where are u? What band?

<Jimmy> Nash*fcking*ville.

<Sean> No way.

Jimmy was Sean's roommate during their less-than-impressive scholarly debut. Both boys were smart enough to have earned better grades, but rather than study, the pair made unusual use of their class time. They sent text messages to girls from the back of the classroom, made cutting comments about the professors, and murmured the answers to the questions without doing the homework or opening the textbooks. After midterms, they stopped going to class.

<Jimmy> We need you on bass, dude. We're gonna make this town the new metal haven.

<Sean> Heavy metal in Nashville = steel guitar.

Sean looked at the directions for the pizza on the box: 450 degrees for 25 minutes. He didn't find microwave oven instructions, so he put it in the microwave and then took it out because it didn't fit. He used a large knife and hacked the frozen pizza in half, then stacked the two halves in the microwave and set the dial to 25 minutes. He stepped outside and tapped on his screen.

<Sean> Let me know when you have a gig.

Sean set the phone in his pocket, assuming that was the end of the conversation. The phone immediately vibrated back. He slid it out of his pocket.

<Jimmy> We have a contract. We're @ a studio now We're ready to cut EP. It's all set.

<Sean> I call bullshit.

<Jimmy> Dude, this is real deal. We start recording tomorrow. You have to come.

<Sean> Prove it. Send me pic.

Sean slid the phone into his pocket again, expecting his request for proof to be the end of the drunken dreams of his former roommate. He looked around at the long shadows from the moonlight across the yard and pasture and then up into the starry sky. He began silently naming constellations, smirking all the while about his failing grade in astronomy. He muttered his dad's favorite dinnertime expression: "The secret to life, Sean, is showing up. Look where it got me."

A long beep from the kitchen called him back inside, and when he got to the microwave, he was greeted by a disgusting, smoky haze and a very overcooked pizza.

"Damn."

Sean grabbed a towel and pulled out the smoldering remains of dinner and then tossed them into the wastebasket under the sink. He turned on the exhaust fan over the stove and then snatched the car keys off the counter. The convenience store in town sold pizza. He'd just get one there and bring it back.

As Sean carried the pizza out of the c-store and into the car, his phone vibrated from his pocket. He pulled it out and clicked on the link in the text from Jimmy. In the photo, Jimmy and two other guys were standing in a studio control room. Sean could make out the racks and knew it was high-end, professional gear. He tapped on the screen:

<Sean> You're legit!

Sean started the car. The gas gauge showed the tank almost full. He looked over at the pizza. He shut off the car, walked back into the c-store, and filled a large fountain cup with a blend of three carbonated sodas from the fountain. He snapped on the lid and yanked a straw from the canister. He paid the girl behind the register for his second purchase in five minutes and walked back to the car.

He started it again, looked back up the road to his parents' house, and then looked right toward the road to the interstate. He turned toward the interstate and picked up his phone, tapping with one hand:

<Sean> I'm so in.

Sean, like his father, David Adams, was a risk-taker. Just the same, the elder Adams liked some safety nets. He had had a feeling Sean might do something impulsive. Since he was unable to keep a daily watch on his son, he had offered the guest cabin on the property to a Joshua Stone. to "keep an eye on Sean, just in case he needs help." What his parents told Sean was that Joshua needed a place to get back on his feet. Sean knew about the shooting on the campus where Stone and his father worked. He knew that Joshua had been shot, another faculty member had died, and that Joshua had saved some lives. And now he was retired and writing in the small cabin at the farm.

As he turned onto the interstate, Sean made one phone call. He left a message on the friend-of-the-family's voice mail: "I'm off to Nashville and will call back in a few days. And hey, Doctor Stone, do you think you could turn off the lights in the big house? I think I left them on."

CHAPTER FIVE

LAST SESSION

TWO WEEKS LATER, SEAN WAS sitting on a stool, looking around at the energy drink and beer can remnants of a recording session bender. He hated being the janitor, but out of respect for the studio owner, he set his bass in its case, walked out to the men's room, soaked five paper towels with water, and returned to the studio. He got down on his hands and knees and began mopping up the blood and dabbing the area rug that ran under the drum kit. He picked up the two halves of the broken drumstick and threw them and the bloody paper towels into the trash can. He then collected the pile of cans, too.

The door burst open.

"Where is that motherfucker? He broke my damn nose!" Jimmy, Sean's former college roommate, was still cupping his nose with his bloodstained hand. "Motherfucker. Here, take my picture—it's evidence."

He tossed the phone across the room, and Sean snatched it from the air with his left hand. Sean set the phone down on a stool. "I'm not gonna take your picture, but let me take a look."

Sean walked over and gently pulled Jimmy's hand down and away from his face. The blood was dried and crusted on Jimmy's lip and nostrils, and his nose, once straight and long, was now a backwards comma on his face.

"Ouch, dude, you need a doctor."

"I don't need a fucking doctor. I need a fucking lawyer."

Before Sean could answer, they both heard the clip-clop of Staci's heels as she scurried down the hallway and into the studio. The door to the normally soundproof room was ajar.

"Baby, oh my God, what happened to you? Oh my God, oh my God."

Sean thought to himself, *If Staci were a band, she'd be named Histrionics.* It was a thought that had crossed his mind before.

Staci continued, "Oh my God, what's your blood type? Sean, we have to go donate blood right now. Oh my God, baby!"

She picked up Jimmy's arm and draped it across her shoulders. Staggering, the two of them turned and began walking to the studio door. Jimmy was now limping. Sean stared at the ceiling to suppress his laugh.

When they had gone, Sean sat down and reached to pick up the bass. As he began to play, the studio door burst open. Again.

"Where is that asshole?"

"Gone."

"I'm taking my drums, man."

Sean got up and stepped to the side of the room. Piece by piece, Scotty picked up part of his drum kit and carried it out the door and out to his waiting van in the parking lot. On his second trip, he picked up the high-hat and then turned to Sean.

"He had it coming, you know." And he stormed out the studio door. Sean picked one-half of the broken drumstick out of the trash can and wedged it to hold the studio door open.

"I mean, the dude has no sense of rhythm." Scotty vanished with the snare.

Scotty reappeared at the door again. "He had no fucking right to say that." Scotty snorted and then picked up the stool behind the kick drum. On his next trip in, he said, "I mean, I played with Megadeth." He grabbed the tom drum and walked into the hall, turned, and then over his shoulder said, "And Slayer."

Sean thought about what Jimmy had said the night before. Scotty wasn't lying. He had played with both bands—if you call being on the free stage with your garage band at the same festival playing "with" a band. In hindsight, that was a pretty big clue.

When Scotty came in for the kick drum, Sean noticed the blood on both his right fist and his shirt. The drum made a ruckus as Scotty tried to squeeze out of the hallway and into the parking lot. Sean drew a big breath.

His phone vibrated. He looked down. The caller ID read SCOTTY.

"Hello?" Sean answered, wondering if someone had borrowed Scotty's phone.

"Dude, one more thing. Tell that asshole I'm not paying any part of the fucking studio time." And then the line went dead.

Sean began talking to himself. His dad spoke aloud every morning while he shaved. He worked on his books early in the day and often made the words come alive between strokes of the razor before he disappeared into his study to write. Now, standing alone in the studio, Sean found himself imitating his father.

"The story of the Nashville metal band named Hubris is drugs, sex, and rock and roll," he said as if he were narrating a documentary about the band that had disintegrated in a profanity-laced tribute to its own name moments earlier. Sean picked up the bass on his left and plugged it into the sound system.

"Scotty was drugs. Not the drugs of our parents' musicians. Prescription drugs. His favorite was his little brother's orange Adderall pills, followed by an energy drink chaser."

Sean continued his narration, all the while changing fingering patterns on the frets of the electric bass and playing silently.

"Jimmy was sex, except that, to be honest, Staci was sex; Jimmy was just an outlet." Sean changed his vocalization, as if he were letting the documentary viewers in on a secret. "I heard Staci and Jimmy together. I heard Staci and Scotty in Scotty's van. And I heard Staci and a doorman at a club in the men's room.

"So that left me, Sean Adams, to be the rock and roll."

Out of habit, Sean began to lay down a funky groove. Between the drama and his own narration, he didn't notice the two women in the control booth behind the glass until he heard Kolby Rae's voice over the studio I/C speakers.

Chapter Six

Yes Sir, Frankie

SEAN SET THE BASS DOWN in a case and walked through the door still propped open by the broken drumstick and into the hall that led to the control room. As he did, he met a man and woman coming from the lobby. They all gathered in the control room and spread out, some sitting on counters, some in the comfy leather sofas designed for advertising agency clients.

Kolby spoke first. "Hey, guys, great news…awesome news. This is Sean Adams. Sean is gonna lay down the bass tracks for us."

The band nodded with approval and murmured some welcomes and kind words.

"So let me introduce you to everyone. This is Skeeter Martin." Kolby waved her hand at Skeeter, whose long salt-and-pepper beard and hair accented his face. Skeeter extended his tattoo-covered arms to shake Sean's hand.

"Skeeter plays rhythm guitar, dobro, banjo, and pedal steel." She moved her hands toward the slender woman with straight, waist-length black hair and soft, pale skin. "This is Kim Hartunian. She plays electric cello."

Kim leaned forward and pointed at the bassist's long black hair and her own, saying, "I see we have the same stylist."

Kolby continued, pointing next at the baby-faced man with short, blonde hair and a gap between his front teeth, "This is Nils Landvik, our drummer."

Nils extended his hand and said, "Hey hey."

The muscular Cuban with thick, dark eyebrows extended his hand and spoke before Kolby could say anything. "I'm Roberto Latas, lead guitar and vocals." Roberto pointed at the T-shirt. "Slipknot. Love their sound. Aren't they like from Des Plaines or someplace?"

"Des Moines," Sean answered back, "but yeah."

"This is Sarah Miles, our tour manager."

Sarah said, "We'll talk about pay and do paperwork later, okay? Come find me."

"And my name is Kolby Rae."

Sean looked around. "So who's the producer?"

"Kolby," the band said, almost in unison.

"I am," Kolby said. "And we're working with Frankie Ryder."

"Frankie Ryder? You mean I can meet Frankie Ryder in person?"

The band looked at each other with a puzzled, embarrassed expression.

Kolby asked, "You've heard of Frankie?"

"Yeah, he came and gave a talk when I was in school. I'm a recording engineer. I just play bass because I like playing in bands."

Kolby gave a patronizing smile. "Well, good luck with that, and in the meantime, can you work tonight and then tomorrow afternoon and then on Friday?"

"Yeah, sure."

"Great. Will you tear down your setup so we can get in there next? Frankie will be here at five o'clock."

Sean nodded, fist-bumped Roberto on his way out of the studio, and then closed the door behind him. The musicians turned their attention to Kolby. Roberto spoke first. "So do you think he can handle what we want to do with 'Goody Two Shoes'?"

Kolby turned to the mixing board and computer keyboard, moved the soundtrack to the beginning of Sean's recorded bass playing, and started the digital file playback. The sound filled the control room speakers and the room. In the first few bars, the band began to move and sway. Nils began drumming his fingers on a countertop, and Skeeter closed his eyes and bobbed his head slightly with the beats. When the digital track stopped, the group hooted and applauded,

Nils held up both hands, grinning: "Where's he been hiding out?

Maybe I can't wait to drink the water in Des Moines."

Kim interrupted. "He's not from Des Moines. His T-shirt is."

Sarah looked at Kolby. Kolby looked at Sarah and nodded.

"Guys, about Des Moines," Sarah began. "The venue had a fire there night before last. It's pretty bad. No one was hurt, but they've canceled all their future shows and ours."

The band let out a collective and disappointed grunt.

"And because of that, it's shuffling everyone's schedule. So we are no longer the front-runner to open for Sherrie Elliot. I just heard from their people. They're saying maybe next spring. In Canada."

"Ugh. Who wants to go to Canada in the spring? Don't they have, like, snow and six months of darkness?" Roberto asked.

Sarah continued. "So I talked with Captain Malcolm. He says hi to everyone. But I told him I called Tommy to let him know we are releasing the bus today. We're not touring this summer. We will keep the eight dates we have scheduled between now and October, but nothing else. Kolby and I are sorry."

Nils was first to speak through his gap-toothed smile. "So that's not so bad, is it? Yeah, yeah, I mean, we can work on the studio album. We don't have to worry about going on the road and blowing our voices and trying to squeeze in mixdowns. Yeah, yeah, yeah? We've always said we wished we could focus on just one thing at a time." Nils looked around at his bandmates and then back to Kolby Rae.

"Nils, you never know when to be blue," Kolby said. She looked around. "There's one more thing. I got an advance copy of *Garden Party* today. I made the cover."

Whoops replaced the momentary disappointment. As quickly as it left, it returned when Sarah held up the magazine, and their eyes focused on the headline next to Kolby's turquoise hatband and pink hat.

"What? Let me see that." Roberto took the magazine and began flipping through the pages until he found the article. He read silently, then out loud, saying, "'Never big enough to be a has-been.' What? Toomey is a moron."

Kolby pursed her lips. "It's the music business. We've been here before. We take the high road."

Sarah interjected, "Yes, so no social media, no interview questions. Leave it be."

Everyone nodded. They took turns reading the magazine, leaning in over each other's shoulders and moving their own instruments into Room C as Sean moved the abandoned gear from the band formerly known as Hubris out of the way and into the halls.

Just before 5:00, Frankie Ryder walked in the back door and into the control room.

"Kolby Rae, if you aren't a sight for sore eyes. Give me some sugar." He puckered his lips and closed his eyes. The balding man with the round belly stooped lower, and Kolby Rae kissed his cheek.

"Frankie, I swear you get younger every year."

"That's not at all true, Kolby Rae, but God bless your lying eyes. Miss Sarah, how's business?"

Sarah arched her eyebrow and nodded. "That depends. Are you on the clock?"

Frankie looked at his wristwatch. "No, not just yet."

Sarah grinned. "Then sit down. Let me tell you all about my troubles. Just tell me when you do go on the clock, and I'll shut right up."

"Who's the new kid?" Frankie pointed through the glass at Sean Adams.

"Just another Nashville dream chaser, chewed up and spit out by the machine. But a bass player for sure," Kolby said.

"Where did you find him?" Frankie asked.

"Here. His band just split up today."

"Oh, really? I need to check with Ross to make sure they paid in advance."

"Frankie…"

"Kolby, I've got to eat like everyone else does."

Sarah stopped short of making an obvious comment about the obese man's eating.

"Maybe you can give him a job? He says he's a recording engineer."

"Don't they all?"

"No." Kolby corrected, "They all say they're singers. He says he's a recording engineer."

"Okay, I'll put him in the chair and see what he can do." Frankie shuffled his feet across the control room, pulled his sagging pants a bit higher around his waist, and pushed his thick, black-framed glasses higher on his face. He was at once trendy and sloppy and too many inches out of fashion to appear in the magazines other than as a head shot.

Frankie leaned over and pressed the I/C button. "Hey, Skinny. Come in here and show me what you can do on the board."

Sean looked up and saw the shape of Frankie Ryder in the window. He stopped, starstruck, before he straightened up and walked out of Room C and into the control room.

"Mr. Ryder, a pleasure to meet you, sir. I heard you speak last year in one of my classes."

Frankie Ryder rolled his eyes. "Son, first of all, call me Frankie."

Sean Adams beamed at the familiar approval from his hero.

Frankie continued, "And second of all, you do not ever speak in this room unless spoken to. Do we understand each other?"

The color drained from Sean's face, and he quickly sat down at the chair in front of the board. He began adjusting sliders and knobs. Sarah and Kolby looked at each other.

Frankie continued, "Sean, I want you to be a success in this business, so I'm just here to tell you some advice. You know what I mean?"

"Yes, Frankie," answered Sean.

"I've fired assistants many times for talking too much, so here's the deal. You and I, we're here to make this lady a hit record. Do we understand each other?"

"Yes, Frankie. I'm ready whenever you tell us to begin."

"Great. Now, I'm going down the hall to make a cup of coffee and find a doughnut. And when the artist is ready, she'll tell me and I'll tell you."

Sarah picked up her phone and began dialing. With her day planner in front of her, she settled in for a night of telephone work.

Kolby walked to the back of Room C and picked up her favorite Larrivée guitar. The guitar's smaller bouts and waist, along with the shorter scale length, made it a comfortable play for her both seated and moving around the stage.

"Roberto, what did Len say about my guitar?" Kolby draped the strap across her left shoulder and fastened the free end to the button.

"Kolby, he said it sounds great. He replaced the pickups and strings. He says the buzz is gone."

"Thank you for picking it up for me."

"Kolby, I know we're not going on the road, so I'm just saying this so you know. About Len—he asked me about being our guitar tech on tour again."

Kolby nodded at Roberto. "He's loyal. Let's find a way to make that happen." She squeezed Roberto's arm. "We need you. Sing your fiery heart out on this song, okay?" She squeezed his arm a second time, then looked at Kim and smiled.

On the opposite side of the glass window separating Room C from the control room, Sean Adams was preparing as he waited for Frankie.

There are two main work areas at the engineer's seat in front of the control board. The first is the mixing board, a flat metal console with sliding faders, rotating knobs, and buttons that control the volume and sound qualities of each microphone or instrument. The second is the computer keyboard and mouse that control the digital audio workstation.

There is a technical skill necessary to monitor the sound, route the cables, and patch the connections so that the vocals and instruments sound as they are intended to sound. But the art that is making music is capturing the spirit and essence of an artist, the ability to capture the recording so that the listener experience is what the artist intended.

Most engineers can make a good technical recording. Beyond good, Frankie Ryder had made a career of making music that sounded great, one of a handful of producers in Nashville who could. Even his critics agreed that Frankie had a nearly spiritual connection from his ears to the mixing board unmatched in most of Nashville. But the same attitude that put Sean Adams off balance had also put off most of the major label executives. And slowly over time, Frankie found himself called in for fewer and fewer jobs. He was working less and eating more.

As computers and digital audio workstations performed more of the adjustments, digital innovation made it possible for almost any studio to make up for what the less experienced engineer lacked. It wasn't Frankie Ryder, but it was good enough to sell 50,000 copies.

These days, Frankie had a new love, or an old love rekindled: vinyl. The twelve-inch LP was experiencing a comeback, and none of the twenty-something producers and engineers on music row had ever engineered for an old-school record. So Frankie was carving a new niche out of an old niche. He wanted to persuade Kolby Rae to consider a vinyl album, so if that meant seeing what the skinny kid could do behind the board, so be it. He decided to let the younger engineer run the mix for a take to see what he knew.

"Sean, when she's ready, she's just gonna start. You never know with this one. You have to be ahead of her."

Sean looked down the row of masking tape labels he had placed above the slider rows for each of the microphones he had set in the studio. He knew the song featured Kolby and had backing vocals from Kim, Nils, and Roberto. Nils, he could tell, had a voice that would overpower them all.

He also knew that Frankie was testing him. Traditionally, a studio engineer would record each part separately, beginning with a simple drumbeat or a click track, then laying in some temporary piano or guitar chords to give everyone something to match. Then, as each musician added his or her instrument to the mix, each track would layer on top of the next. The lead vocal and harmonies would be added on top. If all the tracks were recorded at full volume, the engineer, on final mixdown, would adjust the volumes to be relative and supportive of each other. The engineer typically knew the gear and made a track that matched the producer's musical image of how the song should sound.

But Frankie was asking him to do it live as an ensemble. Frankie knew the band; he knew they played best together. When they recorded tracks separately, their sound just lost life.

Sean had already learned some of Kolby Rae's mannerisms as she spoke and noticed a slight hip shift every time she began. When he saw the hip shift as she sat in the studio, he hit RECORD. Two beats later, she nodded, and Kim, Roberto, and Skeeter began playing. After a four-bar intro, Sean slid the slider marked KOLBY VOCAL up, and the woman's lyrical voice came through the monitoring speakers in the control room. Sean, with a keen ear, adjusted each instrument in anticipation of a buildup or letdown. He had a feel for the song and could predict the direction the band would take the notes.

He saw Kolby shift on her stool and begin to lean in, and on a hunch, he doubled the inputs from her microphone to separate tracks and then adjusted the settings. She began to sing with the famous Kolby Rae whisper, and Sean's instincts made it possible to record the pickup breath and the sound of her lips parting to take it before the second phrase.

Frankie Ryder's eyes opened wide. He turned to Sean at the controls as he listened to the pure sound and mix Sean was creating.

When they finished, Sean brought the levels down and then moved his hands to the computer keyboard. He stopped the recording, and as the system updated the files, he named and renamed the backup files to be sure they had multiple copies.

"What do you think?" Kolby asked over the monitors.

Frankie nodded. "You are an angel. You sound great. The band never better."

"And what about Sean?"

Frankie looked over at the young protégé and said, "He'll do. He did just fine. I can work with him."

CHAPTER SEVEN

LIGHTS OUT

THEIR NEXT DAY AT SIBILANCE began early for the musicians. The session was scheduled to start at 3:00 p.m., and most of the band rolled in between 3:30 and 3:45.

Kolby had been in the control room with Sean and Frankie since 1:00, listening to tracks and mixdowns, becoming both more anxious about the need for a hit and more impressed with Sean's abilities, both on bass and at the control board.

By 6:15, Skeeter was alone in Room C, recording a ride on the steel guitar to lay over the bridge in "Goody Two Shoes." Nils, Kim, and Roberto were sprawled across the control room furniture, Kolby and Sean sitting next to Frankie in rolling chairs, listening to the mix. Frankie had a cellophane-wrapped package of mini doughnuts on the counter next to half a cup of coffee. Sean paused the playback, and he and Frankie adjusted some input jacks behind the console to reroute a compressor and a limiter to new tracks.

Roberto looked out the window and watched the work crew at the road construction. "Isn't that just the way it always is? One guy doing all the work and the others just standing around?"

Everyone looked around the room and then at Roberto. Roberto paused and looked back. "What? I mean them, out there, not us. We're different." They shook their heads at him as he continued. "No, wait. We're not like them. We're working here."

Nils shook his head. "Skeeter's working; we're *avslapning*."

Roberto turned back to the window, fascinated by the crane lifting a large piece of culvert pipe up over the hole in the middle of the street. As it hung just above the height of the workers standing to the side, the band heard a loud twang as one of the metal cables on the crane boom snapped like a guitar string. The workers scrambled away as the culvert pipe spun, tipped on end, and fell into the hole. A quick explosive flash shot from the hole and echoed across the parking lot, and the lights in the studio went out. In the hallway, the single emergency light flickered to life, and an eerie silence fell on the studio and building as the white noise of computers and cooling fans stopped.

"Jesus H. Christ," muttered Frankie Ryder as he stood from his chair and moved across the control room. Skeeter stepped from behind his pedal steel and out into the hallway and followed Frankie through the lobby. From inside, Roberto and the others looked as the workers stood pointing and talking on cell phones. Skeeter and Frankie walked to them, looking up and down the street for an indication of electrical power anywhere.

Nils broke the tension in the room. "Uh oh. I've got a bad feeling about this."

The band and Sean shared a nervous giggle and continued to watch as the workers, Skeeter, and Frankie played a game of charades with punctuated hand gestures and dramatic expressions. After a few minutes, Frankie and Skeeter turned, and everyone saw the dejected looks on their faces.

Frankie didn't waste any time delivering the news. He began as he was halfway through the door. "How in the hell did they do it? I have no idea, but they managed to sever the only electrical feeder line for two blocks."

The bandmates groaned, and all eyes turned to Kolby. "What does that mean?" she asked.

"He's saying no electricity for up to three weeks. He can bring in temporary power for lights and such, but not enough to power for what we need to do here. And it won't be clean."

"Three weeks? We lose another three weeks on the album?" Kolby said.

Frankie waddled to the middle of the group. "Kolby Rae, it's worse than that. I'm having surgery next Thursday. Finally gonna do it.

Gonna do that stomach banding thing."

The room fell silent. They all quietly replayed the events of the last two days: a canceled tour, a returned tour bus, a terrible front-page magazine profile, and now a powerless recording studio. No album, no tour, no money. All eyes looked at Sean Adams.

Roberto said to Sean, "You're jinxed. How can one kid kill two bands in the same week?"

Sean was shifting his weight back and forth, trying to catch Frankie Ryder's eyes. Frankie watched him for a few minutes and snapped, "What the hell is so damn important you have to talk now? Do you need to take a piss? You're dancing like a marionette."

Sean didn't let Frankie's attitude phase his enthusiasm. "I know where we can record. I have a studio at my place. Well, it's my parents' house. In the basement."

Roberto chuckled. Kim and Skeeter looked at each other and rolled their eyes.

Frankie turned, started to yell, and then calmed his voice. "Look, kid, that's really a nice thing to say. I know you mean well, but in case you haven't figured out, this is the big time. This is Nashville. We can't just all pack up and go to your parents' basement."

Sean stood taller and reached for the smartphone in his pocket. As he took it out, he flipped to a photo album. He began pointing at the equipment in the darkened room. "I have one of those, one of those, two of those." He shifted his focus to the control board. "One of these, but mine is the newer model with the upgrades. One of those." He looked around and through the glass. "These mics are good. I have six at my place, but then I have four other 149s and then a whole set of Beyers just for the drum kit. And the Neumanns."

Upon hearing this, Nils perked up and turned his body to face Sean. Sean passed his smartphone around, and the musicians began flipping through photos of the studio. It was—in many ways— nicer than Sibilance.

"The ceilings are ten foot. There are six bedrooms, three baths… and…" Sean looked at Frankie and then at Kolby, took a deep breath, and then almost in a whisper said, "…I've got one thing Frankie doesn't."

Kolby cringed at his cocky attitude.

Frankie said, "Okay, kid, and what's that?"

"Electricity—and a backup generator."

Kim spoke first. "Smoke break. Who's with me?"

"I'm right with you," Sarah said. The men followed her out, leaving Sean, Kolby, and Frankie in the control room.

"Frankie, I can't do this without you," said Kolby.

Sean spoke, looking first at Frankie for approval. "I can do the master; then we can come back here and have Frankie do the mixdown this fall when he's free. Or you're welcome to come up to my place anytime."

Frankie looked at Sean, flipped through the photos on the smartphone, and then looked at Kolby. "The kid's got the stuff. Give him a shot. It's not like you could get in anywhere else in town."

Kolby thought for a moment and then said, "I need to ask the band. This is as much about them as it is me."

When the band returned, the mood quickly shifted from sullen to spastic, each with their own ideas and all trying to invent ways to make up the lost income from the summer as well as focus on the album. It seemed like a quirky formality, but Kolby went around the room looking at each of them.

"Nils?"

"Yeah, yeah, I'm in. I've got some great ideas for drum tracks if we have that many mics." He nodded at Sean, who nodded back.

"Skeeter?"

Skeeter, who, despite his many opinions, was often a man of more tattoos than spoken words, nodded. "In."

"Kim?"

"I'm in, but only if I don't have to share a room."

Sean interjected, "Six bedrooms plus my room. No problem."

Nils grinned. "I wouldn't share with you anyway."

"Okay, junior, it'd better be as nice as your photos," Sarah said.

Kolby turned to Frankie.

"Kolby Rae, you know I believe in you, always have," Frankie said. "I'll ride along and check everything out, and maybe Miss Sarah can give me a ride back to Nashville so I can be with my family before my surgery. Like the kid says, we can do the final mixdown here. And Miss Sarah? I say if the kid screws it up, don't pay him."

All eyes turned to Roberto, who was rocking back and forth, nodding his head. "I've got bills, Kolby. I was counting on this summer. I need the money. I can pick up some club gigs on weekends, but that means I need to be in Nashville Thursday through Sunday. And I could use some studio work. Frankie, can you check around before your surgery?"

Frankie nodded.

Kolby looked at Sarah. Sarah nodded, looked around the room at everyone, and then opened her day planner. "Sean, do you have a car?"

"Yeah, Frankie can ride with me."

Frankie looked at Kolby, rolled his eyes, then replied, "Great, kid. That'll be great."

Sarah began taking charge. "Okay, for this first trip up, let's take the SMILES and KRAEZY and Sean's car. Once we know the lay of the land, we can each drive up or ride along. It's not a tour, so I won't do day sheets or calls, but there will be a recording schedule. Go home and pack for the first two weeks. Load up the gear. Sean, will you, Roberto, and Skeeter be sure we have everything we'll need?"

The three men nodded as they exchanged glances.

Kolby Rae was about to take off on another drive chasing stars in the dark, trying to show the world and Jeffrey Toomey that she could get it right.

Later that night, the headlights from the first of the three cars lit up the curvy blacktop road as the eight of them made the two-hour journey to Crossings, Tennessee, and then a little farther to the Adams family farm and Sean's basement studio in the big house.

PART THREE
THE BIG HOUSE

CHAPTER EIGHT

DAY 399

THE MORNING JOSHUA STONE MET Kolby Rae as she sat strumming her guitar on the step of the big house, he woke up in bed to the sound of meadowlarks and a few geese as they flew overhead. It was still cool enough to sleep with the window open, and he had been waking to these sounds for nearly three weeks.

Fylgja, his German shepherd, was sleeping at the foot of the bed on her dog pad, and Joshua lay still for a moment, adjusting his eyes to the morning sun before getting up and walking across the floor of the bedroom and out into the main room of the cabin. Fylgja rolled over and opened her eyes, content to stay a few more moments on the warm pad before standing, stretching, and going to her master's side. She watched as he flipped the switch on the coffeemaker and then walked to her bowl and sat.

After he started the coffee, Joshua turned and opened the plastic airtight tub filled with dog kibble. He scooped two cups of food into the dish. Fylgja didn't move, waiting for her master's okay. Joshua walked to the far side of the room and then back, testing her response, and the dog kept intense eye contact on the man until Joshua said, *"Nimm Futter,"* German for "eat food," and Fylgja began to bite at her breakfast.

Joshua walked to the small table by the bookcase and looked at the sealed pink envelope and the hard-sided black notebook. He hesitated and began to reach for the envelope but instead, as he had done every day since David Adams had given him the envelope in January, left the envelope unopened, picked up the notebook and a pen, and stepped out onto the covered deck of the writer's cabin. The cabin was a converted horse stable, and the front deck overlooked a horse pasture.

Joshua sat in a high-backed rocking chair and opened the notebook to Day 399, the first blank page. He began journaling at the suggestion of members of his support group in the days and weeks following the shooting and his departure from Grant's Hill College. His departure was publicly called a retirement. *Retirement* was a reasonable word, considering all that had happened. The support group had talked through so many shared issues about pain, loss, and regret. They understood when he told them he was going on the road to take time away. They collectively decided there was a difference between running away and seeking space.

Diane, Joshua's therapist, had said, "Everyone deserves some time to be unplugged." That decision prompted him to call shotgun as he and Fylgja climbed into Dr. Alan Neal's car and rode with him to his summer home in the Rockies. After ninety days with Alan, Joshua rode halfway back, taking a temporary contract at a community college to teach Introduction to Composition. Joshua, who had never learned to drive, took advantage of the tuition discount and enrolled in adult driver's education the first week and struck a deal for a long-term car rental at the insurance agency. He bought a bike rack for his Skeppshult bicycle and stayed in the only pets-welcome, rent-by-the-month efficiency apartment in the small rural town.

Joshua made a three-part pact with himself the day he left Grant's Hill College: to simplify his life, to stop missing opportunities to say what he was feeling to his friends, and to read the Bible from cover to cover. He once heard a priest giving a lecture on campus, who shared that Catholics who attend mass once a week and listened to the readings hear the entire Bible in three years. So that was Joshua's goal, to read the Bible in three years.

"Simplify," he journaled on Day 37, "is in the eye of the beholder. Living out of a backpack with a young puppy and crashing on your best friend's sofa at age forty-three is far from simple."

In January, Joshua had moved to the cabin at the invitation, or rather the insistence, of David and Ellen Adams. Their farm was just outside of Crossings. For the first few weeks, Joshua enjoyed the solitude. By spring, Joshua found himself being less unplugged and more connected to the town, his former students, colleagues, and friends. More and more of his mail was delivered to the Adams address without the yellow forwarding stickers from the post office. He had a smartphone and used it to keep in touch and reconnect. It also made it easy for strangers to find him. Every few weeks, the curious, the lost, and the hustlers all discovered his number, and the unsolicited and unwanted calls began. They knew him from the old news articles and tabloids. The most frequent unsolicited call came each month from Jeffrey Toomey, a writer who wanted to interview him. Joshua at first ignored the calls and then, tiring of that, began swapping each month for a new number, sometimes a new phone, and redownloading his address book.

Joshua glanced over his shoulder back into the cabin at the table with the pink envelope. He considered getting up to retrieve it, then looked down at the notebook, still with the blank page for Day 399 open. The decision about opening the envelope for that day was made easier when Sean Adams walked over from the big house.

"Sean," called Joshua as he set down the journal and looked over.

The twenty-year-old stopped at the first step to the deck.

"Hey, Dr. Stone. How are you?"

"Sean, you've been gone for two weeks. I figured you were on a world tour filled with sex, drugs, and rock and roll. What brought you back? Is everything okay?"

"Hey, yeah, about that. The band broke up, but I've got this gig recording an album. Check it out—a woman, Nashville artist."

Joshua nodded his head. "That's great news." Joshua paused and shook his head. "Good luck with that."

"You know what Doctor Stone? You should drive up and say hi to her. You know, on your way into town."

Joshua smiled, closed his journal and picked up the keys to the Rover from the hook near the door. Sean had sent him four text messages during his two-week absence. It was odd timing; each came just as Joshua was about to call David and tell him Sean was missing.

As he walked to the Rover, he called Fylgja and then said, "We should tell your parents you're okay."

"Oh, they know. I talk to Mom almost every day."

Joshua looked surprised. "What? Why am I the last to know?"

"I didn't want to bother you, Dr. Stone."

And he stared the Rover and asked, "What is it with you people? That's exactly what Forrest and Rooster told me the day after you left on your first trip." With that, he began to drive towards the big house.

CHAPTER NINE

FORREST AND ROOSTER

"WE DIDN'T WANT TO BOTHER you."

That was what the man behind the controls of the skid steer yelled to Joshua on the first day of March. Sean Adams had driven to Nashville to shop for a new electric bass and to hang out in a few clubs, and Joshua assumed he would have the Adams farm to himself. The sound and sight of the skid steer convinced Joshua he was going to have company most of the day. Joshua watched as the tall man drove backwards on the flatbed trailer next to the big house. The shorter, stubby-nosed man next to the trailer nodded in agreement as he flipped down the ramps on the back of the trailer and secured them with a large metal pin. The tall man continued backing the skid steer down the ramps and then spun a quick circle in the driveway before pulling up alongside Joshua and reaching up to the switch, shutting off the motor.

"We didn't want to interrupt your work."

Joshua looked at the two men, the truck, and the skid steer. "I'm Joshua Stone, and you are?"

"I'm Forrest Straight, and this here's Rooster. We keep an eye on the place for Dr. Adams. I'm sure he told you about us."

"Actually, no, he didn't—"

"No problem today, chief. We're here for the driveway. We ain't gonna be too long."

"Driveway?"

The man named Rooster climbed into the truck, fired up the diesel motor, and began turning the flatbed around across the pasture.

"What driveway?" Joshua asked with a bit more ire in his voice.

"Dr. Adams called, said he wanted a rock driveway down to the studio doors around back. Wants to make it easier to get a delivery down there, so that's what we're gonna do."

With that, Forrest turned the skid steer ignition and began backing up with a characteristic warning beep as it went. He lowered the bucket and began swiping away swatches of sod and dirt, maneuvering back and forth. In a matter of thirty minutes, he had the beginning shape of a driveway that curved from the existing driveway to the back double doors opening into Sean's basement studio.

As Forrest smoothed the dirt, a bright red dump truck lumbered up the drive, the motor straining against the weight of the load. As it approached, Joshua recognized Rooster behind the wheel. Rooster turned the truck and backed down the new dirt path to the back of the big house. Joshua listened as the truck's hydraulics lifted the dump box. As the sound of falling rock began, the motor on the truck revved, and Rooster began pulling the truck up the curve, dropping rock as he went. By this time, Joshua had moved to the cabin deck with Fylgja at his feet. He watched as Rooster raised the bed to its top height, then let the box drop, and then drove off down the lane to the highway. In about thirty minutes, he was back with a second load.

Rooster made a total of six trips, with Forrest feathering the surface of the rock with the skid steer. On Rooster's seventh return trip, he was driving the original flatbed, and the moment he set the loading ramp, Forrest was on the ramps and racing across the flatbed until he stopped the skid steer at the end. He shut down the motor and jumped off, and he and Rooster began chaining and strapping it to the flatbed trailer.

Forrest flipped open his cell phone and looked at the time: 11:30. "You got plans for dinner?" he asked.

Joshua paused, not sure if Forrest was talking about the midday meal or the evening meal. Dinner and supper and lunch, he was learning, meant different things in the Rockies, at Grant's Hill, and in Tennessee.

"Hop in. Let's eat at the Roadhouse."

"Can I bring my dog?"

Forrest looked at Fylgja on the deck. "Sure. C'mon, dog, let's go." The three men climbed into the cab of the diesel semi. Fylgja lay on the floor at their feet.

The Roadhouse was a relic from the 1940s when the two-lane road on the edge of Crossings was the major east–west throughway across the state. The parking lot was filled with pickup trucks, mostly dual-lies, and a handful of older cars. Forrest guided the long flatbed down the shoulder just beyond the parking lot, and the three men got out.

"*Bleib*," Joshua commanded, and Fylgja remained on the floor of the cab.

"What did you say?" Rooster asked.

"'Stay' in German," Joshua replied.

Rooster shook his head and shrugged.

The Roadhouse, as the locals called it, was a long, flat building with a covered deck that ran the length of the front. There was a second-story facade that had a few false windows and what was left of a long-faded hand-painted sign. The logo was retro enough to be considered trendy.

They stepped up onto the deck, and Joshua gave a quick glance left and right. Plastic tables and chairs were spaced in a row. A tarp like banner with a beer logo flapped in the breeze. It had handwritten words: *It's 5:00 somewhere. $2.00 bottles, Wednesday nites.*

They stepped through the doors, and as his eyes adjusted to the dark, Joshua scanned the room. It had a bar toward the back, was divided by a half wall, and had two groups of tables and booths that made it feel like two rooms. The tables were covered with plastic pic-nic tablecloths, and wrapped silverware and napkin were set at each chair. The three men sat at a table near the windows and looked over the menus as a man in his thirties wearing wire-framed glasses came up and rested his hand on Rooster's shoulder.

"Hey, Forrest….Rooster." He looked at Joshua and, not recogniz-ing him, extended his hand. "I'm Drew McDonel."

"Father Drew, this is Joshua Stone."

Drew looked oddly at Forrest and shook Joshua's hand.

Joshua stood up, "Father, nice to meet you. No collar today? Are you playing golf?"

"Joshua, they're teasing you. I'm not a priest. I'm their pastor."

Forrest shifted to what Joshua would come to know as his sarcastic "my dumb cousin in Tennessee" voice and asked, "Duh, what's the difference?"

Rooster turned to Joshua. "Drew here is our minister and president of our men's faith league. You've heard of the NFL? Well, we're the MFL. We'd love it if you could come to a meeting."

"Where's your church home, Joshua?" Drew asked

Joshua realized he had stopped going to church after he had left Grant's Hill. "I was in the Church of Christ as a kid." Forrest, Rooster, and Drew exchanged approving looks.

Drew spoke first, "Joshua, we're small but trying to grow. We have seventy-three families as members, and Forrest and Rooster are right, we'd love for you to worship with us and join the MFL."

"Thanks. I think I'd enjoy getting to know more people in the town. I'm out at David Adams's place. It's a bit more rural than I'm used to."

Drew's face focused on Joshua with partial realization. "You're that professor from the college, aren't you?"

"I was. Now I'm just Joshua."

"Rooster, hear that? He's another one of those P-H-D types. Doctor Stone, that's who he is." Joshua laughed at Forrest's three-syllable pronunciation. Forrest proclaimed, "And I can just tell, this man is a one-man pancake machine."

Rooster had just torn open a pack of crackers from the basket next to the ketchup bottle and nodded.

Drew placed his hand on Joshua's shoulder. "Joshua, I hope you will take us up on the invitation. We'd love to have you. You are welcome to pray with us."

"Thank you, Drew. I'll come by on Sunday."

They finished lunch, talking about the MFL and pancakes.

"See, Joshua, the thing of it is, we've done this pancake breakfast every year to raise college scholarships for local kids. It makes good money, and the women, the ladies auxiliary, always help us out. They do the cookin', and we do the cleanup and promotion and advertising."

Rooster interrupted. "But see, they took half the money, so instead of it all going to the kids' scholarships, half went to the auxiliary."

"What did they do with it?" Joshua asked between bites.

"You know how women are. Who knows? But this year, we get to keep it all." Forrest pointed with his fork at Joshua's right hand, and Joshua self-consciously slid his left off the table. "Your hands are too clean to do any dirty work, so I figure you must flip one heck of a pancake."

Joshua tried to remember the last time he had made pancakes. They were sounding pretty good, even on a stomach full from lunch. "When is this pancake breakfast?"

Rooster replied, "It's this June, around the middle of the month."

"Oh, on Father's Day?"

Rooster and Forrest looked at each other with a sly grin. "See, that's why he went to college. You and I didn't even think of that."

Forrest and Rooster stood side by side at the cash register to pay their bills. Joshua waited behind them. The two reminded him of a hipster Laurel and Hardy. The more rotund Rooster was in his sixties and wore both a thick leather belt and bright green suspenders with brass tone clips that had been put on his jeans so many times, they had worn holes through the fabric.

Rooster leaned in. "Joshua, do you carry or just keep a truck gun?"

Joshua stopped before answering. He hadn't talked with anyone about his decision to carry a gun. He could never bring it up when he was at the college. Joshua could tell from the empty holster on Rooster's belt that he carried a gun some of the time.

"Rooster, I carry. I haven't had a truck long enough to have a truck gun. Do you think people around here will object?"

Rooster shook his head. "Joshua, the joke around here is, if the sheriff pulls you over and comes up to the side of your car and asks you if you have a gun and you answer no, he's obligated to write you a summons on the spot." Rooster laughed and slapped the counter next to the cash register. The spindle of tickets fell to the floor. Joshua bent over and picked it up. The waitress, a bit flustered, thanked him.

"Jackie, this here is Joshua Stone," said Rooster. "He's new. Stayin' out at the Adams place. He's gonna join the MFL with us."

Joshua nodded and placed the spindle of tickets on the counter. "Hi, I'm Joshua."

"I'm Jackie Gower. Nice to meet you. You're not from around here, are you? You from Nashville?"

"No, I worked with David…" Joshua already felt as if he had said one line too many.

"At the college? My little girl, Alyson, wants to go there so bad. She has to type her admission essays on the computer. I can't help her. I don't know a thing about essays or computers, but she uses one all the time."

"Does she need some help? I might be able to proofread or help her out."

Jackie Gower beamed as she looked at Forrest. Forrest looked at Joshua, then back at Jackie. "I think it's gonna take some work. He's a little smooth around the edges, but he's gonna fit in just fine around here."

Forrest was in his midforties. He wore short hair and thick-framed glasses. Joshua guessed he was taller than his basketball buddy Dr. Alan Neal. Forrest towered over both Joshua and Rooster. As Joshua got to know Forrest, he saw he always wore a denim shirt, and underneath was a denim self-made holster. Joshua realized that he never would have noticed either man's gun if it hadn't been for his own concealed carry classes. He wondered how many people in his life were carrying guns and he was oblivious. And according to Rooster's joke, most everyone around him these days was carrying.

CHAPTER TEN

THE MFL

THE TWELVE MILES BETWEEN THE Adams place and Crossings made everyday use of Joshua's Skeppshult bicycle impractical. The road's steep climbs, blind hills, and curves were a big change from the pastoral rides to the Grant's Hill college campus. Joshua rode the fat-tired Swedish commuting bike a few times each week, but the bike spent most of the time leaning against a post on the deck of the stable-turned-cabin. To get around, Joshua and his new driver's license made use of the right-hand-drive 1970s Range Rover David Adams insisted on importing to the United States after his first successful African safari. Joshua was drawn to the quirky looks, and the right-hand drive was more like the view of the road he had aboard his bicycle. The folks of Crossings were so used to seeing Dr. Adams and his safari truck running around town each summer that the sight of the new guy in town driving it rarely prompted a second look.

On his way into town for his first MFL meeting, Joshua stopped at the convenience store for gas and walked inside to get a cup of coffee. Two men wearing fishing caps, fishing shirts, and cargo shorts were standing in line ahead of him.

"What they hitting on?" one of the men asked, seeking the local fishing report.

The teenage girl behind the register didn't look up at the men but kept punching keys, ringing up their gas and food, saying, "Number five Shad Raps, back of the coves."

"Really? You'd better give us a couple of those, too."

"Third aisle, second shelf."

The younger of the two men said, "Excuse me," and passed between the shelving and Joshua. He brought back five boxes of fishing lures.

"$79.75. Will that be all?" The girl rang the two men up.

Joshua stepped up as the fishermen walked out to their pickup truck, which had a large bass boat hitched to the back. "Hi. The coffee, and I'm on pump three." He looked at her name tag: Alyson.

She looked up at him, hearing his voice. "Hi. You're staying out at the Adams place, right? I think you met my mom the other day."

"Yes, I am. And is your mom Mrs. Gower?" Joshua set the coffee cup down on the counter and reached for his wallet.

"Yes. She said maybe you could help me with my admission essays. I'm a good writer. She just worries too much."

"That's a mom's job. She has to worry. When is your deadline?"

"I'm applying for a start next year at Grant's Hill, so any time before Christmas." Joshua flinched when she spoke the name of the college, and then the girl hit some buttons on the register. "Twenty-seven fifty-five."

"And the coffee?" Joshua said, pointing to the cup.

"We only charge the tourists. It's free for locals."

"I guess that makes me a local?"

"You are now."

Joshua walked back to the Rover, glancing at the out-of-state license plates on the bass boat and truck, and then the Tennessee plates on the Rover. He paraphrased the checkout girl—"I guess I am now"—and headed to the church.

The Crossings Congregational Church building was a single-story, concrete block, square building built in the middle of a gravel parking lot just off the main highway through town. In a former life, the building was a pizza restaurant, and the current owner happily leased it to the church with the tacit understanding that the restaurant supplies and ovens would remain in the commercial kitchen. The kitchen was put to use for church functions, wedding receptions, and the occasional funeral.

A two-story wood and aluminum cross stood at the northwest corner of the lot, and a changeable letter sign read:

CROSSINGS CONGREGATIONAL CHURCH

F.R. "Fritz" Nordengren

Pastor Drew McDonel

and in script:

All Are Welcome Here
We Are an Open and Affirming Church
Movable letters spelled out:
GOD WANTS SPIRITUAL FRUITS
NOT RELIGIOUS NUTS

Inside, Joshua found a line of fifteen men at a small buffet table, scooping lasagna onto paper plates and talking in loud, conversational tones. Drew McDonel grabbed his shoulder. "Joshua, so glad you came. Let me introduce you around. Grab a plate."

As they made their way through the line, Drew introduced Joshua to several of the men, and when he got to the end of the buffet, he walked over and sat at a table with Forrest, Rooster, Michael Hutsun, and Wayne Baylis.

It quickly became a pleasant routine. Joshua attended church at 11:00 each Sunday, and in spite of being the new guy in town, he was put on the welcome committee, handing out the church bulletin as each family came to services. It was a quick way for others to get to know his name, and he learned his neighbors' names and their stories.

On Thursday nights, he came back to the church for MFL. Each meeting was familiar and comfortable: a buffet dinner, a few funny stories from some of the fishing guides and local farmers, and then Drew led a discussion about the week's Bible verse and how it related to their lives. Each of the men took the scripture to heart, but more than once, there was an implied reminder of a gag or incident that managed to sneak into the mostly reflective chat. After that, the men held a business meeting and talked about how to raise money, how to find more members, and how to move the congregation out of the former restaurant and into a real church.

Joshua liked their company. Michael Hutsun and Wayne Baylis were the money guys, an insurance agent and a retirement plan administrator. Forrest and Rooster were the go-to guys. If they didn't have it or know where one was, they managed to find one before the next meeting. It amused Joshua that it never seemed to matter what the "it" was: metric socket sets, in-line fuse for a jukebox, spring door for a raccoon live trap. If anyone in the room needed it, Forrest or Rooster had it or found it.

The night Joshua met the singer Kolby Rae, he was coming home from an MFL meeting at which they had all voted him to be in charge of the pancake breakfast.

"Guys, thank you. I'm honored, but I'm the newest member, and I've never run a restaurant. I'm a college professor, or at least I was."

Michael Hutsun nodded. "Exactly the kind of person we need. We'll do the cooking; you just watch what we're doing out front and tell us when we need more food. People in town know you worked at a college. They know. Seeing you out pouring coffee and clearing places and being in charge will make them think their money is going to a good cause."

Wayne Baylis nodded in agreement, as did the others in the room.

Joshua nodded. "Okay, so can I make a suggestion?" He looked at Forrest, then Rooster, then Drew. "How many kids do we have that need these scholarships?"

Drew said, "We have five this year, Joshua. All good kids, all who want to go to college."

"Okay, why don't we do this? Let's have them bus the tables and get them some T-shirts that read, *I'm working to pay my way to school*. And then give each one a tip jar that people can toss a few bucks into. And maybe put the kid's pictures and where they want to go to school on a poster?"

The room was quiet. Then Drew said, "And you have to ask why we put you in charge?"

The meeting broke up. Joshua stayed back with Drew and then walked through the kitchen and looked over the utensils.

"Joshua, we like having you in our community. Thank you for your gifts," said Drew.

"I like it here, Drew, and thanks for your confidence in me for this breakfast—I think. I've never done anything like this."

Drew turned to Joshua. "God never gives us a mountain we can't climb, Joshua." He gripped Joshua's shoulder again as he continued. "I know you've done it before."

Joshua reflected on the biblical reference to mountains and asked, "Oh, you mean like Corinthians 10:13?"

Drew laughed loudly. "No, I mean song lyrics. Brooks and Dunn. You need some more country music in your life."

CHAPTER ELEVEN

FIRESIDE

IN THE TENNESSEE DARKNESS, IT was hard to see where the horizon divided the fireflies in the grass from the stars in the sky as Joshua turned the Rover down the private lane and toward the cabin. As he slowed down to make a U-turn and stop in front of the covered deck, Fylgja looked up and gave a quick bark. Sean Adams was walking up the lane from the cabin, and Joshua stopped and rolled down the window.

"Hey, Sean. Nice night."

"Hi, Dr. Stone. I wanted to tell you, we're just hanging out tonight, have a little fire going. You and Fylgja are welcome to come up, get to know the band."

Joshua nodded. "Really? Sure, sounds fun. I'll be up in a bit. Let me walk Fylgja."

The gravel drive to the rear studio doors cut across the grass and then up the left side of the house as Joshua walked toward the covered porch. The porch was an airy three-season room with two open walls. From the chairs, you could see most of the property. It was covered with a hip roof and finished with cedar tongue-and-groove boards and white trim. Along one of the interior walls was a small outdoor kitchen that included a counter and refrigerator. A stone and brick fireplace and oven supported the roofline with a two-story chimney. A large gas-fired barbecue stood at the edge.

Sean Adams introduced Joshua as he stepped under the roof. "Everyone, this is my dad's friend Joshua Stone. He's a writer and used to work with my dad."

"Hey, Joshua, grab a beer. Join us," Roberto called as Joshua walked across the tile floor.

The rest were all seated around the spacious room. Joshua shook hands as he met Roberto, Skeeter, Nils, Kim, and Sarah. He glanced around to see if the guitar-playing woman with the nice legs was there, and when he didn't see her, he sighed and followed Sean to the refrigerator. Sean reached into the refrigerator and pulled out two beers, handing one to Kim and the second to Joshua. Joshua nodded and sat in the large wicker chair next to a low table. Fylgja lay at his feet.

"She's such a pretty dog," Kim said. "How old is she?"

"About two," Joshua answered.

Kolby walked out through the glass-paned door and opened a beer. She looked around at the group. There were several open chairs, including the one next to Joshua and Fylgja. She walked over and began to pet the dog, casually sitting in the open chair and listening as Joshua was talking basketball with Roberto.

"This state has some great teams. You've got Southwood out of Memphis, Oak Ridge, Dyer County."

Roberto recognized Oak Ridge. "I don't think we know the same boys from Oak Ridge."

It was obvious to Kolby neither man quite understood the other's misunderstanding. Nevertheless, their conversation kept rolling along.

Roberto continued, "I didn't play basketball until after high school. I don't know why. I just didn't understand the game. But when I toured with my first band, maybe 1997 or 1998, they taught me how to play. I love it. Nothing better than walking into a gym or a pickup game and just going at it."

"Really? You like pickup games? If you're free, you should come with me into Crossings. They have a community gym, and I work with some of the high school kids. Tuesday night there's an adult church league, but there's nothing churchlike about the way some of these guys play. They get a kick out of watching me try to keep up."

Roberto tipped back his beer bottle. "Get you another?"

"No, not just yet. I just started."

"No? I thought you were a writer, like Papa Hemingway. Don't like beer? Maybe we need to find you the harder stuff."

"Are you a fan of Hemingway?" Joshua asked.

"Hey, I'm Cuban. Of course. He was a great writer. He lived every-where: the U.S., Africa, Spain, France. But where did he live when he won the Nobel Prize?" Roberto slapped his chest twice. "C-U-B-A, Cuba."

Roberto stood a bit taller. "Wait, listen to this, I had to learn this in highschool speech class," and he began to recite Hemingway's Nobel acceptance speech. "'Writing, at its best, is a lonely life. Organizations for writers palliate the writer's loneliness but I doubt if they improve his writing. He grows in public stature as he sheds his loneliness and often his work deteriorates.'"

Roberto nodded at Joshua, who joined him, and together they said, "'For he does his work alone and if he is a good enough writer he must face eternity, or the lack of it, each day.'"

The two men grinned and tapped their bottles together. Roberto then crossed the room to the refrigerator and pulled out another beer.

Kolby and Sarah looked at each other and shook their heads.

"Who memorizes stuff like that?" Sarah asked. Then Kolby turned to Sean, who had just stood up and was reaching across a table for a bag of potato chips.

"Look at his reach," Kolby said. "Oh my word. Sean, let me ask you; how tall are you?"

Sean turned and looked at the short-statured woman sitting be-tween the dog and the writer. "I'm six-eight."

"Really? Six-eight? That's the same height as Trent was."

"Who's Trent?" Sean asked.

Kim and Nils both laughed. "You don't know shit about country music, do you?"

Roberto interrupted. "Give him a break. Sean, it's okay. They don't know Coldplay from Slayer. Trent was"—he paused—"Trent Dixon *was* country music. If you were to name the major men in country mu-sic—Tim, Garth, George—Trent was always included."

Kolby picked up the story. "I met Trent at an awards show with his wife, Rita. Trent was the talent, and Rita was the business."

Sarah raised her glass in a toast of homage. "Here's to TCB: takin' care of business."

Kolby nodded at Sarah, then continued, "Rita said to Trent, 'I think you should sing it with Kolby.'"

Joshua interrupted. "'It'?"

"'Don't Close Your Eyes,' the Keith Whitley classic hit."

Joshua, as lost and confused about country music as Sean, nodded.

"So Trent and Rita arranged for Trent and me to sing a duet at the Opry. We sang this song, originally by a man asking his lover not to close her eyes while she kisses him. And we turned it into a couple having the same thoughts about each other."

Kim interjected, "It was before my time, but it was huge."

Nils beamed. "It was *the* moment in live video performances."

Roberto nodded. "Kolby, you nailed it."

Kolby looked down at her beer, smiling a happy smile. "It was awarded the Vocal Event of the Year at the CMAs. I think you can still download it on online."

Joshua turned and leaned in a bit closer. "Okay, so help me out. I'm not stupid, but if you're on national TV with the biggest male singer in country music and you win Vocal Event of the Year…" He looked quizzically at Kolby Rae and then the others, then back into her eyes. She didn't break eye contact. He continued, "I mean, if that doesn't sell records, what does? What don't I get about the music business?"

Kolby looked back into Joshua's eyes a bit longer. The others noticed, too. Then she continued with her story. "It was big. I'm not boasting, but what we did that night was really rare. So Rita and Trent decided that we would tour together, that I would open."

Sarah said, "Closest yet Kolby's come to a stadium tour."

Nils replied, "We'll get there, Sarah. I believe in you, Kolby."

"So they had this all figured out. Trent and I kept it hush-hush. We made a plan to record his next music video with me in it. Its release would coincide with his tour date announcements, with me as his opening act. The music video with Trent…the tour…we almost got it right." Kolby paused, then nodded once at Sarah. "Tell the rest, Sarah. Back then, Sarah worked for Pier—she was Trent's liaison—so she knew what was going on."

"Okay, sure," said Sarah. "Trent and Kolby were both on the same label. I worked for the label. We put together the whole tour package. The merchandise was hot. Kolby's album was stellar. This was her second album, *Four-Wheel Girl.*"

Roberto chimed in. "That's when I joined the band…and Nils, too."

Kolby raised her bottle and gestured to each of the men.

Sarah continued. "Trent's single was done, and we were on a horse farm in Kentucky shooting the video." Sarah set her drink down and held both hands in front of her as she went deeper into the story. "I'll never forget. Kolby drives up in her truck, gets out, and Trent stands up and walks away from his entire entourage and walks over to her. I see what's going on, so I start walking toward them. So, like, I'm behind Trent, and then Rita walks up, and Trent says, 'Kolby, your trailer is over there, and we have a trailer for your people, too.'"

Kolby took a swallow of beer and interrupted. "No, no, you've got to say it like Trent." She lowered her voice an octave. "'We have a trailer for your people, too.'"

The band laughed at the impersonation.

Sarah continued, "So I'm desperately trying to get Kolby's attention so she would say the right thing, but you know Kolby; she can't make up a fib to save her life, so she says, 'Why, Trent, I don't have *people*. It's just me.'"

Kolby drew a breath, took a sip of beer, and picked up the story. "Well, it was the truth….So Trent leans in to me and says, 'I am so jealous. It must be amazing not to have people. When you make it big, don't surround yourself with people. They take all the love out of the music.'"

Sarah rested her hands on her knees, "So the music video was in two scenes. Trent was filming his part in a barn. They had a cow, a horse, and this rooster brought in by the animal trainers. Well, that rooster scratched Trent's arm. Hell, I think they had three paramedics looking at him."

They all laughed, and then the group grew awkwardly silent. Joshua looked around, and no one made eye contact. He looked down a Fylgja and saw Kolby's hand caressing the dog's ears and fur, seeking comfort from the animal.

Kolby said, "I was walking by when they were all fussin' over him, and he just looks at me and says, 'See what I mean? People!' And that's the last thing he ever said to me."

Sarah took a small sip, drew a drag from her cigarette, and continued, "Filming went awesome. Kolby looked…wow. I still think about how pretty you looked in that dress. The script didn't call for Trent and Kolby to film any scenes together, so when he was done, Trent — against everyone's objection at the label — snuck off the set and off to the Boundary Waters Canoe Wilderness for a two-week canoe trip. Oh, my bosses were so pissed off."

Joshua looked around, still not understanding the story.

Kolby finished the tale. "No one noticed at the time, but remember that chicken? So Trent goes off on this wilderness trip, and the cut is infected, and it turns out to be the bacteria you get in hospitals."

"MRSA?" Joshua asked

"Yes, and he died on that trip, too far from a hospital to do any good. So Rita, both in mourning and still a smart businesswoman, took control of everything of his on the market and locked up the licensing and royalties to his music and his performances. She canceled the tour, bought out our contract for pennies on the dollar, and no one ever knew I was the next rising star in the Trent Dixon lineup."

Kolby looked around the group and then rested her eyes on Joshua. He tilted his head in her direction.

Kim turned to Joshua as she pulled another beer from the refrigerator. "So, Joshua, Sean says you're a writer. What do you write? Are you a journalist?"

"No, no, I'm a retired professor, actually. But I've written a few books."

"Retired? You look too young to be retired. What are you, midfifties?"

Joshua said, "I'm forty-three. I've got a few years."

Kolby began humming and then said a lyric line:

:: Look out, boy, ::

:: You're gonna get a piece of this — sass ::

She didn't think twice about her sudden singing aloud. Most of the time, she didn't notice she did it. Music always played in her head. The rest of the group didn't react. Fylgja raised her head and cocked her ear. Kolby looked over and saw Joshua with the same expression as the pup. She stopped.

Roberto said from across the room, "Joshua Stone — I know I've heard your name. You must be famous for something. I must have heard about your books."

Joshua shifted in the chair. "Hey, maybe. I'm working on a new one right now. I'm calling it *The Rules of Calling Shotgun.* It was going to be funny, but it seems to be finding a darker life of its own. About men making bad choices."

Kim laughed. "Roberto is available if you need any background research."

"I don't make bad choices."

Nils mocked, "If we don't count Mississippi. Or Key West."

Kim chimed in. "Or all of 2007."

Roberto stammered, "Okay, I'll give you Key West, but 2007 wasn't all bad."

Joshua tried his best to keep up with their drinking but gave up and left after midnight. The band seemed to be just getting their second wind. He and Fylgja walked across the grass and over to the writer's cabin. Right before he got in bed, he petted Fylgja and then noticed a scent on his hand. He looked at the dog. "Fylgja, did you roll in something?" He leaned in to sniff. It was the same lavender smell from the meeting with Kolby on the front step of the big house. "Fylgja, did you like that lady? I think she really likes you."

CHAPTER TWELVE

PANCAKE BREAKFAST

JOSHUA WOKE EARLY THE NEXT morning to be out the door and at the church by 5:00 to start the pancake breakfast. He and Fylgja performed their morning ritual in the dark. While the dog ate, the man walked to the table and stared at the notebook and the pink envelope. He thought back to the pained look on David Adams's face in January when David first gave him the envelope.

"Joshua, about what happened that day in the chapel," David began.

"David, we talked it out. There is nothing more to say." Stone clasped his former colleague's hand.

"Joshua, I meant about Liv Olsson."

Joshua hadn't heard anyone say her name in a very long time, and it surprised him to feel his heart flutter as David spoke.

"Ellen and I…well, all of us…every single person who knew you two….we're just so sorry. And we never blamed you for her death."

Joshua looked through the wire-framed glasses resting slanted on the man's face. He felt the compassion and pain in his friend's words. "David, thank you. We all did what we had to do."

"Joshua, there's one more thing…" That was when Adams reached into the deep pocket of his photojournalist-style vest and retrieved a pink envelope. "After the sheriff's department released the crime scene, Grant's Hill let me go into Liv's office and have a look around. There wasn't much there, but somehow, the investigators never looked under her desk blotter. I don't even know what made me look there, but I did, and, well, I found this." Adams extended his hand with the envelope to Joshua. "As you can see, it has your name on it."

Joshua pulled his hand back, not wanting to take the envelope from David. "David, it's been a year. You've kept it from me this long; why even give it to me now? What's done is done, right?"

"I know. I thought the same thing. I almost didn't give it to you, but…Joshua, there's another journalist asking around about you, says he's working on your biography."

Joshua nodded and then shook his head. "I know. Jeffrey Toomey. He calls me nonstop. Most of the time, I just don't answer it."

Joshua noticed that since their time apart, David Adams was looking older, and his mustache was greyer.

"Joshua, I wouldn't want this guy Toomey to get this"

"David, I trust you to never give it to anyone else. I just wonder, why even give it to me?"

"That's just it. Ellen and I had a bit of trouble over the weekend. Someone broke into the house."

"What? In Grant's Hill? Did you report it? Were you hurt?"

"Yes, we filed a report, and other than our sliding door being pushed in, there was no real damage. It was in the middle of the day. Ellen was gone for less than twenty minutes. The sheriff said it was pros who knew our habits."

"David, wow. What can I do?"

"My desk was ransacked, and my laptop was stolen. The sheriff said they were looking for cash or something they could sell quick and cheap in a college town. That's why they left the silver and coin collection."

David held up the pink envelope. "They didn't get this." He pushed it toward Joshua's hand, and this time, Joshua didn't pull away. "As far as I'm concerned, this is yours. I could never excuse myself if someone else—this Toomey character or some petty thief—ended up with it."

Joshua shook his head. "So you give it to me? Tag, you're it?"

Joshua realized he had spoken aloud as he stood in the writer's cabin in the morning darkness, thinking back to his conversation with David. Fylgja cocked her head and looked at him as once again he made a choice between the notebook and the pink envelope.

He picked up the envelope, holding it in one hand and drawing it between the first finger and thumb of his other hand repeatedly as he tried to both remember Liv Olsson and forget their last day together.

Joshua stared at the envelope, and then picked his copy of *One Good Bread Pudding* from the shelf, placed the envelope inside at the back of the pages. He closed it, held it for a moment, then returned the book to its shelf next to David Adams's *Tin Roof Rusted*.

"Fylgja, you're home today. I'll be back after the breakfast." Joshua drove into town.

Three hours later in the big house, Kolby shuffled into the kitchen, hoping to find that Sean or someone had made coffee. She stood there, looking at the sleek countertops and the empty coffeemaker. She stared at it as if by some miracle coffee would begin flowing from the basket and into the empty pot below. It did not. She sighed as Sarah came into the large kitchen from the other hallway.

"Coffee?"

Kolby shook her head.

They began opening cupboards, finding food, plates, glasses, and baking supplies, but no coffee. Kolby opened the side-by-side refrigerator and freezer but found only takeout leftovers and frozen meals. Skeeter walked in with Sean.

"Sean, any coffee?"

"Oh, yeah." He opened the appliance garage on the counter and pulled out a ceramic canister with the word COFFEE fired into the design. He lifted the lid, looked down into the container, and then turned it upside down. A few coffee grounds sprinkled onto the floor. "I think we're out." They all looked at each other. "But you know, Dr. Stone has that pancake breakfast thing at the church today. I bet they have coffee."

They returned to their rooms; pulled on some jeans, presentable T-shirts, and shoes; and met up at the parked SUVs.

"Kolby, I'll drive," offered Sarah. They left and headed into the town of Crossings.

As Sarah pulled into the parking lot of the church, they all noticed children playing on the sidewalks, taking turns tossing coins in the air and catching them. The kids stacked four quarters on their fist and flicked them into the sky, sending the quarters scattering in all directions. They then ran after them, trying to grab them before they became lost in the grass along the sidewalk.

"Who needs video games?"

Once inside, the band followed Sean up to the man taking money. "Four of us, please."

"That's sixteen dollars."

Sean handed him a twenty and said, "Keep the rest for the kids."

A large pass-through window opened into a commercial kitchen. Behind the counter, a motley group of men were stirring mix, ladling batter, and stacking pancakes onto plates along with sausage, bacon, ham, and grits.

As Kolby picked up her plate, she noticed Joshua Stone standing with a group of wide-eyed children sitting around him. He showed the children four quarters and then stacked them on his closed fist. With a flick, the quarters soared in the air, and then he caught them, 1-2-3-4, before they hit the ground.

The children's excited voices cut through the din of the breakfast patrons.

"Me!"

"Me!"

"My turn!"

"Let me try!"

Kolby looked at the band to see if they noticed. Sarah and Skeeter were grinning about an inside joke, and Sean was adding more bacon to his plate. As they picked up their silverware rolled in a paper napkin, Rooster nodded at them all and said, "Y'all are welcome. Thanks for coming."

The band sat at the third table from the food line. As Joshua walked past them, he waved and gestured *I'll be right back* and went through the swinging door and into the kitchen. Kolby looked through the open passage into the kitchen as Joshua patted a few of the men on the back, smiling. He walked back out front, restacked more paper plates, and called over his shoulder, "Forrest, can we get that same amount of bacon as last time? And then let's slow down on the ham. Go ahead and fry that last slice for now."

Joshua brought a pot of coffee to the group. "We just made this. It's fresh," he said as he topped off the cups around the table.

As he finished, an elderly woman with silver-blue hair stepped up to the table. "Dr. Stone? Doctor? I am so glad you are here. My inflammation is still going in my left elbow."

Joshua turned to the woman. "It is? When did this all start?"

"I think it was Tuesday. Yes, it was Tuesday. That's the day the boy next door mowed his lawn."

Joshua turned to the band. "Excuse me," he said and then walked with the older woman as another man in his fifties, wearing his sunglasses on the top of his head, came up to the two of them.

Kolby turned to Sean. "Sean, you've heard our sound. You've heard the band. Tell me what you're thinking."

Sean turned, looking at Kolby and the others. "Is this a test, or do you really want to know what I think?"

"Sean, Frankie isn't here. It's not a test. What do you hear? What if I said to you, 'I want you to produce a song'? How would you cut it?"

"Depends on the song. What are you thinking?"

Kolby leaned a bit closer to him. "How much country do you know?"

"Some. The crossover stuff mostly. I don't know the twangy stuff. Sorry." Sean rocked his head side to side. "I know a few songs."

"Listen to this demo. This kid is a pop singer-songwriter, but I'm convinced this is a country hit."

Sarah and Skeeter both looked away, shaking their heads.

Sean said, "I think you've got some disagreement from the others." He nodded toward Sarah and Skeeter.

Sarah said, "We don't disagree. We just don't see Kolby's vision. It's sung by a guy with a big voice."

"I'd have to hear it," Sean replied.

Kolby reached into the pocket of her jeans and pulled out her phone. She cued up the song and handed it to Sean. Sean pulled a set of custom ear monitors out of his jacket, disconnected them from his own phone, connected them into hers, and began listening. They sat watching him as he nodded.

"It's too big for your voice. He sounds like a big guy, right? So he can sing this song big. Kolby, you're small. You've got a full voice, but these words won't work if you oversing it. To make this song yours, you can't power sing it. You have to sing it like...like you're whispering to someone at three in the morning."

Sarah and Skeeter both cocked their heads and then looked at Sean.

Kolby nodded. "I can sing it like that. The real question is, can you make it sound like that?"

Sean nodded twice. "Yes, I can."

Sarah looked first at Skeeter and then at Kolby. Kolby, as if put up to a dare, looked at Sean. "Okay, you're on. Let's see if you can make us a hit."

Sarah interjected, "Kolby, crossovers and covers don't sell."

"Sarah, when you can explain 'Landslide' to me, then we can talk. You know we would have gotten it right." She stuck her tongue out at her sister, who quickly stuck out her own tongue in reply.

Joshua came back to the table with a to-go carrier and six covered coffee cups. "I thought you might need these, for yourself and the others. Thanks for coming in for the breakfast."

Kolby gave him the same look she used when she told him why he was awkward with women. "Joshua, I saw your trick with the quarters. You had those kids in the palm of your hand."

Joshua nodded. "Thanks."

"Did you used to work with kids?"

"Not this age, I just —"

A shout came from the kitchen. "Hey, Joshua! How much more bacon do we need?"

Joshua looked up. "I'm sorry, gotta go. Thanks for coming by and supporting the town. They, well, we appreciate it."

As they filed out the door, Kolby turned and looked over her shoulder at Joshua rolling up his sleeves in the kitchen and stepping up to the wash sink and the stack of dishes on the counter.

Part Four
Crossings

.

CHAPTER THIRTEEN

MIDSUMMERS

THE NEXT TIME KOLBY SAW Joshua Stone beyond a passing wave in the driveway, he was sitting in the middle of the band, all of them laughing, taking turns telling jokes. In the ten days since the pancake breakfast, the band had all gone home to Nashville and returned, this time with their own cars and Skeeter's motorcycle. None of them noticed Kolby walk in, except Fylgja, who raised her head, wagged her tail, and then rolled submissively to her back, coaxing Kolby to approach and rub her belly. Still unnoticed by the group, Kolby knelt down and gently rubbed Fylgja and then listened as Nils took over the storytelling.

"What day is today? Wait, it's the twenty-third? Today is *Jonsok*. We need to have a bonfire."

Kim pitched her head back. "Oh God, no. Last year you made us all drink that..." She gave a whole-body shudder. "What was that nasty stuff?"

Skeeter, Nils, and Roberto all chimed, "Aquavit!"

Nils grinned, his baby face and wide gap teeth shining like an impish Norwegian devil. "I have just enough for everyone. We'll drink a toast and celebrate *Sankthansaften*."

Kim looked protectively at Joshua, shaking her head and mouthing, "No, don't try it," and giving a second shudder.

Sean looked around. "I don't have enough wood for a big fire. Can we just make a fire in the fireplace?"

Kolby said, "Sean, I think a small fire is better."

Hearing her voice, Joshua turned. He stopped and looked at Fylgja in a submissive pose and the woman stroking the dog's belly.

Kolby continued, "If these boys start drinking aquavit, we need to hide all the sharp objects, small children, and the Patsy Cline CDs."

Sean flipped a switch, and the gas jets began to burn as he laid several precut logs from the stack piled by Forrest and Rooster in the woodbox. The flames took quickly, and even though it was a hot, humid night, the band resettled around the fire.

Nils came back with a bottle of Linie aquavit in one hand and a six-pack of dark beer from the kitchen refrigerator.

Skeeter said, almost barking an order, "Party time, Miss Sarah."

"I'm in," she replied, standing up, setting her cell phone in her chair, then untucking her shirt, tying it in a knot at her waist. "Pour one for me."

"Roberto?" asked Nils.

"I'm in."

"Kolby?"

"Oh Lord, help me. I'm in. Pour me one." She turned to Joshua, paused, then looked into his eyes as she said, "She's such a pretty dog." Then she moved over closer to Nils, who was arranging shot glasses in a neat row, two glasses per person. One he filled with dark beer, the other with the aquavit.

"Sean? Are you in?"

"I'm in."

"Joshua, do you know anything about Norway or Sweden?"

Joshua felt a sudden chill down his back. He shuddered as Kim had done moments before. The image of Liv Olsson in a black dress, walking toward him and smiling, flashed across his mind. "Hey, I'm in. I've got my Fylgja to see me home safe, right?"

The band gave a celebratory cheer.

Joshua looked at the bottle, mispronouncing the aquavit with long *I* vowel sounds, "Line-eye?"

"Lin-ya," corrected Nils as he nodded and continued pouring.

Kim said, "Nils, I can't stand you, but I can't stand the thought of you drinking without me, so set me up."

The band cheered even louder.

"Okay, so drink the beer first and then the Linie. Either shoot it or sip it."

Nils went first, downing the beer and then the shot of Linie. Skeeter, Roberto, and Sarah all shouted *"Skoal!"* The Norwegian grinned his gappy smile, and Skeeter went next.

He, too, tossed back the beer and then tossed back the shot. He cocked his head to the side. "Damn, my grandpap used to make this stuff. Only he called it 'shine.'"

Sarah nudged Kolby, and they both took their glasses together. They stared at each other, and both practice-swallowed as they brought the dark beer to their lips.

"One."

"Two."

They shouted, "Three!" and downed the beer, then immediately grabbed the aquavit and downed it, too, and then both began waving their hands in front of their mouths.

"God, Nils!" Sarah exclaimed. "What is it with you Norwegians?"

"Let me show you how it's done. You rush it too fast," Roberto challenged the group. He picked up the beer and drank it in three moderate sips smiling and savoring the flavor. Then he extended his left hand, palm down, and held it level in front of him. He picked up the second shot glass with the Linie and balanced it on the back of his hand, holding it steady. He brought it to his mouth, balancing the shot until he pressed the glass to his lips, tossed it back, and then returned the glass and lowered his hand to the table with the empty glass balanced and undisturbed.

Joshua did the same, raising the ante, first balancing the shot glass of beer and tossing it back after bringing it to his mouth, and then repeating the trick with the Linie.

Roberto slapped him on the back. "See? He's Cuban like me."

Kim and Sean were last. Sean followed the others' lead and dropped both shots quickly. Kim tossed back the beer and then sipped the aquavit, nursing it for several minutes before it was gone.

Nils put on a playlist of Bob Wills songs from the 1940s and then turned. "Oh, wait, I forgot. We were each supposed to say a wish." He gathered all their glasses and began refilling them.

"Oh God, Nils!" Kim exclaimed. "Let me switch to tequila, anything but this Oslo-vakian jet fuel."

Joshua laughed out loud. "That's funny right there, Oslo-vakian."

"Wait," Kolby interjected. "I'm gonna post that before we get too tipsy and post something stupid." She took their photo, the band around Nils and his bottle of Linie, and tapped the caption on the phone:

<TheRealKolbyRae> *Midsummer's night drinking Nils's Oslo-vakian jet fuel*

Sarah teasingly said, "Crap. There goes our Linie sponsorship for the tour."

Sean went first. "Okay, this isn't really a wish, but I just want you to know that today is my birthday. I'm officially twenty-one, and I just want to say thank you for letting me work with you all. I really dig the sound. We're gonna make a huge record together." He balanced the shot glass on the back of his hand and tossed the aquavit down.

Sarah picked up three glasses and handed one to Kim and the last to Kolby. "Come on, ladies. We can't let junior birthday boy show us up."

The three ladies balanced the shot glasses on each of their hands, Kim's and Kolby's manicures contrasting with the short trimmed and unpolished fingernails on Sarah's hands. Roberto grabbed Sarah's phone and snapped an overhead photo. Then the women each tossed back the shot, Kolby and Sarah both shaking it off and Kim, shrieking loudly, finishing the entire glass in one gulp.

Skeeter nodded at Joshua, Joshua nodded at Roberto, and then the three of them took the glasses from Kim, Sarah, and Kolby and had Nils fill them. Each man carefully balanced two shot glasses, first on his left hand and then on his right. Each with two glasses balanced, the women counted down—3, 2, 1—and the men tossed back the shots, first one, then the other.

Everyone laughed and plopped into chairs as Bob Wills's "Bubbles in My Beer" began playing from Nils's playlist. "We still didn't do any wishes."

"What's your wish, Nils?"

"I got my wish. I got Kim to drink with us."

The alcohol was quickly going to everyone's head as they cheered campy, sentimental cheers.

Sarah went next. "I love you guys. I just…" She stopped and looked at Kolby and then the group. "I just want you to make music."

They nodded. As he sat there, it occurred to Joshua that they all shared the same wish, and there was no reason for them each to repeat it. They were of one mind. He was slipping into the dreamy, woozy influence of the aquavit more quickly than any of the others. In his own haze, he realized they had turned toward him in anticipation of hearing his wish.

"Oh, what? My turn? Um, it's not so much a wish as it is something I miss. You know what I miss? Pizza…really good pizza. I don't mean that stuff they sell by the slice at the convenience store. I mean real pizza, cooked in a brick oven and heated by a wood fire."

They all nodded.

"Oh yeah, where was that place?" Kim asked. "You know. What show was that? Where they had that guy who had the wood-fired oven cater the show?"

"Seattle. That was killer pizza," Roberto told her.

"Yeah, yeah. I remember his name was Russ," Nils added. "Something Wood-Fired Pizza"

"Gusto. It was Gusto Wood-Fired Pizza. I remember he said he named the business after his son, Gus."

The band let out a sentimental "mmm," and then Sean offered what they thought was a non sequitur. "Mom had Dad get her a brick oven."

They all turned to look at Sean. "What? Where?"

Sean pulled his hair back and then stood up and pointed. Just to the side of the porch was a brick and stone oven. "Mom was in this organic homemade bread phase for a while. But the oven I think still works."

Joshua got up and walked over to look at it. "Hey, this could work. Do you guys want pizza some night?"

Skeeter nodded. Roberto answered, "Yeah, you bet."

Kim nudged Kolby. "Oh my God, he brings coffee, and now he cooks? Swear to God, if he cleans, too, we're introducing him to my mother."

Kolby looked over at Joshua and then nudged Kim back. "He's not that old."

Roberto turned to Skeeter and then to Joshua. "Yeah, they were telling us that you were kind of running the show at the pancake breakfast," Roberto said. "Are you thinking about a new career in the restaurant business?"

"Who, me?" Joshua laughed. "Me? No. I was just helping out for the kids. You know, they don't teach that stuff in high school anymore. Kids don't learn how to work in a kitchen, how to budget food, you know…life stuff."

"Neither do musicians. That's why there's catering," Roberto replied.

CHAPTER FOURTEEN

FOUR-WHEEL GIRL

THE STUDIO CREATED BY SEAN'S dreams, his father's money, and Forrest and Rooster's labor was styled like a loft in an old warehouse. It was a striking contrast to the refined, elegant finish and furnishing in the rest of the big house. Growing up, Sean was an indoor kid. When the family spent their summers at the Tennessee farm, Sean preferred to ride his pedal car, then later a small bicycle around in circles in the unfinished walk-out basement with ten-foot ceilings.

The Adams big house became the home of impromptu band rehearsals, loud rock and roll parties, and more than a few family arguments about the meaning of "clean up." The basement was where Sean felt most at home. David Adams had Forrest and Rooster build a small bedroom and full bath as Sean entered his teen years, and now, with his guests upstairs in the six bedrooms, Sean was content to crash in his basement room, play bass in the studio, or listen to mixdowns and tracks.

The studio had four rooms. The control room was similar to the control room at Sibilance. It included a large table with both a mixing board and a computer station. Four big flat-screen monitors sat across the back of the table in view of those seated at the workstations and those behind who were sitting in leather lounge seats. Sean had moved a few chairs from the upstairs down into the control room so everyone could sit and listen.

The second room was the recording studio, with a brick and glass wall between the control room and studio. The surrounding walls were double thick for soundproofing, and there was a solid door that led from the control room into the studio. To the left was a small equipment room with digital equipment racks and panels for electricity and sound cabling.

The biggest room was the playroom. It had a pool table, a few arcade games, and the glass doors that led to the driveway scooped by Forrest and Rooster. The musicians hung out in the control room, adding their thoughts and ideas as each track was laid down. Sarah had taken over a small table near the back of the control room, spreading her files and notes across part of the wall and onto the floor in neat stacks.

Before Frankie had left and returned to Nashville, he paid Sean two compliments. He loved the design of the studio: its aged brick wall with full-length draperies that could be slid over the hard surface to warm the sound in the room and minimize echo; the hard, solid maple floors; and then the placement around the room of the jacks, both for electrical power and audio cables.

He gave the second compliment to Sean in the form of an order as he stood next to the SMILES SUV with Sarah and Kolby after they spent most of the first week laying down new vocal tracks. He kissed Kolby on the cheek and said, "The kid here reminds me of me when I got started. Sean, I missed my chance at a Grammy with this lady. Don't screw it up for her a second time."

But Frankie's endorsement, the studio design, and Sean's prodigious talent were not helping Kolby Rae as she struggled in the studio with the song written by the pop writer that Sean was producing. Every time she began a new take, she overpowered the notes in the chorus and took it terribly flat. Sean was trying to coach the more experienced singer with his own ideas, and the band was offering encouragement. Their words surrounded her through the headphones as they spoke from the intercom in the control room. Because the microphones in the studio all led to the monitors in the control room, it was easy for everyone there to hear what Kolby said. For her to hear them, Sean needed to push the I/C button on the console to activate the intercom microphone.

"Kolby, it's the vowel sounds," Sean said. "They're making you go nasal and flat. You've got to open up more and bring the volume down. The energy is right; now give me less volume."

"Sean, if I give you less volume, this might as well be an instrumental track."

"Yes ma'am, I'm just —"

Roberto offered a tip. "Sing it like 'Kissed with a Lie.' Be real."

Kolby's voice snapped, "Roberto, I *am* real."

Sarah interjected, "Guys, maybe this is just all wrong. Sean, you've got great ideas, but this just isn't working. Kolby, we're doing an album, not a single. Are you sure you want to put all this energy into this one song?"

"Cue it up, Sean," Kolby barked and picked up the lyric sheet with her notes and rested it on the music stand.

Sean moved the marker to the beginning of the digital track and pressed RECORD. In an unusual move, they had laid down all the tracks, and now all Kolby had to do was sing in the main vocal. Sean was looking for a three-in-the-morning sound, not a front-of-the-stage concert sound.

Kolby recorded the entire track and then left the studio to sit in the control room for playback. They listened to the song, and when it was finished, Kim spoke first. "Kolby, it's too karaoke."

Nils nodded. "I liked the second chorus, but the rest was a bit pitchy."

Roberto shook his head. "This isn't your song. You know who you are, and this isn't you, Kolby. It's time to let this one go."

"One more. Cue it up, Sean."

Kolby sang it slightly better, almost good enough to call good. Near the end of the chorus, she brushed the bracelets on her right arm against the sensitive microphone, ruining the take. The musicians cringed. It was a rookie mistake.

Kolby Rae didn't say a word. She stood up, walked out of the studio, up the stairs, and down the entryway of the big house. She was headed to KRAEZY and a drive, and as she stepped into the driveway, she heard the Rover wheels skid on the gravel as Joshua hit the brakes. She walked to the left side of the vehicle, opened the door, climbed in, and slammed it shut. Without making eye contact, she said one word: "Drive."

Joshua looked over at her. She couldn't disguise her anger, so she let him see it. Her teeth were clenched, her breathing a short, staccato huff. Joshua put the truck in gear with his left hand and headed down the lane. Rather than drive into Crossings, he turned the opposite way, down the road that led deeper into rural farmland. They rode in silence for about five miles when Kolby turned to him. His pace was killing her. She was tempted to slide her leg over and jam his foot and pedal to the floor but dismissed that thought and curtly asked him, "Would it be okay if I drive?"

Joshua turned as he slowed down and pulled to the side of the road. "Yeah, sure. Ever driven a right-hand drive?"

"Nope."

She got out, and they paraded around to each other's side and climbed back in.

"Okay, this is different," she said. Then she punched the gas, popped the clutch, and flung gravel and dust behind them as she ran through the gears.

As Joshua looked over, he was flustered and excited by what he saw. Her short skirt had now slid fully up her thigh, and as she slammed the clutch and shifted gears, he wasn't sure if she had any more leg left to expose. He didn't want to miss anything but looked up at her face and saw the beginning of a smile cross her lips. They hit a bump, and he felt himself lift out of the seat, hit the limit of the seat belt, and slam back down into the cushion. Then she cut the wheel, and the next thing he saw was green—lots of grass and pasture—and then mud.

Kolby had turned off the road and was driving though a semidry creek bed, spewing mud on the windshield and flinging it far behind them. She spun the wheel and shifted gears, and they were sliding. Joshua slammed hard against the door and then flung the opposite way, almost landing in her lap, and then back upright as she topped a bump. He felt the bottom fall out of his stomach. He imagined they were airborne. And then the *ker-thump* confirmed, yes, they had been, and she spun the wheel again.

Joshua felt almost as dizzy as the week before drinking aquavit with the band, but now Kolby was grinning, her bare legs working the clutch and the gas, her arms twirling the wheel and the Rover in circles.

She was spinning the truck around and around. She spun the wheel in the opposite direction. At the top of the hill, she stopped, tumbled out of the Rover, and lay down in the grass, staring up at the sky, laughing as hard as Joshua had heard any woman laugh.

Joshua scrambled out. His heart pounded. So caught up in the thrill, he collapsed in the grass next to her, her laugh infecting him and he laughing with her, harder and faster until it almost hurt. Still laughing, they turned and faced each other, their faces inches away and still laughing out loud.

To Kolby, this was just fun. This was two people having a good time and blowing off steam, to be free of worries and cares and records and studios. And then…

Joshua Stone kissed her.

When Joshua opened his eyes, he looked into her face and saw a fire he had never seen in a woman. Kolby Rae knew there was just one thing to say to him. "Take me back."

The drive back to the big house was silent. Kolby refused to look at him, even when he tried to look at her. She just sat looking straight ahead. When Joshua pulled up to the big house, she threw open the Rover's door before he had completely stopped and dashed across the drive, up the walkway, and through the doors.

In the basement studio, everyone was waiting in the control room. Sarah was on her cell phone with the crowdfunding company, brainstorming ideas to ramp up pledges. Sean was sitting at the control board, flipping the volume slider on track seven up and down to an imagined rhythm in his head. Nils was gently tapping his drumsticks on the arm of the sofa.

The door flew open and crashed into the doorstop on the wall. Kolby stormed through the room past them all. "Cue it up," she said curtly and yanked the door to the studio open. She walked behind the partition and sat on the stool, refusing to look at anyone in the room.

Sean set the levels on the sliders, pressed the record button, and muttered, "Take nineteen."

The instrumental track began.

Chapter Fifteen

Let's Not Cross This Line

As Kolby Rae sang the first line, Joshua walked sheepishly into the control room, ready to take responsibility for her mood. He glanced around and saw the band was mostly ignoring the activity in the studio.

:: Let's not cross this line ::

He stopped when he heard what he took as a personal reference in the lyric. There was something different about her voice, a power he hadn't felt before.

:: We've both been here before ::

Joshua looked up. He didn't know the song, but the words certainly had meaning in context. He was self-conscious that she was talking about crossing lines after what he had just done with her.

As she sang the third and fourth lines, she gave a tiny growl, an attention-getting vocal effect. It worked.

:: Don't close your eyes ::

:: Please don't give me one more ::

Sarah said, "Just a second; let me call you back," and set the phone down on the table. She looked toward Kolby Rae. On the next two lines, the tension built. Joshua kept his focus on her face. He felt like it was just the two of them, alone, still in the middle of their kiss.

:: If you kiss me here, I might not know where I'm at. ::

:: If you hold me close, I might not ever look back. ::

At the end of the line, Kim reached over and laid her hand across Nils's drumsticks. He looked at her, and she nodded in the direction of Kolby.

:: Who will find out, if we don't tell? ::

: Let's just stop right now, maybe it's just as well? ::

The first time through the chorus, Kolby's skin was just beginning to glisten. Sean noticed her slight breathiness and decided to double the tracks to capture it rather than filter it out. The first lines of the chorus built the tension, and with each line, Kolby became more breathy.

The last lines of the chorus pushed her deeply into a physical connection with each word. The glistening on her chest increased, and Joshua began to notice a few splotches of red on her neck and chest. He'd seen the same pattern on nervous freshman girls speaking in his class.

:: Your kiss ::

:: Just set me on fire ::

:: Your kiss ::

:: Just flamed my desire ::

:: If all that means what I feel ::

:: Will you kiss me again? ::

As she sang the bridge of the song, Kolby nailed a whispered growl. No one knew where in her vocal repertoire it came from. The newfound restrained power in her voice caused everyone to lean forward and nod with approval and encouragement.

:: I make it look so easy, being alone and strong ::

:: I take on the world, when I sing my songs ::

:: But that didn't slow you down, we just kissed ::

:: Now what am I to do 'bout this? ::

At the end of the line, her voice quivered. Joshua had moved forward to the glass partition between the control room and the studio space.

:: Who will find out, if we don't tell? ::

:: Let's just stop right now, maybe it's just as well? ::

:: Your kiss ::

:: Just set me on fire ::

:: Your kiss ::

:: Just flamed my desire ::

:: If all that means what I feel ::

:: Will you, kiss me again? ::

Her volume was building to an incredibly big and loud finish, and then, at the very height, she shifted her voice to the famous Kolby Rae whisper:

:: If all that means what I feel ::

:: Lover, kiss me again? ::

She was exhaling, deep, heavy breathing, slow and steady. The studio was silent. Finally, Roberto said, "I need a cigar."

Sarah said, "I need a drink"

Kim said, "I need to get laid."

Kolby Rae looked up and over at Joshua through the glass.

Nils offered an idea. "Drinks!"

Through the speakers, Joshua heard Kolby Rae's voice. "You go on ahead. I just need to gather my wits, and I'll be up." Kolby Rae didn't break eye contact with Joshua as she spoke.

The others left, gigging and talking, interrupting each other as they walked out and to the kitchen upstairs. When they left, Joshua said, "That was amazing."

Kolby pointed to her headphones, shrugged, and then pointed at the mixer board. Joshua walked over and looked at the sliders and the blinking lights. It was as foreign as the controls of a jet airplane, but the letters I/C caught his eye, and he pointed. Kolby nodded. He pressed the button, and a green light glowed above his finger.

"I said, wow, that was amazing."

"Why, thank you, Joshua Stone. That's very kind of you."

Joshua wasn't sure what to do or say next. Kolby had ended their kiss abruptly and stormed out of the Range Rover. And then, she just…he stopped his thoughts. What did she just do? And in front of everyone? His finger slipped off the button as he began to speak. "Listen, I'm really sorry about the kiss. I shouldn't have done that."

Again, she pointed at the headphones and grinned, not hearing his words. He realized he had been given a second chance, so he changed his words and pressed the I/C button.

"I said I would like to take you to dinner tonight, and I hope you will say yes."

Her head turned ever so slightly to the side, and she made a subtle smile. "Joshua Stone, I would be happy to have dinner with you tonight."

They stood, staring though the glass that separated them, both smiling. The band returned carrying wine and beer bottles and cascaded into the studio surrounding Kolby Rae.

Sarah wrapped her arm around Kolby. "Damn, girl, nineteen takes but…love it."

Chapter Sixteen

Dinner

Joshua Stone opened the bedroom closet. He looked over the hanging clothes and the folded stacks on the side shelves. He'd dressed for dinners out at the college for years; looking at his clothes now, he had no idea what to wear. On campus, he had an assortment of jackets, some dress shirts, and a few nice suits for the important parties. Every day, he wore a jacket, trousers, shirt, and tie. Now, his everyday closet looked weekend-ready.

He ran his fingers down the stacks of dressy T-shirts—one stack of dark, one stack of light—and pulled a long-sleeve black one from the pile. He took a pair of blue jeans with a button fly from the hanger, pulled them on over his boxers, and then pulled on the T-shirt, tucking it in. He thought back to Alan Neal laughing at him the first time he asked for an iron to press a few wrinkles from his jeans when he had stayed at Alan's cabin in the Rockies.

"Joshua, no one irons blue jeans."

He had a couple of dress shirts and a sport coat he wore to church on Sundays. The rest of his shirts were outdoor shirts sold at a fancy sporting goods store he and Alan had stopped at during their drive east after the summer in the Rockies.

Joshua pushed up the T-shirt sleeves to his elbow, then pulled the sports shirt over it and neatly folded the cuffs back three folds on both sleeves. He looked in the mirror. He turned and opened the dresser drawer, retrieved his holster, and slid it in the waistband of the jeans. He skipped a belt, walked to the pistol safe, swiped his finger over the biometric sensor, and unlocked it. He thought about his friend in

Grant's Hill, Sgt. Jessica Addison, and quietly mimicked their conversation when she asked if he was carrying his pistol. "Gear check?" she would ask him. "Every day," was his reply.

He left the sport shirt untucked because it concealed the pistol and holster easily behind his right hip. He turned and saw Fylgja staring at him. He recited some anonymous dating advice as if it were coming from the dog. "I know. Be on my best manners, listen more than I talk, and don't order anything with garlic...or onions."

The dog made a whine-yelp as if mocking her master. She made the sound twice more and then stood, wagging her tail.

Joshua looked around the cabin. It was tidy. A couple of David Adams's books were on the bookshelf, along with his own book, *One Good Bread Pudding*. When he had first come to the cabin, Joshua was flattered to find a copy of his book along with some highlighted passages and a few handwritten comments in the margin of some of the pages. David had never commented on Joshua's writing, but it was clear from the scribbles that he enjoyed it very much.

Joshua looked one more time in the mirror and turned his head to each side. He shrugged as he saw the scar on his left cheek and then picked the keys from the hook near the front door, closed the cabin, walked to the Range Rover, and climbed in the right-side door.

In the big house, Kolby Rae had taken two sundresses from their hangers and, having put them back, was standing instead in a pair of jeans with rhinestone trim on the back pockets and a pearl-snap Western blouse. She left her room and walked to one of the big house's shared bathrooms. As Kolby began putting the finishing touches on her eyeliner, Sarah walked by the open door. She stopped, stuck her head in, and interrupted Kolby.

"You know what? I knew you believed in that song, but I never understood why until I heard you today. Girl, that is our hit."

Kolby put some lip liner on and pressed her lips together, watching in the mirror.

"I was thinking," said Sarah. "Maybe tonight around the fire, maybe we should talk about album names. I was thinking about *Crossroads*—" Sarah stopped midsentence, and her eyes opened wider. "Kolby Rae, you're going on a date. Where are you possibly going to go on a date up here? There's no one—" She stopped again and looked down the hall and toward the front door. "Wait. No. No way. You? And that writer? You and Joshua?"

Kolby blushed slightly in the mirror.

"Kol-by?"

"It's not really a date-date. He just" — Kolby puckered her lips twice and looked over the top of the lipstick tube at her reflection — "asked me to go to dinner with him in town."

Sarah reached across Kolby's front and gently pulled the placket on the pearl-snap blouse apart to expose a pink lace camisole underneath. "No," Sarah said with a mocking tone of denial, "no, this isn't a date-date."

Kolby slapped her hand away with a laugh. "Okay, but you've already seen more than Mr. Stone will see, so don't make this more than it is."

Sarah turned toward the living room of the house and then stopped. "All I can say is" — she turned around and made eye contact with Kolby in the mirror — "if he can make you sing like you did this afternoon, he'd better keep taking you to dinner…and breakfast…and lunch. Girl, that was awesome."

As Sarah walked out the front door of the big house, Joshua Stone was walking in. She looked him up and down, made a *tsk-tsk* sound with the side of her mouth in a playful scold, and said, "No flowers? Mmm, mmm, strike one."

Joshua's face fell. He started to back up. His mind tried to picture any flower beds around the big house or the guest cabin. "Oh man, seriously? Really?"

Sarah giggled at him. "Joshua, I'm joking. Besides, it's not a date-date, right?"

Kolby came down the hall, and as she did, the recessed lights in the ceiling alternatively lit her face and body and then teased Joshua with their shadow. He felt her shine in each step. She was wearing boots. Her jeans accented her curves. She wore the same pink cowboy hat with the turquoise band as when they had first met, the same one in the *Garden Party* cover photo.

"Kolby Rae, I hope you are ready for a night out in the" — he paused — "big city."

"I'm very ready, and after today, I'm ready to be out of here. I think we were in that studio all day other than our little adventure." She winked at him and immediately blushed. She walked past him so he wouldn't see.

"I suppose it's okay if I drive?" he asked as they both walked to the left side of the Rover.

"Sure, but I get to drive home."

He opened the door, and she climbed up and slid into the seat. "Deal," Stone said.

"I know," Kolby replied.

When they pulled up to the Roadhouse, Joshua waved at Forrest and Rooster, who were sitting with Warren Edlington in plastic chairs at a table on the outside deck. After he parked the Rover, Joshua got out, walked to Kolby's door, opened it, and took her hand. The two crossed the parking lot toward the front door of the Roadhouse.

Warren Edlington nudged Forrest. "You see that? He opened her truck door for her. You know what that means, don't you?"

Rooster nodded and Forrest asked, "No, what's it mean?"

Warren whistled and leaned in as if revealing a secret. "Either the truck is new or the girl is." He laughed as he slapped the table, jiggling the beer bottles.

Rooster chuckled under his breath and then kicked Forrest under the table. Forrest looked at the couple as they walked inside the Roadhouse. "Well, I think both are. To tell you the truth, I think both are new."

Joshua and Kolby were seated in the middle of the restaurant, in a booth just out of view of the television screen on the opposite side of the bar. The waitress, Jackie Gower, called Joshua by name and handed them both menus. Joshua silently clicked through the advice he pretended Fylgja was telling him: best manners, listen more than talk, don't order anything with garlic or onions.

"Oh my, look at this. They bread their own onion rings. Joshua Stone, do you like onion rings? Do you know how long it's been since I had onion rings? Let's start with that. Then I want to hear all about you."

Michael Hutsun and Wayne Baylis walked by the table, followed by their wives. "Joshua, hey," Wayne began, "did you hear the total?"

"Hi, Wayne, Michael. No, I didn't. Where did we end up?"

Wayne nodded at Michael and then looked at Joshua. "$1,743. All of it goes to the kids' scholarship fund."

Michael leaned in and said, "And we don't have to split it with the women's auxiliary. It all goes to the kids."

Joshua beamed. "That's great. That's really great. You guys were really flipping those pancakes fast."

Joshua looked over at Kolby, unsure how to introduce her to the men. He stood up. "Say, Michael, Wayne, I'd like you to meet a friend of mine. This is Kolby."

"Miss Kolby, nice to meet you. We're friends of Joshua from church. I'm Michael Hutsun. This is my wife, Elizabeth."

Elizabeth Hutsun waved from the back of the group, and Wayne put his arm around the other woman. "I'm Wayne Baylis, and this is my wife, Katy."

"Hi, Kolby. I'm Katy. Are you just visiting?"

Kolby nodded once, enjoying the moment of anonymity. "Yes, I'm visiting."

"Y'all have a nice supper," Michael said as the group moved to a table near the far wall.

On her way past, Katy said, "Be sure and order the onion rings."

Joshua sat back down and turned his attention to Kolby. As he began to speak, Jackie Gower returned. "Are you ready to order?"

Joshua looked up. "We'd like to start with the onion rings and a drink, then decide. I'll have ice tea." He looked over at Kolby.

She looked back at him with a dumbfounded look and cocked her head. "I'll have *sweet* tea." She paused. "Joshua Stone, you aren't from around here, are you?"

Jackie laughed, "No, he ain't, but we're sure glad he came here. He's helping my daughter write her college entrance essay, so we put up with his funny talk."

Kolby and the waitress grinned at each other. The waitress looked at Joshua, then at Kolby. "Hon, you may need to do the ordering for the both of you. He's still not sure if chicken-fried steak is chicken... or steak." The waitress laughed as she walked away.

Joshua was crossing off a mental checklist: no flowers, strike one; onions, strike two; please don't let me spend the night talking about myself.

Across the table, Kolby Rae sat back in her chair. She felt her shoulders relax as she turned her head and looked around the Roadhouse restaurant. No one was staring at her. It was a room full of couples and families enjoying their dinners and laughing and talking. This was a long way from Nashville's chain restaurants and music industry power bars.

She looked at Joshua. He was on time, to the minute, when he picked her up. He didn't argue when she asked to drive. He opened her door for her. Momma would be proud. She had asked to drive home partially because the Rover was fun, but also because she didn't know how much he drank and didn't want to have the "give me the keys" argument on their first date.

Kolby stopped midthought, reminding herself it really wasn't a date-date. When Joshua turned toward her, she saw his eyes, a rich blue, and then she looked at the shape of his lips and remembered the sensation of his kiss. Just as she began to speak, an elderly woman with silver-blue hair stepped up to the table with a fifty-year-old man behind her, calling to her.

"Mama, Mama, please don't bother Dr. Stone."

"Dr. Stone, I am so glad you are here. My inflammation is still going strong in my left elbow."

Kolby recognized the woman from the pancake breakfast.

"Mama, he's not that kind of doctor."

"Mrs. Packard," Joshua said as he reached out and clasped both of the woman's hands in his. "Mrs. Packard, are you still dating these younger men?" he said, pointing to her son, Tom Packard, behind her.

The old woman laughed. "Dr. Stone, that's my son. He's not my boyfriend."

Joshua mocked surprise. "Mrs. Packard, you can't possibly be old enough to have a son his age."

The elderly woman batted her eyes at Joshua. "Oh, you are such a charmer."

Tom Packard looked down at the floor, still a bit embarrassed by his mother. "C'mon, Mother, let's go home and let Dr. Stone enjoy his dinner."

Kolby shifted her gaze from the woman to Joshua and with dubious eyes asked, "Doctor?"

He looked up. "It's not what you think. She's harmless. I think early Alzheimer's. I saw the same thing with my dad."

"You are so sweet. And you know what? That's what I want to hear. I want to hear the entire Joshua Stone story."

He looked back into her eyes. He didn't blink. He didn't look away or down her shirt. He looked at her and began talking.

"I was a late bloomer. My dad was former Army, and my mom was a Sunday school teacher. And I always got good grades and liked school. No, that's not true. I didn't like school. I loved school. I loved everything about school. So…" He rested his arm out across the table. The scar on the back on his left hand caught Kolby's eyes, and she wondered if it was from the same accident that had scarred his face. Joshua's scars were not easy to hide.

Kolby became wrapped in her own thoughts, admitting that some scars are easier to hide, and then she listened as he continued. "I never quit going. High school, college, then a master's degree, and then my Ph.D. I was so busy studying, I never learned how to drive a car."

"Joshua Stone, you stop that. Don't tell me lies." She glared across the table at him.

"No, I'm serious. I mean, yeah, I figured it out, but I got my first driver's license just last fall. First time."

She paused. "Wait a minute. You're not a forty-year-old virgin, are you? Oh my God, you said you were awkward with women."

He grinned. "No, I'm not the forty-year-old virgin. Awkward, yes. Virgin, no. And I'm forty-three."

She sighed a dramatic and comic sigh. "So a Ph.D. That makes you 'Doctor Stone'?"

"I used to be. Now I'm Joshua to everyone, except to Forrest. And Mrs. Packard." Joshua looked down at his silverware and then turned back to look at Kolby. She watched him hold his head up and his shoulders a little straighter as he continued. "I was good. I brought the best out in kids. So my life for the last fifteen years was get up, go to work, teach my classes, write my books, come home."

Kolby leaned slightly forward, and as she did, she noticed him lean slightly closer. She took that as a good sign.

"What else was there?" she asked as Jackie brought a large platter of onion rings fresh from the fryer. Steam was rising from the pile.

Kolby jerked back quickly, and the waitress set a stack of two plates on the corner of the table.

"These look so good," Kolby said. They both reached for a plate at the same time, their hands lightly touching. As they took onion rings from the platter to their plates, Kolby urged Joshua to continue.

"That was pretty much my world, and then Rex came into my life."

Kolby's heart sank. She almost silently whispered, "Oh, of course." And then louder said, "Rex? So you're gay?" She spoke faster from her heart than her brain could filter. "I mean, it's okay."

Joshua laughed out loud. "What? Wait." He coughed as a bit of onion ring lingered in the back of his throat. He quickly grabbed his tea glass and drank several swallows. When he took the glass away, he was still grinning, his voice a bit hoarse. "No, no. Rex was my dog, my beautiful black dog. I found him on the side of the road after he was hit by a car. I ended up taking him to the vet, and I paid for his operation." Kolby noticed a sentimental glow in his face when he added, "And we were inseparable for five years."

With slow, deliberate nods, she spoke again. "Okay, but I'm still checking." She took a sip of her sweet tea and looked across the top of the glass at him. "You do like women, right? Tell me I'm not misreading all this attention, am I?"

She watched as he raised his hand and reached across the table. They were close enough to touch, and he touched his hand to her forehead, then lightly touched her curls. His finger brushed her cheek.

"Yes, I like women. I like…this…woman. And no, you are not misreading my attention."

Kolby felt her heart rise and a lump in her throat. His touch was soft and strong at the same time. His confidence made her heart pound faster and do what she called the flippy-flop thing.

"So tell me about Rex. What happened?"

Joshua shifted in his chair. "For a long time, I didn't know. I mean, I didn't understand why he had to die. It wasn't until a former student gave me Fylgja that I had some perspective. And when she did, she told me that all dogs are a gift; we just don't know how long they will be with us. I guess I gave Rex a second chance at life. And when he died—"

"Would you two like a refill? Are you ready to order?" Jackie looked at Kolby, ignoring Joshua.

Kolby was hanging on Joshua's words. She felt the moment had just slipped past them both. She reopened her menu and spoke up. "Doctor Stone"—she giggled as she called him that—"must have the chicken-fried steak. And I think I'll have the catfish platter."

Jackie slid the ballpoint pen behind her left ear and said, "Okay, sweetie, thanks. Y'all help yourselves to the salad bar." She turned and took their order ticket to the window into the kitchen.

Both Joshua and Kolby got up from the table and walked over to the line of ice-filled coolers holding pasta salads, lettuce, cottage cheese, and an assortment of toppings. It was pressed against an interior wall, leaving more room on the open wooden dance floor. The tiny stage at the edge of the floor looked to Kolby like it hadn't been used by a house band in twenty years. A digital jukebox was next to the stage, casting a neon glow over a stack of soft drink cases and empty bottles. A man in a motorcycle leather vest walked up to the jukebox and began looking over the display.

Kolby turned to Joshua. "So, Joshua Stone, what does a smart Ph.D. have on his playlist these days? Do you like any kind of music in particular?"

Joshua laughed. "I really like all kinds of music but not any one kind enough to know much about it. I mean, I know some country, I know some R and B, I know some blues, and pop and classic rock. I mean, music was a very weird place for a kid in the eighties. Think about it. The fifties: Elvis, right?"

Kolby nodded.

"The sixties: Beatles, Stones. The seventies: Led Zeppelin, Aerosmith."

Kolby was impressed. He knew more music than he let on.

"But for me, when I went to the record store in 1984, I could buy Lionel Richie's 'Hello,' a Julio Iglesias and Willie Nelson duet, and Duran Duran's 'Hungry Like the Wolf.' See why I'm musically confused?"

Kolby scooped some salad greens on her plate and looked over at him. "Okay, this one's for the million-dollar prize. Which one did you buy?" As she said the word "buy," she leaned in with her shoulder and nudged him.

"None. I wanted only one album: Springsteen's *Born in the U.S.A.* We had MTV at my house, and I saw the video to 'Dancing in the Dark.' I was hooked. I wanted to be Bruce. But there was one problem: I can't sing."

"That might make it hard to be Bruce," she said.

"We had a VCR—remember, with tapes? I recorded that video. I must have watched it every day, maybe twice a day. I had this huge crush on that girl."

"What girl?"

"Remember, near the end, Bruce reaches down and grabs a girl from the audience and pulls her onstage to dance with him? I was fourteen years old and thought, 'If that's how I meet girls, that's what I'm gonna do.' I wanted to dance with that girl—to that song—so bad."

Kolby laughed. "Joshua Stone, since you can't sing and that was your plan, I see why you're awkward with women. I hope you figured out other ways to meet girls."

"Not really. But hey, you know what? You know who that girl was, right?"

Kolby looked up at him. "Which girl?"

"The girl with the body and the haircut and the eyes? That girl was Courteney Cox—you know, Monica from *Friends*. It launched her career."

"How do you know this so much?"

"I had a student who went to the same high school as she did, Mountain Brook High School. She went there, and so did one of the first MTV veejays, Alan Hunter."

"You knew that much about your students? You know about their high school?"

Joshua nodded, and they walked back to their table. As they sat, the jukebox began playing Bob Seger's "Old Time Rock and Roll." "So what about you? What was the first album you bought?"

Kolby took a bite of her salad and then dabbed her mouth with her napkin. "I honestly don't remember the album, but I know the first song I learned to play on guitar. I was fourteen, and I learned Alan Jackson's 'Don't Rock the Jukebox.' I must have listened to that song ten thousand times to learn the chords." Joshua gave an understanding nod.

As they finished their meals, Drew McDonel walked by their table returning from the salad bar, paused, and nodded to Kolby and then Joshua. "Joshua, good evening." He turned to Kolby, "I'm Drew McDonel. I think we saw you at our pancake breakfast. It was very kind of you to come and support the kids."

Joshua stood and introduced them. "Kolby, this is Pastor Drew McDonel from my church. Drew, this is my friend, Kolby."

"Kolby Rae, it's a pleasure to meet you. I hope you've found out that Crossings isn't a starstruck town. We all respect your work, and we also respect your privacy. And I hate to interrupt your dinner, but Joshua, there is someone I want you to meet. I know this is impolite, but he's leaving on vacation tomorrow, and it would be nice for you to meet him before he leaves. It's Darrell Burrow from the high school."

Joshua looked at Kolby and then Drew. "You go on ahead," encouraged Kolby. Joshua left the table, and Kolby watched as the two men walked to a table near the back. She took out her phone and snapped a photo of the menu cover of the Roadhouse and posted:

<TheRealKolbyRae> *The best onion rings. Ever.*

She closed the phone and got up from the table.

When Joshua came back from talking with Drew McDonel and Darrell Burrow, Kolby was gone. He looked behind him, thinking she may have gone to find him, and then he heard a long-forgotten but unmistakable drumbeat and opening notes to Springsteen's "Dancing in the Dark."

Alone on the dance floor and in the neon glow, Kolby Rae was starting to wiggle her body in a controlled rhythmic imitation of the dance done by Springsteen and the future *Friends* star on the stage of his music video. She cocked her head and motioned a come-hither gesture with her right hand as she coyly touched her cheek with her other hand. Joshua looked around the restaurant. There were still customers sitting at the table. He hesitated, then bent slightly forward, touching his left hand to his chest and looking up at her. He then joined her on the floor.

She didn't know what to expect. He had said he didn't dance. She didn't want to embarrass him. She planned their escape. She would dance and then tug him off the floor, and they would sit down. But she watched his hips, she watched his hands, she watched his arms...and then he turned his back to her. This was a new view, a tight-jeaned sway that caught her off guard. Then he turned again, facing her.

Kolby looked back into Joshua's face. Maybe it was the blue neon from the jukebox, but his eyes were bluer, and his smile was so damn cute. She wanted it to go on, and it ended too soon. He laughed as the next song started. Kolby had also picked "Don't Rock the Jukebox."

"I just wanted to play this for you. We don't have to dance to it. I don't expect you to know how to two-step."

"Try me."

She turned, and he was standing, facing her, his arms outreached.

"I hope you can follow."

"Joshua Stone, if you don't beat all."

And they began, quick–quick–slow–slow, in a counterclockwise circle. By the end of their first loop, the vested man and a woman in a matching vest had joined them, and by the end of the first chorus, there were five couples two-stepping around the Roadhouse dance floor. By the end of the song, nine couples filled the tiny space. The Roadhouse employees and customers all applauded, and the circle of dancers turned, bowed, or curtseyed to Joshua and Kolby. Joshua took her hand. He put some cash on their dining table, and the two of them walked and swayed out to the Range Rover in the parking lot.

"Keys?" she said playfully.

He dug in his pocket, stepped back, and tossed them using a high-arcing jump shot. She swiped them from the air backhanded and got in the driver's door.

They laughed during most of the drive back to the big house and the cabin. They were silly laughs about nothing in particular. One of the pair would look at the other and giggle.

"Okay, okay," Kolby said as she made the final turn that led them to the big house lane. "This thing is a classic. I get that. And driving on the wrong side is just plain fun. I get that, too. But for a guy who never had his driver's license, why in the world did you buy this?" She stretched both arms out in front of her.

"I didn't. It belongs to Sean's dad. I think he shipped it back to the States from Africa after his first safari back in the seventies. The thing is as old as I am. And for me, it's perfect. I've spent my entire life as a passenger in the shotgun seat or riding in the bike lane. This is what the road looks like from my point of view."

"It's a good thing we're not on a real date."

Joshua looked back. "Okay, if it's not a real date, what is this?"

"I don't know. You're the Ph.D. You tell me what it is."

"I don't know, either, but if it were a date…?"

"Well, first off, bucket seats. I can't sit next to you and distract you while you drive," she said confidently. "But that only matters if this were a real date and if I were that kind of woman."

"But you're driving."

"And second, the controls are all backward. You shift with your left, and your right hand is clear over here."

She extended her arm out the open windows and mock waved at him.

"Well, that's what you get with me—a right-hand Rover."

Kolby looked up away from the road for a moment, in her mind, playing with the brand and the word: Rover and rover.

:: Right-hand rover boy ::

"Joshua Stone, you maybe just wrote your first song."

He burst out laughing, and the sight of his eyes dancing with his laughter made her laugh, too.

Kolby drove up the lane past the big house and stopped the Rover in front of the cabin. Joshua started to get out, and Kolby told him to sit. She got out, walked to his side of the truck, and opened his door.

"Well, this is different."

"I *am* different, Joshua Stone." And to prove it, she stepped up into the covered deck and touched the doorknob. "I'm inviting myself in for a nightcap, so you don't have to go through all those awkward hints and suggestions."

"Well, like I said, I'm awkward around women."

"Joshua Stone."

Fylgja immediately came to Kolby's side and sat when she walked in the door. Joshua flipped on the light and commanded, "Fylgja, *geh voraus*." The dog looked at Joshua, then at Kolby, who nodded, and Fylgja walked outside.

Joshua reached under the corner shelf in the far end of the kitchen to get a bottle of wine left by David and searched for a corkscrew in the drawers. Kolby wandered around the cabin. She looked at the

106

books, stacked neatly and arranged by size along the shelves.

"Your name is on this one," she said, pointing to Joshua's book *One Good Bread Pudding*. She took the book down and leafed through the pages, finding the pink envelope with his name written on it in a woman's handwriting. She closed the book and put it on the shelf.

Joshua looked up. "It's David's copy." Kolby continued looking. She wanted to rummage through his drawers to see if he was neat or messy, if the clean main room of the cabin was his life or just a facade for date night, although she reminded herself, again, this wasn't date night because this wasn't a date-date.

CHAPTER SEVENTEEN

MAKING OUT

KOLBY WAS SITTING ON JOSHUA'S left, and he was careful to angle his body to keep her out of contact with the pistol in the small of his back. He was already trying to find a reason to excuse himself and lock it in the bedroom when she turned her face to him.

Her eyes reflected the flicker of the candle on the table, and he looked into them as he gently raised his right hand and lightly touched her cheek. She tilted her head ever so slightly to welcome his touch, and they both moved in together for their second kiss. He felt the same electricity in her lips as they wrapped their arms around each other.

These were tender and timid kisses. Neither of them felt the intoxication of the wine or a rush of forgotten passion to move any faster. He kissed her mouth, her nose, her cheek. She nibbled at his ear. They pressed tighter together, and he slowly moved his left hand down the right side of her back. She arched closer to him, and just about the time his hand reached her belt line, she reached behind, took his hand, and pulled it away.

Joshua Stone began to second-guess himself but thought maybe this was part of her coy nature. Was she testing him? Was she saying no? In his memory, he heard her telling him that she knew why he was awkward with women.

The second time he slid his hand down her back, she was kissing him more deeply than before, and he took that as a sign of encouragement. When his hand got to her waist, he felt it. Hard, flat, and sticking out of her belt, just behind her hip. He knew the feel of the pistol grip the moment his hand touched it through her shirt. She felt his hand there, too, and immediately pushed him back and away.

"I can explain. Just don't think the wrong thing," Kolby told him in a hurried rush of words.

Joshua tried to act surprised, but he knew. For once tonight, he was one step ahead of her. But he decided to play it out. "What is that?"

"I don't let everyone get that close to me. I'm sorry. It's nothing personal against you. I carry a pistol every day. It's part of who I am, and if you don't like it, then we need to end this right here."

Kolby was breathing heavily, and Joshua knew she had no desire to end anything. Her words were oddly familiar because he had practiced the same speech all afternoon.

"So, what you are telling me is"—he paused, hoping to add suspense to his delivery—"there is a gun...in your jeans...right now? While we're making out?"

"Yes." She wasn't sure what to say next to him. Her eyes scanned around the room. With no clear reply, she went on the offensive. "And what kind of a writer says 'making out'? No one has said 'making out' for twenty years."

"So what would you call it, petting? Kissing? Hooking up? How about groping for words? Pawing? Foreplay?"

"Joshua Stone, stop it." Kolby pulled a small pillow from the back of the sofa and held it close to her body. "I'm sorry you had to find out this way, but someday, if you really want to know, we can talk about this."

She wanted him to say something and he knew it, so he remained quiet, adding to the tension. After a few moments, Kolby dropped her shoulders, set the pillow aside, and said, "I'd better get my things," with a bit of regret in her voice. She began to stand up.

"No, Kolby. I've got a better idea."

She looked at him and saw his devilish smile. She hadn't seen it before and wasn't sure what it meant.

Joshua stood up and hooked his thumbs in his own waistband. "I think we should play a game....It's called, 'I'll show you mine if you show me yours.'"

"Joshua Stone, just because I feel bad for not telling you doesn't mean you get to look at me naked."

"Nope," he scolded. "I insist."

Slowly, he moved both of his hands across his crotch in a suggestive fashion and then back up his shirt and across his chest. He'd seen some dancer do the same move in a music video, and he hoped it looked erotic enough to throw her off.

"Oh, puh-leeze," she complained.

Joshua turned his right side to her and slowly raised his shirt. Kolby covered her face with both hands, partially out of play and partially to tell him not to go further.

"No cheating," he said. "You have to look."

She took down one hand, opened her eyes, and saw his pistol in the holster at his waist.

"Oh my!" she shrieked and tossed the small pillow at him. "Joshua Stone, I can't believe you. You made me think…"

He interrupted, holding up one hand and looking at her. "Now, now. It's your turn. Turn around. Let me see."

She looked into his eyes, and then she seductively stood up and slowly turned around. She untucked her own shirt and lifted it high enough for him to see the pistol. And her bare-skin waist and the shape of her ass. Joshua said nothing and just grinned.

"How about this?" He took his pistol from the holster, unloaded it, and set it on the table next to the flickering candle.

Kolby nodded and did the same. And then he took both of her hands in his. "Let's sit outside?" The two of them stepped out onto the deck and sat on the steps. Fylgja looked up from her nap at the end of the deck and then rested her head back in her paws.

Kolby squeezed his left hand. Joshua hesitated, self-conscious of the scar there, and almost pulled it away. Instead, he remained still, and after a few quiet moments, she let go and pulled her legs up halfway to her chest as she sat on the step. She rested her elbows on her knees, made a steeple with her fingers, and pressed them to her lips. It was Joshua's turn to admire the shape of her lips. He wanted to kiss her more.

"So tell me, what do I need to know about Joshua Stone?"

His expression made her think there were several things he could say and wasn't sure if any of them was the right place to start.

"I told you everything at dinner. I'm a writer, novels mostly. I used to teach at a college, but I took an early retirement."

She didn't move her head but looked at him out of the corner of her eye. "And?"

"And I spent last summer with a friend of mine and fall teaching in a community college—mostly because I miss the classroom." He stopped, adding, "God, I miss the classroom." Then he continued, "And I've been here ever since. The man we met at the end of dinner, Pastor Drew? He and the high school principal are talking to me about working with the kids. No real ideas, just some brainstorming."

"So why did you retire if you miss the classroom so much?"

Joshua looked away at the light on the hill. "It's complicated."

"Try me. You don't seem like the complicated sort. You're pretty easy to figure out. You're the writer who can't write, the babysitter who lost the baby, and you don't dance, play cards, or fish." She turned and stuck her tongue out at him.

Joshua said nothing in reply.

"So where did you used to work? What did you teach?"

"I taught creative writing and the American short story." As he said the words, he realized they did similar jobs and added. "I guess what you do in songs, I do in books."

Kolby pressed on. "And this was where?"

Joshua hesitated. He'd had this conversation with dozens of people. This is where it usually ended. He knew the looks and the responses he received from people when he said "Grant's Hill." It had become synonymous with "change the subject."

"Did you ever hear of a small college called Grant's Hill?"

He saw her take a breath, but the rest of her body remained firm and unmoved. He waited for her to say something. She just looked ahead, elbows still on her knees. After a minute, she took her right hand, slowly picked up his left hand, and traced the scar on the back of his hand with her thumb.

"That's where you got this, isn't it? You're him. You're the guy who saved all those kids."

She turned and looked him in the eyes. He looked back at her. It was never easy to remember that day or say the words.

"Yes," came out as a hollow whisper.

They both sat in the quiet.

Joshua drew a breath and posed a question back to her. "So just because I've never heard of your music doesn't mean I'm not interested. Tell me about you. Tell me what I need to know about Kolby Rae." Then he quickly added, "And no offense, but is Kolby Rae your real name? Or is it your stage name?"

He noticed she didn't let go of his hand and actually pulled it closer as she inched her body toward him.

"The Kolby Rae story. Except you're the writer, so you probably would tell it better. I grew up singing, and all through high school, I sang in the choir and did 'The Star-Spangled Banner' at football games."

"Where did you go to high school?"

"You've never heard of it—Tremont, Mississippi."

Joshua interrupted. "Sure, Tremont Eagles. They had a female basketball star there back in the really early sixties. Hey, she went on to be a big entertainer. Tammy Wynette? Maybe you've heard of her?"

Kolby looked surprised. "Well, Joshua Stone, if you don't beat all. Maybe I didn't give you enough credit." She held his hand tighter. "So I started writing songs and I sang in a few bands, and finally, I got the nerve to come to Nashville to try to sell a few songs and be a singer. I was twenty-four years old, and I didn't know a thing about the music business. But with luck and some help from Him"—she glanced up and then back at Joshua—"I got a record deal, and my first albums was called"—she paused, then thrust both of her arms out in a fake show business pose and said—"*Kolby Rae*."

Joshua grinned at her.

"Yes, it's a stage name. Daddy was a coal miner before he met Momma and moved to Mississippi. So they named me Kolby. That's my given name. My middle name is Ruth, but the record company insisted on Rae instead of Ruth. So my real name is Kolby Ruth Miles, but I've been Kolby Rae for so long, I like that name just fine."

"Ruth is a pretty name," Joshua told her.

"And so I've recorded four records. The first two did okay. The third was awful. The record company gave up on me after the fourth, so now I'm my own record company and everything."

"But I don't understand. Even though I don't know your music, I mean, four records is a big deal, right? And you have this band and, what? You tour, sell records, earn royalties?"

She sighed. "This is a hard business, Joshua, and if it wasn't for 'Dance on Your Shoes,' we wouldn't be anywhere. I think you have a kind heart, so thank you for saying that. The band and me, we're having a rough time right now, but we'll get through it. We've been through a lot together."

It was coincidence, but their timing could not have been worse. When she said the word "band," the two of them looked up to see three flashlights shining from the big house, their dancing beams zig-zagging around the yard, accompanied by some drunken men's voices calling her name in a falsetto yell.

"Kol-by! It's past curfew, honey child. Time to come in and get your beauty rest."

Nils, Skeeter, and Roberto had been drinking shots of bourbon most of the evening, and when Sarah mentioned that Kolby and Joshua were having dinner, they concocted a very drunken idea that it would be funny to catch the couple together. By the time they stumbled to the cabin, Kolby had already retrieved her pistol and pink cowboy hat from inside, and Joshua had walked over to Fylgja. The dog became alert, and Joshua assured her it was okay.

As the three drunken band members came into the glow of the cabin light, Kolby came out on the deck with her pink hat in hand. Ricardo shouted, "Young lady! Do you know what time it is?" The other two men snickered.

Fylgja reacted quickly, stood up, and immediately moved to put herself between Kolby and the three drunken musicians. The dog sat, nonthreatening but positioned to protect the woman on the deck.

"Fylgja wants me to stay," Kolby said.

She looked at Joshua across the deck. He made a face and cocked his head, trying to say the same thing with an expression and not words. He was suddenly self-conscious about where he was standing, across the deck away from her. No way to give her a good-night kiss, no way to tell her anything else about the way he felt. He sighed. Another Joshua Stone missed opportunity. Strike one: no flowers. Strike two: onions. Strike three: he talked about himself all night.

Before Joshua recalled Fylgja to his side, Kolby bent down, petted the dog, and whispered, "This is for your man." She gently kissed the side of the dog's face.

The three amigos, as they were now calling themselves, were attempting spinning dance moves in the grass, oblivious to the dog, woman, and man.

Joshua called, "Fylgja, *hier!*" She obediently moved to his side and sat.

Kolby Rae whispered, "Thank you," and walked into the grass. Then she disappeared into the dark as the boys escorted her to the big house.

CHAPTER EIGHTEEN

WINDOW

JOSHUA LAY IN BED LISTENING to the sounds of the night and Fylgja's breathing. She started to growl and then let out a murmured yip in her sleep. She was chasing something, having dog fun in her dreams.

Joshua's mind danced in the sleepy haze between now and memory. He was thinking of first meetings: how Kolby looked as she walked down the hall of the big house. He thought back to his first meeting with the Grant's Hill English Department. He remembered meeting Liv Olsson and the first time he met Sgt. Jessica Addison. He thought about the shooting. He could still smell the room and see the faces of his students and the blank, lifeless stare the shooter had the entire time. He thought back to Kolby's kiss and the way it felt when she touched his hand. And then the rowdy band bringing an end to their date.

He switched on the light. It was 3:33 a.m. He got out of bed, pulled on the jeans he had hung on a hook in the closet, and took a shirt from the hanger. He pulled on his socks and shoes. By then, Fylgja was up, ready for breakfast.

"Not now, back to bed."

Fylgja paced back and forth, expressing her uncertainty at the new routine. Joshua quietly opened the door to the cabin, stepped out into the cool Tennessee night, and shut the door behind him. Fylgja ran to a window and sat down, watching him walk across the open space in the moonlight to the big house.

From the outside, Joshua wasn't sure which bedroom window was Kolby's, but he had narrowed it to two. As he walked up to a window, the moonlight lit up the room enough for him to see her pink cowboy hat on the dresser. He saw a shape in the bed and decided to tap on the glass. At first, the shape moved ever so slightly. He tapped harder and then knocked.

With the knock, Kolby Rae sat up and looked toward the window. Through her half sleep, she recognized Joshua. She got out of bed wearing only a long T-shirt, walked to the window, and opened the sliding glass.

"Joshua Stone."

"Kolby Ruth."

"What brings you to my bedroom on this fine night? And it'd better not be with the idea you're coming in the window."

"The truth?"

"Yes, I always expect the truth."

"I, uh"—he paused and then looked into her eyes—"I've let a lot of really good moments pass me by in my life. No regrets. I just didn't say things I should have when I wanted to."

Kolby arched her back and listened.

"I just didn't want tonight to end without telling you that I think you are very sweet. And I really like the way you kiss me."

Joshua noticed a slight blush. "Joshua Stone, you walked all the way over here at three-thirty a.m. just to tell me that?"

He tipped his head. "Yes. Yes, I did."

She smiled a sleepy smile and whispered, "Well, Joshua Stone, if you don't beat all."

Kolby touched her lips and made a kiss, then pressed her hand to the windowpane. Joshua reached his hand back and touched the glass, smiled, and walked back to the cabin.

:: Mama always warned me, be careful where you play ::

:: You know how people are and what they say ::

Kolby sat down, leaned over the guitar case, unfastened the latches, lifted the guitar by the neck, and took it back to bed. From her purse next to the bed, she pulled a hard-sided pink notebook, opened it to a blank page, and wrote the lyric she just said out loud.

:: But you know what it's like—when you barely turned eighteen ::

:: He's a boy with a truck—in a pair of tight blue jeans ::

She remembered the Western swing playlist from midsummer's night as she continued into the chorus.

:: Climb in, ::

:: jump on, ::

:: my right-hand rover boy ::

:: Take me down the back roads to your heart ::

:: Climb in, ::

:: jump on, ::

:: my right-hand rover boy ::

:: Take me down the back roads to your heart ::

CHAPTER NINETEEN

THE PICKERS

AFTER BREAKFAST, JOSHUA AND FYLGJA hiked up the drive and through the front door of the big house, turning down the side hallway to the large office. The north and east walls of the Adams family office had three-panel French doors, and a tapestry area rug lay across the dark wood floors. In the center was an ornate desk with an equally ornate but uncomfortable chair. Behind the desk was a black leather tufted sofa, and in front were two overstuffed chairs. The built-in bookcase on the west wall included in small minibar. The tray vaulted ceiling held recessed lights. Joshua looked around thinking it was the ideal showplace office, but he couldn't imagine getting any real work done there. It helped Joshua understand why David had built the writer's cabin. This could never be David's office.

Joshua sat at the desk, turned on the computer monitor, and was greeted by a log-in screen with a GUEST option. He chose that, opened a web browser, and searched for the online store that carried his books. He typed his name, and all five books displayed in a neat row:

Bottle Rocket
Our Final Days
Hoop
The Fistfight
One Good Bread Pudding

Joshua put them all in the store's shopping cart, and on checkout, he updated the shipping address to Kolby Rae in care of the Adams farm in Crossings. He pressed the button and finalized the purchase, paying extra for overnight delivery. He had second thoughts; overnight might seem too forward. But the bits of data were long gone across the Internet.

Joshua had two other items of digital business to conduct. He logged into a pay-as-you-go phone company and ordered a new phone and new number. After the shooting, he had become a public figure. With the fame came a barrage of stranger's phone calls and solicitations. As he typed in the delivery address at the Adams farm, he hoped he could have a permanent phone number someday, once he was free of the salesmen, evangelicals, dubious organizations seeking him as a spokesman, and the haters.

He opened a new browser window and logged into his last item of business, his e-mail account. He waited as the counter tallied the new messages. As usual, there were multiple messages from Jeffrey Toomey.

Joshua thought about David Adams as he looked around the house David had bought with the money he'd earned as an adventure writer. Back in the pre-Internet days, the David Adams byline was one of the most recognized. He was as strong a writer now as then. *Faith Shattered*, his book about the Grant's Hill shooting, pulled no punches. It was candid and frank. It highlighted missteps and the multiple factors leading up to the shooting. There were only two people who knew that the book omitted an essential truth. But no one seemed to care about the real truth. They were content with the one grieved by the media and eulogized by David Adams's book.

Jeffrey Toomey was a modern David Adams. Joshua clicked on the link in his e-mail signature and jumped to Toomey's blog displaying a colorful, riveting photo of a dead junkie lying in a Georgia gutter. He clicked on the link to the story. It was solid writing. He quickly fact-checked a few of the assertions, realizing he was as much grading Toomey's work in the context of his freshman composition class as he was reading the story out of human interest. Toomey's writing was accurate and punctuated with enough slang to be hip.

Joshua thought back to his own book sales and the sales potential for *The Rules of Calling Shotgun*. In a fleeting marketing fantasy, he considered how David Adams's connections and Jeffrey Toomey's fan base could accelerate the launch of his own book. Maybe there were new sales horizons now that Joshua was a recovering academic. So maybe talking with Toomey could boost his own work, too.

Joshua reread Toomey's e-mail. It was the same as the others. Toomey wanted him to talk about Grant's Hill, talk about his life growing up, talk about Liv Olsson. Nothing in it gave him any hope to talk about his novels or future projects.

Joshua skimmed the e-mails, deleted them, logged out, and wandered into the hallway and past the stairs leading to the basement studio. He heard the band talking downstairs, thought about saying hello to them, and then decided instead to drive into Crossings.

When he came to the four-way stop, Rooster pulled up opposite and waved. Joshua turned the right-hand Rover around to pull up alongside Rooster's truck, driver door to driver door.

"This is backwards," said Rooster. "We're supposed to talk going opposite directions, and you've got it all turned around."

"What's new, Rooster?"

"Forrest is halfway to Nashville, and I need some help out at my place. Could I get you to follow me out there and give me a hand?"

Joshua nodded. "Sure, lead on. I'll bring up the rear."

Rooster led Joshua down several back roads and across some of the oldest bridges in the county before finally turning down a twisty gravel lane and ending up in the middle of a collection of metal farm buildings. Rooster backed his truck up to the sliding door of one of the buildings in the center. Beyond the buildings, Joshua saw eight or ten antique tractors. It was hard to tell which were for parts and which were complete tractors. Along the fencerow were seven International pickup trucks, parts to half a dozen more, and at least two Piper Cub airplanes.

Joshua imagined the insides of the buildings were much like his garage in Grant's Hill. He pictured his own labeled and numbered plastic tubs, and the sealed and numbered cardboard moving boxes, all forty-two of them, ready to go to his new home, wherever that would be. Though he missed teaching, he was in no rush to leave the Adams farm, and Crossings felt more like home every day. Rooster slid the door to the building open. Joshua had seen picker's barns only on television. The building was filled from floor to the rafters with stuff.

To his left was a pile of medical standing scales. As Rooster went deeper into the building, Joshua passed stacks of magazines, cases of food cans, and some kind of military surplus crates. The stenciled labels used the typical reverse sentence structure of the military— TABLE, FOLDING LEGS, FIELD—and a fifteen-digit inventory number.

Joshua walked carefully down the narrow aisles, around pallets, and over piles that were scattered along the way. At the end of the last pathway, Rooster stopped.

"Here it is." He pointed to a medical table that looked like it dated to the early 1900s. A padded leather top rested on a chest of drawers.

"Wow, great relic."

"It's a W. D. Allison, with original stirrups. I gave fifty bucks for it." Rooster scratched behind his cap. "Got a buyer for thirteen hundred 'n' fifty."

Joshua nodded.

Rooster nodded back and then said, "Which end?"

Joshua gave a dumbfounded look. "Which end?"

"Yep, we're taking it to the truck."

Joshua looked over his shoulder at the narrow path back to the door on the far side of the building where they came in. Rooster grabbed the opposite end, "You take your side."

For the next twenty minutes, they stopped every few feet, dragging, lifting, wedging, and otherwise humping the two-hundred-pound exam table out to the sunshine and Rooster's truck. Winded, Joshua looked at the tailgate, which, after lugging the table, now seemed to be dozens of feet in the air.

"Don't worry. I'll get a fork, and we'll set it in there."

Rooster was gone and a few minutes later was back with a propane-fueled forklift. He guided the forks under the table, lifted it, set it in the back of the pickup, and then was gone, putting the fork lift wherever it originated.

Rooster returned, slammed the tailgate of the truck, and then turned to Joshua. "You a NASCAR fan?"

Joshua nodded. "Not a huge fan, but I watch Daytona and Tallade-ga when I can."

Rooster grinned, motioned, and turned to the building opposite the one they had just explored. He slid the door open. The inside looked like a racetrack warehouse. There were tools, boxes, hoods of cars, doors, engine blocks, banners, and an entire wall of collectible miniature cars in original boxes. Hanging from the ceiling was what looked like a vintage 1979 stock car.

"The tranny's over there," Rooster said, pointing to a dark corner. "The engine's over there, and the tires…" Rooster looked around. "Oh yeah. I sold them last August to a fella out of Austin. Nice kid. Some kind of computer geek."

Joshua looked around. "How do you get all this stuff?"

"Forrest and I go every winter. We go from town to town, Alabama, Mississippi, Louisiana, Georgia. We go looking. People give us a list of what they're looking for, or we just look for what we want for ourselves. It's a father–son business, you know."

Joshua looked back. "What do you mean father–son?"

"Forrest, he's my boy. Didn't you know?"

Joshua grinned. "I had no idea."

"I've done this for fifty-three years. And there is nothing—and I mean nothing—I haven't been able to find. It took me nine years to find a left-hand flipper for a certain Japanese pinball machine, but I found it." Rooster stared off. "What do they call that? Patchniko or something." Rooster shook his head.

Joshua looked around at the floor-to-ceiling stuff. "So you can find anything?"

"Ain't been beat yet. Forrest is gonna inherit a great business, don't you think?"

Joshua stood staring at the stacks until he realized Rooster had walked away and was honking the horn.

CHAPTER TWENTY

BASS DRUM

IN THE MIDDLE OF THE next morning, Joshua heard the alarm beeping of a truck and looked out the cabin window to see if Forrest and Rooster were returning to do more dirt work. Instead, a big brown delivery van was backing up and came to a stop in front of the cabin porch.

Fylgja alerted Joshua and barked. He quieted her and the delivery driver got out, tossing two dog treats on the ground. Fylgja stayed perfectly calm, waiting for Joshua's release to get the treats. The driver stopped. "Wow, I've never seen that."

"You're okay," said Joshua. "You're safe. She won't move. She'll go when I release her."

The driver handed Joshua a box. "Here you go."

Joshua looked at it. It was an overnight delivery addressed to him from the online bookstore. He shook his head. "What did I do? I shipped these to myself?"

He walked in and set the box on the table. He would have felt better if they had arrived as a gift, but he resigned himself to carrying them to Kolby so she could read them at her leisure. He picked up the box, deciding to open it and seek out a nicer gift box in Crossings to give them to her.

Joshua slit the tape with a kitchen knife, put it back in the drawer, opened the box, and removed the packing materials. It wasn't his books. It was four music CDs: *Kolby Rae, Four-Wheel Girl, Other Side of the Tracks*, and *Tequila Temptress*.

Each CD had a cover photo of a different Kolby Rae. She was beautiful and sexy. The first to catch Joshua's eye was her debut, *Kolby Rae*. She was younger. Not quite as pretty as he found her today but still very cute. The sex appeal was undeniable. She was wearing a denim jacket over a white lace dress with a scoop neck and a cameo pendant. Her right arm was closest to the camera and bent, so her closest hand was near her chin. The line of her arm pulled his eyes up to her face and smile. Her left arm extended out and back at an angle.

But it was her legs with the boots and the bare thighs that drew Joshua's eyes. He felt voyeuristic. The dress was open and her knees partially bent. Her eyes looked straight at him, and he felt what every other man must have felt: she was looking only at him.

He opened each disk, loaded them into the CD changer in the cabin, and spent the next four and a half hours on the couch listening to the music anthology of Kolby Rae and reading her liner notes over and over again.

Around 2:00, Joshua walked up to the big house, stopped in the kitchen, and made a sandwich. He took his sandwich on a plate and walked down the stairs and to the basement. He could hear the group talking over the I/C with Nils. Kolby was telling Nils what she wanted from the drum sounds for their backing vocals.

"Nils, just use the kick drum for now. We'll sing the chorus, and then when we find the right sound, we'll layer it in."

Niles nodded, and his eyes rolled up as he listened for the song's playback in his headphones. Before the playback began, he stuck his tongue out the side of his mouth, making everyone giggle, and then he became more focused. His head and neck became set; his hands gently pulsed with the playback of the other instrumental tracks. His mind was silently singing the lyrics on the vocal track. As it got to the part with the kick drum, he beat the drum's foot pedal: *bom bom bom*.

"Great, okay, let's set up for vocals, and we'll all do the harmonies," Kolby ordered, and the laid-back and casual band hopped into motion. One by one, they gathered behind the microphone stand, crowded together so that their shoulders overlapped. They were all looking above Joshua's head and smiling. Joshua looked back, wondering what they were smiling at, and then realized they were just in the moment, focused on the harmonies at hand.

It amazed Joshua each time to see the passion and energy they put into every take. Roberto shook his head back and the focused on the mic, Kim swept her hair out of her face, and Nils and Kolby were pursing their lips, silently listening to the playback in their headphones and nodding with the beats.

Nils's drumbeats played, and they began singing the harmonized vocals. As they sang, they didn't just sing with their voices; their entire bodies emoted the feeling and energy they were trying to capture.
Bom bom bom.

:: Yo-oo-oh-h-h ::

:: Yo oo oh-h-h ::

:: Yo oo oh-h-h oh-h-h-h ::

Kolby silently mouthed, *One, two, three.*

:: Yo-oo-oh-h-h ::

:: Yo-oo-oh-h-h ::

:: Yo oo oh-h-h oh-h-h-h ::

"Hey, stop." Kolby waved her hands. Sean pressed some keys and then looked over at the monitors. Kolby continued, "What if we add in a hand clap between the second and last one?" She sang it solo.

:: Yo-oo-oh-h-h ::

:: Yo oo oh-h-h ::

CLAP

:: Yo oo oh-h-h oh-h-h-h ::

They nodded, and Sean started the playback again.
Bom bom bom.

:: Yo-oo-oh-h-h ::

:: Yo oo oh-h-h ::

CLAP

:: Yo oo oh-h-h oh-h-h-h ::

Kolby nodded her head up and down dramatically.

:: Yo-oo-oh-h-h ::

:: Yo oo oh-h-h ::

CLAP

:: Yo oo oh-h-h oh-h-h-h ::

"Okay, let's play it back," said Kolby. All came out of the studio and into the control room. Everyone filed past Joshua. Roberto reached over and took a potato chip from his plate.

Kim turned to watched Kolby's reaction as she came out.

"Why, welcome, Joshua Stone." Kolby's voice, her smile, and her eyes lingered just a bit longer after the others' attention returned to business. Kim nudged Roberto.

"Nils, do you want to try that sound?" said Kolby.

"Sure, Kolby. Let me get settled. Give me a sec." He opened the door to the studio, and as he reached his drum kit, Nils walked around his drum stool once, then around a second time, and then he sat down.

Joshua looked over at Kim and made a face. "It's just what he does, every time," she said.

Sean brought up a Beyer mic near Nils. "Okay, so this is the kick drum."

Bom bom bom.

Kolby nodded and pressed the I/C button on the board. "Okay, great. That's kind of *bom bom bom*. I want a more metallic ending. Sort of a *bomt bomt bomt*."

Nils looked at her. "What if we suspend a cymbal and let it ring?"

Sean got up, walked into the studio, and jury-rigged a cymbal in the center of the kick drum. Nils hit the foot pedal for the kick drum and created a resonating sound in the control room.

BOMSST BOMSST BOMSST

"No, too much," Kolby said, and the other musicians nodded in agreement. Joshua leaned forward, intrigued by her path down an invisible trail. He felt as if he knew exactly what she was seeking but had no idea how to make the noise with the drum kit.

"Want me to pad it?" Nils asked, undaunted by the wrong sound.

"Sean, do you have any Moongel?"

Sean and Nils experimented with the removable sticky pads on the drumhead as they listened to the modified sound.

BOMP BOMP BOMP

"No, that's not it. It needs more slap and then a short decay—*bomt bomt bomt*."

Joshua got up. "I'll be right back."

No one acknowledged his comment, and he went out to the fire pit patio. He looked in the cupboards, under the chairs, and then out in the grass until he found the basketball. He picked it up and carried it back inside and downstairs.

"Hey, Joshua," Roberto said, smiling. "Yeah, let's get a game up, but not now. We've gotta get this track right. It may be an hour or so."

Kolby was looking over Sean's shoulder as they were playing back the different drum sounds, and he was electronically manipulating the audio files to create a synthetic sound.

Joshua opened the door of the studio, and Roberto looked over. "Joshua, Nils can't play, either." Kim looked up and then back at her book.

Kolby looked at the soundboard and the computer monitor when the sound over the speaker boomed into the room.

BOMT BOMT BOMT

"Sean, yes, that's it," said Kolby. "That's the sound. What did you do?"

BOMT BOMT BOMT

"Kolby, I didn't do…" They looked up at Joshua standing in front of the microphone with Nils holding the mic close to the floor. Joshua dribbled the basketball three times.

BOMT BOMT BOMT

"Damn," Roberto said.

The basketball on the wooden floor echoed just enough to give the crisp, driving, familiar sound Kolby was seeking. Sean quickly layered the new track in place of the old kick drum and hit playback.

BOMT BOMT BOMT

:: Yo-oo-oh-h-h ::

:: Yo oo oh-h-h ::

127

CLAP

:: Yo oo oh-h-h oh-h-h-h ::

Kolby jumped and cheered. "Oh my word, you guys sound so great. Yes, oh my, that is so awesome. I think this is my new favorite song."

Sarah grabbed her smartphone. Nils and Kolby posed and did a thirty-second impromptu video of making the basketball sound to post on the crowdfunding website. Each day, they were attracting about three new pledges. They were thirty-five percent funded.

PART FIVE
STEAM

CHAPTER TWENTY-ONE

PIZZA PARTY

JOSHUA PULLED THE COPY OF *One Good Bread Pudding* from the shelf in his cabin and opened it to leaf through the pages for the pizza dough recipe. As he did, the pink envelope fell to the ground from the back where he had put it the day he had his date with Kolby.

He picked it up, looking at the shape of each letter in his name written by Liv Olsson. As his eyes crossed over the letters, he could almost hear her voice saying his name. *Joshua*. It was an odd contradiction. He wanted to tell her he was sorry and would never have the chance. What she wanted to tell him was in this envelope.

So she had had the last word, and she would never hear what he wanted to tell her. Joshua looked around, ready to either open it or hide it. He thought about flipping a coin. Ironic, he thought, in light of the trick he showed the children at the pancake breakfast and the freshmen in his classes at Grant's Hill. He held it for several minutes, thinking back to his life on campus. The farther he was from Grant's Hill, the harder it became to remember and the less important remembering seemed to be. He looked down at his journal on the table. He decided against the coin toss and committed instead to opening the letter. Just not today. He picked up the weekly calendar from his desk and blindly slid the envelope between some pages near the end of the year. His decision was clear—when he got to that page, regardless, he would open the envelope and read what she had to say. He turned the calendar back to the correct week, set it back on the desk, and walked to the big house kitchen with *One Good Bread Pudding* tucked under his arm.

Joshua pulled the pizza dough together, let it rest and rise, and punched it down to rise again. While the dough waited in the kitchen, he drove to Crossings and found Drew and some other members of the congregation in the parking lot of the church hosting a small farmers' market. He wandered through the selections and found some fresh herbs, some tomatoes, onions, and peppers.

"Joshua, that's way more food than you'll eat. Who are you cooking for, an army?"

"Worse…musicians," Joshua joked as he shook his head and reached out to shake Drew's hand.

"You've been a kind host to them, Joshua. People around town have told me how polite they are and how highly they speak of you. Musicians can be a tough lot. Be sure you let them know they are always welcome in Crossings. Kolby Rae is a good role model for our girls."

"She can be a bit wild, Drew. You know that, right?" Joshua added.

"Sure. So can our teenagers. Wild is fine. Just stay this side of the line." Drew was looking into Joshua's face. "Joshua, you have a gift that you're keeping from us. And I understand. So I'm not asking you to do anything other than to listen to your heart. These kids need a role model. We have a splendid group of families, and your joining us is wonderful. You could add something to our kids, our older kids."

"Drew, what are you saying? Another basketball camp?"

"Sure, next year. But I'm just asking you to listen. You'll find your role. You remember high school. It's a time when you love your parents but don't want to listen to their advice anymore. These kids like you." Drew grabbed Joshua on the shoulder. "Just tell me you'll listen."

Joshua smirked. "Yeah, listen. Okay, I will, Drew."

"Doc-tor Stone." Joshua turned and found Forrest and Rooster holding plastic bags filled with produce and grinning. "Say, it's none of our business, but since you brought it up, we couldn't help but notice you had a pretty little lady on your arm at dinner the other night."

"Hey, Forrest, Rooster. I don't think I brought it up, but yes, I did, as a matter of fact."

Forrest and Rooster both nodded, and without indulging their curiosity any further, Joshua put his produce in the Rover, got in, and drove back to the big house.

Kolby was the first to come to the kitchen as Joshua was rolling out seven-inch pizza crusts. Kolby looked at the counters—meats, cheese, garden vegetables diced and in bowls, all neatly arranged down the center bar in the large kitchen with room on each side for the band to walk, build their pizzas, and carry them out to the covered porch.

Joshua's back was to Kolby and as she snuck behind him. She pressed a chilled beer bottle to the back of his neck.

"Oh-h-h-h, that's cold." He turned and was met by Kolby's grin. He took the bottle from her and began pushing her backwards, much in the same way they had two-stepped at the Roadhouse. She saw hunger in his eyes. It was not just a dance he wanted. She let him press her against the wall. She parted her lips, inviting him to kiss her, when Nils walked in the other door to the kitchen.

"Wow, look at all this stuff."

Kolby and Joshua quickly separated, murmuring half excuses, moving apart, and looking away from each other.

Sean led the rest of the band into the kitchen. They were in mid-conversation about the order in which to lay down tracks when they stopped at the sight of the spread of food in front of them.

Sarah came in after them, and they all looked at Joshua with a chorus of, "What? You made this for us?"

"Yeah. So here's the deal. There's some sauce on the stove; it's ready. I grated a couple of different cheeses, and the veggies are from the farmers' market in Crossings. So just choose your crust, put a little olive oil on it, and then make whatever pizza you want. I'll be outside at the oven. Bring it over, and it'll be ready in about seven minutes."

Roberto handed his phone to Sean, who connected it to the outdoor speakers. Salsa music flowed across the patio and out into the grass. Joshua stole one more longing look at Kolby from the door. She was talking to Sarah, and she snuck not one but two looks his way, and then turned back to Sarah's conversation.

They kept the across-the-room glances up all night, and the longer the looks became, the closer they found themselves standing together.

Joshua took a cheese pizza out of the wood-fired oven, cut it into slices, and slid it from the pizza peel onto a plate. Kolby took one slice, the cheese making a long string. As it stretched from the plate, she held the pizza high above her head and nibbled up the cheese string and then turned the pizza slice, offering Joshua a bite. She began swaying her hips to the salsa song and then led Joshua by the pizza slice out onto the middle of the room, and they began dancing. Kim patted Roberto twice on the shoulder, and he swept her up into salsa moves of their own. Sean had his bass and began playing along with the song. Nils put together a collection of boxes, empty cans, bottles, and a flower pot to make an impromptu drum kit.

Roberto said, "I'll get my guitar," and dashed off. Sarah stood up and took Kim by the hands and waist and danced with her. When Roberto came back, he switched off the playlist on his phone and then called a singer's name and song title to Nils: "Celia Cruz, 'Oye Como Va'?"

Nils began dragging his drumstick across the tiles of the counter, making the rhythm of a guiro.

Sean asked, "What key?"

"G, try it in G," answered Roberto. Sean laid down the staccato bass beats, and Roberto's guitar screamed.

The girls quickly huddled around a beer bottle as if it were a microphone and sang the song's title, "Oye Como Va," and the intro verse in Spanish. As they sang on, Skeeter crossed the floor and handed Joshua a beer.

"Great pizza, man." He lingered a moment longer as if he had something more to say. Joshua looked back with anticipation. Skeeter watched as Kolby, enjoying life in the moment, was strutting around with the other girls, all the while looking directly at Joshua. Skeeter looked at them each one more time and then finished, "I'm really glad you're here." He tapped beer bottles with Joshua and sat down, clapping in time to Sean's bass rhythm.

When they started the next song, Skeeter had his dobro in his lap, and they played "I Think I'll Just Stay Here and Drink." Roberto took the lead on the first verse and then nodded to Kim to take the second. Kolby whooped and hooted as they sang, clapping her hands, swaying her shoulders and hips, and Skeeter began the solo break.

Skeeter nodded at Sean, "Go, man." Sean laid down a funky bass riff, and then Nils picked up the final verse.

They were just getting started. The singing, and drinking went well into the night. Sarah stuck to lemonade, and Kolby switched to water halfway through the party. Joshua slowed down, unable to keep up with Skeeter, Roberto, and Kim.

At the end of the music jam session, Sarah said her goodbyes to everyone and walked out to the parked SUVs with Kolby Rae. She hit the remote start. SMILES woke and the running lights blinked twice. She turned to Kolby Rae.

"I'll finish the details with the rental people in the morning. Take care of the bank stuff. I'll get the crew lined up and confirm all the dates."

The two women hugged.

"Drive safe," said Kolby. "Text me when you get in, okay?"

"Sure."

Sarah got in the SUV, and Kolby felt Joshua at her side. She reached over and took his hand and then waved at Sarah's truck as it disappeared down the lane. She waved for another few moments.

"What are you doing?" asked Joshua.

"I'm waving goodbye."

"Okay, but why?"

"Where are you from? You always wave goodbye."

"I don't think I've ever waved goodbye. It's not like she can see you."

"Joshua Stone, it's just good manners. Didn't your momma teach you any good manners?"

"My momma—my mother taught me manners. We just didn't wave goodbye in our family."

"Here, try it. Don't you miss Sarah already? Wave. It'll make the hurt go away."

Kolby watched as Joshua sheepishly looked around to see if the others were nearby watching, then shook his hand once or twice in the air and returned the hand to his pocket.

Kolby waved a bit more just to make her point and then turned and grabbed Joshua's left arm with both of her hands. "Let me walk you home, Dr. Stone?"

"Sure, that would be nice. Fylgja, *heir*." The dog came running and walked around beside Kolby's.

"I think she likes me."

"She does, and she's protecting you. You're part of her pack. See? Watch this." They stopped. Joshua turned around and faced behind them. Fylgja shifted her paws in the grass and turned more to be opposite of Joshua, looking directly ahead of them. Joshua turned around and took a footstep forward. Without command, Fylgja turned to her right and was now watching behind them. "She's protecting you. She's working with me to keep you safe."

They kept walking until they reached the cabin door.

"Let me see the other room."

"What? The bedroom?"

"Don't you think it's time?"

Joshua took her by the hand, and they walked into his bedroom. She lay down on the bed and patted the pillow.

"Come lie down here." Joshua kicked off his shoes and crawled into the bed next to her.

"Is this okay?" Kolby asked.

Joshua gave her a pleasure-filled look. "Oh yeah, very okay."

"Are you comfortable?"

"Yeah."

"Excited?"

He nodded. "Yeah."

"Nervous?"

"A little."

"Good." Kolby sat up. "Well, that's that. Now you can tell your friends you've been to bed with Kolby Rae." She got out of the bed. "It was good for me. I hope it was good—"

Joshua reached up and grabbed her arms, pulling her backwards onto the bed. She laughed so loud, Joshua was convinced they would hear her in the big house.

"Oh my word, Joshua Stone, you should have seen the look on your face. Oh my word, if I only had a camera."

He rolled over onto his back, laughing with her, and she rolled onto her back. They lay there watching and listening to the ceiling fan in the darkened room.

CHAPTER TWENTY-TWO

STEAM

"I LIKE LAUGHING WITH YOU, and so if that's going to bed with Kolby Rae, what would a guy like me have to do if he wanted to make love with Kolby Ruth?"

Kolby Rae scooted back against the pillow and the headboard. She looked at him and cocked her head to the side. "Is that what you want? Do you want to know me in that way? Because I do. I want you to know me. I want you to know who's lying in your bed. Will you listen? I don't want you to say anything. I just want you to listen…"

Joshua rose up on his left side, propping his body with an elbow. He pulled the blanket at the foot of the bed up over both of their bodies. "Tell me," Joshua said. "Start with your father. Tell me about him."

"First off, he was never my 'father'; he was always 'Daddy.' My daddy was a wiry man with an opinion about everyone and everything in town. Some folks would say his bark was worse than his bite, but he never said a word in anger to Momma or me."

Joshua lightly brushed a single hair from her forehead.

"When I was growing up, he took me everywhere. The men in town called me Kolby Coon Hound because I was always at his heels trying to be just like him, dressed in our matching camo pants and mud boots. I learned how to cut cards and deal five-card stud by the time I was twelve, and I'd sit with him at the town bar, and he'd smoke his cigarettes and drink beer and talk with the men about politics and too much government bullcrap.

"It didn't matter which party was in office. Daddy hated 'em all. By the time I was sixteen, he'd never said anything good about Bush and threatened to move us all out of the country to Canada if Clinton was elected. On election night, my girlfriends and I sat around crying and hugging each other over an atlas of Canada. We knew they spoke French in Canada, and the girls told me I needed to get better at French kissing. I lied to them and told them I knew all about French kissing and even some other kinds of kissing, too."

Kolby leaned forward and kissed Joshua, playing with her tongue just inside his lips. When she stopped, he was looking intently in her eyes.

"We weren't poor, but we weren't rich. Mostly, Daddy worked on people's cars and small engines out of a metal building on the back corner of our lot. I'd wake up first thing in the morning and go to the kitchen and pour him a cup of coffee and carry it to him. The steam from the cup would dance across my face, and I took a whiff and then down the steps, very slowly so I wouldn't spill, and then across the grass to his shop.

"Sometimes I'd be barefoot and the dew would get my feet wet, and I'd try to spell out my name with my footprints on the concrete driveway while I sang him the songs I learned in Sunday school that week. I could always find him there with the radio playing country music, lit up by the amber glow of a trouble light under the hood of someone's car turning a wrench."

She sat up and turned her body, crossing her legs and facing Joshua.

"One night when I was fourteen, I was playing my guitar when I heard Momma and Daddy talking, so I went down the stairs and sat on the last step and listened. They were talking about money, and some man owed Daddy a lot of money. I don't know how much. They weren't having a fight, but I could tell Momma was telling Daddy what he had to do, and Daddy didn't want no part of it.

"Momma said, 'You have to do it. He owes you, and you've been good to let this slide so long, but if he ain't gonna pay you cash money, you have to do what you need to do to keep this family going.'

"'But what's he gonna do if I take them tools?' Daddy asked her. 'It ain't the Christian thing to do to take a man's tools.'

"'They are your tools, and he is no Christian.'

"Years later, Momma explained to me that Daddy had worked in the man's auto repair shop, and Daddy was buying tools from George Harding, our neighbor who drove the big truck for the tool company that sold to starting mechanics. Daddy had worked hard, and the man told Daddy he would match whatever tool Daddy bought and paid for with his own money with an equal amount, dollar for dollar. And then the man said he needed some time for Daddy's paychecks, and after three months, Daddy didn't have any paycheck, and the man closed and locked the doors on the shop.

"I don't know what happened, but I remember two things: first, the look of pride on my daddy's face when he backed the pickup into our metal building with the huge, bright red tool chest strapped to the back, and second, that night when we went to the bar and Daddy just said, 'Kolby, you don't say nothin' no matter what happens in here.'

"I was scared, but we opened the door, and a bunch of the men were huddled around a table in the back. They whispered and pointed at Daddy when Daddy and I sat at the bar. Daddy acted like he didn't care, but the whole time, I could see his eyes watching them in the reflection in the mirror on the back wall of the bar. In a little while, Daddy finished his beer and started to put some cash on the bar to pay up. The waitress walked over and handed Daddy a fresh bottle of beer, a whole bottle, not just a glass, and she pointed to the guys at the table. Daddy looked over, and they all raised a glass at him.

"They knew what he did, that he went and stood up for himself. He took what was rightly his. Later that night, he let me use his electric engraver and write our family name and the year on the back side: Miles 1991."

She paused as Joshua rolled over to his back, staring at the ceiling as he pictured every scene she described. "Miles 1991?" he asked her. Kolby nodded. Joshua encouraged her to go on. "How about your momma?"

Kolby nodded when he got the word right.

"Momma and me were just as close but not in the same way. We'd stand outside and hang the washing and then take it down and fold it, all the time talking about the ladies at the church and the things they organized for people, mostly funerals. She would talk about faith, and she'd quiz me, like a game, about people and places and stories of the Bible.

"Momma sang with me every night and got me to join the church choir. Church choir was awful. Most of those women and men couldn't carry a tune in a bucket, but we sang all the hymns, and my first singing break came the year I turned fifteen. Momma talked the choir director into letting me sing a solo on Christmas Eve. I sang 'What Child is This?' I brought my guitar, and when Pastor Ray finished his sermon, it was my cue to go on.

"One of the ushers placed a stool right up front, and I stepped across the wooded floor and my boots went *click-clack* with every step. Momma even gave me some of her lipstick to wear. She said it was so the older people could see my mouth better, but I think she wanted the boys in town to take notice of me, but in a church and not a high school dance so they would get the right message."

"I bet you were very pretty," Joshua said.

"Sh-h-h, just listen, okay? I was so nervous, but I wanted to be in the center of that church so bad that I just started playing and singing. The first two lines, I barely spoke a whisper—and that's the first time the Kolby Rae whisper came out. Everyone thought I did it on purpose, so I just told them, 'Yes, I did.'

"Momma and me stayed up that whole night making Christmas cookies and talking about life and boys and the Bible and what I wanted to do next and how many babies I wanted to have. I knew that night that I wanted to be a singer. I didn't care about boys or babies; I wanted to be in front of a crowd. I didn't care if they were all old and hard of hearing; I wanted an audience. I wanted to be the next country singer from Tremont, Mississippi.

"So I joined the high school choir, and I sang at everything I could sing at: state contests, school concerts, 'The Star-Spangled Banner' at every home game for football and basketball. I would've sung at a track meet if they would've let me. And when I was seventeen, I entered my first professional competition, a Christian music contest, and the winner got a recording of a one-song demo with a real studio band and a thousand dollars in cash. And I won it singing 'Hallelujah,' which then no one had ever heard."

Kolby stopped and looked at Joshua. His expression was vague, so she sang:

:: It goes like this the fourth, the fifth, the minor fall, the major lift ::

Joshua nodded with a glimmer of recognition.

"That night, I came home and Daddy was working on a truck in the metal shop building. I loved being in that shop with him. That big red toolbox—his toolbox was amazing. There were twenty-one drawers, and I knew what was in every single one of them. Daddy could be under a truck, hands caked in grease, and yell out, 'Kolby Ruth, I need a three-eighths crescent wrench,' and I knew where it was: third drawer down, third wrench in. And I'd get it and hand it to him.

"He never heard me sing in the contest, but we were talking and he was working underneath, looking for a leak in the radiator. He said, 'Kolby, sing that song for me.' So I did. I sang it for my daddy a cappella. And while I sang, he listened, and when I was done, he told me I was an angel. My daddy called me an angel. Then he said, 'Sing it again while I look for this here leak.' And he rolled back underneath while I stood next to the truck.

"'Kolby, shine that light down here.' His trouble light was hanging from the latch on the truck hood, so I stood up over the bumper to reach for it. It was just out of my reach, and I leaned a little farther, and that's when the hose split on the radiator.

"That truck had been running for a while in Daddy's shop, and that hose was just old and tired. It was a tiny split, not much more than an inch, they tell me, but it sprayed my shirt and my chest with two-hundred-fifty-degree steam. God was watching over me that day; all that hot stuff missed my face and my eyes. And everyone says I must have slipped, but I know it was the hand of God that reached down and pushed me away as I fell back on the ground."

Joshua sat up. "What happened? Were you hurt?"

"I don't remember much of what happened after that except I know we were in the back of Daddy's pickup, Momma was cradling my head in her lap and her hair was flying in the wind, and it was like Momma and me were flying. It was dark, and all I could see was Momma's face surrounded by all the twinkling stars in heaven. I knew this was how I was going to die.

"Momma says it broke her heart to hear me scream the whole forty-minute drive to the hospital. She says Daddy scrambled out from under the truck and picked me up in his arms and started hollering. She looked out the kitchen window, and there was Daddy running as fast as he could, carrying me to the back of that truck. He laid me down. By that time, Momma had come running out, and Daddy yelled at her to get in back with me. He drove so crazy out of town that he ran three people off the road.

"Momma said she'd never been in a truck that moved so fast, and Daddy would never say how fast he drove. Later on, the state trooper told Daddy it took him seven minutes to catch up to our truck. It was a good thing that trooper was Daddy's friend Junior Watson. Daddy and Junior were part owners in a stock car one year. Junior didn't know it was Daddy and Momma and me in the truck, and when we finally pulled over, Junior got out with his gun drawn, and Daddy came flying out of the driver's seat.

"After it was all over, Junior and Daddy laughed, saying that he almost shot Daddy until he saw me and Momma and the fear on Daddy's face. Then Junior said, 'Follow me and stay close.' And Daddy told him to 'stay the hell out of my way.' So these two good ol' boy rednecks made a drag race out of the last five miles of my trip to the hospital.

"I didn't stay there long. In an hour, they packed me into an ambulance and drove me to a bigger hospital, and from there, they transferred me to Children's Charity Hospital. I had third-degree burns and some second- and first-degree. The third-degree, the worst ones, didn't hurt. My nerves had been steamed clean off. It was the smaller burns that hurt most.

"The middle of my chest and the top half of my left breast were all destroyed. The pain shot clean through to my heart. And I said, 'Okay, the worst is over.' They gave me pain medicine. I said, 'Okay, I'll be home in a couple of days and go record my demo and be off to Nashville.' I said, 'The worst is over.' I was seventeen years old, and I had no idea of the hell I was about to live."

Joshua was rubbing his own scars, first his cheek and then his left bicep with the bullet injury.

"When your skin gets burned off, before the new skin can grow, the old skin needs to be taken away. And they don't just do it once. They have to do it over and over again. The first time they did it, two nice nurses came and took me to a room. It had a steel table and a steel tank like a horse trough. It had the hoses and water jets that blasted into my chest and ripped the dead skin. It tore at my flesh, and they held me down while I screamed in pain. The first time I thought I was going to die. Every time after, I begged them to let me die. I begged them to stop. I begged and I pleaded for them to stop. They just held me down, opened the water jets, and then blasted my open wounds. When they were done, they rinsed my old dead skin and my blood down the drain."

Kolby shivered, and as Joshua pulled the blanket higher on their bodies, a tear formed in the corner of her eye. She drew a breath and continued.

"The pain was so bad, I asked God every night why he didn't tell me to jump out of the back of Daddy's truck and die on the side of the road. Why did he let me live to come to the hospital and then leave me to suffer?"

When she spoke those words, Joshua remembered the night he saw his first dog, Rex, injured and lying by the side of the road. In his mind, the images of Kolby lying next to him and Rex mingled. His body shuddered, too.

"They did this to me so many times, I stopped counting. But it was nights alone in the dark that left deeper scars in my heart.

"They measure burns by the percent of your body that is hurt. My burns covered only six percent of my body. The other kids on my floor were living, if you call it that, with twenty, thirty, even seventy percent of their skin burned off. The smell was horrid. The screams were awful. Every night, before I fell asleep, I would lie there and listen to the beeping rhythm of the heart monitors. Some fast, some slow, never the same beat twice. So at night, I would lie there and listen to the beats and try to make up a song to go with the rhythm, to make it not so awful. And some nights, a heart monitor would stop beeping and emit a solid tone, a long, lonely cry that the heart in the next room had stopped.

"And I would close my eyes and pray until I heard the shuffle of feet and the rolling wheels of the cart that looked like Daddy's toolbox. I could hear them talking. It's nothing like on TV. It's just controlled talking and the sound of drawers opening and closing and packages being torn apart and a bed mattress creaking, kind of like the sound of sex, as someone pumped away, trying to force life into a charred body, counting 'one and two and three and four' as they tried to call another lost soul back.

"When it was over, there was a lonely silence. Every time, I cried. And to this day I don't know if I was sad or jealous.

"I stayed in that hospital for twenty-nine days. Momma stayed home, taking care of Daddy and Sarah. It broke her heart not to be with me, but I lied and told her Sarah needed her more. The day I got out, Momma, Daddy, and Sarah picked me up, and I hugged them all so tight, I didn't want to ever let go. Momma smelled like she was going to church and looked all pretty. Daddy never looked me in the eye, and when I hugged him, he smelled like the old men at the bar who drank bourbon all day. Sarah and I stuck our tongues out at each other, but it was never the same for us after that."

Joshua interrupted her. "Wait, you mean Sarah? This Sarah and you? You're sisters?"

Kolby nodded. "When I got home, Daddy had boarded up the metal shop building and put a padlock on the door. Daddy dropped Momma and me off at the house and drove to the bar to drink away the guilt and shame he felt because he thought he hadn't protected me.

"Momma and me stayed up and talked. After a while, she asked me to undo my shirt and let her see the final scars. The skin on my chest and breast were discolored and misshapen. Part of my breast was gone. The hospital had years of surgery planned for me. Momma tried to smile, but she looked so sad. Seeing me like that at home, I guess, made it all real. She said she was sorry that I would have to hide my heart away forever.

"The contest people mailed me a check for my thousand dollars, but they gave my studio time to the runner-up. So for three years, my songs were silent. I stayed home and helped Momma take care of Daddy as he slowly drank himself to death. I never went to a swimming pool and stayed inside on the hottest days, which was pretty much half the year in Mississippi. I was ashamed of my scars and hated the looks I got from people who didn't know me. I learned what to wear to hide my scarred heart. In between my surgeries and skin grafts, I took care of Momma, Momma took care of Daddy, and we survived like that. Sarah went off to college and never came back home.

"One July morning, Daddy just didn't get out of bed, and when I walked upstairs to check on him, I knew he was gone. So I came down and told Momma. We said a prayer and then called the funeral home. I sang for the first time again at Daddy's funeral shortly thereafter, started singing in my cousin Buddy Mitchell's band. Buddy was Momma's sister's son. Buddy had big dreams and ambitions. He was even my manager a few years ago, but Buddy was a little light on follow-through, but he was nice. Momma always taught me to put family first.

"But in Buddy's band, it was easy to be in front of strangers because I always wore cowboy shirts with pearl snaps up the front and long sleeves, and all the boys thought I looked sexy. I stayed two more years folding laundry with Momma and singing with the band. Sarah beat me to my own dream and got a job as an assistant at a big Nashville record label.

"On my last night in that house, Momma came to me with tears on her face, holding an envelope full of hundred-dollar bills. She had sold Daddy's tools. She told me it was time to stop hiding my heart. She said, 'Kolby Ruth, your time has come.' She gave me the envelope full of cash and said, 'You and I are moving to Nashville so you can live your dream. You're gonna be a star.' We packed our things and left the next day. She lived with me until she died three years ago."

Joshua was silent for a long time after Kolby finished her story. He lay there, holding her hand. They listened to each other breathe.

Kolby leaned up, looked at Joshua, and rolled her body on top of him, straddling his hips, beginning to undo the pearl snaps on her shirt. When she unsnapped the last one, she hesitated, then slid the blouse off both shoulders, then reached down, pulling the camisole up and over her head. In the moonlight, Joshua could see the curves of her waist, her chest, her breasts, and the discolored skin from the nearly twenty-year-old burn. The skin on her chest and breast was blanched white, some pink, some red. The skin was wrinkled in places, like prune fingers from swimming. It covered much more of her chest and breast than he imagined possible. He recalled some of her more revealing photographs in her CDs and magazine layouts, and there was never a hint.

Kolby reached out, took both of Joshua's hands, and slowly raised them to touch her breasts. She watched his face for the slightest hint of revulsion or disgust. He gently caressed her skin, slowly touching and nuzzling her. He pulled her closer, kissed her warmly, and they were both trembling as they finished undressing each other. She lay on top of him, naked, and they kissed more, sweetly, softly, and then as if some new hunger overcame them both, he was inside her, and they consummated what they began in the recording studio days earlier, no longer separated by a wall of glass.

CHAPTER TWENTY-THREE

PILLOW TALK

FOR THE REMAINING DAYS AND nights of August on the Adams farm, Kolby Rae and Joshua became an item. They never made a formal announcement and avoided public displays of affection, but the band knew. Sean Adams figured it out, and most of the men of the MFL figured it out as the couple spent more and more time together. The couple shared and talked about everything except love.

The night before the band rolled out for their Saturday show and the tour, Joshua and Kolby were kissing in the threshold to the bedroom and, as they had done so many times, performed an erotic dance with their bodies intertwined as they kicked off their shoes and landed on the bed in a pile of hugs and caresses. Kolby was the first to roll over to her back, and Joshua followed her lead and rolled to his back as well. They lay there in silence, listening to the *click whirr click click* of the ceiling fan.

"Do you remember my telling you about Rex?"

"Your dog…yes, I remember. What made you think of him now?"

"Popcorn. We used to—okay, don't laugh—some Friday nights, I would make popcorn for dinner, and that's all we would eat."

"What, in the microwave?"

Joshua propped himself on his elbow, looking at her.

She stopped him from talking. "Oh Lord, that look. Why do you give me that look? You know what that does to me."

"No, not in the microwave. Real popcorn…in a skillet…on the stove. You know, shake the pan?"

She looked back at him. "I have never had that."

He was laughing. "Oh no, here we go again with the words. Don't start with me. This is not one of the pop versus soda, sweet tea versus iced tea things. Everyone has had popcorn. So okay, what do you Southern girls call it?"

"No, we call it popcorn, and I had it at the movies with Momma and Daddy. Then when I got my first apartment in Nashville, I had a microwave oven and made it in that. I've never had popcorn made on a stove." Kolby propped herself on her arm, and they stared at each other, noses inches apart, daring the other to blink or move first.

"Seriously, why do I have to teach Southern girls everything about life?" With his dismissive phrase, Joshua rolled off the bed and left for the kitchen. Kolby lay there, giggling and a bit surprised at his willingness to always go into the kitchen. She rolled over and looked at the stack of books by his bed. And the stack of her CDs. They were all open, and some of the liner notes were askew. He had read them.

Next to the books, she found his black, hard-sided journal. Before she reached for it, she called to him. "Joshua, is this journal something you would share with me someday if I asked you?"

In a moment, he appeared at the door, smiling. "You're in for a treat. This is going to be great. Which journal? That black one?"

"Yes."

"Read it now if you like. No secrets. I write daily, mostly creative ideas or capturing scenes that I see or like. You won't find any midforties angst there. I think I have a few years before that whole midlife bitterness sets in. Whaddya think? Me? As a grumpy old man?" He pulled his jeans as high on his waist as he could, made a duck face, and then in a raspy voice pretend-shouted, "Hey you kids! Get offa my lawn!"

He pulled his jeans back down as Kolby rolled over, grabbed a pillow, and threw it at him.

"You scare me some days, Joshua Stone. You have a crazed mind."

Joshua nodded and pointed at the journal. "Go ahead. Read all you like." And then he asked, "Where's yours?"

Kolby pretended to be coy. "Why, Doctor Stone, what would ever make you think that I keep such a thing?"

"Because I've heard your songs. You don't get to be that kind of a writer unless you practice every day. What you do with words is..."

148

She waited for him to finish.

"What you do goes beyond poetry. It goes beyond art. You capture emotion, and you don't do that unless you write every day, so will you share your journal with me?"

Kolby pointed at her purse. "Pink book, inside the main flap."

She was dozens of pages into Joshua's journal when he returned to the bedroom with her pink journal and a giant bowl filled with hot popcorn.

"Fylgja will beg us nonstop," he warned her.

"Then, Joshua Stone, get her her own bowl."

Joshua looked at Kolby and then returned to the kitchen to find a bowl for the dog. He came back and sat on the bed, the popcorn between their legs.

"Wait, we have to take a picture." Kolby grabbed her phone and made a photo of her feet, complete with the gold ring around her third toe, and the bowl of popcorn. She tapped out a caption and posted it live to a photo-sharing site.

"What did you type?"

\<TheRealKolbyRae\> Nothing better than popcorn and a friend. Hope your Thursday is awesome.

She looked at Joshua's face, and he approvingly cocked his head to the side.

For the emotions they shared, the pages of their two journals showed the differences in their minds and styles. Kolby's pages were more often scattered phrases in clouds and shapes, and connected with streaks, squiggles, and arrows. Sometimes there would be snippets of lyrics and some musical notations.

Each entry of Joshua's journal was numbered with the day, beginning at Day 300 through Day 450. He wrote words, lots of words, with the occasional bulleted list. Every few days, the journal included a checklist, ordered and neat, with tiny hand-drawn boxes with X's through them.

Kolby was leafing through and stopped on Day 337. She read the words out loud. "There is a certain agony in surviving." She put her hand to her chest, feeling a fleeting flash of phantom pain. She caught her breath, then spoke. "Oh, I love this. Is it yours?"

Joshua looked over her shoulder, taking a piece of popcorn and placing it on her lips. "No. It's by Cathryn Prince, from *Death in the Baltic*. It's an amazing truth, don't you think? When I read that line…" Joshua stopped. He realized he was rubbing the back of his left hand.

"Will you write it in my journal?" asked Kolby. "At the back?"

Joshua leaned across her body to the nightstand, took a pen from the drawer, and wrote in the back of Kolby's journal under a list of other quotations. He scanned the list. Some were one-line quotations; others filled an entire page. He flipped a few pages and then read:

The winter snow receded, revealing the contours of the landscape as if it were a white sheet, drawn away from a sleeping lover's body the morning after.

"I think I recognize that," he said to her with a sheepish smile.

Kolby looked over at him. "You should. You wrote it. It's the opening line from *Our Final Days*."

"You wrote down something I wrote?"

Kolby winked and then turned another page.

It was just after 3:30 when Kolby woke up, rolling over and feeling the popcorn bowl between her body and Joshua's. They were both dressed, the popcorn long gone, their journals in between them. She got out of the bed, undressed, and then covered Joshua with a blanket and tucked her own body under the covers.

Kolby wondered if Joshua would call out as he had the first night they slept together. He had shouted, having a dream. He sat up, and she asked him what the dream was about. He was confused, and it was clear he wasn't awake. She didn't ask him about it the next morning. This night, as she lay there listening to him breathe, she wondered if and when he would have the dream again.

She fell back asleep to his gentle breathing and was awakened by his kiss and smile, offering her a cup of coffee.

"Good morning. Have some coffee. I need to jump in the shower, and then I need to meet with Drew. He has some more ideas about my running a pizza restaurant. But I'll go listen as one of his faithful."

Kolby rolled over. "Wait. Let me take a shower with you. You can scrub my back."

The shower was cozy and gave them both ideas about what they could do on another day when they had more time together, but Joshua was quick under the water and back out, drying himself before Kolby finished rinsing her hair. He was shirtless as she emerged and stood next to him wrapped in a towel, and they stood looking into the mirror. In the light of the bathroom, the burn scars on her chest and breast were visible above the terrycloth wrap around her body. The bullet wound in his left arm and his hand and the scars across his cheek and forehead were all highlighted by the less than flattering light above the vanity. The two of them looked, first at themselves, then at each other in the reflection.

Joshua was the first to speak. "Nothing better than popcorn with a friend."

Kolby heard him say the words, and she smiled at him. She didn't pick up any sarcasm or inflection. Now in the light of morning, she didn't like the way it sounded. "Friend." It felt as incomplete as a dissonant chord.

He gave her his warm smile, and he kissed her, first gently, then passionately. "I want to see you later. When do you leave on the bus?"

"We're going into Nashville today. We'll be back tonight, and we're loading out the bus from here. So I'll see you sometime after midnight."

Joshua hugged her. "Have a great day in the city. I'll be back midday. I think the guys and I are grilling out some steaks and shooting some hoops tonight before you leave. You know, male bonding time. Me and my posse. Well, me and your posse."

She stifled a smirk at his out-of-date attempt to be trendy.

And he left, taking Fylgja with him.

Kolby loosened the towel around her body and hung it over the back of the chair. As she glanced around the bedroom, she noticed Joshua had done the same with his towel, hanging it over the back of a chair. She sat down on the bed and looked at the image of their two towels as if they were the shadow of their parting embrace. His shirt from the night before was lying on the edge of the bed, so she put it on, rolling the sleeves up and fastening one button. She and Joshua had stood before each other, nearly naked, unashamed, scars exposed. She lay back on his bed and took in the lingering smell of his freshly washed body. His pillow smelled a bit like the sweetness of his sweat. She lay there half dressed, realizing that Joshua Stone was much more than her friend. And she resolved to tell him that night before she left exactly how she felt about him.

CHAPTER TWENTY-FOUR

GIRLS WILL BE GIRLS — BOYS WILL BE BOYS

SARAH AND KIM WERE GLAD to be free of the guys for the day. It didn't take Kolby long to match their enthusiasm for a girls' day in Nashville. The three of them, wearing large-framed dark glasses, had a Matraca Berg playlist blaring "Back in the Saddle," and they were singing harmony on the chorus.

Kim looked at her phone and then growled as she slapped it down in her lap.

Sarah asked, "What's wrong? Forget something?"

"No, it's my mother."

"What'd she do?"

"She's texting me." Kim picked the phone up and then slapped it down a second time. "O-o-o-oh, I wish she would give it a rest."

Kolby looked over her shoulder. "Why? What did she say?"

"I told her we were going on tour and that I would be gone for the next few weeks and I would call her every day…and she replied with" — Kim picked up the phone and read in Korean — "*Wae gyeolhonhaji? Nan amu sonjaga eobsoda!*"

Kolby and Sarah exchanged looks, and then Kim translated, "Why not get married? I do not have any grandchildren!"

Sarah looked at Kim in the backseat, and Kim looked back at her in the rearview mirror. She cocked her head twice in Kolby's direction and then raised her eyebrows. Sarah looked back with a questioning expression. Kim repeated the head cocking and eyebrow raising, then cleared her throat.

"Kolby, Sarah wants to ask you a question," Kim blurted out

"What? Who wants to ask?" Sarah said, making a snarl in the rear-view mirror at Kim.

Kim protested, "You brought it up!"

"I'm driving. You're making faces in the rearview mirror."

"Okay, okay, so, Kolby? Miss Kim is making me ask you about… Joshua." Kolby pretended not to hear. "I said, about Joshua?"

"You girls know I never kiss and tell."

Kim, from the backseat, said, "Okay, since you're not telling, then the two of you are officially kissing?"

"Oh my, you two are worse than sisters. Why don't we just pull off here, I'll get the empty Coke bottle out of the trash, and we'll play Spin the Bottle and Truth or Dare?"

"I am your sister. It's my birthright," Sarah proclaimed.

"Wait, we did that. Remember? That time in Atlanta?" asked Kim.

"Oh my God, and those guys with the nose rings. They came by and wanted to take a picture with us."

"I have never seen a redneck with a nose ring."

"Ewwww, they were so disgusting."

Sarah prodded her sister. "So, c'mon, girl talk here. Kolby, what is it about Joshua? Are you suddenly into scars?"

Kim chimed in. "I dunno. Scars are kind of a turn-on. I mean, as long as they're not from something lame like falling off a barstool."

Sarah replied, "Sorry, not my thing. I mean, Joshua is very nice, but…"

Kolby felt her skin flush, thinking of Joshua's arms around her and the feeling of their cheeks touching.

Sarah looked over. "Oh girl, look at that look….Look at that glow. I've seen that before. It's over. Kim, we've lost her."

Kolby interrupted. "You two, stop it. Okay, one question, one question. You can ask me one question, anything you like about Dr. Stone, and I will tell the truth."

The two women looked in the mirror at each other. Kim spoke. "So how do you know? How do you know he's different? That he's just not Mr. Right Now?"

Kolby thought of his touch, his kiss, the things they did together when the lights were out. She didn't dare tell them some of the things they did when the lights were on. She settled back in the car seat.

"His kiss. When he kisses me."

"Oh, girl, they all kiss."

Kolby sighed. "But you know how guys are after you've been to-gether, every time they kiss you? It's all about the hands. It's like kiss—*bam*. And the hand is on a boob or your ass?"

"Yeah, that's just what guys do," Kim replied.

"Not Joshua. Sometimes…he just kisses me. He just kisses me and holds me. And my whole inside does this flippy-flop thing."

Kim sat back. Sarah picked up her cell phone and placed a pre-tend call. "Hello, merchandising? This is Sarah Miles. I need to cancel those ten thousand Kolby Rae T-shirts and place a new order....Yes, print them as *Just Married*."

"Oh, we are so done talking about this." Kolby turned the volume louder on the stereo.

Around 6:00 p.m., a large tour bus climbed the small hill on the lane and made the turn into the circle drive in front of the big house. From its nose to the rear of the trailer behind it, it filled the loop and came to a stop near the front door. The doors opened. Five men in their late twenties and early thirties stepped out and were greeted at the portico by Roberto and Skeeter. It was a loud reunion.

Nils and Joshua were on the porch, supervising Sean as he fired up the gas grill for the steaks. Fylgja kept careful eye on the twelve thick T-bones, unwilling to move or turn her head, even when a rabbit came out from under a bush next to the deck. Sean had a pile of sweet corn he was planning to grill as well.

Roberto introduced the new men to Joshua. "This is Graham; he's FOH. Tim is our backline tech. Len is new; he's our guitar tech. Rob is our LD, and Captain Malcolm has driven Kolby almost since she left Pier Records."

Joshua pleaded, "I have no idea what you just said."

Nils chimed in, "You'll catch on."

As they each took a steak and put it on the grill, Roberto and Nils began explaining what the crew did. "We're lucky. We do small shows and have a small set, a bus and a trailer. It's not big time, but it's still fun."

"What's big time?" Joshua asked.

"A big tour, a huge stadium act? Maybe doing a long summer tour, they could have a hundred and sixty people on the crew, ten buses, a few semitrucks."

"Wait, what can a hundred and sixty people possibly do?"

Rob, the man Roberto introduced as the LD, was the lighting director. He answered, "On a big show, you've got huge video screens, staging, steel rigging to hold it all up, lighting installations, computers, monitors, stages to build and tear down and build again. It goes on and on."

Tim continued, "It's like you have this rolling town, and you come in, unload, build it up, play, tear it down, load it back up."

Nils nodded. "Yeah, yeah. I would love to do that one time with Kolby just to say we did it, but give me a small venue where I can feel the people."

"Small venues, small egos, everyone gets along better," Roberto said as he ground pepper onto his steak and then passed the grinder around the group. Roberto pointed. "Rob works miracles since we stopped traveling with a big light kit. He's got a few for Kolby, Kim, and me. Nils and Skeeter are left to the mercy of whatever the venue has. Most of the time, that's okay. If we use our own lights at every show, the color is the same, and then Kolby and Kim don't need to reinvent their makeup color for each show."

Graham pointed. "Captain is the man. He's the only driver I've ever toured with who has this superhuman ability to miss the rumble strips." The band and crew all nodded. "If Captain is up front, I know I'll sleep through the night. Just pop in the bunk, listen to the sound of the road, and gently rock to dreamland."

Over dinner, the group continued to tell Joshua about life on the road and then continued as they huddled around a bottle of bourbon in the afterglow of their steaks. Roberto pulled out a small box of Cohiba cigars.

"I need everyone's help. You must perform your patriotic duty." The alcohol was giving Roberto's normally full voice a few extra decibels of volume. "The last time I visited my *abuela* in Cuba, she gave me these cigars. They are illegal contraband in the United States, and so when I flew home through Mexico, they stopped me at customs and asked me if I had anything to declare."

Nils nodded. The customs stop was a familiar experience for the Norwegian citizen.

"And I could not lie," continued Roberto, "so I showed him these cigars. I told him they were a gift from my grandmother. The customs man told me they were illegal and that they had to be destroyed." Roberto made a sad face. "I asked him, 'Destroyed?' He said, 'Yes, and the best way to destroy them is with an open flame or a match. You are on your honor to destroy these.' So I say to you all, we must now do our patriotic duty and destroy these cigars."

Roberto passed the metal cigar box, and each took a single cigar. Then he passed the candle, and each man lit his cigar, puffing Cuban smoke into the night air.

Graham asked, "What was that Willie Nelson song? 'To All the Girls I've Loved Before'?"

Nils took an exaggerated and theatrical drag on the cigar, blew the smoke out, and grinned. "So many women, so little time."

Roberto grinned. "Nashville is getting too small these days. You can't throw a guitar without hitting an ex."

The men chuckled.

"So are there lots of women on the road?" Joshua asked.

"Joshua, there are so many women, you stop looking. Blondes, brunettes, redheads." He took a long, slow drag on the cigar, blowing the smoke in front of him. "Twins, cougars, MILFs, mother–daughter pairs."

Joshua interrupted. "No, wait, that's a joke, right? I mean, you're making that last bit up."

"No, for real." Skeeter and Nils both nodded.

"That's just creepy weird."

Roberto shrugged his shoulder partway. "Sometimes the local crew might look for a jump-off. Each of us," he said, waving his cigar around him, "has a girl now."

Tim, whose job as backline tech included setting up and tuning Nils's drums, looked over. "Nils? How is your girl these days?"

"She's great. We're great."

Tim continued, "That's awesome. Hey, Joshua, do you know what they call a drummer without a girlfriend?"

Joshua shook his head.

In unison the others all said, "Homeless."

Joshua looked at Nils. They had both been made the butt of the joke. "Yeah, with girlfriends at home, we don't hook up as much as other years."

"As much?" Joshua pressed.

"Boy, you don't miss anything, do you?" Roberto said, smiling.

"Hey, I'm not judging. It's just not in my frame of life. This is a whole new world for me," Joshua said, standing up and reaching for the bourbon.

Roberto challenged the former professor. "Really? You think we're so different? So weren't there certain professors who always seemed to have college girls hanging outside their offices? Or helping with projects?"

"Well, sure, but they—"

"Joshua, it's the same thing. Groupies are groupies. And guys are just as bad."

Joshua stopped. "What, there are guy groupies?"

Nils grinned. "Oh-h-h yeah."

"Just look at this photo." Robert took out his phone and showed Joshua a photo of Kim and Kolby posing in dresses they were trying on. Kim had posted the photo to her social media fans earlier in the day. The photo had been shared by other viewers 719 times in the last hour. "This is, seriously, every man's dream come true. The guys drool over these two. Just like the ladies all like the Latin lover in me. Who's up for some hoops?" Roberto left Joshua holding the phone, looking at the two women. "Joshua, you pick your side; I'll pick mine. I take Nils."

Joshua looked up. "I take Skeeter."

Roberto hollered, "Graham!"

Joshua looked to Sean. "I'll take Sean."

Roberto answered with, "Tim."

"Len," countered Joshua.

Roberto, "Rob."

Joshua, "Captain."

Roberto pointed. "You're skins." Joshua nodded at Skeeter and his team, and the men took their T-shirts off. Skeeter's tattoos extended up his arms, sleeved out.

"We'll be out first," Joshua said, and Roberto tossed the ball to Joshua. As he caught it, the outdoor light lit up his left arm, revealing the bullet wound scars. Roberto stared for a moment, and then the game began.

When the men stopped, they were tied, eighteen to eighteen. Joshua was reaching for a glass and another shot of bourbon. Roberto had lost some of his bravado. Joshua attributed it to being tired or the extra shot Roberto had managed to stay ahead of Joshua.

The others were mingling around, and Roberto leaned in close to Joshua. "Now I know why I know your name. I am so slow. You're the professor from that school. You saved all those kids' lives in that shooting."

Joshua looked at him and shook his head. "Don't believe everything you read in the papers. We just did what we had to do."

Roberto held out his hand to stop Joshua from talking. "I thought about that day a lot, man., I thought, *What would I do if a man like you rushed into a room and saved my daughter's life?*"

Joshua leaned back a little and looked around. "Yeah, it was a tough day, but tell you what." Joshua looked at the back of his left hand, then back at Roberto. "When you get to that point in your life, maybe you can tell me about it. I'm just glad you don't have a daughter who was there that day."

"2007."

"Excuse me?"

"Remember the other night, when I said 2007 wasn't all bad?"

"Oh yeah, right. About making bad choices. Sure, I remember."

Roberto looked straight at Joshua. "There's a brown-eyed girl with my nose and her mother's chin out there somewhere. She must be six years old now."

The basketball flew between them, and Roberto put his hands in front of his face, catching it before it hit. He stood up, switching moods, shouting, "Okay, first team to thirty wins!"

The fire in the game began to dwindle after twenty-six points, and by thirty, Roberto's team was ahead and all were willing to return to the chairs, the beer, and the bourbon.

"So how about you? What's next, Sean?" Roberto asked.

"I've got two women who want to record a bluegrass album coming in next week, and then I want to work with Frankie on the final mix-down on *Crossroads*."

"How about you, Joshua? You gonna finish your book?"

Joshua paused. He hadn't written for his book since Drew had brought up the restaurant and Kolby came to town. It was clear that Kolby and the band were moving on, so he talked about the restaurant. "Well, believe it or not, I'm going to open a pizza restaurant."

Nils gave his gap-toothed grin. "Congratulations, Joshua. You'll be great at it."

Roberto chimed in. "Hey, I know what you can name it. You can call it the Pizza Stone…get it? Stone?"

Joshua continued, "So I'm sourcing ingredients, developing the menu, and hiring local high school kids to work and run it."

Malcolm turned with a big, excited face. "Joshua, I know lots of growers and farmers around. Let me know if I can help hook you up. Meats, herbs, vegetables. I do a little barbecue on the side."

The band and crew laughed.

"What's so funny?" said Malcolm.

"A little barbecue? Captain Malcolm isn't captain of the tour bus; he's captain of the barbecue world. This man has won more prizes than Nashville has tip jars."

Malcolm handed Joshua a business card. "Let's stay in touch. If I can help, let me know. I love food and cooking."

Roberto looked at his phone. "Sorry, gang, it's been fun, but Sarah just texted me. They're in Crossings. It's time to load up."

The men got up and started moving to the house. Joshua, Sean, and Fylgja were left, looking at each other. Roberto stopped, turned around, walked back, and extended his hand to Joshua. "It's been a pleasure meeting you, Joshua. I hope our paths cross again someday. Best of luck with your restaurant."

Nils was behind them. "Hey, hey, Joshua. You're a fun guy. Thanks for your basketball idea. If you ever come to Norway, let me know. I can introduce you to some people. Some pretty girls."

Skeeter fist-bumped Joshua and nodded. The crew waved, and they disappeared into the house.

Joshua looked at Sean, then at Fylgja. "I guess the party's over."

Chapter Twenty-Five

Wave Goodbye

REFRESHED FROM A DAY WITH the girls and excited to be going back to live shows, Kolby approached the small cabin with some trepidation. It was easy to imagine telling Joshua her feelings as she lay on his bed that morning. Now, closer to departure time, opening her heart felt difficult. Once she started, it would be easy. He always made it easy for her to talk. She was unsure how to bring up the subject. She saw him sitting on the deck, stroking Fylgja's fur.

"Joshua Stone, you waited up to say goodbye to me?"

She showed him the double chocolate chip cookies she had bought for him in Nashville. She was stunned when she heard him speak.

"Great, the consolation prize. Some lovely parting gifts for our contestant."

Kolby paused and cocked her head slightly, not sure if she had misunderstood his words or if he was joking. She took a timid step forward and asked, "May I come in?"

Joshua nodded and took the box from her hands as she walked ahead of Fylgja into the big room of the cabin. The incandescent glow painted them in warm orange light. She took off her hat, laid it on the table, and turned to him.

She made a soft plea. "Please don't make this any harder than it has to be. Give me a kiss. Hold me close."

Joshua kissed her. It wasn't his best kiss. They kissed a second time and then a third, each one growing in passion. Then he stopped and pulled away.

He spoke finally. "Kolby, I understand. I know what this is. It's been, well, amazing."

She pulled her head slightly back and opened her eyes wider. "You know what 'what' is?" she asked.

"Look, I know what goes on, and I understand." He thought back to the boastful conversation between Roberto, Skeeter, and Nils.

Kolby dropped her arms from around his neck and took a half step back, still searching his face for clues, but she had not seen this look before. He looked determined and unwavering but somehow lacking confidence.

She asked him to explain. "You know *what* goes on? *What* do you understand?"

"Kolby, I get it. You and I, well, it is what it is. Now you're going on the road. Lots of places…fans…long nights." He paused, and she looked at him blankly. It was a stare down, and each was determined not to let the other win. "Loneliness…temptation."

Kolby felt the red splotches on her chest and neck, and her breathing became a bit faster. "Joshua Stone, what are you saying to me?"

"I'm saying that I thought you meant more to me than maybe I should have let either one of us believe. But that's okay." Joshua fiddled with his hands and lightly rubbed the scar on his left hand. "You're a big star, and I can't think for a moment that you won't…" He couldn't find the courage to say the words. He didn't want to picture the image of her doing what the words implied. He closed his eyes, and when he opened them, she was still staring at him, her left hand twirling her hair.

"What?" she said loudly. "Think for a moment that I won't what?"

He looked back, implying that she knew what he meant.

"What?!" she demanded. "Think for a moment that I won't what? Tell me!"

"You know what I mean."

"No, I don't know what you mean, and you'd better tell me. Think for a moment that I won't what? Tell me."

"The truth?" he asked her. He knew what she would say next.

"I always expect the tru—"

Before she could finish, Joshua blurted the words. "Fuck someone. Get laid. Make love. Hell..." He looked around the room, unsure where to focus or what to say. "All of it for all I know."

He stopped and looked above her, then settled his stare on her face and saw rage in her eyes—not the glow of passion, not the fire of anger, but rage. Her body stood firm. Only her left foot jiggled. She fiddled with her hair, twirling it, and then turned away from him and walked to the sink, turned back around and walked to the far side of the table, then turned to face him.

"Sex? This is about sex? This isn't about Joshua Stone and Kolby Ruth Miles?"

He didn't back away and stared intently at her.

"Sex, okay, fine. You want to know about my sex life? You think life on the road is one big jump-off while I drink a beer and sing you some songs?"

Fylgja looked at the two and paced back and forth.

"I'm getting ready to leave here tonight and be gone for more weeks than we've been together, and you want to spend it talking about me sleeping with other men?"

She tipped her head down and stared at the table. She audibly blew out three breaths.

"Fine, you wanna talk about sex? You got it. Get out your notebook, writer boy. Get schooled." Kolby held up one finger. "One time. One time. One time I gave a cowboy a— " She stopped herself in midsentence. "I gave a cowboy a good time in the parking lot of a show in Austin because he had a cute ass and I had one too many tequila shots. And you know what? Yes, it was fun. Okay? Happy now?" Joshua looked up at her, and she scolded him. "Turn the page; keep writing."

Kolby was just warming up. She shoved her hat off the table and walked around to the end. They were three feet apart.

"And don't tell me for a moment that some young college girl never walked into your office in a short top and skirt, and you didn't think about giving her some private lessons. But you want to talk about me?"

She reached out and shoved his shoulder as if she was making a point. She continued, "Okay. Yes, I've been with other men. Yes, they were great in bed. I know what you're thinking. Because we're all out there onstage, we're able to have the pick of the crowd? You're probably right.

"I never slept with Roberto, but look at his body, look at his eyes. You think there isn't a woman in America who would say no to him if he asked to get in her pants? And I'm not blind. I know what Kim looks like. You and every other wild-eyed Southern boy would give anything to be the electric cello between her thighs." Joshua was stunned she could read his erotic thoughts. "But Joshua Stone, that is not who you and I are."

Kolby stopped, drew a deep breath, and then slowly punctuated the next seven words. "I…don't…make…my…bed…that…way."

Joshua didn't move. He didn't blink. He stared at her mouth and nose as her nostrils flared with each breath. Fylgja moved next to him and sat, then stood up and sat next to Kolby, then stood up again and walked to the far side of the room and then out the open door.

Kolby looked at Joshua and realized she knew more about what he wanted to say than he did. So she said it for him. "Joshua Stone, yes, I've been with other men, but they all came up short."

She saw Joshua's neck and jaw relax a bit. She kept reassuring him. "None of them, not a one, could go the distance. None of them was you. I feel things with you I've never felt before. I know this is true. You are my one and only, Joshua Stone. I came here tonight to tell you how I feel about you and what you mean to me." As she said the words, she rested her hand on his chest.

From her napping place on the deck, Fylgja heard more muffled sounds and heard both of them raise their voices and yell each other's name before it became quiet. The dog got up and walked back into the room several minutes later. She looked around for the arguing couple and only found two pairs of jeans crumpled on the floor where they had been arguing moments before. The dog looked around the floor and in the corners of the room before she found the couple, out of breath and lying on top of each other on the dinner table.

Kolby was the last person on the bus, and as the doors closed, with Joshua and Fylgja standing on the drive as they pulled away, she asked Captain Malcolm to turn on the rear-facing camera. In the black and white monitor, she saw the dog and Joshua. And then he raised his arm and waved goodbye, just as she had taught him to do. The smirk on her face stayed with her all the way to Mississippi.

PART SIX
ALL ACCESS

Chapter Twenty-Six

The Kolby Rae road show had one star: Kolby Rae. That's not to say the musicians didn't get well-deserved praise and appreciation from the fans; they did. It's not to say that when times were good and Kolby could afford them, the crew they took with them from city to city wasn't respected, appreciated, and reasonably paid. They were. And when cash accounts were lean, the local crews, the dayworkers, and the volunteers made the Kolby Rae show magic.

Showtime meant the spotlight was focused on Kolby, with occasional highlights for each member of the band. For the remaining twenty-two hours and eleven minutes of show day, it was Sarah Miles who was the center of attention. Sometimes arbitrator, sometimes tour guide, sometimes mender of broken souls, and once or twice bail bondsman, Sarah ran the show.

It was little sister Sarah who had opened the Nashville door for Kolby when she signed with Pier Records. Kolby's demo, complete with "Landslide," was "accidentally" mixed in with the final stack of demos to be approved by the label's A & R team. Kolby never knew and Pier never knew; it worked out well for everyone in the beginning. As the years went on, their career paths seldom crossed. Sarah's job took her on the road with Trent as assistant tour relations manager, a powerless title that was as meaningless as most of the duties that went with it. But titles and duties don't matter when your résumé includes one of the biggest names in the industry.

As Kolby struggled, Sarah's successful tours contributed to their drifting apart. They hadn't spoken since their mother had died. Kolby cared for their mother till the end, often canceling shows to drive her to chemo and doctor's appointments. Sarah was on the road and didn't attend the funeral.

Oddly, it was Pier that reunited them. Sarah's boss, Joey Fitaldi, told Sarah that the label was not renewing Kolby's contract and that Sarah had to deliver the news. The first conversation the sisters would have would be a cruel homecoming. Kolby came in wearing her denim shirt, a dark denim skirt, and brown leather boots with the cuffs turned down. Sarah always loved the boots. She looked Kolby in the eye and told her the news. She swallowed twice, hoping Kolby would say something. She didn't. Locked in a sister-to-sister stare down, they sat in silence for nearly ten minutes. Then Kolby stood up, walked out the door, and into the hall.

Sarah let out a deep sigh and turned to face J. D. Siggins, the vice president, who kept his back turned during the entire meeting. Sarah next looked at Joey Fitaldi as he shook his head, boasting, "You must have ice water in your veins."

Sarah didn't know if it was a compliment until they continued, telling her that the ice water in her veins made the rest of their conversation easier. Sarah was also terminated. Her desk had been cleaned out while she had been in the meeting. A security guard would escort her to the front door.

Sarah remembered two other things from that day two years ago and never forgot them. The first was the blast of heat and humidity from the Nashville summer as the lobby's glass door opened and she walked out onto the sidewalk unemployed, a payment behind on her new car, and fresh out of a heartbreaking relationship. The second was the sound of Kolby's voice. "Well, this day is a complete waste of makeup. Wanna go get drunk?"

And they did. It brought out a decade of resentment. At one point, they were screaming at each other in the middle of the Music Row roundabout at the base of the bronze sculpture *Musica*.

"You abandoned Momma!" Kolby yelled, attracting the attention of more than one passerby, several of whom called 9-1-1.

"She never accepted me for who I am," Sarah protested.

"She was our momma."

"She disowned me as her daughter."

They stopped yelling long enough to hail a cab before the Nashville PD arrived on the scene.

They woke up in Kolby's living room, neither of them sure how or when they got there. Hung over and with more listening than shouting, they reopened the argument and began healing old wounds dating back to Kolby's accident, Sarah's leaving home, and the final days of their mother's cancer. They struck a deal and shared a pinkie swear.

Sarah remembered that day as she stepped off the tour bus in Tunica Resorts, the new name for Robinsonville, Mississippi, as the heat and humidity rolled across the casino parking lot. Sarah lugged behind her the three bags she had with her at all times: a briefcase, a messenger bag, and a rolling pilot's case. More than once, TSA began to wave her through security lines in airports before they realized the well-dressed woman in the black pants and blazer lacked a pilot's ID badge and redirected her to the passenger lines.

Sarah's briefcase held the paperwork, the contracts, the paper checks, and the few bits of business detail that for some reason or another were not yet digital. It also carried a paper printout of her current phone directory sorted by name, state, and job skill. In any town, Sarah had access to a road crew who were looking for work and came recommended either by past work with Kolby or the other managers Sarah spoke with weekly. While musicians tended to stay in one or two music styles and genres, crews were genre agnostic.

The messenger bag held Sarah Miles's digital life: the chargers, laptop, cables, and adapters to connect and log on anywhere in the world.

The third and largest bag was the lifeline of the band. Sarah had dozens of laminated signs with arrows and directions:

THIS WAY TO BUS
THIS WAY TO STAGE
THIS WAY TO DRESSING ROOMS
THIS WAY TO MEET & GREET
CREW ONLY
VIP ONLY

There were manila envelopes full of laminated ALL ACCESS passes with Kolby Rae's photo on one side and the band's photo on the other. She had school pencil pouches full of pens, markers, and office supplies; a single pink case held Kolby's personal stash of pink Sharpie markers for meet and greets and autograph sessions.

The rolling pilot's case held a first aid kit, maps, city guides, playing cards, and an emergency stash of cash. In towns when they had time, usually while Kolby was buying her endless stack of postcards to mail to fans from the road, Sarah bought greeting cards. On the road, one day seemed like the next; one month blurred into another. It was easy to forget to buy a birthday card, an anniversary card, or a get well note. Sarah's supply in the pilot's bag meant sentimental salvation for members of the band and the crew who lived out of backpacks for weeks at a time.

Show day routine was the same in every town. It began on the bus. Sarah posted the day sheet, a printed itinerary and schedule for band, crew, and Kolby. It listed who was to be where and when: the time of the sound check, catering, meet and greet, and showtime. To band and crew on the road, the day sheet was their life.

The day sheet lived behind an acrylic panel on the back of Malcolm Lapis's driver's seat. When Sarah left the bus, she met the venue house manager and did a quick inspection of the front of the house, the back of the house, the stage, the dressing rooms, and the green rooms. Each venue was different, some better, some worse. Sarah dreaded looking at the bathrooms. In the two years she had been manager, she worked hard to get Kolby into better and cleaner halls. Even if it didn't improve the cash flow, everyone enjoyed their work more.

Their contract was straightforward; the show logistics were as simple as they had ever been. Rob put together a small light kit. They traveled with a riser for Nils's drum kit, amplifiers to reinforce any venue sound, their own monitors, microphones, cables, instruments, and the controls and consoles to make a trailer full of work cases turn into showbiz. They could set up a performance in a mall or on a large theater stage.

Inside the venue, day sheets were posted on the work boxes for the backline crew and in the dressing rooms:

DAY SHEET — KOLBY RAE

Tunica Resorts/Robinsonville, Mississippi

Crew Lobby Call	1:00 p.m.
Load In	1:30
BAND Lobby Call	3:30
SOUND CHECK	4:00
KOLBY Meet & Greet	5:00
DINNER–CATERING	6:00–
DOORS:	7:30
OPENER: Dirt Road Dreams	8:00–8:45
KOLBY RAE:	9:00–10:45
BUS CALL	6:00 a.m. tomorrow

Robinsonville to Nashville: 239 miles, 3 hours 4 minutes

The crew lobby call included Sarah, Graham, Tim, Rob, and Len in the lobby, or the closest thing to a lobby, at each venue. At outdoor shows, it meant on the bus or just outside the bus. In Robinsonville, it was just inside the casino's performance theater.

Sarah spoke first. "I've got signs up in the back of the house. This is where you can set up for front of the house. All of us have been here before except maybe Len. Len, have you worked here?"

Len nodded. "A couple of times, and I've been to a couple of shows here. Setup is pretty easy, and the locals are nice."

The men were all dressed the same, wearing black cargo shorts. Each had a black Kolby Rae "Candlelight and Chaos" shirt with CREW printed on the back. They resisted Sarah's uniform at first, but Sarah insisted, purchased the clothing for each of them, and paid to have it laundered along with the show clothes. After some initial grumbling, they all complied.

"Kolby and the band do their call at three-thirty. We do a sound check at four o'clock."

Graham rolled his eyes as Tim nodded. The difference in reaction was a clue to their different opinions about the value of artist sound checks.

Tim, Rob, and Len went to the back of the house and began moving cases from the bus and trailer parked outside. First, they set up the platform riser for Nils's drum kit. Next they paced off the distances between each musician's normal playing area onstage, placed white gaffer tape markers, and then unrolled the gel mats for Skeeter, Roberto, and Kolby's center-stage position.

They rolled the big, black road cases with reinforced metal corners and dolly wheels. The smaller and thinner cases, holding guitars or control panels, were carried by hand. Since they had loaded the trailer together in Nashville, they all understood the packing and unpacking system. Still, the first day–first show load in was slower than the pace they would learn as they moved on.

"Radio check, talk to me. Who's not on?" crackled Sarah's voice over the radio dangling from Graham's belt. Sarah was standing next to Graham. He nodded at her as they heard her voice over his radio speaker.

"Tim's on. You're good," replied Tim, rehanging his radio to his belt next to the red lens flashlight he used during the show to preserve his night vision.

"Rob's live," came a second reply.

"Len's on."

The other's quickly decided to initiate the newbie. Rob pressed his walkie-talkie push-to-talk button. "Len, this is Rob. I can't hear you. Turn your radio on."

Len's voice came back a bit louder. "Can you hear me now?"

Graham grinned, picking up his radio from his belt and keying the push-to-talk button. "Len, I can't hear you, either. Check to be sure your radio is on."

Sarah smirked and looked down at her clipboard.

"Can you hear me now?"

Tim's voice was next. "Graham or Rob, do you hear Len? I don't think he has his radio on."

"It's on! Can you hear me?" Len's frustration and volume were growing.

Tim took his radio and set it near a stage microphone. He nodded at Graham, who raised the volume on the control board just as Len keyed his radio button. Len's words filled the theater with a booming plea of desperation.

"It's on! Can anyone hear me?! Over!"

The word "over" echoed, and Len stormed onto the stage, red faced and looking quickly from corner to corner of the stage as the others on the crew stood in a mock standing ovation, clapping an arrhythmic beat.

Len had his nickname now. For the rest of the tour, he would be Over.

CHAPTER TWENTY-SEVEN

SOUND CHECK — RALEIGH, NORTH CAROLINA

GRAHAM CARR, KOLBY'S FRONT-OF-HOUSE ENGINEER, sat at the mixing board in Raleigh, North Carolina. Graham cued up a playlist that began every PA test with an Eagles song: "One of These Nights."

Graham had a new challenge every show. Each room had its own unique dead spots, its own collection of sometimes crappy sound systems, and always the potential for broken gear. As FOH, front-of-house engineer, he needed to be able to mix "Tequila Temptress" loud, roaring, and full. He also had to make a softer "Kissed with a Lie." At full volume, he had to capture the Kolby Rae whisper as authentic, quiet, and intimate as he could. Graham queued a second CD when he was in venues he'd never worked. It began with a track from Steely Dan: "Hey Nineteen." The mix was ideal and gave a good dynamic overview of the PA and the room. Graham also loved the looks he got from younger locals, most of whom had never heard of Steely Dan, Donald Fagen, or Walter Becker.

Next, he played a classical track of Vivaldi's *Four Seasons'* "Summer" for cello. For vocals, he added Kid Rock and Sheryl Crow's "Picture."

During the recorded playlist, Skeeter Martin was holding court from the top of Nils's drum riser, watching them lay cords, connect microphones, and test and line up monitors and loudspeakers. Skeeter had more opinions about how to set a stage than his use of words would suggest. Instead, he used his general presence, expressions, and body language. He was the newest in years played and oldest in years lived. Pier Records hired Skeeter to do some session work on "Tequila Temptress." Everyone loved his sound and his versatility, switching from pedal steel to dobro and the occasional banjo riff. Kolby asked him to go on the road with them.

When the final song in the mix was finished, Skeeter stepped from microphone to microphone, speaking into the mic and waiting as Graham adjusted his levels and patched the cables to his liking. Both Graham and Tim appreciated Skeeter's willingness to help out; it meant they could both work their individual mixing boards at the same time, each creating the blend they needed for their mix.

Most people who met Skeeter took him to be a forty-year-old who looked fifty, the result of a hard life on the road. The reality was he was fifty-nine; life on the road was kinder than most assumed. Skeeter's sleeved-out arms were all that gave any clue to his brief time with the military service he called Uncle Sam's Misguided Children. He left the Marines and their short haircuts, job-hopped up a few part-time gigs, and spent the rest of his life as a musician, touring with five bands before Kolby Rae.

The tour to support *Tequila Temptress* was the worst tour he'd been on. They played a string of bars and clubs, and a summer of Tilt-a-Whirl and cotton-candy-filled county fairs. The fair shows meant they changed clothes in tents in the dirt and dust.

The bar shows reeked of sour beer and stale smoke. After a while, the toughest decision of the day was choosing between drinking beer to numb the experience or being able to last the entire night without having to use the bathroom. Club bathrooms were disgusting, filthy, showerless cages. Skeeter and Kim, both drunk and both exhausted, got into a heated shouting match one night about which was filthier, the men's or the women's restroom. The club owner heard them, and it took Kolby's cousin/manager Buddy Mitchell several minutes to calm everyone down. The young and slightly psychopathic club owner took their words as a personal insult to his family and refused to pay them for the night. It put everyone in a jam, and Skeeter, who had sobered up enough to realize the desperate situation, saw an opportunity to let everyone save face.

In front of the club owner, Skeeter confronted Buddy, escalating their argument to a standoff where Skeeter threatened to quit. Buddy, who was at first dumbfounded, finally caught on and fired Skeeter on the spot in a noisy, expletive-laced shouting match. Skeeter picked

up an empty guitar case, flipped over a chair, stormed out of the club, and began walking down the highway. With a smug attitude, the club manager paid up the cash, the band piled on the bus, and they picked up Skeeter a mile down the road.

During the early weeks of the *Tequila Temptress* tour, it was clear to everyone that Buddy was in well over his head.

In those days, when they played a show, they had three hotel rooms: one for Kolby, one for Buddy, and a third room shared by the crew and band. It was a shower room, meaning the crew and band used the same room to take a shower, and then the band could use the room to change into and out of show clothes.

Under her cousin-manager's direction, Kolby did only meet and greets with radio station contest winners. Buddy insisted they treat Kolby like a star. Everyone had to refer to her as "the artist." After sound check, a limo would take Buddy and Kolby to the hotel, and then they would return, making a splashy, flashy appearance for her fans lined up to get into the venue. Buddy always timed it so he could release the limo still inside the four-hour minimum. He was good at cutting corners and scrimping cash.

The food sucked.

The bus broke down more times than Skeeter could count, but they never missed a show, and the magic onstage made up for the mayhem on the rest of the road.

Skeeter puzzled over Kolby's lack of success. Artistically, she was a strong singer. The show they put on was tight, entertaining, and fun. Kim's energy, Roberto's number two lead onstage, and Kolby's timing should have had her opening stadium shows for superstars and headlining midsized venues year round. Skeeter put all of the blame on Buddy; his heart and DNA may have been in the right place, but he was way out of his league and had no clue how to push the label for more support or how to negotiate a solid deal. He set up one show at a time, never thinking about leveraging larger promoters into multiple-city shows. Skeeter knew from the beginning that Buddy was a short-term player and started to talk with Kolby about it one night over a shared bottle of wine. She quickly rebuffed him. Skeeter had been on the road long enough to know there were two ways to argue with an artist, and neither one worked.

When the end of the tour came, Buddy ran off with a daughter of a rich club owner he met backstage during the final wrap party, and no one on the crew or band ever heard from Buddy again. Their final paychecks were signed personally by Kolby. Skeeter called that time of his life BS. So did everyone else. BS was Before Sarah.

Today's stop in Raleigh reminded Skeeter how far they had come. Everyone had a single room in the hotel, crew and band alike. Kolby had bought them all dinner the night before. And the theater, even though it was older, was clean and all the equipment worked.

As Skeeter finished working with Graham, he spied Sarah moving from empty row to empty row, listening to the sound and trying to limit the number of seat kills, which were seats that could not be sold because the band's monitoring gear blocked the view of the stage. If the venue had already sold the seat and it was a seat kill, the fan was relocated to a better seat. Sarah looked up and called Skeeter and motioned for him to join her near the FOH board and Graham. She lined them up and snapped a photo. As she did, her phone lit up:

<Sean> *I just finished the mix of Cross This Line with Frankie. It sounds awesome.*

Sarah sighed after reading it and looked at the men, "It's for the crowdfunding site—today's update. We've still got a long way to go."

CHAPTER TWENTY-EIGHT

MEET AND GREET—CHARLOTTE, NORTH CAROLINA

THE MEET AND GREET IN Charlotte, North Carolina, began between the sound check and catering call. One of the first things Sarah Miles changed was Buddy's approach to meet and greets. The limo arrival grand entrance was gone. Kolby began to reconnect with her fans and with each show became more at ease with the personal touch she shared with fans when she first began. At some shows, Kolby stood in front of a giant banner with the phrase *We ♥ Kolby Rae* in pink. She stood there usually for an hour, posing and shaking hands with fans as they walked in and met their star with cameras and tickets in hand.

In other venues, Kolby sat at a table signing anything—ideally T-shirts and merchandise bought from the merchandise team. The more she signed, the more they sold.

A young woman came to the table and Kolby asked, "How should I sign this?"

The woman offered, "Just put *To Deena Phillips*."

Kolby started to reach for a Sharpie and then paused. "Deena, where do I know you from? This isn't the first time I've signed something for you, is it?"

"No ma'am. You signed my shirt in Tuscaloosa, and—"

Kolby spoke at the same time. "And in Memphis. Darlin', this is the third show of mine you've seen this year?"

"Yes ma'am."

Kolby signed the shirt and motioned for Sarah to come over. "Deena, where are you sitting? Where are your seats?" Kolby asked.

Deena looked at her tickets. "My two girlfriends and I are in Section GG."

Kolby looked at Sarah, and Sarah pinched her nose—Section GG was the nosebleed section, high and in the back of the house. Kolby lifted her finger and made a number 1 and nodded to Sarah, who walked up to Deena.

Sarah asked, "Hi, I'm Sarah Miles. Have you seen Kolby live before?"

Deena nodded. "Yes ma'am. I've been one of Kolby's GRITS since 2007."

The GRITS, Girls Raised In The South, made the most noise at Kolby's shows, bought the most tickets, and collected the most show merchandise. Kolby's on-stage question—"Where's my GRITS at tonight?"—usually stopped the show, sometimes as long as a minute filled with hoots and screams.

"Deena, why don't you come with me? I think there's a mix-up with your tickets. We want to move you and your friends a bit closer."

"Oh my God, no way. You're joking, right?"

And Kolby returned to do the rest of the signing.

At the end of her day, from her bed in a Charlotte motel, Kolby called Joshua. She had called him the first time the day after she left Crossings. In truth, she waited until he called her first. He did, leaving her a message early in the morning, saying he and Fylgja were on a walk and that Fylgja missed her.

Kolby had pulled the phone away from her ear and looked at it with disbelief: he was awkward with women. The silence in his message made her think that was all he was going to say. And then she heard him take a breath, and she pressed the phone back to her ear.

"God, I suck at this," Joshua began. "But Kolby, I miss you, too. And I want you to know, Kolby, I love you. I should have told you the night you left instead of in a lame voice mail. But I love you, Kolby Ruth."

Before she dialed his number, she played the message again, felt her heart do a flippy-flop, and then pressed CALL.

Joshua's voice was drowsy. Kolby liked the way he sounded. She listened as he tried to suppress a yawn and said, "So tell me about it. What was it like being Kolby Rae today?"

"Oh, I have to tell you about this cute little boy. We were doing the meet and greet, right? And up comes walking the cutest little boy. He must have been six years old. He's wearing a cowboy hat and boots and two pearl-handled six-shooters on his hips. His mom is kind of behind him and off to the side. She's just lettin' him go for it. He has no fear.

"So I say, 'Howdy.' He doesn't talk well, makes funny sounds, so you know me, I just swoop him up in my arms and put him on my lap while I talk to his momma. But as we're talking, he keeps pulling my hair away from my ears and looking at his momma and then back at my ears. The more he does this, he starts getting very agitated and concerned. I do my best to keep talking with his momma, and finally I ask, 'Is your little boy okay? Is something the matter? Did I do something to upset him?'

"His momma looks and says, 'He wears hearing aids in both ears and only hears a few sounds. He saw you on TV and saw the earplugs in your ears.' You know, my stage monitors? Anyway, his momma tells me that he saw those and thought I was so cool because I wear hearing aids, too. She said, 'He's worried because you don't have your hearing aids on now.' Isn't that sweet?"

"Kind of special. I guess being so public, you don't know what will touch people."

Kolby continued, "So I ask his momma, 'If he can't hear, how does he hear my music?' And she says, 'We turn it up real loud, and he can feel your music, the *thump thump thump*.'"

Joshua murmured, "I can feel your music, too. I like that."

"It gets better. Wait till you hear. So you know the set break when we do 'Right-Hand Rover'? I kinda stopped the band....I thought Roberto was gonna die. But I stopped them. And I told the audience I have a new boyfriend, and I pointed to that boy's momma, and the security men lifted that little boy up on the stage.

"So I start the band and start singing 'Right-Hand Rover' to him. And you know how I have those in-ear monitors? We also have monitor wedges on the stage so the band can feel the music like that little boy. So all the while, he dances and jumps up and down on the stage."

"And you wonder why they love you?"

Kolby sighed, staring at the ceiling. "Do you ever think about kids?" she asked Joshua.

"I spent fifteen years thinking about kids. I thought about them every day, morning, noon, and night. And now I've got a wait staff and kitchen staff filled with kids."

"No, I mean little kids. Babies." She paused. "Little Joshua Stone babies?"

"Wait, you're not telling me that you're…"

"Joshua Stone, do you think I would tell you I was pregnant like this? No, I am not pregnant." Her voice returned to her sweeter, questioning tone. "But we never really talked about it."

"Well, I don't know. I mean, I'm forty-three. Kolby, I'd be the oldest dad in the PTA. I mean, he'll get his Cub Scout card and I'll get my AARP card in the same year."

"Joshua Stone, you are not old."

"Well, maybe not. I know you'd be a pretty hot soccer mom."

"Maybe, Joshua Stone, but right now, this pretty hot soccer mom is pretty tired. Can I wake you up tomorrow morning?"

Joshua murmured and rustled the phone in his hands as he passed it from one to another. "Sure."

"Good night, Cub Scout Leader Joshua Stone."

Then she realized she had done what he had done. She meant to tell him how she had felt before they had their stupid argument about sex. And she hadn't said the words yet, even during their daily phone calls.

"Joshua?" she blurted.

"Yeah, I'm here."

Kolby drew her own breath for confidence. "Joshua Stone, I love you."

CHAPTER TWENTY-NINE

"HALLELUJAH"—PELHAM, ALABAMA

WHAT GRAHAM DID FOR EVERYONE in front of the stage, Tim Richards did for everyone onstage. Monitorland was his home during the show, where he served as the band's personal mix master. Each musician wanted to hear different things. Kolby wanted to hear Roberto's guitar in her ear monitors and feel Nils's drums through the wedge monitors onstage. Kim wanted to hear Nils, Skeeter, and Kolby. Roberto wanted to hear Kolby, Kim's and Skeeter's playing, and Kim's and Nils's vocals. Tim needed to feel Nils, too. Tim Richards often complained he worked harder than Graham and got less recognition. But he also admitted that if he screwed up, he just upset the band. If Graham messed up, it ruined the show for hundreds of fans.

As part of his routine, between the meet and greet and catering, Tim printed the set list, a list of the songs, in the order the band would perform them. Tim made certain that each position— Roberto's, Kim's, Kolby's, Nils's, and Skeeter's—had a taped-down copy they could see while playing. Graham got a copy, Tim kept a copy, and two were posted in the stage wings on work cases next to the day sheets.

Next, Tim and Len would tune the drums, set Skeeter's pedal steel, and restring and tune the guitars. The final thing Tim did was to cut a strip of gaffer tape, place nine guitar picks onto the tape, and then affix the tape to Kolby's mic stand. Then it was time to eat.

The casino shows usually included a meal at the buffet, and often the crew and band smuggled leftovers onto the bus for the next day or even the day after. Catering was unpredictable. In their bar days, it was all greasy fried foods. The smaller upscale clubs they played had the same food but charged their customers twice as much for it. Tonight, in Pelham, Alabama, the promoter had a decent selection of sandwiches.

About twenty minutes before each showtime, the band gathered together with Kolby for their preshow warm-up. Their tradition had its roots in 1994 when the seventeen-year-old Kolby Ruth Miles won a Christian music contest singing a mostly unknown Leonard Cohen song. Kolby had never heard of Cohen but heard the song on Jeff Buckley's album *Grace*. She liked the strong ties to biblical stories and the appeal of the music and mix. It wasn't until later that she fully grasped the overtly sexual nature of Buckley's version.

It became their ritual after Kim joined the band and they were touring in support of the nonselling *Other Side of the Tracks*. Kolby was pacing, working through preshow jitters as they waited in the green room, a musty converted storeroom of the old theater that was reserved for the opening acts. Suddenly, without being aware she was doing it aloud, Kolby began the first verse of "Hallelujah":

:: I've heard there was a secret chord ::

:: That David played, and it pleased the Lord ::

:: But you don't really care for music, do you? ::

As she sang the line, Nils, Roberto, and Kim nodded and waited to see if she would continue:

:: It goes like this ::

:: The fourth, the fifth ::

:: The minor fall, the major lift ::

:: The baffled king composing Hallelujah ::

Nils stepped forward and reached his hand to Kolby's, and she squeezed back. The two of them sang the chorus:

:: Hallelujah, Hallelujah ::

:: Hallelujah, Hallelujah ::

Nils sang another verse, slightly out of order:

:: Baby, I've been here before ::

:: I know this room, I've walked this floor ::

:: I used to live alone before I knew you. ::

:: I've seen your flag on the marble arch ::

:: Love is not a victory march ::

:: It's a cold and it's a broken Hallelujah ::

With the word "hallelujah," Kim walked up and took Kolby's free hand, and the three of them sang the word four more times. Despite her personal dislike of Nils, Kim stood strong and loyal with him whenever they worked. Kim's voice was smooth and strong as she began:

:: Your faith was strong but you needed proof ::

:: You saw her bathing on the roof ::

:: Her beauty in the moonlight overthrew you ::

:: She tied you to a kitchen chair ::

:: She broke your throne, and she cut your hair ::

:: And from your lips she drew the Hallelujah ::

Roberto stepped forward, taking Kim's and Nils's hands and forming a circle as the "hallelujah"s grew louder:

:: Hallelujah, Hallelujah ::

:: Hallelujah, Hallelujah ::

Roberto's bass voice echoed in the cold room as he sang, looking into Kim's eyes, the lyrics suggesting to Nils and Kolby there may have been more going on than they saw:

:: There was a time when you let me know ::

:: What's really going on below ::

:: But now you never show it to me, do you? ::

:; And remember when I moved in you ::

:: The holy dove was moving too ::

:: And every breath we drew was Hallelujah ::

The final four "hallelujah"s encouraged Kolby to think of a prayer that was fitting to the moment and to the new collection of singers standing with her in the circle. What came out was this: "Lord Jesus, please let us into your heavenly presence." And then she added, "As we all raise a little hell tonight!"

And the tradition was born. When Skeeter joined two years later, he stood with them, sometimes singing a verse but mostly joining in only on the chorus.

Once, just before a benefit concert for a children's hospital, the green room was filled with cancer patients and their parents. The very sick children with sunken eyes and shaved heads both motivated and saddened the group. On that night, Kim led off with the verse that referenced both David and Samson, needing proof of faith and cutting hair.

Despite its presence on so many artist's repertoire lists, for Kolby and the others, it remained a very private, personal, and spiritual warm-up for what was about to occur onstage. The lyrics were both spiritual and secular. It was the one song that captured the complexity and ambiguity of Kolby Rae. It was a very intimate sharing of their pact with each other. It was the bond of the band.

They sang "Hallelujah" in Alabama. Kolby had them all pose for a photo, and she uploaded it to the crowdfunding site with the caption:

<TheRealKolbyRae> *Help us bring our show to your town. We need your pledge and a miracle.*

Kolby looked at Sarah. They were seventy-seven percent funded to produce the album with a week to go.

Chapter Thirty

Lights Up—Noblesville, Indiana

From the green room, no matter where they were, the procession was the same. Kim Hartunian, dressed in tight fitted black pants and a black woman's-cut tuxedo jacket with a starched white shirt and cuffs, and her cello were first onstage. A single spotlight lit her chair. She walked on, sat, and began a cello solo.

It was a unique sight. Kim's straight and flowing, long, black hair accented her light-colored face with her lips and eyes brought out in vivid detail by the stage makeup. Kim's mother was born in Korea; her father was an American diplomat born in Hawaii who met her mother at the U.S. Embassy in Seoul. Kim's mother raised her to stay out of the sun and nagged her daily to use her very white skin as the focus of her beauty to catch a husband.

Kim listened and followed her mother's advice intently until freshman year of high school when the orchestra director asked her to come to tryouts for instruments. He was short of cellists and was hoping to find a student willing to lug the instrument home and back at least twice a week for rehearsals and practice.

Kim's mother sobbed in Korean for the entire night when she brought it out the school doors and struggled to get the cello into her mother's car. As a fourteen-year-old girl in search of a parental button to push, Kim had discovered hers quite by accident. But the payoff was golden for a sheltered girl who was sometimes teased by her peers and always looking for a way to be the center of attention, another trait her mother neither understood nor forgave.

It was, however, the friction that kept the two of them close, and the more her mother objected, the harder Kim worked at the cello. She sat in the eighth chair, meaning there were seven other cellists who performed better during their auditions. By the end of her freshman year, Kim sat first chair and held the chair until she played "Pomp and Circumstance" during her own graduation ceremony.

Kim left home for the Jacobs School of Music at Indiana University. While there, she discovered the music scene in Memphis and Nashville during weekend road trips. She moved to Nashville the summer she graduated college and shared a house with five other musicians. They taught her to smoke. They taught her to drink. They showed her how to get on the short list of names for session work in town. She showed up to play two parts on an album called *Other Side of the Tracks* by a singer named Kolby Rae. She was paid by the day, and it was two days' work. It wasn't going well. Two days turned into four days, then ten. The producer of the album tended to leave the studio—a lot. The artist, Kolby Rae, spent most of her day giggling on her cell phone and talking in a soft voice. When she sang, she seemed distracted, but Kim didn't care; the other musicians were great and the money good.

Kim met Nils and took an immediate dislike to his impish mannerisms and childlike face. Everything he did bothered her. What bothered her most was that he always said something positive. Their dislike was palpable until they shared harmonies. The blend of Kim's alto with Nils's high baritone, combined with their own unique vowel sounds, created vocal duet perfection normally reserved for siblings. If they added a bit of Nashville twang, the kind of sound that made it possible for words like *thrill* and *deal* to rhyme, they could take it all the way to George and Tammy and still keep it their own.

Roberto, the Latin guitar player with dark skin and bushy eyebrows, was something else. She called him *oppa*, the Korean equivalent to what a little sister might call an older brother. There was an erotic and romantic overtone to the way she said it. Roberto, too, took a liking to the light-skinned, long-haired cellist who was four years younger. Roberto had an opinion about everything, and, unlike Skeeter, shared it openly, loudly, and often. Kim told herself that when they were done working together, she would go with Roberto to his apartment and let him show her his moves. She imagined the look on her mother's face. Fate took an interesting twist. On her final day working in the studio, she made it a point to open two extra buttons on her shirt, and when she finished playing, Roberto came up to her, very close. He was always standing closer to her than most men anyway, and she knew she had captured his full attention. She wanted to surrender herself to him and was waiting for his initiation. And when he said he wanted to ask her a question, she felt her lips quiver, and she looked up from her chair, the cello clutched between her legs.

"Yes?"

"I wondered if you might be interested in hanging out some more."

Kim kept a polite expression, her mother's influence, while inside, she was picturing them doing all kinds of lovers' dances in his bed.

"I'm going to ask Kolby if she will take you with us on tour. I think you would help us bring the album sound out on the road."

Kim was at once frustrated and destroyed. But her mother's grace and public cool took over and that was the last time she thought that way about Roberto. But they both took the underlying and unspoken sexual tension and made it shine onstage. It added a sizzle Kolby Rae had never taken on the road before Kim joined the band.

As the show opener, Kim sat in the chair with the lights up and began her solo, the Prelude from

It was novel. Kim was brilliant and also an experienced showman. She knew she couldn't hold a restless preconcert crowd for more than twenty seconds.

As she finished the first lyrical line of the solo, a second spotlight came up on Roberto, dressed in black jeans and a denim jacket, his trademark curly hair sprung out from under a beret. He struck a power chord. This was his time to shine, and Roberto wanted the crowd's eyes on his face and hands and not some flashy guitar. He opted for the timeless electric guitar looks of a Gibson Les Paul Standard. He relied on his artistry to make the music stand out. And there was no doubt he was ready to play as he did a fifteen-second shred, which was immediately interrupted by Kim on cello. They dueled with a cello/guitar version of the fiddle battle from Charlie Daniels's "The Devil Went Down to Georgia."

After Kim did a back and forth with him, Roberto stopped and ripped off his jean jacket, revealing a white muscle shirt. His broad shoulders, tan skin, and powerlifter biceps immediately brought the girls, wives, and moms to screams. Roberto began to make his guitar imitate a police siren.

Kim, not to be outdone, stood up and removed her tux jacket, revealing a bodysuit that from the audience looked as if she were wearing only the starched shirt front and cuffs. They were a hot contrast. At each show, Roberto and Kim faced off, close enough to breathe the same air. The look said, *Take me now*, even if most nights the two of them were desperately trying to suppress laughter. Kim was a woman who enjoyed sex as much as Roberto. What they expressed onstage was better than any sex either of them had shared with another. And it fueled the tension and display.

At the fall of Roberto's police siren on the Les Paul, Kim began playing a cello version of Michael Jackson's "Smooth Criminal." It was the second odd choice in the context of country music; the King of Pop was a few doors to the left of mainstream country. Kim had seen the online video of 2Cellos from Croatia and thought it worked, especially with her aggressive bow thrusting across the cello and passionate eye contact between her and Roberto. And as the tension built between them, Skeeter stepped in the dark behind the pedal steel, and Nils made his ceremonial two loops around the drum stool. At the height of the seductive musical intercourse, the stage went dark for a split second, and then the spotlights lit up each player in rapid succession—Roberto, Kim, Skeeter, Nils—and the volume exploded as they began "Goody Two Shoes."

They played eight bars on their own, and then Kolby Rae walked on from stage right wearing a short white dress with an off-the-shoulder neckline and a gold cross, accented with a wide belt and boots. The band played four bars through the applause, and then Kolby began the opening chorus lyrics:

:: She's a goody two shoes in cowboy boots ::

:: Got her daddy's new truck and somethin' to prove ::

:: The radio blasting gonna turn it loose ::

:: She's a goody two shoes...in cowboy boots ::

Kim had conceived the ideas for the show opener for the band their first summer touring together in 2007. *Other Side of the Tracks* was stalled in the sales charts. Kim, who knew little about Kolby Rae as an artist and even less of her as a woman, noticed her change as the tour moved from state to state. Kolby whispered on the phone less and less and had a stare-out-the-window-as-the-miles-roll-by emptiness on her face most of the day. On that tour, Kolby didn't hang out with the band much after the shows, usually having a single drink and then going back to her room on the bus or hotel for the night.

But as Kim added more heat and passion to every show, Roberto began playing stronger. Kim and Nils's vocals added depth to even Kolby's oldest songs, and audiences were rediscovering "Next of Ken," "Piece of This—Sass," and "Candlelight and Chaos." Local reviewers were giddy about the sound and the intimate experience of Kolby Rae live.

It was during the July Fourth party at Kolby's condo that Kolby thanked Kim for bringing passion back to their live show. Kolby confided over the top of a margarita, saying only, "I lost focus this year. But you brought it back. Thank you." And then she added a reflective, "You know what? I turned thirty today, and I'm still not married."

Kim made her laugh by replying, "Damn, girl, you sound like my mother. Are you sure you're not Korean?"

By New Year's, Kim and Kolby were blocking out a new set list for the band. Kim's idea was to do a three-act play: the girls set, the boys set, and the couples set. For the girls set, Kolby would be dressed to please the women, to look like the cool, pretty, fun, party girlfriend to go out and hit the clubs with. During the guys set, after a wardrobe change, Kolby would be dressed to please the boys, a little rowdy and showing an illusion of more skin: lots of legs, lots of bare back and bare arms. If they could get guys to sing along, the band and Kolby knew they would own the house. The last set had the love songs, the ballads, and by 2009, they added the rowdy "Tequila Temptress" to finish out the show.

The encore since tour one was "Dance on Your Shoes." For Kolby Rae fans, it was better than the recoded hit by Sherrie Elliot. Reviewers and fans told Kolby and the band that time and again.

Kolby often led up to the song by asking the audience, "Where's my GRITS at?"

The GRITS answered back, loud and proud. The music came from

Kolby's heart. The words told of love for her father, and her vocals echoed the emptiness of his absence. It was something felt, a young girl's longing to dance with her daddy one more time. The arrangement was acoustic, with Kolby alone on her other Larrivée twelve-string guitar for the first verses and choruses, with Nils, Kim, and Roberto on harmonies as each chorus built in volume. The final chorus was backed with a full-on country instrumental as Kolby walked to each side of the stage, bowing, blowing kisses, and usually receiving a rose or two from adoring fans as the band finished out the song. Before leaving the stage, Kolby touched two fingers to her lips, formed a fist and touched her heart, and then raised an open palm to the sky in praise.

CHAPTER THIRTY-ONE

LOAD OUT AND HOME—CUYAHOGA FALLS, OHIO

It was a straight haul back to Nashville from Ohio—seven hours and thirty-seven minutes, according to Sarah's day sheet. Their part of the daylong festival concert began at noon, and they were clear of the festival show at 2:00 and loaded by 4:00 p.m.

The crew knew they had cleaned only half the gear. The worst of the mud-caked cables and cases were clean before they went into the trailer. The rest of the gear would have to be cleaned once they got back to Nashville. Kolby was crashed, napping in her bed at the back of the bus, when Nils brought up the idea of food. Captain Malcolm grinned and shouted back to Nils, "I know a place. How about if I call them and see if they can take a tour bus?"

The band had told Joshua Stone that Malcolm Lapis was known for two things in the music tour industry: his near-psychic ability to miss rumble strips and barbecue. The money others on the road might spend on beer, pot, harder drugs, or alcohol, Malcolm splurged at the butcher, sometimes reserving specific cuts of meat from specific animals on local farms. He negotiated briskets and ribs and carefully bought spices by the ounce from preferred markets and growers around the country as he traveled. His dry rubs ruled the handful of Kentucky competitions he entered. His pork did well all over Tennessee, and in Memphis, he kept his homemade malt vinegar under lock and key; his tomato vinegar sauce always resulted in a prize. Once, a fill-in crew member overheard Malcolm negotiating for a few ounces of herbs, so he offered to share a baggie of marijuana. Malcolm politely declined.

Above his driver's seat in the front of the Prevost bus hung a string of four-by-six color photos: Malcolm and his family, close-ups of his daughters, and his barbecue trailer. The trailer was a rolling refrigerator, prep kitchen, barbecue grill, and smoker. The photo was snapped two years ago when he had competed at a national contest shortly after Pier Records fired Kolby and Sarah. It was also where Sarah met Malcolm. Malcolm was serving barbecue, and somehow their conversation turned to driving buses. They exchanged cards, and that fall, Malcolm began driving for Kolby.

It was Malcolm's love for and contacts in the food business that caused him to grin widely. In response to Nils's suggestion for food, he said, "Let me make a call. I know a place you all might like."

From his cell phone headset, Malcolm dialed a number. The teenager at the other end of Malcolm's phone call was confused. "A bus? A tour bus? Yeah, I guess so. We're busy now, but the crowd will thin out some." They disconnected the call.

The bus and trailer pulled into the parking lot a little before 9:00, and Captain Malcolm parked it near the back. Inside, the teenage hostess looked out and then remembered that she had forgotten to tell the owner a bus was coming. She turned and tapped him on the shoulder.

"Oh, I am so sorry. I totally forgot to say anything. I forgot to ask. Can we take a tour bus? They called me an hour ago and said they were coming, and I forgot."

It was at that moment that Joshua Stone looked up to see Roberto, Nils, and Kim walking in the front door of the Pizza Stone.

"Hey, Joshua. This pizza any good? Or should we go up the road to that convenience store?"

"Roberto! Kim! Nils!" Joshua walked over, shook their hands, and slapped them on the back. Kim's eyes twinkled, watching his face to see where he would look next. He stepped outside, and they all walked toward the bus.

"So, is it just you? Or everyone? Or…?"

Joshua watched as the crew stepped off. Finally, Sarah stepped off with a very sleepy-looking Kolby behind her. Kim nudged Roberto as Joshua's face filled with a huge grin. They all looked across the parking lot at Kolby, who looked around and then, realizing where she was, looked over and spotted Joshua.

Kolby shrieked and began running across the parking lot. Joshua stepped forward and caught her midrun, and they spun around the parking lot, arms twisted together, and then he lifted her higher, kissed her, and then set her down on the ground. Their deep stare into each other's eyes was replaced by sheepish expressions as they realized the band, the crew, and all of Joshua's employees were gawking at the two of them.

"Get a room," Nils joked.

"Feed us first, then get a room," added Roberto.

They piled into the restaurant, Kolby and Joshua holding hands. The restaurant workers set their tables, took their orders, and began baking pizzas. Sarah's phone rang. She waved her hands at Joshua and Kolby and walked to a quiet end of the restaurant. Joshua was holding both of Kolby's hands and smiling. Kolby was smiling back and took a quick look at Sarah. Kolby read her sister's body language; something was up. Sarah was nodding and motioned to Kolby.

"Joshua Stone, hold that thought," said Kolby. "Don't move. Do not leave. Just stay right here. I'll be right back."

Kolby walked to Sarah, who disconnected her phone, and the two women began talking. Kolby turned, and everyone looked her way to see what was going on.

"Change in plans, everyone," Kolby said. "We've got another gig."

It was Friday night, and no one had plans beyond cleaning gear, but still it was odd to add one more show to a tour.

"Where?" Asked Nils between bites.

"Missouri. St Louis. Afternoon set at the Heartland Benefit Concert. They had a crisis. Tanner Thomas has appendicitis and had to cancel. He's just out of surgery. He's okay, but they dropped him. So as a favor of a favor of a favor, we're on. We perform at five-thirty."

Nils spoke first. "Stadium show, national TV. Sarah, I knew you could do it."

Kim made a face, mimicking, "'I knew you could do it.'"

Nils replied with his traditional insult. *"Mor di svetter lite til å være så feit."*

Kim tossed a hunk of pizza crust at him. Sarah, Kolby, Skeeter, and Roberto all looked at each other, trying to hide their snickers. Some of the teenagers from Joshua's crew were laughing, too.

Malcolm was walking in the back door of the restaurant when Sarah called to him. "Malcolm, dinner's on us tonight. And we need to be in St. Louis by tomorrow midday."

"I think we can do that. Give me a minute with Joshua first."

Joshua got up, and Malcolm handed him a large shopping bag. "I got you the oregano. Wait until you taste this stuff. It's so fresh, and it's nothing like what you've been using. You give this a try. And then"—Malcolm pulled a business card out of his pocket—"this butcher makes this great Italian sausage. He's about an hour from here, and he'll deliver to you. Give him a try."

Joshua nodded and handed the bag to one of the teens behind the counter.

Sarah and Malcolm sat down to calculate his driving hours, DOT-required rest hours, and the schedule.

Kolby got up and stood next to Joshua. "Look at you—what you've created. The last time I was in here, this was a church. And look at these kids. They're all happy."

Joshua nodded. "I think they're starstruck by you. But yes, they like working here. Can I give you a tour?"

He took her arm and walked her through the doors leading into the kitchen.

"Guys, this is a friend of mine, Kolby. Kolby, these are my team leaders: Curtis, Jason, and Caleb." The high school boys turned, nodded, and said hello. "Curtis and Jason are my seniors. They lead the kitchen crew. Caleb is my junior. He'll probably run the crew next spring."

Kolby lingered with her look at Joshua before turning to the boys and giving them her attention. She said, "Nice to meet you. Is Dr. Stone treating you all right?"

The three young men nodded and gave a polite "yes ma'am."

Kolby turned to look at Joshua. She recognized the look in his eye. She remembered how long it had been since she had seen it.

"I didn't know you were coming," said Joshua.

"I didn't know, either. I was asleep, and when I woke up, here we are. Is this a dream? If it is, don't wake me." Joshua reached over and pinched her. "Joshua Stone! You stop that."

The teenage boys stared for a moment, then quickly turned around and pretended to be busy.

"I want to kiss you," Joshua said to Kolby.

"What's stopping you? It never stopped you the first time."

He touched her face and then kissed her, pulling her closer. When they both pulled away to catch their breath, she asked him, "Can you come with us?"

Joshua looked at her. "When? Where?"

"Tonight, tomorrow. Come to the benefit. You'll be back on Sunday." She looked at him with a wild expression. "Ever done it on a bus?"

He looked back at her. "Have you?" And then quickly added, "No, wait, don't tell me. No, Kolby, I haven't done it on a bus, but you can be my first."

She looked at him. "Joshua Stone, neither have I. You can be my first, too."

Joshua's phone lit up, and he felt the vibration in his pocket. Two of the teens in the kitchen were snickering, and when he looked at the display, he was greeted by a photo of himself and Kolby kissing.

"All right, boys, show's over. Back to work."

Kolby winked at the two boys and mouthed, "Nice one," to them.

Joshua was about to lead her out of the kitchen when his attention was turned as Caleb slid a dirty chef's knife into the soapy dishwater. Joshua moved toward Caleb and in a warm, comforting tone spoke. "Caleb, excellent initiative, good cleanup. Can we talk for a moment?" Then he and Caleb whispered a few moments. With his hand still on Caleb's shoulder, Joshua called his team. "Hey, Pizza Stone! Team huddle."

Kolby stepped back, and servers and kitchen crew immediately gathered around.

"I want to share a success that Caleb just pointed out, a quick lesson. When we've got sharp knives, what we don't want to do is drop them into the dishwater." Kolby looked on with curiosity as Joshua worked the face of each employee, making eye contact and drawing out their answer. "Why is that?"

One of the waitresses spoke up. "Because you can't see them and might reach into the water and cut yourself."

"Great, Alyson, that's right. So Caleb wanted to show everyone a

196

quick way to get them clean."

Kolby watched as Caleb, who moments before had made a mistake, was now leading the others on the crew in a safe way to wash and return a knife to service.

"Excellent, Caleb. Excellent work, everyone. One more thing—our guests tonight are leaving for St. Louis. Can we see what we can put together for them as a to-go basket?"

The teens huddled around a counter, firing off ideas and making lists, scurrying to the coolers to pull together some salads and to make some pizzas that could be cooked and then shipped along to eat later.

Kolby squeezed Joshua's hand. "Look at the life you're building for these kids. This is what you do, isn't it? This is what you've always done."

"I like this. I really do. We make a small pizza, and it makes people happy in just seven minutes. And the kids like the work, and they get to show off a bit. Folks who want to drink can go up to the Roadhouse. With no beer or alcohol, I don't have to worry about permits, rowdy customers, or issues with underage kids and drinking."

Kolby thought back to their first date and Joshua's leaving the table to talk with Drew and Darrell Burrows, the high school principal. "I guess I was there at the beginning, at dinner that night."

Joshua grinned. "A lot of things began that night."

Kolby bit the corner of her lip and winked at him.

It was just after 11:30 p.m. when Joshua locked the restaurant and boarded the bus. Kolby, the band, and the crew had been aboard for a while. Sarah and Kim were enjoying a final cigarette in the parking lot. When they stepped up to the coach, Malcolm closed the doors, and they began the trip to St. Louis.

Somewhere near the Tennessee line, Joshua used the bathroom on the bus. Ordinarily, no one would have noticed, but when he opened the door on leaving, a strong odor overpowered everyone in the bunks and the front lounge. All eyes turned to look at Joshua before Roberto spoke first. "Joshua, newbie, man. That stinks. Bus rule number one—"

The entire crew and band shouted, "No number two!"

Joshua blushed and looked around. "But, um, I mean, I didn't—"

At the same time, Nils stood up and looked around. "Hey, where did my pizza go?"

Nils looked around some more and then looked up at Joshua. Together they looked down on the bottom bunk where Fylgja had made herself a bed. Beside her was a chewed pizza box. The dog passed gas a second time. The stench quickly spread through the bus.

Joshua laughed. "You didn't let her eat pizza, did you?"

Roberto threw his pillow at Nils. "Nils!"

Soon everyone threw their pillows at the boyish Norwegian. Joshua looked at the still-sleeping Fylgja and shook his head.

Chapter Thirty-Two

Ruth 3:9

Two hours before showtime, Kolby was wearing a white terrycloth bathrobe and was seated at the makeup table in the small room at the back of the bus. There was room for Joshua to sit. She looked up at his reflection of the mirror. "What are you looking at, Joshua Stone?"

"You. I want to watch. I've never seen you perform. I've never seen you in your stage clothes and makeup. I want to watch you get ready."

"You do? Well, okay, but you can't laugh. No, wait, stop. Raise your right hand and repeat after me."

"What?"

"You heard me, Joshua Stone. I'm about to break every rule of the women's secret code by letting you watch me. You have to swear you will never reveal what I show you."

"You're just putting on makeup."

"Joshua Stone, raise your right hand."

He sat straighter and raised his hand.

"I, say your name…"

"I say your name…"

"Joshua Stone!" She looked at him, tapping a makeup brush on the tabletop, the *tap tap tap* growing more impatient.

"Okay. I, Dr. Joshua Stone…"

"Do hereby swear…"

"Do hereby swear…"

"And affirm and pledge my undying loyalty and devotion…"

"And affirm and pledge my undying loyalty and devotion…"

Kolby then strung all the other words together in a long, rambling phrase, "That-I-will-never-reveal-the-secret-rights-of-womanhood and how-to-put-on-makeup…so help me God."

Joshua laughed and repeated as many of the words as he could remember, ending with "so help me God."

Kolby set the makeup brush down and removed a small tube from the case next to the table.

"First, I start with a moisturizer. This has sunscreen in it, too. Not a big deal for normal shows, but I always use this anyway." Joshua watched as she daintily covered her face, around her eyes, down her nose, and then lower as she opened her bathrobe and applied the moisturizer to her chest and the visible burn scar on her breast.

"This helps be sure my skin stays moist before I put the makeup on." She batted her eyelashes in the mirror, watching his eyes as they traced her hand around her face and chest. "Next, I put on a primer. This helps keep my makeup on, for the whole show or the whole day if we're doing a long show or a series of shows."

He watched, and she applied the flesh-toned cream across her skin.

"So, ready? Here's where the magic begins. I make a concealer by blending a couple of colors that I know work for me, and these go under my eyes…even on days when"—Kolby looked at Joshua with a mocking expression—"my boyfriend didn't keep me awake most of the night, like he did last night." She winked at him. "I still want to hide anything that looks like dark circles under my eyes."

She put two large drops of each color on her wrist and then blended the two shades into a new one that was very close to her natural skin tone. She lightly applied a dollop with a fingertip on the upper and lower eyelids and then a final bit just at the edge of her discolored chest to mask the uneven skin tone.

Kolby reached into another bag, pulled out a headband, and pulled her hair back and out of her face.

"Next is my foundation." She took another bottle, opened the thick cream, and dabbed some on her wrists with the concealer. She added a small bit of moisturizer, plucked the makeup brush from the bag, and began blending the creams on her wrist to a smooth, even color. From her neck up, Kolby began to apply and smooth the foundation with a brush, hiding the slight differences in skin tone, smoothing the lines, and giving a uniform glow to her skin.

"This is way, way too much for every day, but the lights are so bright, they would wash me out. I'd like look a ghost, so you'll see where the expression *painted lady* comes from."

Joshua rolled his eyes and leaned back, watching as she moved into the mirror and then back out, talking all the while.

"Next is a bronzer, a skin tone," she said, waving a new brush with a shorter handle. She applied the powder beginning at the base of her neck and working up and across her face. "It gives me that fun-girl-in-the-sun look.

"So, next"—she looked down at her bottles and tubes, then at her reflection, and then at Joshua—"to be a beautiful, blushing woman, I add a blush." She held up a pink container. "This is way over the top for every day, but it looks so good onstage." She swapped to the smallest brush and began to brush the pink rosy color to her cheeks. "I put on a lot because if I don't, once those lights hit me, it looks like I don't have any cheeks at all. So this goes on very, very heavy."

With each swirl of her brush, Kolby gave more distinction to her cheekbones. She was looking beautiful in a new way.

"Ready for my eyes?" She pulled her headband off, fluffed her hair, and then brought a small container of eye color to the table. "I use a bunch of different colors. I start with this, which I could use alone if it was just every day. It's cute. I love the color."

Using her fingers, she applied a tiny bit to each upper eyelid and then smoothed out the color. She then took three other colors, adding them layer by layer. She applied the lighter shade below her eyebrow and in the crease along her eye, working from the outside in. With the next darker shade, she used a brush along the crease and working across the eyelid. She turned around, and they looked at each other. She was beautiful, entirely over-made-up for a night out, but for the stage, she looked dazzling.

"Kolby Rae, you are just the most amazing woman. I think I'm in love."

"Joshua Stone, if you don't beat all."

He stood up, hugged her, and then pulled slightly away. "I don't want to mess up your makeup."

"You can mess it up later," Kolby assured Joshua.

"Really?" he asked her with a wink.

"Now, go. The band and I need to do our warm-up. We've got to find our way to the stage. You can be up there with us. I want you to see the whole show the way we do it. It's only three songs, but you can be right there on the stage, just in the wings."

Joshua picked up his Grant's Hill varsity jacket and put it on. As he opened the door to the main area of the bus, the band and crew were moving around. Sarah waved to Joshua. He walked forward with her off the bus. She handed him the ALL ACCESS laminate, and he hung it from his neck.

It was just after 5:30 when Kolby took to the stage.

Her set was three songs. She planned to finish with "Right-Hand Rover." The band was doing the musical filler at the end of her second song, "Next of Ken," when she scooted off stage right behind the speakers. Kolby thought Joshua looked at home standing there, wearing his ALL ACCESS laminate and his Grant's Hill varsity jacket.

"You make a good-looking roadie."

"You make a better-looking star."

"Joshua Stone, I'm so cold. Why didn't you warn me?"

Joshua looked at the denim miniskirt with the rips and the thin top she was wearing. "I should have, but I was enjoying the view.....So are they." He gestured to the crowd, who were up on their feet. Kolby's music and energy had turned the restless crowd into a chanting and dancing mob. She was making the show catch fire in the early chill of the autumn night.

"Give me your jacket," she said.

"What?"

"You heard me; give me your jacket. Put it around me like a cloak."

Joshua slid the jacket off his shoulders one at a time and carefully draped it around Kolby. She briefly leaned into him and then started walking to the stage. The band was playing the intro to "Right-Hand Rover," and the crowd responded with applause and cheers.

It was showtime. This moment was for everything that mattered. This was what Kolby had been thinking of for weeks, and after Joshua had agreed to come with her, she knew the one and only time was now.

She yelled at him, and he didn't understand.

"What? I can't hear you!" He cupped his hand to his hear.

"Ruth three nine," she said again. She could see by the look in his eyes he was confused. She mouthed the words and made hand gestures. "Ruth," she mouthed as she pointed at herself. "Three." She held up three fingers. "Nine." She held up nine fingers.

Joshua stood looking at her, and she lingered for a brief moment before she skipped and ran to the center of the stage in time to hit the opening line.

The crowd erupted when they saw her. The image of her in the denim miniskirt and varsity jacket filled the Heartland Benefit Concert screens. Cameras and cell phones blinked as photojournalists and fans snapped photos. Over the opening bars, everyone began to recognize the jacket from Grant's Hill.

Joshua repeated what she had said. "Ruth 3:9." Kolby glanced sideways as he took the smartphone from his pocket, and she guessed he was searching for Ruth 3:9.

As she began singing the lyrics, she knew what he would find, and she knew he would understand what she was saying.

"Who are you?" he asked.

"I am your servant Ruth," she said. "Spread the corner of your garment over me since you are a guardian-redeemer of our family."

She had just proposed to him. Kolby Rae just asked to be his wife. Her vocals filled the arena:

:: Mama always warned me, be careful what you do ::

:: You might not like what happens when you're through ::

:: Mama always warned me, be careful where you play ::

:: You know how people are and what they say ::

:: But you know what it's like—when you barely turned eighteen ::

:: He's a boy with a truck—in a pair of tight blue jeans ::

CHORUS

:: Climb in, ::

:: jump on, ::

:: my right-hand rover boy. ::

:: Take me down the back roads to your heart ::

:: Climb in, ::

:: jump on, ::

:: my right-hand rover boy ::

:: Take me down the back roads to your heart ::

Kolby was reluctant to look at Joshua, unsure of his response. Roberto moved to the middle of the stage, his beret-covered curls now filling the large video screen. Kolby looked past Roberto to Joshua, who, with a slightly humbled and confused look, was pointing at himself with a questioning expression. She smiled at him broadly and nodded a very enthusiastic yes.

:: Daddy always warned you, treat my baby like a queen ::

:: You have her home by ten and don't be late ::

:: Daddy always warned you, she's her mama's precious child ::

:: Thank God he never caught us by the gate ::

:: You pull me close I push away—we drive another mile ::

:: You want it fast, we'll take it slow, but boy I make you smile ::

:: Climb in, ::

:: jump on, ::

:: my right-hand rover boy. ::

:: Take me down the back roads to your heart ::

:: Climb in, ::

:: jump on, ::

:: my right-hand rover boy. ::

It was Kim's turn to dazzle the standing and dancing fans. Far up on

the grass hill all the way down to the closest seats, the benefit support-
ers and fans were dancing, taking photos, and singing along. Kolby
looked once more toward Joshua, who was looking at her, and when
her eyes met his, he nodded as agreeably as she had nodded during
the first break.

:: Climb in, ::

:: jump on, ::

:: my right-hand rover boy. ::

:: Take me down the back roads to your heart ::

:: Climb in, ::

:: jump on, ::

:: my right-hand rover boy. ::

When they were done with the song, the band went stage left, and
Kolby ran to Joshua at stage right and jumped into his arms again.

"C'mon, let's go celebrate," she said.

"Where?" he asked.

"I don't know. Get a cab. We'll go find a motel."

And they did, leaving Fylgja on the bus with the returning band.
Somewhere, Joshua and Kolby managed to find a liquor store and a
motel.

Part Seven
Stone Unturned

Chapter Thirty-Three

No-Tell Motel

Kolby heard the ringtone and the vibration. She covered her head with a pillow. She felt Joshua's arm across her back, and he wasn't moving to answer it. She hoped that meant he didn't hear it.

"Kolby, love, let's pretend we don't hear it."

A second ringtone and vibration began.

"Is it just me, or do they sound like mechanical locusts?" Joshua began to slide his arm off Kolby's body.

"Don't move," said Kolby. "Please, just a few more minutes?"

As Kolby became more awake, she realized she was naked. She gently felt Joshua's body; he was naked, too, except for one sock. She slowly opened her eyes and looked around at the room. The window blinds were pulled tight, but a small crack near the top revealed enough light to make her guess it was the middle of the day. The next day.

Kolby looked at the nightstand made of cheap imitation wood-toned plastic with water rings and a sideways bottle of bourbon on top of it. She rolled over and searched the room. There were clothes everywhere. Joshua reached over and picked up his phone.

Kolby groaned, "Uhh uhhhhh."

Joshua looked at the display. "Why would Sarah text me?" He stared at the display again. "Seven times?"

Kolby sat up and rolled over, pulling a sheet up to cover herself. "Hand me mine?" She took it from him. It was open to her photo album. She didn't remember taking the selfie of her and Joshua. Or the other selfie of the two of them. She looked at the next one. It was just Joshua.

"Oh, you look so good. Look at this." She held it out and showed Joshua the photo, then advanced.

"Oh my word, when did you take this?" she said. "We're deleting this right now."

There were two more of Kolby. And one of Joshua.

"Okay, we're deleting all of these."

She flipped the phone to her message screen.

<Sarah> Awesome set, way to go.

Kolby flipped to the next message.

<Sean> Super show, it sounded great.

Kolby flipped to the next message.

<Sarah> Hey, did you see this?

And the next.

<Sarah> OMG #TheRealKolbyRae is trending. So is #RightHandRover.

<Sarah> They love the jacket, the Grant's Hill jacket. There must be hundreds of pix of you online.

<Sarah> We've added 10,000 followers in the last two hours.

<Sarah> Where are you? They want you to do an encore.

<Sarah> Kolby!!!!! We just funded the album! We've gone way past the goal! We're so over the top!

<Sarah> We've added 20,000 followers tonight.

Joshua held his phone up for her to see. They were all messages from Sarah:

<Sarah> Please call.

<Sarah> Please CALL.

<Sarah> Where are you?

<Sarah> Funny ha-ha now call me now.

<Sarah> Where is Kolby? Please tell me the two of you are together.

<Sarah> *Now it's not funny. Please let me know you two are okay.*

<Sarah> *If you two broke up, I'm not keeping this dog. Come get her.*

"I think we missed curfew," said Kolby. "Little sister is gonna be mad." She pressed CALL and called Sarah.

"Kolby, is that you? Where the hell are you? Please tell me you're okay."

"We're fine; we're fine. I have some news."

"Great. I have bigger news. You stole the show. We need to get you to New York first thing Monday. You're going on the *Good Morning Country* show. They want you to perform 'Right-Hand Rover.'"

"Wait, what?" Kolby began to pick out which of the clothes scattered across the room were hers.

She mouthed to Joshua, "Where's my underwear?" He shrugged and got out of bed. She looked at his naked body and then tried to concentrate on what Sarah was telling her.

"So New York tomorrow," said Kolby. "What, do we all fly there?"

"We're booked," said Sarah. "You, the band and me. The crew will have to dead head back to Nashville. I took the cash from the tour account. We'll figure it out. We leave out of St. Louis at three o'clock. Kolby, you are still in St. Louis, right?"

Kolby muted the phone. "Joshua, where are we? St. Louis?"

Joshua looked around. "I don't know." Kolby opened a drawer and found a Bible. He opened another and found a St. Louis phone book and held it up, nodding.

"Of course we are." She laughed and then said, "Sarah?" Kolby twisted her hair around her free hand and then said, "Joshua and I are getting married."

Sarah paused. Her silence was long.

"Did you hear what I said? Joshua and I are getting married."

Sarah replied, "See you at the airport. Oh, and bring Joshua. We're feeding Fylgja, but she can't fly with us. He has to take her home on the bus."

Kolby hung up the phone. "Oh my word, Joshua, I am gonna be on the *Good Morning Country* show. I've got to get dressed, and we've got to get to the airport."

Joshua looked around. They took turns handing each other articles of clothing to put on. They found everything of Kolby's but her underwear.

"Did you wear any?" Joshua asked her.

"Joshua Stone, I can't go onstage in a skirt this short and not wear cheerleader spankies. I can't have a wardrobe malfunction. They're the same as what cheerleaders wear at football games. Did you look in the bed? Under the bed?"

Joshua nodded.

"I give up," Kolby said. They walked out to the hall and looked at the giant mirror with a large elaborate wooden frame. The pair of cheerleader spankies were dangling from the top left corner.

"Oh my word, Joshua Stone, if you say anything about this to anyone, I will make sure you never say another word to anyone again."

Joshua nodded. "It's kinda coming back to me now. I think that was your idea."

"Joshua Stone!" She glanced at herself in the mirror—hung over, half-worn-off makeup, and unbrushed hair. "What would Momma say if she saw me now?"

CHAPTER THIRTY-FOUR

CALLING DR. ALAN NEAL

BACK IN CROSSINGS, JOSHUA TOOK a new phone out of the box, turned it on, and followed the on-screen instructions to authenticate and activate his new account. He was sitting on the covered front deck of the cabin. The morning light threw crisscross shadows over the browning grasses. Joshua and Fylgja both looked up to watch a rabbit hop out from under a cedar tree and then scurry back under cover.

As usual, it took only a few minutes to activate the new phone and number. Once live, Joshua logged online and restored his backup data and phone directory. The phone's new number had a North Carolina area code: 828.

He typed Alan Neal's name and then tapped a text message.

<Joshua> Alan, it's Joshua, new number, delete the old one.

He waited several minutes; then the phone lit up.

<Alan> Dr. Stone, must be that time of the month?

<Joshua> Yeah, and I'm cramping, too.

<Alan> How's things in <wink>. Where is 828?

<Joshua> Good, really good. 828 is in NC. Alan, I've met someone.

Joshua hesitated before pressing SEND. He moved his thumb to the DELETE key, then moved it back and pressed SEND. The reply came quickly.

<Alan> Pics?

Joshua looked in the newly downloaded photo storage. He found a photo of Kolby Rae from her website. It was his favorite pose, so he attached it and pressed SEND. Kolby was standing in a yellow print dress with large white daisies in the pattern. It had cap sleeves, a scoop neckline, and a high waist that tied below her breasts. Her hair was down and tussled. She was looking directly into the camera with her right hand and arm tucked behind her, her left hand brushing the hair out of her face. He couldn't help but leer as he sent the image.

<Alan> Stone, you are so busted. Here's a pro tip…if you're gonna scam your best friend with a pic of a famous hottie, don't pick the woman who is on the cover of every magazine this month. After that deal at the Heartland Benefit Concert, her photo is everywhere. Stone, that's Kolby Rae. Busted!

<Joshua> Why, Alan, you math guys do have some culture. Yes, it is Kolby Rae.

<Alan> Okay, okay, fun joke.

Joshua looked through the photos on the phone in his online album and found the picture of the two of them sitting on a bench before the Heartland Benefit Concert show. Joshua was wearing the Grant's Hill jacket, and Kolby was still in her everyday clothes: a pair of jeans and a sweatshirt. He selected it and pressed SEND.

<Alan> Stone, I'm impressed. You've learned Photoshop. Can you make one with me and Gaga?

Joshua looked again and found the picture the teen boys had taken of them kissing in his restaurant. He pressed SEND.

<Alan> Get out of here, dude. Are you serious?

<Joshua> Yeah. Can you believe it? So will you come here for New Year's? I need a best man.

Joshua's phone lit up with a call from Alan. "So is this a yes?" Joshua asked as he connected the call.

"Joshua, are you telling me you met Kolby Rae? You actually met her? And you two are getting married?"

"Yes, yes I am."

"Is that where she got the Grant's Hill jacket? That was yours?"

"Yes. Crazy, isn't it?"

"Joshua, that song is everywhere. 'Right-Hand Rover'? I mean, the kids on campus play it nonstop. The cheerleaders here have a dance routine to it. It's huge."

"Seriously?"

"Joshua, when did you meet her?"

"June. We started dating a little later. We got engaged—get this, at the Heartland Benefit Concert."

"Wait, so you just met this woman and you're getting married after four months? And she's what, ten years younger than you?"

"Seven. I thought you were the math professor."

"Man, I don't know what you're doing down there, but whatever it is, keep it up. You still looking for a teaching job?"

Joshua laughed. "Wait till you hear this. Remember those pizzas I used to make?"

Neal replied, "Yeah, I remember."

"I opened a little place here. It's a funny deal, but the place was all ready to go. I just needed to walk in and turn it on. I've got all these great high school kids who want a job."

Alan Neal paused and then asked, "Don't make me rain on your parade, okay? I'm happy for you, but are you sure you want to get married after knowing this woman only a few months? I mean, you've been single forever."

"Yeah, can you imagine that? I don't know. I can't explain it. It just feels right. But I'm serious; I want you to stand up with me. I'd love to invite a bunch of people, but we've kind of got limited space. Wait until you see this house and farm. I think publishing paid a whole lot better than academia. This place is amazing."

There was silence. Then Alan continued. "So how you doing? I mean, now that people are thinking about Grant's Hill and all. You okay? Still having the dreams?"

"I think I'm okay. Not as bad as that one night back at your place."

Neal laughed. "Joshua, okay, count on me. And I just have to say, you sound happy."

"Yeah, I am."

Joshua hung up the phone and sat for a moment. He sent a text to

Kolby, gave her his new number, and then sent a text to Sarah. To his surprise, she answered right away.

<Sarah> What would you think about doing a book reading in Nashville?

<Joshua> Might be fun. What are you thinking?

<Sarah> I'll set it up. Details later.

Joshua stood up and walked into the bedroom and opened the closet door. He found a moving box he had packed before he left Grant's Hill. Joshua unfolded the flaps and began to sort through the belongings from his former home office: his address book, some office supplies, the stone desk plaque from his mother.

Joshua 1:7 Be Strong and Very Courageous

He took the plaque out, set it on the shelf, and then returned to the box. Near the bottom was a lockbox. He pulled it free and carried it to the table in the main room. He looked around for his keys, found the ring next to his wallet, and sorted through them until he reached the lockbox key. He sighed, looking at the keys to his house in Grant's Hill, his bicycle lock, the Rover, the cabin, and the lockbox. He opened the lockbox and began taking out a few envelopes of savings bonds, some insurance papers, and his retirement account statement from last year. Near the bottom, he found a faded velvet box with gold trim around the hinged opening. He gently lifted the lid. The box held a simple strand of pearls. His father had bought them for his mother in the base PX and had given it to her on their wedding day. His mother said she saved it for him to give to his bride. He paused on the word *bride*. It wasn't a word he used often, if ever.

CHAPTER THIRTY-FIVE

KIND OF ALIKE

SARAH MILES WAS COMFORTABLE IN her own skin and sure of who she was. Her devotion to a career and a sister who was now receiving the attention of a lifetime overfilled her calendar with two lives. It left her double bed empty on one side.

Sarah's twice-loved, once-broken heart was always open to possibilities, and as the cute barista wiping the counter looked up and over at her, Sarah nodded. Their eyes lingered. Maybe the woman liked her deep brown eyes and wavy black hair. Or her laugh as they spoke about the tea of the day and the weather. Or the gentle touch of her hand as she took her change.

It was a moment. Sarah nodded a second time and watched as the barista brushed her hair behind her ear with her fingers. Their look continued, and then the moment Sarah was about to say something more personal, the barista tilted her head to one side and slightly shrugged with a disappointed expression. She then called to another young woman in a short denim dress with noisy bracelets in line. "Karrie, hi." The two clasped one another's hands and kissed.

Sarah watched them with a pang of regret. *Right key, wrong note,* she thought. She picked up her phone and scrolled through the voice messages. There was a new one from Kolby.

"Hi, it's me. This is too long and complicated for a text, so I'm calling. Frankie called me and asked to go up to Sean's to listen to the mixdown, so I'm already on my way there. And you've got me on a flight to do that photo shoot, and I won't be back until day after tomorrow. Joshua was coming to meet you to talk about the bookstore appearance. He was going to stay at my place, but now I'm up here. Can you take him to the condo and let him in? Thanks."

Sarah dialed her back, unaware that Joshua had come in and was watching her as he got his coffee from the cute barista.

"Kolby, okay, phone tag. Yes, I'll let Joshua into your place. I've got three other things. We're set for New Year's at the Ryman. I think we need to add to the crew and start looking at tour dates for next year. I'd like to bring in a production director and a second backline tech for guitars. The Ryman acoustics are awesome. What do you think about bringing Sean in and doing a live version of one of the songs? Not 'Rover' but maybe 'I Don't Make My Bed That Way'?"

Sarah looked down at her day planner and was ticking off her checklist.

"Kolby, the song downloads this month are totally off our charts. I think we need to have a meeting with DJ. This is, like, a lot of money. And already I have some people calling me about tours next year. Do you want to open? Or do we want to headline our own state fair tour? I mean, Kolby, these are the players, and they're moving fast. We need to make some decisions."

Sarah sighed. "Kolby, we need to catch up, and I need some help. I need to hire some help….Love you."

As Sarah disconnected, Joshua walked up to the table. "Hi. Great place." He looked around at the eclectic surroundings. "How was your day?"

Sarah looked at the phone, the barista, and then at Joshua. "My day was good, but now I get to deliver the bad news: you're on your own tonight."

"Excuse me?"

"That was Kolby. She and Frankie went to Sean's, so she's spending the night in your cabin before she flies out to the photo shoot. I'm going to let you into her condo." Sarah jingled her keys in one hand as she took a sip from her teacup.

Joshua looked at her before sitting down. "You know, I've never been there."

Sarah nodded, "It's nice. I think you'll see you guys are kind of alike. I'll run you over there when we finish up."

"So does she know?"

"What, Kolby? I told you, she called and asked me to let you in."

"No, I don't mean that." Joshua turned and looked at the barista and then turned back to Sarah and raised his eyebrows.

Sarah took a deep breath, gently twisting the gold bands with PEACE, HOPE and LOVE on her right hand, and then nodded. "Yes, Kolby knows. It's no secret."

"I hope I wasn't being rude. I can be slow on the uptake. It took me a while to figure out you two were sisters."

"She said you were awkward with women."

Joshua grinned. "It's become kind of a running joke. Seeing anyone?"

Sarah shook her head. "Not for a while. I thought—well there was someone, but I misunderstood. I never quite figured us out."

Joshua thought about the pink envelope from Liv Olsson. "Yeah, I know how that can happen."

Sarah changed the focus of their talk. "Ready to do this book reading?"

"Sure, I guess. I did a tour with each of my books, usually at colleges and campus bookstores, and I did a series of chain stores with *One Good Bread Pudding.*"

"This is the same deal. You go in, you talk, you do a reading, then you sign books and T-shirts and whatever people bring along. This is the Tennessee Author's Series, and it usually gets a pretty good turnout. You'll do great. But we need to think about the future, too. Have you thought about your life now that you're going to be married to a celebrity?"

"Not quite that way. What do you mean in particular?"

"I'd like you to meet with me, Kolby, and her attorney so you understand how the business runs. And then, once things calm down after the wedding, I'd like to get you involved in some Nashville groups. Not a lot, but a few volunteer things and fund-raisers. Kolby says you play a pretty mean game of basketball."

"For a guy who's only five-eight, I can hold my own. Three-on-three."

Sarah jotted some notes. "And you cook. What about this pizza restaurant thing?"

"Crossings has become home for me. I like the kids; I like the town.

I'm gonna give them a chance to learn life skills and give it my best. Besides, I need something to do when you've got Kolby out on the road."

"We should talk about that. Maybe there's a way to tie it in, bring in some celebrities."

"Sarah, I like the idea, but can we go slow at first? I'm really doing this for the kids. I want them to learn about work and responsibility. I'm not saying no; just let me figure it out first."

"Sure, Joshua, sure."

They finished the planning, and Sarah handed Joshua the key to Kolby's condo. He drove off to let himself in for the night.

In Kolby's living room, Joshua turned her *Other Side of the Tracks* to play at half volume. Joshua really wanted to like it but understood why Kolby said it wasn't her best work. Each performance was just a bit…off. Joshua didn't have the musical vocabulary, but he had seen the same results in freshman writers. And in his own work. He thought for a moment about his half-written *Rules for Calling Shotgun*. *Sometimes, the muse abandons you,* he thought. He was in Kolby's kitchen, looking through the cupboards.

Two hours away and in the kitchen of the cabin, Kolby Rae was looking through cupboards, too. Despite Sarah's proclamation that "you guys are kind of alike," they each found something totally unexpected. Joshua arranged the food items in his pantry by size; it was easy for Kolby to quickly see everything in a cupboard. She opened a drawer; the spices were alphabetized. She closed the drawer and looked up, as if some friend would empathize with the shock in her eyes. She opened the drawer again in disbelief, whispering, "Allspice, basil, cumin…" She closed the drawer.

Joshua found a hodgepodge of containers and boxes in Kolby's cupboards: Karo syrup, a container of a long-dried-out "one-step garlic chicken rub," an open bag of pine nuts that smelled like they were rancid, some kind of cheese spread in a can, and a bottle of a greenish oil.

He turned around, and perfectly centered atop the stove was a small placard:

I kiss better than I cook.

Joshua left the kitchen and walked down the hallway and was surprised to find two bedrooms. One was clearly Kolby's—he recognized some of the clothes and the photos. The second was a mystery, the door partially closed. He pushed it open, thinking it was a guest room. There was a small makeup table, a bed with a flower print bedspread, and a window with a small bird feeder on the window ledge. There was a photo frame with two black and white photos of a man and woman taken decades ago. The woman had Kolby's hair; the man had Kolby's eyes and chin. Another frame held faded square color photos, one of a young teen with a guitar, the other a girl in a bathing suit standing at the beach. Joshua picked up the young girl photos and recognized a much younger Kolby and Sarah Miles. The makeup table had a handheld mirror and a purse-size, well-read Bible.

Joshua noticed a funeral card stuck in the mirror from a Nashville funeral home and the name Barbara Miles. Joshua picked up the card, which was dated February 23, 2010. Joshua opened the closet door. The clothes looked like a mix. Some of the clothes were Kolby's show clothes, and some belonged to an older woman. There was a long, tan trench coat with a plastic hair protector draped around the collar for rainy weather. A red polyester shirt with puffy sleeves had been reserved for special occasions. It hung covered in dry cleaner's plastic along with a long black skirt. Joshua thought for a moment about the idea of holding on and letting go, standing in his own mother's bedroom and cleaning out her closet. He thought again about the pink envelope from Liv Olsson, unsure of the last place he put it.

In Crossings, Kolby left the kitchen and moved into Joshua's bedroom, opening drawers and finding the same kind of order and structure as in his kitchen. His socks were in a neat line, his underwear folded. His T-shirts were not only folded but stacked and sorted by color, dark and light.

On his desk, Joshua's calendar was a week behind. Kolby thought it was odd, so she flipped the page and found the pink envelope facedown between the pages. She turned it faceup and read Joshua's name in a woman's handwriting. She was certain it was the same woman's handwriting as on the envelope she saw the night of their first date. Her heart was filled with both curiosity and concern. Hadn't he told her they were getting married? Didn't this woman know that whatever she once had with Joshua was now over? Kolby shrugged. Maybe it was a final goodbye, sort of sad, sort of sweet. She placed the envelope at the very back of his calendar.

She sat down with her pink journal and jotted down ideas for a new song.

:: There a box of pretty papers wrapped in ribbon 'neath our bed ::

:: I found them once while you were gone ::

:: I read what each one said ::

:: She spoke of love so deep and true, she spoke of passion's flame ::

:: It broke my heart when there she wrote ::

:: "I know you feel the same" ::

:: Why can't you send your—old flame up in smoke? ::

:: Why can't you end it—so my heart ain't broke? ::

:: You loved her then—and she loves you ::

:: And still you lie with me ::

CHAPTER THIRTY-SIX

MEET ME?

BETWEEN BAGGAGE CLAIM AND HER truck, Kolby's phone lit up.

<Toomey> Meet me?

Kolby glared at the display and continued tugging the roller suitcase behind her as her boots clicked across the pavement. She touched the door opener on her key chain. The SUV's head and taillights blinked twice, and she heard the driver's door unlock. She pressed the opener again, and all the doors unlocked. As she raised the tailgate to lift the suitcase into the back, the phone display lit up again.

<Toomey> Please? It's important.

She loaded the suitcase, turned around, and leaned against the bumper before closing up the truck. She tapped on the screen:

<Kolby Rae> So is my beauty rest.

<Toomey> It's only 1:30 and you are always beautiful.

<Kolby Rae> You want something. I know you.

<Toomey> Meet me at Skip's.

Kolby glared again at the display. She unlocked the security compartment in the back of the SUV and retrieved her holster and pistol. She looked around and opened the front of her jeans in the parking lot, slid the holster behind her hip, and zipped again. She closed the back of the SUV, climbed into the driver's seat, and set the phone on the console between the seats. She pulled away, paying the man in the parking booth as she drove out and on to Terminal Drive. The night wind blew against her face with the window down, and she pushed the SUV faster. She evened her speed at eighty-five and glanced at the phone again,

<Toomey> Please.

His text ended with a crying emoticon.

"Oh, for God's sake, Toomey," she exclaimed and picked up the phone.

<Kolby Rae> I'll give you 10 minutes — 1 drink.

Jeffrey Toomey waved across the crowd from a stool at the bar just around the bend that led back to the bathrooms. A line of women was behind him, waiting their turn in the stalls.

"Hi. Thanks for coming." He gave Kolby a quick hug and a small kiss on the cheek.

"Seriously, Toomey, who's that show for?"

"No one. I'm just happy to see you. Look at you." He paused as he squeezed her again and then looked down her blouse as she pulled back. "My article did you wonders."

"Your article damn near ended my career."

"Really? How do you figure?"

Kolby looked at him, and the bartender interrupted. "'Never big enough to be a has-been?'" Kolby turned to the bartender. "Jack, straight, and put it on his tab. But run his card first to make sure he's not over his limit."

Toomey looked back. "It's true. It was all true. And look at you. What you did on that stage at the Heartland Benefit Concert. Genius. Pure genius. Look at the song? Most downloaded on the Internet. Top twenty in every major market. And a New Year's show at the Ryman. Come on, give the Tooms some credit."

"I give my credit"—Kolby looked up—"where credit is due."

The bartender returned with her drink and a receipt for Toomey to sign.

"You need to speak fast, Toomey. I'm gonna shoot this, and then your one-drink limit is over."

"Kolby Rae, always the feisty Christian. Warm a barstool on Saturday night and a church pew on Sunday."

Toomey reached out and touched her arm. His touch was cold, his fingers damp from the beer bottle he had been holding. "So how are you and Joshua Stone these days?"

Shocked that he knew Joshua's name, Kolby kept her expression neutral and waited for Toomey to say more.

"I'll take that as a 'no comment.' Okay, fair enough. I know about your little summer fling. And I know he was with you at the Heartland Benefit Concert. Was the jacket your idea or his?"

"Toomey, are you just talking to meet your word quota, or is there a point to all this?"

"Kolby, I know you may not like me, but we need to watch out for each other. You're the reborn star, and I'm the guy who writes things about you that people talk about. You think I didn't see the bump in your online mentions the moment *Garden Party* came out?"

"You're a parasite."

"Could be, but I'm *your* parasite. And I'm the good Dr. Stone's parasite, too, except he wouldn't talk to me."

Kolby snapped. "You leave Joshua out of this. This has nothing to do with Joshua Stone."

Toomey grinned. "The lady doth protest too much, methinks? No, maybe not, but this does pertain to the good Dr. Stone." He reached into a black, beat-up messenger bag and retrieved a file folder.

Kolby turned the folder over to see a mock-up of a book cover. She saw a photo of a younger and more frazzled Joshua. She read the title: *Stone Unturned: The Story of Joshua Stone and the Grant's Hill Shooting.* At the bottom of the cover was the phrase *An Unauthorized Biography by Jeffrey Toomey.*

"What the hell is this?" she said as she picked up the shot glass of Jack Daniels. She stopped to listen as Toomey answered.

"I'd say 50,000 copies and a book tour in five-star hotels. Their advance is paying for our drinks."

Kolby frowned, set the full shot glass on the bar, and scooted it toward Toomey.

"Hear me out," said Toomey. "For your own good. Something about this guy Stone doesn't add up."

Kolby's mind jumped to the pink envelopes with his name on them. Toomey began, "He's the victim here. My God. He figures out there's trouble, runs to a roomful of college kids, all the while he's on 911, and he tells the kids to take cover. He gets shot, for Christ's sake." Toomey slapped the photo of Joshua with his flat palm. "It's an amazing story."

Kolby shook her head and looked up. "The Lord works in mysterious ways, Toomey. You should go to church on Sunday instead of blabbing on those talk shows."

"Kolby, this guy is an author of five books. I've seen some online videos from his classes. He's funny. He likes to be at the head of the class. I mean, he's no Johnny Depp in the looks department, but he's a personable guy."

Kolby felt her skin flush and brought her hand over her mouth to try and hide it.

Toomey continued, "He's a writer with the story of the century. But he hasn't said anything to anyone about what happened. Not even a 'no comment.' He's vanished from social media. He's totally off the radar. He switches cell phones every month. He's totally unplugged." Toomey looked into her eyes. "And then a year and a half later, he's on the arm of Kolby Rae? Even Nashville isn't this crazy."

Kolby looked the writer over and reflected on his words. As much as she disliked his cover article about her career, it contained no lies. He was honest in his words, even if they painted an unflattering portrait. Joshua had never talked to her about the shooting; she had only read *Faith Shattered*.

"Toomey, just for a moment, stop being a famous jackass and just be a normal one. How many people do you know who could watch kids get shot up and ever want to talk about it?"

"This goes beyond that, Kolby." He took the file from her. "Look at this." Toomey handed her a printed newspaper article with a photo of Grant's Hill and the victims. He pointed at a photo of a young woman in a sheriff's uniform. The photo looked like a driver's license or ID photo. Underneath was the name: Sgt. Jessica Addison. Next to her photo were photos of two other deputies: Bill Simmons and Sgt. David Wiggans. "They never publicly identified which of the three deputies killed the shooter. The grand jury records are sealed."

Kolby handed the article back.

"I've looked at the official records that were released and listened to the dispatch tapes. This chick here, Addison?" Toomey placed his finger on the photo of Sgt. Jessica Addison and tapped it three times. "She had to be the first one in the door. She had to be the one who shot. She's the one who saved your boy's skin."

Kolby shrugged her shoulders. "She's cute, Toomey. You got a cop fantasy? You into handcuffs?"

"Just hear me out. Look at this." He pulled a photocopy of a state record and handed it to her. Across the top, she read the words,

APPLICATION FOR PERMIT TO
CARRY CONCEALED WEAPON

and the applicant's name: Joshua Stone. "Did you know your boyfriend carries a gun?"

Kolby subtly felt her hip. The holster and pistol she had placed there after getting in her truck at the airport were still unseen. "If I'd been shot at, I'd get one, too," she said.

"But look at the date: December. This was four full months before the shooting. And look who attested to his firearms proficiency."

Kolby looked at the signature on the bottom of the application: Sgt. Jessica Addison, GHSD. She tried to remember the handwriting from the pink envelope to see if it matched. And then she realized she was buying into Toomey's hyped fantasy to sell his book.

"Toomey, our time has been so great, let's not do this again anytime soon." She stood up, and he stood up with her.

"I need to know what happened in that chapel, and no one's talking about it," Toomey said.

"Kids were shot, Toomey. A woman died."

"Please, for me, ask lover boy to talk to me and tell me his version. Or I'll find someone who will, like his other girlfriend, Jessica." Kolby began walking away. "Or maybe her husband, Larry, wants to dish a little dirt before he divorces her."

She walked to the truck, started the engine, locked the doors, and sat there thinking of what to text to Joshua. She dropped the truck into gear and headed down Broadway and turned north on George L. Davis. She took the on-ramp to I-40 and pointed the SUV toward Memphis. She wound the truck's engine up, hitting ninety miles per hour as she passed the first sign that read, *Speed Limit 65*. The truck effortlessly climbed over one hundred miles per hour. She sped on, into the night.

Kolby opened the sliding glass roof and let the wind dance with her hair around her face. Away from the glow of Nashville, the night sky was clear. She closed her eyes and imagined her momma's face surrounded by all the twinkling stars in heaven. The wind ruffled her shirt against her camisole and the tortured skin protecting her heart.

When Kolby reached Memphis, she dropped her speed and blended onto I-240. She got off at Madison, turning another block south onto Union Avenue. She stopped the truck on the street in front of Sun Studios. She looked at the clock: 4:30 am. She'd made the 211-mile drive in a little less than two and a half hours. As the sun came up, she got out of the truck, stood in front of the sun, and held her phone out at arm's length. She took a selfie and then sat down on the sidewalk and tapped the screen, sending the photo to Joshua. She added a message:

<Kolby Rae> *Good morning from sun. And me.*

She pressed SEND, got in the truck, and drove back to her Nashville condo.

Chapter Thirty-Seven

Book Reading

Sarah parked SMILES in the parking lot of the bookstore, and she and Joshua went in the back door. There was a line of patrons at the cash registers and a collection of chairs, all full, in an open space near the center of the store.

A giant banner read, *Welcome, Joshua Stone* across one wall. Joshua had never been to a reading this large. Sarah had done well.

"Joshua, I'll be at the back of the crowd," said Sarah. "I know you'll be fine. In case anyone asks something and you are not sure what to say, look at me. I'll give you a sign. Just remember, smile. We will blitz social media with this tonight and all weekend. We'll move every copy of your book sitting on shelves."

"Really? You can do that?"

"No, not a chance, but I have to say these things because I'm your manager." She grinned.

"You are?"

"Yup, package deal. I'm like a kid from a previous marriage. You marry Kolby, I'm along for the ride…and my ten percent."

A woman from the bookstore staff rang a small chime and began to speak. "Ladies and gentlemen, I want to thank you all for coming, and I am so sorry we ran out of chairs. This is a wonderful turnout on this gorgeous night. I'd like to welcome you to our Tennessee Author's Series, and while he's not a native of Tennessee, he now calls Tennessee his home. He lives just outside Crossings. Please welcome the author of five novels, including *One Good Bread Pudding* and my personal favorite, *Hoop*, Joshua Stone."

Kolby Rae

The audience politely applauded, and several women in the front row took photos with their smartphones. Another woman holding a large camera and long lens was crouching near the side aisle, taking photos of both Joshua and the audience members.

"Hello, and thank you for having me. My name is Joshua, Joshua Stone. I tried to think of some opening remarks. But I figured no one wanted to hear any of my old lectures from Freshman Composition."

Some giggles filled the room.

"How about if we just go straight to any questions? And then, if you don't mind, I'd like to read from a couple of my books."

The group applauded enthusiastically. A woman with a small child who was reading a picture book raised her hand. "Joshua…is it okay if I call you Joshua?"

"Sure."

"I think my favorite book of yours is *One Good Bread Pudding*, and I just wondered, did you actually create the recipes in the book? I've made all of them, and they are really good. I just wondered if you made them or if you had someone help you."

Joshua laughed. "I started with some basic recipes and then improvised. At the time, my coworkers all thought it was great because I was bringing in all these desserts. and we would eat them at the office during coffee breaks." The audience chuckled. "As I said, at first. But they pretty much banned me after they all put on weight. But yes, they're my twists on some fairly traditional dishes. Which is your favorite?"

"Oh, the bread pudding." The audience giggled with her.

"Yes, mine, too, and the judge's in the book."

The audience giggled again.

"I'll do a reading from that in just a little bit. Next question?"

"Joshua, I have kind of the same question, but it's about the pizza dough recipe." The crowd laughed. "I've tried it dozens of times, and I never get it to bake up right. Got any tips?"

Unseen by both Joshua and Sarah, Jeffrey Toomey walked from the register and stood just to the left and behind Sarah near the back of the crowd.

Joshua laughed. "Okay, forget the readings, let's just go into the test kitchen." The crowd laughed with him. "It's not the dough. Although

230

to be honest, there are so many things that affect a dough like that—heat, humidity, water content in the flour—but it's the cooking temp. How hot is your oven when you bake the pizza?"

"Hot, very hot. Four hundred fifty."

"Okay, yep." Joshua nodded. "That's what I did, too. I thought, *That is hot.* But that dough does best in a pizza oven, seven hundred degrees. The pizza will cook in a few minutes. Actually, I made that a few weeks ago for some friends. They have an outdoor wood-fired oven. They built it to bake bread, but let me tell you, it makes a killer pizza crust."

"Joshua, I wondered about *Our Final Days.* You seem to have such an understanding of love and the devotion of partners. Even though your characters were dogs, what about real life? Will you write a love story?"

Joshua gasped with mock shock. "What, you don't call *The Fistfight* a love story?"

Sarah was grinning from the back of the room. He owned the crowd. She had had no idea he was this charismatic in front of a group. He knew how to work it. His timing was great. She was thinking ahead to promoting a dual career couple: Kolby in the spring, summer, and early fall, and Joshua fall through early spring. Maybe Joshua was a better fit for big sister than she first gave him credit for.

"I, ah, wow. Thank you for your words, but to be honest, what I know about love you could put on a matchbook. Give me another forty years, and I may have something to say."

"So does that mean you're single and available?"

Joshua looked back to Sarah for guidance. She nodded up and down twice, then shook her head side to side twice.

"Nashville is a very friendly city, isn't it? Yes, I am single, and thank you, but no, I'm not available."

The woman nodded and gave a disappointed smile. "Whoever she is, she's a lucky woman."

Joshua smiled back, touching his left hand to his chest. Sarah gave him a thumbs-up.

"Joshua, I know we're here to talk about the books, but I just wonder, do you ever talk with any of the students whose lives you saved?"

"No, I don't. How about another question?"

As the questions returned to his books and their characters, Jeffrey Toomey sidled next to Sarah. "He's good. How much did you coach him?"

"Jeffrey, how nice of you to come. Which book did you buy?"

Toomey held out a bookstore bag with all five of Joshua's books. "Let's say I'm a huge fan of Professor Joshua Stone."

"You must want something, Toomey. Let me guess, an exclusive interview for *Garden Party* on life with Kolby?"

Joshua was wrapping up the Q and A and was moving to a table set up with a water bottle and several pens as the crowd formed a line at the table.

"Sarah Miles, you do know all the angles, and that would be wonderful, but I have a prior engagement: *Stone Unturned: A Biography of Joshua Stone*."

"Interesting, Joshua never mentioned it."

"That's because he won't return my calls, so it's the unauthorized biography."

Sarah suppressed a laugh.

"Sarah, what do you know from that day?"

Sarah turned to face Toomey. "I read the newspapers for days, Toomey, as we all did. I read the tabloids. What he did was..." Sarah paused, then added, "There are no words." She looked at Toomey's face, trying to understand where his questioning was going.

"Sarah, do you know Joshua was attacked two separate times?"

"Twice?"

"Yes. And isn't it interesting? About five months before the shooting. He was jumped in a parking lot and left for dead. The attacker killed his dog."

"I had no idea."

"They left that detail out of most of the reports. Have you read *Faith Shattered* by his friend David Adams? You should." Toomey looked over at a smiling Joshua Stone looking up at a reader before he signed her book. "You can't really make out the scar on his forehead anymore, but that cheek one, well, that's on his permanent record."

"Nice." Sarah expressed her displeasure by stepping back and frowning.

"Sarah Miles, love, I need your help. Please convince Dr. Stone. After all, he is your client now. Please convince Dr. Stone to meet with me. Just tell me his story and confirm the things I already know."

"Why don't you stand in line and ask him yourself?"

Toomey nodded. When it was his turn, Jeffrey Toomey seized the opportunity. "Dr. Stone, I'm Jeffrey Toomey."

Joshua laughed. "Mr. Toomey, nice to meet you. That's funny, you're much taller on e-mail. I didn't know you were so short."

Sarah shook her head from the back of the room and to the side, just out of Toomey's view, trying to catch Joshua's attention.

"You haven't returned any of my phone calls or e-mails, so I hope you don't mind that I came to this public reading, I, too, wondered if you talked with anyone from that day. How's Jessica?"

"You might ask Sergeant Addison."

"I've tried. I've spoken with her husband. He doesn't know if you two talk or not. But then, she probably wouldn't tell him if she was still talking with you, would she?"

Joshua scanned the room. The few remaining guests were turned in their chairs looking at the famous Internet journalist, and some were taking photos with their cell phones.

"Ahh, that's right; I forgot. The pretty lady sergeant is so last year. You have a new flame in your life, don't you? Kolby Rae?" The crowd murmured. "I mean, she looked so hot at the Heartland Benefit Concert in that Grant's Hill jacket." Toomey looked around the room and then added, "It was your jacket, right? Or do I have the wrong single, retired Grant's Hill professor?"

Joshua looked around, half-smiling and half-seeking Sarah to bail him out.

"I don't want to take these wonderful people's book signing away from them, so why don't you and I set up a time to talk about this? How is next week?"

Sarah watched as the crowd slowly thinned and, other than Toomey, ended a nearly ideal book reading. She and Joshua mingled a few more moments as he signed some books and personal items for the bookstore employees, and then she walked him to the main entrance and out to her SUV. Joshua slapped the top of the SUV.

"Wow, that was, special," Sarah said, hoping to break his tension. She was impressed he'd kept his public face so unaffected. Joshua opened the door and climbed in, slamming it closed. She sat in the silence, her hands in her lap, and then asked, "Wanna tell me about it?"

"There's nothing to tell."

"Right. Jeffrey Toomey just picks you at random in all the bookstores in all the world, and he happens to walk into your reading and ask you about an old girlfriend?"

"She was not my girlfriend."

"It doesn't matter if she's the Virgin Mary, Joshua. If Toomey is on to you two, she was your girlfriend now."

"She wasn't."

"My first boss told me, never pick a fight with someone who buys ink by the barrel."

Joshua corrected her, "That was Mark Twain."

Sarah corrected him back. "No, my boss's name was Joey." She added after a pause, "But to be specific, that quote is often misattributed to Twain. It originated with an Indiana congressman." She stuck her tongue out at him as Joshua had seen her do many times with Kolby. He took it as an odd compliment.

"Joshua, I'm on your side. I love Kolby because she's my big sister, and I treat her like she's my biggest client. What the two of you do between the sheets is your business. What you do on the streets is my business. I don't care if you had a harem full of women, Joshua, but beginning now, you do not ever break her heart, and you don't ever let it come out in public."

Sarah pointed at him and then softened her expression. "This is my facts-of-life speech. From little sister. Not quite from Daddy with a shotgun, but the reality is, if you cross my advice, you'll wish I was only Daddy with a shotgun."

Joshua leaned slightly back in the seat.

"Joshua, they all like you. I don't know how you did it, but even the band really like…"—she paused—"…likes you. They have always been very protective of Kolby, a little bit family and a little because she's their meal ticket."

"That's great. I like them all, too. I've had friends before, but at times, they do feel more like family than friends. You said 'they.' Does that mean you don't like me?"

"I like that Kolby likes you. I like that you two are getting married."

She shrugged. "Sort of. It's just that…" She paused and then looked over at him. "Joshua, Nashville, music, fame. I don't know if you're cut out for this. It's not the same as being an author or a college professor."

"I think I'm beginning to figure that out."

Sarah continued, "I'm assuming you've told Kolby about your life. Maybe your past loves, whatever. One of the things I'd like you to think about is your past love life. We could do a background check. We can pretty much find out anything about you. We have those kinds of connections."

"You mean at Grant's Hill?"

"Grant's Hill, a summer fling, a conference, a public bathroom. Joshua, you're entering a world where there are no secrets. At least not yours. You don't need to tell me, and I'm not going to go looking. But if there is something…" Sarah made sure he was making eye contact before she continued. "You need to tell Kolby before Toomey or someone else does. If you're still married to your high school sweetheart or have a mail order bride in a third world country or a son or daughter you haven't seen in a decade, they will be found by someone, and it won't be pretty."

Joshua nodded. "I understand."

Sarah continued, "It's very easy to get caught up in the moment and…."—she looked at Joshua and took a deep breath in and out through her nose, her lips pressed together—"and stray, Joshua. Men have a habit of straying."

"What? You don't think that I would—"

Sarah interrupted. "Joshua, no, and neither does Kolby. This isn't my test of your fidelity. This is me helping you out. You can't give off the appearance of doing anything wrong, or it will become wrong. Never, ever. No clubs, no parties, no coffee dates. You can't have lunch alone with another woman. Only in threes or more, but never one on one."

"Sarah, Kolby knows she can trust me."

Sarah replied, "She can and does. But her fans will never forgive you. She's not just the girl next door. She's country music's girl next door."

Joshua rubbed his tongue across his teeth and felt a twinge in his hand and arm. He lightly rubbed his left bicep over the old bullet wound. He lowered his voice. "You had more people here than I have ever had at a reading."

Sarah nodded. "Thank you."

"But Sarah, they weren't there for me. They wanted to know about recipes from my fictional characters and then Toomey and then Kolby Rae."

"Oh, Joshua, I thought you understood. You've been here before, right? You were in all the tabloids after the shooting. You and I never talked about it, but I saw them all. I searched you online. Call it the due diligence of a sister and manger. Surely you must have known that when you and Kolby Rae hooked up, it would be like this. And now you will be everywhere. Everyone will know this new Joshua Stone."

She cocked her head at him. "My friend and my client, Joshua Stone. Welcome to the glass house."

CHAPTER THIRTY-EIGHT

HOUSE HUNTING

KOLBY SET THE PHONE ON the counter, propped up by the microwave oven, and pressed CONNECT. "Hi. Can you see me?"

A rectangle with a silhouette filled her screen and then was replaced with an image of Joshua and Fylgja sitting outside. "You look like you're outside. Can you hear me?"

"Yeah, I can hear you and see you. Are you in the kitchen?"

"Yes, I'm warming up some awesome Chinese food. It is so good. There's this place down the street. I have to take you there sometime. You'd love it."

Kolby watched Fylgja's nose fill the screen, and then the dog's tongue licked it, turning the image dark. When the dog leaned back, the screen image was blurred and Fylgja whined.

"I think she wanted a taste," said Joshua.

"Aww, she misses me. Hi, baby. Hi, baby. Do you miss Mommy?" Fylgja whimpered.

Joshua leaned in close in the frame. "Hello? What about me?"

"Ewww, you're all slobbery now."

She watched the image as he wiped off the front of the cell phone screen, and she asked her next question as he finished. "What don't I know about Joshua Stone? Surprise me. What should I know? We're getting married in two weeks. There must be some secret you're dying to tell me."

"Okay, how's this? I don't just live out of a backpack. I know, you probably thought it was kind of weird, my living out of a backpack and crashing at my friend's house like I didn't have a home of my own."

"Weird? Joshua, I'm a musician, and my world is musicians. It's what we do. It would be weird if you didn't. You know what they call a drummer without a girlfriend, right?"

He laughed as he remembered the joke on Nils as they both said, "Homeless."

"But you have the condo, right? Well, I actually own a house," said Joshua.

"A house? Really? With a yard and your own mailbox?

"Yes, a house and a yard and my own mailbox. It's for sale. I have a renter living in it, and all my stuff is packed in forty-two boxes in the garage."

Kolby bent down in front of the cell phone camera as she looked in the microwave oven and then looked back into the camera. "Joshua Stone has stuff? You mean you're not really this nomad?"

"No, I'm hardly Zen minimalist."

"Don't get me wrong, honey. Nothing about you says Zen. You're more of a-place-for-everything-and-everything-in-its-place kind of guy. Put away is more important than aesthetic display. So prove me wrong. Tell me about your house. Would I like it?"

Joshua shook his head. "I don't know. Probably not. It's a nice house, small, two bedrooms; one is an office. It's Tudor style, great big heavy front door. Single car garage."

Kolby grinned. "So where would you park your car when mine is in the garage?"

Joshua laughed. "I'd go back to my riding my bicycle. But I don't think I could go back to Grant's Hill."

"So I never asked, but how long are you planning on staying at Sean's place?" She stopped. The question made her feel very impulsive about their marriage. They had not talked about where Dr. and Mrs. Stone would live. There were hours of conversations they hadn't had time to have.

Joshua was quiet. Kolby looked down to the phone screen and gave a tentative shrug. He was looking back at her.

"It's kind of funny you mentioned it," said Joshua. "I was wondering what you thought about us looking at a few houses between here and there. Maybe out in the country? Maybe some room to grow?"

"I haven't lived in a house since I left Mississippi. I've been in apartments and condos. I've lived here for ten years."

"I understand. I wasn't asking you to give up your condo. But you never really invited me to move in with you."

Kolby watched as Joshua turned his head, looked away, and then turned back to look at her. "What if I told you I found a place? Would you come see it with me? This week?"

"This is real, isn't it? We're like grownups making big decisions."

"Grownups? Kolby, you're thirty-six. I'm forty-three."

"Oh, so you've done this before?"

"No, not like this."

The microwave beeped and Kolby opened the door, knocking the phone over. Instead of displaying her face, the phone was now sending Joshua live-streaming video of her ceiling.

"I'll set it up," said Joshua. "You come up Monday night, and we'll go see it on Tuesday."

On Tuesday morning, Kolby stepped out of the cabin bedroom dressed in a sweatshirt with her hair pulled back under a baseball cap.

"Dang, girl, you look good."

"Why, thank you, Dr. Stone. You look very husbandly today yourself."

"I printed off the real estate listings from the computer," he told her, "and when I called the real estate agent, I left a message, and then she called me back and left a message. Here, listen to what she said."

The perky voice over the speakerphone began after a moment of background noise. "Hi, Dr. Stone, this is Regina Winfield, your Homeland Real Estate agent, returning your call. I would be happy to show you the property you mentioned. It's four bedrooms with a very contemporary and open floor plan. It's a two-story. It sits on six acres, and there's a forty-by-one-hundred outbuilding. It's very…interesting inside…but the seller is willing to work with the new buyer to make some changes there. They're ready to sell. Now is the time to buy! Bye bye."

Kolby looked at Joshua. "What does 'interesting' mean?"

"I don't know. I was hoping you would tell me."

"Let's take your truck." Kolby put on dark glasses and pulled her ball cap down.

"Oh, we're going incognito?"

"You just be Dr. Stone, and we'll let it all go at that."

Just before their scheduled viewing of the property, Joshua and Kolby pulled into the driveway, went through the gate, and then followed the tree-lined drive a quarter mile back to the yellow contemporary house sitting in a wide open lawn. To the right side was the outbuilding. A large four-door car was parked in the circle loop that led to the front door. Joshua said, "I bet you could turn a tour bus around in that loop."

"Joshua, I'm a terrible shopper. I love it all ready. Don't let me say anything. She'll know I love it. She'll take advantage of us."

They toured the house. The main floor was a large great room with honey-colored wood floors, spacious windows, and an open kitchen with granite counters and commercial-style stove, oven, and refrigerator. There was a staircase leading up to the second floor. Regina Winfield pushed open a thick steel door on the wall under the stairwell and revealed a small storeroom.

"The previous owner built this as a storm shelter. He called it his safe room. It's concrete reinforced and anchored to the foundation. If we ever have a huge storm, you're as safe here as in a bank vault."

Joshua and Kolby looked inside. It was clean and dry, and they were both able to stand under the stairs.

"This is where we hide from paparazzi?" Joshua joked.

They walked up the stairs. There were four bedrooms upstairs, all of reasonable size but small in comparison to the bedrooms in the Adams big house. The largest bedroom had two closets; the other bedrooms had single closets. In a classic and traditional arrangement, the bedrooms were in the corners of the upper level with shared bathrooms in the center and a master bath attached to the largest bedroom.

"I want you to pick one for your office, a place that's all yours," Kolby said.

Joshua gestured toward the room on the east side. "This one gets the morning light. I like that."

Kolby, Joshua, and Regina Winfield walked to the outbuilding. "Now, Dr. Stone, the current owner had some interesting hobbies, and so this was his playroom. But they know this won't work for most people, so they are offing a five-thousand-dollar cash allowance for you to make any changes to the floor so you could actually use the building."

Joshua looked at Kolby, and Kolby shrugged.

Regina pulled the door wide enough for the three of them to see. It was dark, and when she flipped the light switch, some slow-to-start mercury vapor light began to reveal the floor: a regulation-size hardwood basketball floor complete with clear acrylic backboards and a scoreboard. Kolby squeezed Joshua's hand so tightly, she was afraid she would break his fingers.

"Yes, well, it'll be hard for me to change the oil on my truck in here," said Joshua.

Kolby did all she could to keep her snickering quiet.

They walked back to the main house, stood in the kitchen, and asked Regina Winfield to draw up an offer to purchase. She started at the bottom of the form, asking them if they had any special considerations or needs. She worked through the terms and the date of possession. Joshua looked at Kolby and suggested January second.

"Will this be in both of your names?"

"Yes," answered Joshua, looking at Kolby.

"Dr. Stone, what is your first name?"

"Joshua."

"And Mrs. Stone?"

There was a long awkward silence as Kolby was looking around at the kitchen cabinets. Joshua nudged her. "Mrs. Stone?"

"What? Oh my Lord, you mean me?"

Regina Winfield looked at the two of them.

"We're getting married January first. I am so sorry. Kolby with a K, Ruth, Mi—" She stopped and then smiled, looking directly into Joshua's eyes. "Kolby Ruth Stone."

They signed the papers, and Regina Winfield asked if she could call them later that afternoon. On the drive home, Joshua told Kolby the house was theirs.

"How do you know?"

"She's going to call us this afternoon. It's been on the market a long time, and we didn't make a fuss about the gym floor. Can you believe that?"

Kolby clenched her fists in hopeful excitement and looked down at the photos she took on her phone of the lawn, house, and interior.

"Can we talk about something? I need your opinion," Joshua began.

She turned and set the phone in her lap. "Do you know how sweet that is?" Kolby wondered where he was leading the conversation.

"Drew had me meet with Darrell Burrow again. Remember, from the high school?"

"Sure, yes, I remember. What's up? What do they want? Do they want you to teach high school?"

"No, but this pizza thing is getting more interesting every day. There is this company that makes these wood-fired ovens on a concession trailer, right? Just like you see at the county fairs and events, only it's really good pizza."

Kolby nodded. "Like the man who catered our concert in Seattle, yes."

"So Darrell is saying I would have an exclusive at the football and basketball games if I agree to hire and pay kids in the voc-tech program in the restaurant."

Kolby looked at him. "I thought you were going to hire kids anyway."

"I am. So I need to invest in this trailer, but then it's like having two places open on weekends. The kids learn the restaurant side first, like as a junior, and I let the seniors run the concession, with a parent to supervise."

"You care so much about kids, don't you?"

"Yes, I do."

Kolby smiled, picking up their clasped hands. "Joshua, what are you asking me? What can I do? How can I help?"

"I don't know. I guess things are moving fast in both our lives. How will we know if we're too busy?"

As Joshua finished, his phone rang. The display read FORREST. Kolby's phone rang. Her display read SARAH.

Both Joshua and Kolby laughed. "You answer your phone, and I'll answer mine."

Kolby was listening out of both ears, jumbling the conversation with Sarah and trying to hear Joshua's to tell if it was the realtor. When she heard Joshua say, "There's something I want you to look for," she began to ignore Sarah until she heard him say Forrest's name and talk about Forrest and Rooster's annual pickers' trip down South. She then turned her attention back to Sarah.

"So, Kolby, we're booked and committed for the New Year's show. It sold out in thirty-nine hours. We could have picked a bigger venue."

"No, Sarah, I'm going to be nervous enough as it is. It's perfect."

Kolby saw Joshua hang up and heard his phone ring again. She looked over at him as he looked at the display and then nodded at her.

"Sarah, let me call you right back."

Kolby hung up as Joshua spoke. "Hey, Regina. What? Um, sure, let me hand the phone to Kolby." Joshua handed her the phone, and he pulled the truck over to the side of the road. From the right-hand side, he said, "Can you flip it onto speaker?"

Kolby pressed the icon, and Regina's voice boomed, "Can you two hear me?"

"Yes, we can," they answered together.

"Congratulations! You own the house. It's yours."

Kolby shrieked and lurched at Joshua, dropping both of their phones on the floor of the Rover. They sat there giggling, and then Kolby reached for her phone, picking one of the photos she took of the front gate and another of the deck of the house. She attached them to her social media post.

<TheRealKolbyRae> OMG, we love our new home.

CHAPTER THIRTY-NINE

PRENUPTIAL DETAILS

THE MEETING THAT SARAH SUGGESTED for Joshua to meet with the lawyer came together the next week. After arranging for movers to collect his boxes in Grant's Hill and deliver them to the new house after the closing, Joshua made the drive into Nashville.

Kolby Rae and Sarah met Joshua in the main lobby of the Fifth Third Building and rode the elevator to a law firm with a large conference-room view of the city. A young, well-dressed receptionist led them to the room and offered them coffee, and the three waited a few moments before they were joined by Dewayne Jefferson, Partner, as Joshua would read later on his formal business card. The greetings were much more familiar and informal.

"DJ, look at you. That suit must have cost two thousand dollars," exclaimed Sarah as she saw the attorney enter the room with an assistant directly behind him.

"Sarah Miles, you look fabulous." DJ turned to Kolby and extended his arms, and she embraced him as if he had been missing for years. Their hug lasted a few more moments, and then Kolby turned and introduced the two men.

"Joshua, this is my longtime friend and trusted confidant, DJ Jefferson, and DJ, please meet Joshua Stone, my fiancé."

"Dr. Stone, it's my pleasure. It's an honor to meet you. I've read your books."

Kolby watched Joshua's expression. A bit of disbelief lingered in his smile until DJ continued. "I think I was hooked with *Bottle Rocket*, but *The Fistfight* and *Hoop* were terrific." Kolby squeezed Joshua's hand as his look turned more genuine, recognizing that Jefferson had at least skimmed the titles.

DJ turned and extended his palm across his body, pointing to a young woman who looked to be just out of college. "I'd like you to meet Lynn Callaway. She's a law student at Vandy who's doing some part-time work here."

"Dr. Stone, can we get you a beverage or a snack?"

"Please…Josh. Call me Josh. And no thank you."

"Well, let's have a seat," said DJ, "and I can't begin to tell you how happy I am for the two of you." He paused and grinned widely at Kolby Rae. "Kolby Rae, as I sit here, just think, you getting married."

She beamed at Joshua, rocking her crossed leg and boots, and then turned to DJ.

"So, Joshua, I don't know how much you and Sarah and Kolby have talked about this," said DJ. "Let me tell you what my role is and what we'll do today, and then what might happen in the future. Sarah is pinch-hitting these days as Kolby's tour manager, and I am the attorney for her trust. What that means is if you and Kolby decide you need a prenuptial agreement or any kind of legal understanding about your assets, you each need to hire an attorney because I represent the trust, not Kolby and not you. Now, true, Kolby is the sole beneficiary of the trust, and so it will always seem as if I am protecting her, but my role is to protect the trust, even if it is against Kolby's wishes."

DJ paused and took a sip from a teacup his assistant brought him. "I think maybe some history is in order. I met Kolby, I think, the second week she was in Nashville."

Kolby interrupted. "It was the first week, my first weekend here, but we really didn't talk to each other until the second."

Jefferson continued, "I was just a kid, killing time to take the bar exam, fresh out of Vandy, and I was cruising the Nashville bars."

Kolby turned to Joshua. "It's not what you think. He was looking to get acts signed, not laid."

"I had a dream to be partner by age thirty, and thanks to a few artists and Kolby's 'Dance on Your Shoes,' I was partner at twenty-seven."

Kolby interrupted. "Here's this guy, talking to me over the top of his beer glass, who looked like he was going to hit on anything with boobs and hair, talking all the legal mumbo jumbo at me, telling me I needed to be my own publishing company and rights and the future of the Internet and recording contracts. I don't know what about him made me believe him, but I guess it was because he didn't want any money, and he was always a gentleman. So I had this stuff all set up and wrote 'Dance on Your Shoes,' and he told me what to do and I trusted him."

"Nine and a half million sales later, plus all your other music, you have a nice nest egg," said DJ.

For the next forty-five minutes, DJ and Lynn presented a series of financial pictures, trends, and asset descriptions. It was an amazing picture. Kolby earned a modest income, and the money generated by the tours and merchandising funded a modest salary for the band year round. When they toured, the band did very well.

At the end of the presentation, DJ paused. He looked at everyone before continuing. "All this was true until the Heartland Benefit Concert. Beginning the day after, we saw this." DJ's on-screen presentation showed a column chart that was mostly flat and then three consecutively grown columns on the right side. "The simplest explanation is your net worth has doubled. Your licensing income alone for the last three months exceeded the last three years' combined."

DJ looked at Sarah and then Kolby. "You need to think about a new approach to business. Financially, you're a midlevel star now."

Sarah spoke again. "DJ and I have a plan. We want to double the crew. We want to hire some administrative help." Sarah sighed. "Kolby, I'm out of hours in my day."

Kolby held up her hands. "Is this the real deal?"

DJ looked at Sarah. "Kolby, you're not wealthy. This is not Sherrie Elliot piles of money, but you need to grow the business. I can't find a single thing wrong with Sarah's plan. Kolby, it's smart business." DJ smiled and nodded at Lynn, who stood, walked to the doorway, and flipped the lights back on. "Sarah tells me the two of you are thinking about a house and some land up by Crossings?"

Kolby nodded at Joshua, and he began speaking. "Yes, we saw it the other day. It's not big, not small, four hundred thousand dollars and some change. I guess we need to ask you and Sarah if we can buy it."

Sarah and DJ both laughed.

DJ replied, "Ask as in get our permission or can you afford it?"

Kolby laughed. "The money, sillies."

Sarah nodded. "Yes, Kolby. Both of you could swing this on your own, and together, it's not a problem."

DJ added, "This is outside the trust, so this is a marital asset. Joshua, when you publish your next book—and I hope you do—we should talk about a trust. And if you are not comfortable with me, I can refer you outside the firm to a friend who is almost as good as I am."

The meeting appeared to be ending when Sarah and DJ looked at each other and nodded, and then DJ asked Lynn to invite the other guests in.

The men with short military-style haircuts and suits nearly as nice as DJ's walked in and stood. DJ rose to greet them and then turned to make the introductions. "Dr. Stone and Kolby Rae Miles, I'd like you to meet two representatives from Flanigan Associates. Bryon Mc-Mahon…" Byron reached out and extended his hand to Kolby and to Joshua. Kolby noticed Joshua staring at the second man. DJ continued, "And this is —"

"Dwight Evans," Joshua said, surprising everyone in the room except Dwight.

"Joshua, it's really great to see you again, and congratulations on your upcoming wedding," Evans said.

Kolby looked at Sarah, first unsure who the men were and, second, how Joshua knew Dwight. She looked to DJ, who was equally surprised.

"You two know each other?"

Dwight took charge. "Joshua and I did some classes together back in his Grant's Hill days." Dwight looked at Joshua with a confident look that implied "that's all they need to know; you can tell them more if you like." Joshua remained quiet.

Sarah took a sip from her teacup and then rose from her seat. She took off the dark-framed glasses she had been using to read with during most of the meeting and looked first at Joshua and then at Kolby. "Kolby, Joshua, just as DJ's job is to protect the trust, my job is to protect the Kolby Rae name. The brand, the image. And we've all worked so very hard to build Kolby and the whole band into something really special and popular. And we all have had our ideas and dreams about what that means. But there is a dark side to popularity, too, so I've asked Flanigan Associates to give us a briefing about our risk exposure and how they work with clients."

Kolby interrupted with a stomp of her boot. "We are not going to have bodyguards. I won't have goons hanging around the meet and greets. I won't have bodyguards. I am my own security." She turned. "Sorry, gentleman, I didn't mean that. I'm sure you are very nice goons with a nice Mrs. Goon and cute little goonettes."

"I can protect her," Joshua said. He shifted his weight enough in the chair to feel his holstered pistol press against the leather chair back.

Sarah restrained her frustration. "Nope, no bodyguards and no goons, but what I've asked them to do is talk about what we can expect and what our risks are, and to do an assessment of the way we tour and do things so we can be one step ahead of any trouble. And I have hired them to consult us on the wedding and to provide a security detail. We don't want paparazzi there. We want to sell the rights to the wedding photos exclusively, and by banning paparazzi, we actually will increase their desire to get photos of you." As an afterthought, she added, "And Joshua is no slouch, either."

"Wow, thank you," Joshua said with a sarcastic smile.

Kolby began thinking about Jeffrey Toomey. She considered bringing him up but didn't get the chance before Sarah continued.

"I'm kidding. But your book sales are up, and you were in the news before. Several media would love to do a 'whatever happened to' follow-up story."

Kolby watched Joshua and Dwight quickly exchange a look and then return their focus to Sarah.

Sarah continued, "So let's hear them out—with an open mind—and then we can explore some options."

Byron McMahon began speaking first. "First off, thank you. I don't know that I've ever been called a goon by a woman with such an amazing voice. I'll be sure and give Mrs. Goon and the little goonettes an extra hug tonight." He said it in a very disarming way, accepting the skepticism from his potential client. "My name is Byron McMahon, and I am a partner in Flanigan Associates. We're fond of saying we're the company who runs a top ten list no celebrity ever wants to be on: the top ten most at-risk celebrities. And I appreciate that you don't want to be on our list.

"We provide our clients with a number of services, and we are very, very good at what we do. We've prepared a plan for the wedding that we can share with you."

He handed a one-inch binder to each of them. Kolby kept hers closed; Joshua began leafing through the pages.

McMahon continued, "We've looked at the Adams farm and the big house, and we feel we can provide a level of security and screening to keep the atmosphere open and feeling free, as well as keep the paparazzi at a distance and control access to you."

Joshua, looking at the pages and half-listening, smirked and stopped him. "Code names? You gave us code names?"

Kolby quickly opened her book. "Oh for Lord's sake, seriously?"

"Jamaica? I'm Jamaica?" Joshua said in a mocking tone.

Kolby looked over. "I'm afraid to ask. What's mine?"

"Kolby is Kingston," McMahon replied.

Kolby made a face at Sarah, then turned to the men, "That's the best you could do?"

Joshua looked over at Dwight Evans and recognized the look he had seen many times during their pistol training together.

Evans began to speak. "Ms. Miles, Dr. Stone, the good news is, you are not on our top ten list. I would love to sit here and tell you that only the biggest celebrities get stalked, that only the most outspoken opinion leaders are hated, and that only heads of state are shot at." He looked at Joshua. "I'm afraid we all know that is simply not true. Sometimes good, everyday people get attacked." Kolby looked down and fiddled with the cuff on her right sleeve.

"If we talked about our client list—which we never do—it might be fun to brag about this NBA star or this Oscar-winning actress, but as I said, some of our celebrity clients—and I mean no offense when I say this—just aren't that big. They are hardworking entertainers, and for whatever reason, some nut job latched onto them."

Evans paused, then continued. "What we know is that to most of these nut jobs have multiple targets. The goal is to strike a target, and they may be setting up two, three, or more possibles. Our goal is to discourage them from keeping you on their list of possibles."

Sarah looked at Dwight and then leaned into the table. "Kolby, when I worked with Trent, we had a lot of obsessed fans. They were moving from show to show, parking in front of his house, sending him…"—she paused and rolled her head side to side—"sending him things in the mail. They weren't killers. They were just weirdly obsessed. But that was before online really took off. The Internet was nothing like it is today."

"My fans aren't like that."

"Kolby, they didn't used to be, but do you understand how popular you are now? Remember when we had thirty thousand followers?" Kolby nodded. "We have over one hundred sixty-two thousand, not to mention the other social media sites. There is probably a lot of overlap, but easily another fifty thousand. I didn't tell you this, but I talked with Flanigan after we started getting the letters and daily e-mails."

Joshua spoke first. "What letters?"

McMahon interjected, "Let me reassure you, we've evaluated them, and we're monitoring. It's someone who thinks Kolby is in love with him."

Joshua said, "Now I'm fully reassured."

He placed his hand on top of Kolby's.

McMahon spoke again. "We'd like to do the security audit, and we'll outline some suggestions. We'll provide a detail to keep the people you don't want at the wedding out, and it will all be good."

"Why?" Joshua asked. "The only people who will be at the wedding will be the people we invite. It's at the Adams farm. Who wants to drive to Crossings on New Year's Day?"

Kolby began to understand. She looked across the table at DJ, then to Sarah. She looked one more time at Joshua. "Do we need to move the wedding?"

Dwight spoke quickly. "Absolutely not. Our job is not to make you change your lifestyle; our job is to protect your lifestyle. That's why we want to do the audit, and then we'll make it possible for you to enjoy this day with your friends and guests. We've looked at the aerial photos, and we can keep it secure. It's what we do best."

"I can protect her," Joshua said a second time. They all looked at him.

Dwight looked at McMahon, then back to Joshua. "Joshua, I know what you can do." Joshua and Dwight stared at each other. Sarah and Kolby looked at the men and then at each other.

Dwight continued, "Joshua, any other day is a different story. This is your wedding. You are in the spotlight. You can't be the protector and the protectee. Not this day."

Kolby watched as Joshua moved back in the chair, looking first to her eyes, then down at the table.

"Joshua," Sarah began, "I don't want to leave you out of this discussion. I know you won't be offended when I say authors don't enjoy the same celebrity status as singers. But your followers have doubled, too."

Joshua looked at her. "Oh, you mean I have two now?"

Sarah mocked him. "No, three. I followed you this morning." They all laughed. "You're not Joshua Stone, author and retired professor anymore. You're Joshua Stone. The day we announced you and Kolby were getting married, the two of you were neck and neck for trending topics. Sure, your fame flame has dimmed a little, but you need to think in terms of being a public figure. And I think we need to have an offline discussion about getting you a social media team. The last time you posted an update was four hundred seventeen days ago."

Kolby turned to him and leaned in to whisper. "Joshua Stone, I want all your attention on our wedding day. Let them protect me then, and you can protect me the rest of our lives."

Joshua looked back at her, gave a partial nod, and then turned to Dwight. "Just for the wedding?" He waited for someone to say something and then added a reluctant, "Okay, we'll follow your plan."

On their way out the door, Joshua and Dwight stopped in the hallway. Kolby continued down the hall and looked over her shoulder as the two men shook hands and didn't release their grip.

"Dwight, thanks for your vote of confidence, but I don't think you do know what I can do." Joshua's voice was mixed with bravado and hesitation.

"Josh, I know you can't say anything about Grant's Hill."

Joshua nodded. "You have no idea what I'd like to say to you."

Dwight raised his eyebrows in an understanding expression and pumped his grip on Joshua's hand. "Remember, I used to work for that three-letter government agency. I still have a few friends. I just want you to know, regardless of what happened there, I'm on your team. We'll keep it that way."

When Joshua finished with Dwight Evans and walked to join Kolby, she slid her arm though his as they waited for the elevator. "Why don't you take me to lunch, and we can read through this together and talk?"

Sarah and McMahon were huddled together in the glass conference room. Kolby hesitated, waiting to invite her, too, and then turned and pressed the elevator button, still hanging on Joshua's arm.

When they walked in the trendy and open-kitchen restaurant, Joshua turned and kissed Kolby on the cheek and then lightly on the lips. Kolby gave a self-conscious look around at the patrons, who didn't react to their public affection. As Joshua wrapped his arm around her waist, she felt him pull her close, and then they walked to a table and sat down next to the glass windows. Kolby tried to remember the last time she was kissed in public. Her life in Crossings, on the road, and in the studio was much more sequestered than she had realized. She and Joshua were a couple. It was becoming more real.

They ordered. Joshua had his back to the wall and was scanning the room as they waited for their food.

"Would you still marry me if I weren't Kolby Rae?"

"Would you still marry me if I weren't Dr. Stone?"

She objected, "But you told me you're not Dr. Stone anymore, that you're Joshua."

"And you're Kolby Ruth. At least it was Ruth who asked me to marry her, so that's who I'm marrying."

Kolby picked up Joshua's hand. "Okay, it's a deal." She played with his hand, flipping it over and back, stroking the back side with her thumb. "So how do you know that guy from Flanigan? You two were having a pretty serious conversation in the hall."

Joshua looked around the room and then back into her eyes. "It's like a whole 'nother life ago. I did some pistol training with Dwight."

Kolby thought back to his speed and focus when the two of them went to the quarry for some pistol practice before the fall tour began. She had never asked where he took his classes. "You do have some secrets, don't you, Joshua Stone?"

"Me? No secrets. I'm just saving some stories for when you get tired of me so I can recapture your interest in—Jamaica." He rolled his eyes.

"Oh my Lord, I thought I was going to die. Seriously, Kingston? They want to call me Kingston? Oh Lord, I always wanted to be in love with someone and have him give me a pet name, but Kingston? I sound like a cigar!"

"How about me? Jamaica? Why can't I have a macho name like Barbados or Bar Bad Ass?" Joshua made a tough grimace with his face, turning his scar toward her. She laughed loudly. Heads from other tables turned and then returned to their meals. Joshua held the pose and then asked Kolby, "So you wanted a pet name. Do you have one for me? I don't think I've heard you say one."

Kolby reflected. "No, not yet. What about for me? Do you have a pet name you call me?"

"Ruth."

"Yes, I know that." Then she added, "Do you know you call me Ruthie in your sleep?"

"I do?"

"Yes. You've done it a few times. And then sometimes you just yell. Like you're awake but not really. I ask you about it, and you don't remember."

"Really?"

"Yes, you did it the first night we were together. Scared me so bad I thought I was going to scream, too. But I looked at Fylgja, and she was calm and unconcerned, so I figured you must do it a lot."

"Really? I didn't—"

"No, I ask you when it happens, and you act like you're awake, but I can tell you're still sleeping. It's about Grant's Hill, isn't it? You dream you're back there?" Kolby stopped short of asking him about the other woman, Jessica. He called her name, too. Kolby wanted to know if she was the woman who wrote his name on the pink envelope.

Joshua looked away. "Let's not talk about that. Let's talk about pet names."

"Joshua?" Kolby waited until he looked at her before she continued. "I think every man is entitled to a secret. But it has to be a secret that he keeps to remind himself of how good he has it now. Is that your secret?"

Joshua bit his lip, and then she watched as his tongue slid across the front of his teeth behind his lip. "I told you, I don't have any secrets. But there isn't a day that goes by that I don't remind myself how good I have it now." As he said the words, he tilted his head to the side. He took his hand and lightly brushed her curls and her cheek.

"Um-m-m, oh, that is so sweet." She felt her body begin to surrender to his touch as her phone chimed with a notification from her calendar. She looked at the display and said, "I've gotta go. Try on a dress. You can't come."

"And that's your secret? I hope it reminds you of how good you have it now."

Kolby left the table as the waitress brought their order. She turned, blew Joshua a kiss, walked out the door, and turned back down the sidewalk, passing the window and their table. As she looked in, she watched as Joshua turned his hand, palm out, and pressed it against the window glass. She reached up, met his hand on the opposite side of the glass, held it there for a moment, smiled at him, and then continued down the sidewalk.

CHAPTER FORTY

NEW YEAR'S EVE

THEY WERE STANDING IN THE middle of the Ryman Auditorium stage with the crew hustling around. Graham Carr was overlooking the stage from his seat at the guest Front of House mixer high in the back of the auditorium just beneath the line of paired Gothic-arch stained-glass windows. Sean Adams has a separate audio mixer, next to Graham and the two were routing cables to feed both boards, Grahams for the house and Sean's for the live recording. Tim Richards was finishing the final setup of Nils's drum kit. Skeeter was standing tall and in charge, enjoying the bustle of the larger crew. The newcomers were hustling to prove themselves, hoping to impress Sarah to be picked up for the spring and summer tour. Sarah was at the doors, talking with the house manager and promoter. In midsentence, Kolby changed the subject, turned to Joshua, and reached over to touch his arm. He shifted his attention from the stage to her.

She whispered, "Joshua Stone, do you realize you're marrying a woman who is more concerned about seat kills on the night before her wedding than bridesmaid flowers?"

He whispered back, "Kolby Ruth, do you realize you are marrying a man who has no idea what seat kills are?" Then he added, "Why are we whispering?"

"'Cause this is hallowed ground. This is the Ryman." Joshua looked around. Kolby took him to the center of the stage. "This is all new, but there was so much respect for the stage when this used to be the Opry that there is a circle of the old stage boards that they cut out and took over to the new Opry House."

They looked at the new teak floor. Joshua whispered, "What do you think? About two-thirds the size of a basketball court, not as deep and not as wide?"

"Joshua Stone."

"What? You could get a good half-court game in here."

She slugged him. "Do you know who met here?"

Joshua watched as Tim motioned to a new member of the crew, who dashed across the stage and then dashed back. "No, who?" he asked.

"Johnny and June." She looked into his eyes, and he just grinned back at her.

"Are they new?"

Kolby slugged him again.

It was the last night for so many things: the last night of their fall tour, the last night being single, and the last night of the year.

The show started off great with a full house and a fired-up and receptive crowd, but Kolby felt something was just a bit off. It seemed as if the band was stalling and lacked their normal focus. Their sound was full and rich, their timing in the songs was tight, but between songs, they acted a bit immature and unsure. At first, Kolby wrote it off as her own perception, just nervousness about the wedding, but as the night progressed, it became more and more clear something was amiss. The audience, however, was in a party mood and was thrilled by the casual and impromptu timing of the show. At the end of the couples set, the final set of the night, Sean Adams was working at his own mixing console next to Graham, recording "I Don't Make My Bed That Way" while Kolby was singing and looking at Joshua at the side of the stage. The song came from a line she said in the middle of their fight and grew into a romantic ballad.

:: There are lots of party girls ::

:: You can take out on the town ::

:: There are lots of pretty girls ::

:: Who will love you all night long ::

:: Kiss you in moonlight ::

:: and be gone before the dawn ::

:: But I don't make my bed that way ::

:: I don't make my bed that way ::

:: I don't make my bed that way ::

:: I don't make my bed that way ::

:: Just let me spend my life with you ::

They led into the chorus a final time. Roberto stepped back, nodding to the others.

:: I don't make my bed that way ::

:: I don't make my bed that way ::

:: I don't make my bed that way ::

Roberto signaled Nils, Kim, and Skeeter to stop. Kolby looked over at Roberto. He had missed the cue, and this wasn't the right ending to the song. She paused. Rob changed the lights, and she was alone center stage. She grasped the microphone and followed Roberto's lead. In the Kolby Rae whisper, she looked at Joshua and sang:

:: Just let me spend my life with you ::

The applause was intense, and Roberto and Nils led the band offstage, and Kolby stepped off and tapped Sarah.

"Roberto never misses a cue," said Kolby. "We're late. We have eight minutes, and we're on overtime. We've got to cut a verse on 'I'll Be There for You,' or we're in overtime."

On a tour, the opening act plays a joke on the headliner on the final night, a live show tradition. Since they were solo, the band had decided to play a trick on the audience. Their planned encore was Bon Jovi's "I'll Be There for You." The plan was for Nils to come out with a big-hair wig and kick off a drumbeat, followed by Roberto doing a power slide in long hair and tight leather pants. And Kolby would do a hoarse Kolby Rae whisper of the lyrics, singing the "I'll Be There for You" lines looking directly at Joshua, who was standing stage right. The crowd would love the gag, and Kolby wanted to say something publicly about the marriage after the song. She'd asked Joshua to join her onstage, but he refused. But now, Roberto had moved the whispered line too early in the show and they were late, and the night at the Ryman was fast becoming a nightmare. All they needed to do was exit together stage left and make the quick wig attachments, and they would be set. Except when Kolby went stage left, the rest of the band went stage right.

"God bless, this is gonna be one of those shows," she exclaimed to Sarah, who seemed unruffled by the band's growing lack of attention.

"Kolby?" Sarah placed both her hands on Kolby's shoulders, trying to get her full attention and break her tizzied mood. "Just watch. This is for you…."

The lights came up on Nils wearing a huge big-hair wig as he strutted across the stage, waving to the crowd. He walked around his drum stool once and then around a second time, and then he sat down. The audience cheered and laughed at the sight of the comical Norwegian drummer with the baby face in a glam rock, big-hair costume. Nils began a raucous rim-shot drumstick solo.

Roberto's guitar screamed a rock and roll power chord and then a riff, and he ran across the stage wearing a big-hair wig and aviator sunglasses. He dove into a classic rock and roll knee slide. Kolby began to panic. This was not Bon Jovi; this was the David Lee Roth era of Van Halen.

Nils's high baritone voice began speaking into the microphone, improvising a spoof of the spoken introduction to "I'm Hot for Teacher." "You know how the song goes, so we all want to know what the teacher's gonna look like…"

Two models in schoolgirl outfits rushed up from the green room where Sarah had them in hiding and handed Kolby a stack of schoolbooks.

Sarah shouted over the guitar, "Follow their lead!," and then the three of them strutted onto the stage and sat at school desks brought out by the crew, sitting center stage under the glow of a pink spotlight. They sat just behind the semicircle on the front face of the Ryman stage, looking out to the crowd.

On the opposite side of the stage, Skeeter, Tim, and Over handed Joshua Stone a graduation cap and gown. Skeeter urged, "Joshua, put this on now." Joshua looked around, unsure. "Now, Joshua, now." He zipped up the gown and had the cap mostly in place when the small platform he was standing on began to slide. "Hang on! Look ahead! And smile!" Skeeter yelled and then ducked behind the work cases to sit at his steel guitar.

Kolby looked over and saw Joshua hanging onto a prop lectern, being pushed to center stage. She put her hands over her mouth, trying to hide the laughter, but couldn't stop.

Nils continued, "Ladies and gentleman, you've heard the rumors. You've seen the tabloids. Tonight we're here to tell you it's all true!"

The audience stood on their feet in front of the classic Ryman Auditorium wooden pews.

"Kolby Rae and Dr. Joshua Stone are getting married tomorrow!"

The GRITS cheered loudest.

"But tonight, Nashville, in the Ryman Auditorium, we welcome you to be a part of history: the world's biggest bachelor and bachelorette party ever. At midnight, they're cutting the cake, and you all get to have a slice." Nils yelled into the microphone, "Class dismissed!"

Balloons fell from the room as confetti cannons exploded, and glitter and confetti filled the air.

Nils began chanting, "Kiss! Kiss! Kiss!" as the house lights came up. Kolby stood, and Joshua began walking toward her. They both stopped center stage.

"Did you?" She asked Joshua.

"I had no idea."

"Oh my God, what are we doing here?"

Kolby took Joshua in an embrace and began to kiss him. They kissed and swayed. His cap began to fall, and he grabbed it, first with his hand to hold it in place, and then, while kissing her, he flung it out to the audience. They were standing center stage on the now-torn set list.

Nils finished, "Ladies and gentlemen, Kolby Rae and Joshua Stone!"

The stage lights went out, the house lights down, then the house lights went back up, and the mix tape normally played during setup and teardown began. Skeeter, Kim, Nils, and Roberto rushed the couple with Sarah not far behind.

"Congratulations, you two!" exclaimed Kim.

Kolby nodded. "Okay, okay, now I get it. But we're on overtime."

"It's in the contract, Kolby. We're here until one o'clock. Go have fun, dance. We cut the cake at midnight."

"I can't believe you guys did this."

Dwight Evans crossed from the opposite side. "Congratulations to the happy couple," Dwight said. He then brought his hand casually to his mouth and said something into a microphone attached to the sleeve of his jacket. He turned his attention back to the couple. "Joshua, Kolby, this is a big crowd. Nashville PD has the streets outside, but it's New Year's Eve. They're busy. Ryman security is on the doors, and our detail is inside. Sarah and I have gone through the plan. Here's what you need to know: The receiving line is on the stage. You'll cut the cake after you pose for some photos. We have men at both stage stairs, four men onstage with you at all times."

They looked at the band crew and realized four additional men had stepped onto the Ryman stage near the back wings. Unlike Evans, who was wearing a business suit, the Flanigan team looked like concertgoers.

Evans finished his prep talk. "The exit is stage left, over my shoulder. If anything goes wrong and we have to go…we go." He said the second "go" with a forceful tone of voice. "And stay with me and the team to the back door and out to the SUV. Otherwise"—he grinned— "have fun, and enjoy your party."

Dwight looked up to where Graham and Sean were at their mixing board. One of the Flanigan team members was standing, overlooking the stage. "All posts. Kingston and Jamaica are briefed," Dwight said. Kolby and Joshua looked at each other and shrugged at the use of their code names.

By midnight, the crowd was as much lost in the party as they were with the thrill of being in the room with Kolby Rae. The receiving line had dwindled, and Nils stepped to his drum kit, did his twice-around-the-stool routine, and then played a loud drumroll followed by a cymbal crash.

Rob dimmed the house lights to half, and the spotlight lit up a rolling cart with a guitar-shaped, two-tier wedding cake with pink frosting and a tiny bride and groom on the top tier.

"We're doing this backwards," Joshua whispered in her ear. "Does this mean—?"

Kolby snapped her elbow back to Joshua's rib and through her grin said, "Don't get any ideas, Joshua Stone. You have to wait until after the ceremony. We're just cutting the cake tonight."

Joshua was silent and then leaned in. "Like you weren't having the exact same thought I was?"

She squeezed his hand tightly.

One of the staff handed Kolby a cake knife, and she and Joshua stood behind the two-tier guitar as cameras flashed from across the theater.

The photos from the event spread quickly. Even though #NewYearsEve dominated the trending topics and the updates, the most popular photo from the Kolby Rae–Joshua Stone party was of the two of them holding a piece of cake just in front of each other's open mouths. It was both romantic and campy, and the following shots revealed that neither bride-to-be nor groom-to-be had smeared cake on the other's face.

Chapter Forty-One

The Wedding

Dwight Evans and the Flanigan detail took Kolby and Joshua to the Adams home in Crossings while Malcolm drove the band. Malcolm parked the bus near the writer's cabin, and late in the morning, they all went to separate rooms to get ready for the wedding.

Flanigan Associates was working their event protection plan to the minute, with members of their detail at the entrance and the end of the road that led to the Adams farm. The local police and sheriff's department had stationed an off-duty officer at each end of the road, and only residents and guests with invitations were allowed access. At the entrance to the lane, guests were checked against the master list, and the flow into the Adams farm was orderly and smooth.

Kolby, Kim, and Sarah were standing in the large bedroom of the Adams house. The bride was putting the final touches on her makeup, and then they helped her with her dress. They each posed for a photo with Kolby, and Kolby took one of each of them. She stood near the edge of the king-sized bed. Then Sarah opened the door and Skeeter, Nils, and Roberto came inside.

In a rare circumstance, Skeeter spoke before any of the others. "Kolby, we all wanted to say how much we appreciate you keeping us together, you know, like they say in the wedding ceremony, in good times and bad. So we wondered if instead of that old something borrowed, something blue, well, we wanted you to carry something from each of us today. So you know that we not only love you, but we are fully behind you and Joshua. We're in this with you, always."

Skeeter took off his hat, held it for a moment, then took out the hat-pin that had been in the side of it as long as any of them remembered. "This belonged to my grandmother." He took it out and handed Kolby the silver pin with the tear-shaped turquoise stone surrounded by silver scrolls with black patina from age and tarnish in the recesses.

Kolby felt a small tear in her eye and said, "Thank you," to Skeeter. She gave him a kiss on the cheek.

Kim handed Kolby a bracelet woven from the strings of her cello. "These are from this fall at the Heartland Benefit Concert. These are the strings I used that night. That night was so amazing for us as a band, and then to know you and Joshua got engaged, too. So I don't know if it goes with your dress or not, but I hope you remember that day forever and what it meant to all of us."

Roberto was next. He reached into his pocket and pulled a silk embroidered handkerchief. "This was from my *abuela*. She told me my *abuelo* wore it in his suit coat pocket when he went to Havana on business." He handed it to her. "Just in case you begin to cry."

Kolby was fine until Roberto said "cry." Then the small tear became a flood, and she wrapped her arms around him.

Last was Nils. He looked at the other gifts, and everyone saw the slight hesitation. Then he took out his box. Kolby dabbed her eyes with Roberto's gift handkerchief and then looked up at Nils.

Nils began, "I don't know what to say except that when you asked me to join your band, the very first night we played live, there were still two of your guitar picks taped to the microphone stand. So I kept them. I don't know why. I thought maybe someday they might have sentimental value. So when you and Joshua said you were getting married, I remembered them and had them made into earrings for you to wear."

Kolby opened the box holding two pink, leopard-pattern guitar picks drilled with earring hoops to let the picks hang free from her ears. Kim helped her take each one from the box. Kolby carefully took out the simple pearl earrings in her ears and replaced them with the new guitar pick earrings. Kolby and Nils hugged and kissed.

Sarah looked at her phone. "It's time. We need to be out front."

Sarah held the door for the band members and then closed it, staying with Kolby a few moments more. In so many ways, they were a long way from Tremont, Mississippi.

"A long time ago…," Sarah began, "…you probably don't remember, but a long time ago…you told me he was out there for you. And I knew you believed it. And I never once saw you lose faith. And you turned twenty, and you turned twenty-five, and you turned thirty, and you turned thirty-five."

"Okay, okay, we don't need to count all the numbers, Sarah."

"I know, and I just want to say that now that I've spent time with Joshua, I'm glad you waited for him."

From her right hand, Sarah slid the three slender rings off her finger. Her fingernails, always short and rarely painted, were colored a soft rose. Each ring, made from a different tone of gold, was engraved with a different word in block letters. One ring read HOPE, the next LOVE, and the third read PEACE. She slid the three rings on the ring finger of Kolby's right hand, aligning the words, and read them: "Hope, Love, Peace."

Through tears, Kolby said, "Sarah, these are wonderful."

Sarah looked at her big sister. "I am so happy for you."

Kolby hugged her and then whispered, "I will give these back to you when you find the one woman for you. She's out there. I know she is."

Sarah paused at the door, lifting and dropping the hem of her navy blue dress. "I can't believe you made me wear a dress for this."

"Thank you. It's the only time I'll make you, I promise."

Sarah stuck out her tongue, and Kolby stuck out hers back.

As Sarah left, she saw Joshua in the long center hallway of the big house, close to where she saw him the night of his first date with Kolby. She looked him up and down and made a *tsch* sound with the side of her mouth in a playful scold.

"No flowers? Mmm mmm, you just never learn." Joshua shook his head. Then she said, "Give me a kiss, brother-in-law. You're marrying the best woman in the world."

Joshua lightly kissed her on the cheek.

"She's in there," said Sarah. "You guys have fifteen minutes before showtime."

"Showtime? You never quit, do you?"

"Neither do you. That's why you won her heart." And with that, Sarah slipped out the side door to walk around to join Alan Neal. She and Alan would step up on the portico after Joshua and Kolby walked out the front door. They would serve as best man and maid of honor.

Kolby was adjusting the beaded lace that layered over the strapless top of her dress when she heard him knock on the door. She stepped to the knob and placed her hand there and waited. Kolby and Joshua had never really talked about what the other would wear for the wedding. She had no idea what to expect. No, that wasn't true. She knew he owned a suit; she had seen his photos. She turned and stared at herself in the mirror, feeling a moment of doubt, wondering if she looked good enough for him. In her reflection, where a moment ago she saw a beautiful mature, sexy woman, now she saw a gangly girl with curves in all the wrong places, with every hair out of place and a horrid scar on her breast.

She closed her eyes and turned back to the door, twisted the knob, and opened it. She took a step back and then stopped. Joshua Stone cleaned up nice. He wore a black tuxedo jacket with a thin shawl collar of black satin. He had a crisp white shirt with a wing collar and gold studs in place of buttons. The jacket fit him well.

But all that blurred to the background when she saw the expression of awe and pleasure on his face. He was mesmerized by her looks. His eyes locked on hers, and then he looked at her shoulders, bare under the beaded lace scoop neck. The empire waist, tea length dress had two lace fabrics, a net lace and flowered lace guipure at the waist, midskirt, and hem. Joshua followed her legs to her white boots and back up her body, stopping again at the earrings, dangling free and fun.

They both began to giggle, a nervous, happy, I-don't-know-what-to-do-next giggle.

"There are..."

"Sh-h-h-h," Kolby said. "Just let me look at you."

Joshua stood there, then reached into his pocket and pulled out the slender case containing his mother's pearl necklace. "There are so many gifts I want to give you."

"Me, too," she told him.

"These were my mother's," he said as he opened the box. "My father gave them to her, and she gave them to me to give to you."

"But Joshua, I didn't know your mother."

"She knew you. I didn't know you, but she knew you. She knew you were out there for me."

Joshua stepped around, draped the pearls around her neck, and fastened the clasp behind her.

"No, wait. I have something for you." Kolby turned to the night-stand and retrieved a black box with a white bow.

Joshua opened it to find a silver cross with gold wire wrapped at the ends and at the loop where it connected to a masculine neck chain.

"Turn it over. Read what it says."

Joshua flipped the cross. Engraved on the back was *Ruth 3:9*. His eyes twinkled.

"Joshua Stone, I love you with all my heart. But I have never been so nervous to go out in front of a crowd in all my life."

"You, nervous? What about me?"

"Joshua, what if your friends don't like me? What if they don't think I'm smart enough? What if…?" She felt his fingers touch her lips.

"Kolby, there's one more thing I need to say to you."

"What?"

He looked at her and said, "Yes."

"Yes?" she asked him back, unsure of what he meant.

"Yes. You asked me to marry you and then ran onstage to sing your song and steal the show, and I never got to tell you my answer, so I figured I'd better tell you now before it's too late. Yes, I want to marry you."

She began to giggle again, which made Joshua giggle, and then they held each other.

"The band came by and gave me some things," she said.

"Really? That's sweet. They stopped by and handed me this flask, said it was Linie—just in case we needed a boost."

Kolby looked at Joshua, and he looked back with a devilish grin. "We shouldn't yet," she said. "What would Drew think?"

Joshua was unscrewing the top and then tilted it her direction. "Mrs. Stone?"

Kolby took the flask, touched it to her lips, and tossed back a mouth-filling shot. She felt a tremor and offered the flask back to Joshua, who raised it as she said, "Dr. Stone?" He, too, downed a shot, returned the cap, and slid the flask inside his jacket.

The outdoor temperature hovered just at fifty degrees as Sean and David Adams, who were serving as host and ushers, urged everyone outside at 2:45. By 3:00, the assembled crowd was sitting in chairs facing the front door where less than six months ago, Kolby and Joshua had had their first conversation.

The main door opened. Kim walked out, cello in hand, and sat at a small chair with a white cover tied with bows at the legs. As the first notes of the wedding march flowed from the cello, Drew stood up and moved to the side. Joshua and Kolby walked down the main entry hallway, through the door, and onto the covered front porch of the big house.

David, who had moved to sit next to Ellen, commented, "We can see them. Why aren't all weddings like this?"

Drew was slightly to the left and turned to face either the audience or the couple as he spoke. He read from the Bible, I Corinthians: 13. Next he read from Joshua's novel *Our Final Days*: "In the amber light of the setting sun, they sat side by side, a wordless day that was filled with every expression they knew. Two hearts: older, wiser, long on years, and committed for life."

He then read Kolby's romantic lyrics from "Looking Glass Memories":

"Looking glass memories, faded with time. Looking glass memories, remind me you're mine. Whenever I see me, I see you. Looking glass memories, of love that is true."

Drew paused and then said, "We are gathered today for a very special purpose. We are gathered here today for these two people. This man and woman have come before us to publicly declare their love for one another. But who are these people?"

Drew repeated the phrase. "Who are these people?

"We know the singer; we know the author. We know the star, we know the hero, but neither of those people is getting married today.

"We're here because two people fell in love....Kolby Ruth and Joshua Stone fell in love."

He asked the rhetorical question again, "But who are these people? We know the Bible story of Ruth, loyal to her mother-in-law, faithful to the end, who stood strong against adversity and sought protection and redemption from her protector.

"And who better to protect her than Joshua, the warrior of the Old Testament? We all know about the man who parted the water and led his people to safety. We know that man as Moses. But Joshua did the same strong and courageous thing, and yet another gets the fame for parting the waters.

"So the faithful and strong woman"—he nodded at Kolby—"marries the humble and mighty warrior." He nodded at Joshua. "Her protector. His faithful servant."

Drew turned to Alan Neal. "At this time, I would like to receive the rings."

Alan Neal reached into his pocket and pulled out a double ring box, handing it to Drew. He opened the box, took both rings, and set them on the open Bible.

"I ask you two to hold hands and repeat to each other the vows I am about to share with you and these witnesses."

Kolby and Joshua clasped hands. She traced the outline of the scar on his left hand with her index finger.

Drew mouthed, "Smile," at them and made a cheesy grin. "Joshua Stone, do you take this woman, Kolby Ruth, to be your wife, to love her, to cherish her, to honor her, in sickness and in health, in good times and in bad, as long as you both shall live?"

Joshua looked at Kolby, smiled, and said, "I do."

Drew turned to Kolby. "Kolby Ruth Miles, do you take this man, Joshua, to be your husband, to love him, to cherish him, to honor him, in sickness and in health, in good times and in bad, as long as you both shall live?"

Both Joshua and Drew saw the quiver in her lip. And then she said, "I do."

"As witness to these vows, I now turn to our gathered friends and ask you the same." Drew turned, facing the gathered guests. "Will you love this couple, will you cherish them, will you honor them in sickness and in health, in good times and in bad, as long as you all shall live?"

Roberto, Skeeter, and Nils overpowered the other voices as all the guests answered, "We do."

The boisterous response made Drew laugh. "I need to talk with them about joining our church choir."

And everyone else joined the laugh.

"It is my honor, right, and privilege to pronounce the two of you husband and wife in the eyes of God and the laws of the state of Tennessee. You may seal your love with a kiss."

Joshua and Kolby embraced, and their lips touched, as they had done on the grassy hill following Kolby's drive across the farm fields a few months earlier.

Drew ended the ceremony with Ephesians 3. "I pray that Christ will live in your hearts because of your faith. I pray that your life will be strong in love and be built on love. And I pray that you and all God's holy people will have the power to understand the greatness of Christ's love—how wide, how long, how high, and how deep that love is.

"Ladies and gentleman, I have no greater honor in this life than to introduce newlyweds. Please join me in congratulating Dr. Joshua and Mrs. Kolby Ruth Stone."

PART EIGHT
GLASS AND STONE

CHAPTER FORTY-TWO

DRIVEWAY MOMENT

KOLBY RAE WAS SEATED IN the studios of *AirTime*, a syndicated public radio music show, being interviewed about her latest album.

Several hours away, Grant's Hill Sheriff's Sergeant Jessica Addison was having a driveway moment. She was listening to *AirTime* in the patrol car at the farm she and her husband, Larry, had operated since they were married. Both Addisons had been fans of Kolby since her debut album. Jessica bought Larry every disk Kolby recorded and accepted that even though he loved the music, his relationship with her packaged CDs was like many men's relationship with *Playboy* magazine. He told her he liked sound of her voice, but in reality, he was equally mesmerized by the pictures. With the release of her second album, *Four-Wheel Girl*, Kolby had changed her hairstyle, and it matched the short, parted-on-the-side pixie cut that Jessica wore. It was Jessica's only brush with look-alike status. The two women didn't look much alike at all, but for a few months, they shared a haircut.

Addison had stopped the car just in front of the walk to the house and flipped the key to accessory so she could hear the interview.

The female interviewer began her question:

You show a lot of skin in your performances, but somehow you manage to stay sexy and not [pause] not slutty.

Thank you.

How do you do that?

Well, first, I love being sexy. I love being a woman, and I love to show off, but there's a way to do it and a way not to do it. I don't wear anything onstage that any mother or father in America would be ashamed to see their daughter in.

Their grown daughter.

Laughter

I do show a lot of skin...but you don't see what you think you see.

Okay, so this is interesting. I mean, you are very attractive. You were voted in the top fifty sexiest entertainers by *Country Music Weekly*. You have curves. I mean, I notice that in your album covers, I can't find one with you showing much cleavage.

Oh my — can you say that on public radio? I can't believe we're going to talk about my boobs on *AirTime*.

Laughter

But what I mean is, a lot of women in the music industry with your body would probably show even more of it off.

I know, but that's not who Kolby Rae is. I show my legs. I show my back — I show a lot of my back. I show my shoulders. With Kolby Rae, you get wiggle, a lot of wiggle; we just leave the jiggle offstage. I'm not judgmental. If others in the industry want to show their moneymaker onstage or on camera, it's showbiz. I don't think that's wrong. It's just not me.

So we won't be seeing a nude photo layout?

You know what? Young girls need to hear this. Moms, turn up your radio. I've never sunbathed naked. I can count on one hand the number of men who have seen me without my clothes. That's just who I am. My momma and daddy raised me as a Christian, and I do my best.

But you raise a little hell. You've covered Merle Haggard's "Stay Here and Drink." You've opened for some of the biggest party acts in country.

Yes ma'am, I can warm a barstool on Saturday night and a church pew on Sunday morning.

You do a lot of benefit shows for children's hospitals.

I do. I think that any time you share a gift with others, it's a good thing.

We're talking with country music artist Kolby Rae. This is *AirTime*.

Break

I want to talk about the early years. You came to Nashville in 2001.

Yes, and I wrote my first song and took it around.

It was the major hit "Dance on Your Shoes."

It was, and I am so honored that Sherrie Elliot listened to my demo and then recorded that song. I was so young, and it really gave me the boost in confidence I needed.

That song is the best-selling and most downloaded song of the last twenty years. So did Sherrie help you?

She did. I'm sure she opened the doors for me. I had been singing since I was a teenager. My demo also included "Landslide."

The Stevie Nicks classic?

Yes ma'am, the Stevie Nicks song. She had a hit with it twice. Same song, two times. So the label loved my demo. I mean, other people in the industry told me they had never seen the label so excited. Even Sherrie told me that they were excited.

But you didn't know at the time? You didn't know how excited your label was?

No, I was so new to the business, I just figured that's how it worked. So we were all set. They were burning the disks...when the Dixie Chicks released their version of "Landslide."

What happened?

The Chicks had a major hit. I was so happy for them. But my label didn't want to muddy the water. They destroyed the disks. We released the album without "Landslide."

And it sold?

Yes, it sold. It got to thirty-five on the top one hundred albums.

But no singles.

We released "Next of Ken," and I think it got to seventy. But Pier Records believed in me. If we had been a month earlier on "Landslide," things might have been different. So I went on tour. I opened for some big acts. And the reviews were great. So we went back in the studio and recorded *Four- Wheel Girl*.

Let's talk about *Other Side of the Tracks*.

I loved the concept. But it's not my best work.

Why?

I don't know. My producer and I never agreed on anything. I don't know if it was him or me....but we never ever agreed. We're friends now. We still see each other...but we could not work together.

Were you romantically involved?

Yes, just not with each other. He was engaged, and I was seeing someone. Maybe we were both distracted. Pier pushed, and the tracks were shallow. But we've done those songs live, and audiences and critics have said they were great. They aren't that great on the album.

Give me an example.

"Kissed with a Lie." I think a lot of fans don't recognize the song when we do it live. They think it's new.

My guest has been Kolby Rae, and her new album is called *Crossroads*.

Sergeant Jessica Addison quickly scrawled the title on a note and then turned off the truck. Her husband Larry's pickup was gone, so he still wasn't back from his trip to the capital. She wanted to run her idea past him first before she took it to her boss, Sheriff JB Jardine.

Jessica plucked the copy of the tabloid she bought at Royal's Grocery, carried it in the house, and set it on the kitchen table. Later that night she looked over at Larry, who was reading the tabloid as she finished putting away the dishes and walked into the living room.

"I figured you might want to see the article about Kolby Rae. I didn't get a chance to read it, but I saw the headline. She got married."

Larry looked up. "Really? That's some lucky guy. Let me look."

"I heard her on the radio today."

"Who?"

"Kolby Rae. Nice interview. It got me thinking—what if we could invite her to come do that concert fund-raiser at the college that JB is working on? Wouldn't that be great? She'd do a great show, don't you think?"

Larry Addison dropped the tabloid and exclaimed, "You must be joking."

Surprised, Jessica looked back at him. "Okay, I know it's a long shot, but I'm serious."

"No, babe, not you. I mean this. No way. No way."

Larry picked up the tabloid and began to read the article to her.

"'The 36-year-old singer and writer of the daddy–daughter dance wedding song 'Dance on Your Shoes' celebrated nuptials of her own on New Year's Day, marrying Joshua Stone.'"

Jessica stopped moving and listened as Larry read on.

"'Stone, 43, is an author, now retired from Grant's Hill College, where he intervened in a campus shooting, saving the lives of dozens of students. The couple will live near Crossings, Tennessee. On the heels of the surprise single success of 'Right-Hand Rover,' Kolby Rae's new album, *Crossroads*, completed a successful crowdfunding campaign in October and will be released this month.'"

Larry and Jessica Addison stared at each other. He turned the paper around and showed her the photos. Jessica took the paper and looked closer at the photos, saying, "They look so happy."

Jessica sat down. Larry draped his arm around her. "There's your in, babe. Doc knows you. I bet if you call him and ask, she would come sing here." He paused. "Maybe he could even get us backstage passes."

They sat there in the quiet. After a few moments, they turned to each other with confused expressions before murmuring, "Joshua Stone?"

The next morning, Jessica Addison knocked on the door to the sheriff's office in Jefferson in the combined city–county building down the road from Grant's Hill. "JB, Got a minute?"

"Sure, Jesse. I always have time. How're your sisters? How's your dad? He ought to be proud of all three of you girls."

"Dad is, well, you know, Dad. And my sisters are fine. My niece starts at Grant's Hill High next year."

"Oh my word, I remember when you started there, Jesse. The last of the Nystrom girls. I still think of you as Jesse Nystrom."

Jessica nodded and pointed at a chair. "May I sit down?"

JB's politician grin turned to paternal concern. "Jesse, what is it? When my lead sergeant asks, 'May I sit down?,' I know it's trouble. Is it department or family?"

"No, no, nothing like that. JB, it's about the memorial fund-raiser."

"Oh Jesus, that poppycock? Jesse, who's idea was it that I join their board of trustees? Never mind, don't answer that. I know it was my own doing."

Jessica Addison laughed. "I have this idea. What if you could bring a rising country star to perform at Grant's Hill for a concert to kick off the fund-raiser?"

"Well, now, wouldn't that be something? It would bring the town people over, that's for sure. I'm not sure dueling grand pianos is gonna pull the crowd from Mike's Pale Blue Moon Tavern, if you know what I mean."

JB turned around and looked at a stack of music CDs on his desk and plucked out Kolby Rae's *Four-Wheel Girl*. He pointed at the liner notes photo of Kolby Rae as he held up the disk. "Did you see this little lady at the Heartland Benefit Concert?" he asked. "She was wearing the Grant's Hill jacket. If we could bring her to town, now that would be the trick."

Jessica knew she had him. Whenever it was JB's idea, it was always easier to sell him than trying to talk him into an idea of her own. "I know someone who might be able to help us do just that, if I can get him to your meeting on Tuesday."

"Jesse Nystrom, if you can get him to our meeting, and you can get Kolby Rae to perform here, I'll buy you a brand-new patrol car, anything you want."

Addison nodded. Small town politics were great.

Chapter Forty-Three

Safe Room, Now

"HEY, COME TAKE A WALK with me," Joshua said to Kolby as they parked in front of the house after their dinner at the Roadhouse. He jumped out his side and walked around to her door. He opened it, and as she got out, she leaned in.

"Give me a little smooch," she said.

They kissed lightly, and then Joshua took her by the hand. "Come, show me where you want the garden plowed. I was thinking maybe I'd bring Forrest and Rooster down with the skid steer, and they could dig out the sod and maybe fill in some dirt or compost or something."

"Joshua Stone, a skid steer? How big of a garden are you thinking of?" She took off her shoes.

"I don't know, but we might as well do it up right, right?"

Kolby began skipping across the grass, still damp from the rain shower while they were at dinner, and then ran back to the driveway. "Look at me." She began spelling out her name by making footprints on the driveway.

Joshua stopped her. "Come on." He took her hand, and the two of them walked around to the back of the house. Joshua walked an imaginary line straight out from the deck and started pacing steps across the lawn. Kolby looked at him and then glanced back to the deck as she put her shoes back on.

"I was thinking maybe here. It gets full sun."

Kolby looked at the spot in the grass and then back to the sliding glass doors that led from the patio into their kitchen. Something was worrisome and wrong. She saw the frames of the sliding doors knocked free and the sliding panel lying sideways on the patio. The house had been broken into.

"Joshua, break-in. Stop." Then she said their emergency word, "*Gib laut*," crisp and clean.

The first time she heard Joshua say the German command, they laughed about it. She and Joshua had just finished shooting at targets in Crossings's stone quarry when Joshua spoke to Fylgja in German.

"Why do you talk to her in German?"

"Because she's a German shepherd."

She slugged him in the arm.

"Okay, okay, no real reason, I found some commands on a website and figured if I ever need her to be a tough dog, speaking commands in German might be better than in English." Kolby's face was skeptical. "Here, try this one." He whispered in her ear, "*Gib laut.*" She repeated the phrase with a commanding tone, and immediately Fylgja began barking, standing in a guarding position.

"Oh my, that is so amazing. Did you teach her that?"

"Yes. We started when I was out west with Alan. Then when I was at the community college, I worked with Fylgja every day."

Kolby shook her head, partly in disbelief and partly in amazement. The day in the quarry, she wondered what writing a song about Joshua would include. In those early days, he wasn't in the category of lover. He was still an enigma, except that you can't say words like *enigma* in country songs. In retrospect, their conversation showed her a new emotion: he was her protector.

"We should use that word," he said to her.

"What word?" Kolby asked.

"*Gib laut*. In case there is ever a situation, you know, if somebody gets too close to you or you don't feel safe. Or one of us thinks we're in danger. That should be our emergency word."

When Kolby said the words "*Gib laut*" in the dark behind their new house, Joshua reacted without hesitation. Joshua's hand was back on his pistol, and he was running the twenty feet to her side. He stepped between her and the house, and then she pressed up against him, back to back. Her hand came across their hips, and she drew her own pistol. The two stood there, he scanning the house and she watching the yard, motionless.

Joshua whispered, "Oh shit, oh shit."

Kolby echoed. "Double oh shit. I've got your back."

"We're too exposed out here. We need to move, now. We can make the truck, or we can go in."

Kolby pressed harder against his back. "Let's go for the truck."

Then they both said, "Fylgja."

"We have to go in," she told him. "Joshua, we have to."

Kolby felt his arms and shoulders move as he brought his pistol up to a high-ready hold.

"Kolby, do you feel like a two-step?"

"Joshua Stone, this is a hell of a time to ask me to dance."

"I'm not. Just move with me. Come up next to me. We'll walk together, just like a two-step. Slow slow. Quick quick slow."

Kolby shifted to be on his right side, and like a side-by-side two-step, they made their way to the deck, then up the steps, and then across to the outside wall of the kitchen next to the broken patio door. Joshua whispered to Kolby as they came up to the side of the door, "Up against the house, now." They both moved and pressed their backs to the side of the house, Kolby looking to her left, Joshua looking to his right and trying to see inside the door. He dropped his left hand and fished the flashlight from his pocket. He shined it in the room and then quickly switched it off.

"The place has been flipped upside down," he said.

Kolby tipped her head back against the side of the house and then looked his way. "Dwight. Let's call Dwight. He'll know what to do."

Kolby leaned back against the side of the house and dialed the phone. As Joshua peered in the house, Kolby was whispering to herself, "Pick up, pick up, pick up."

A voice interrupted the ringing. "Dwight Evans."

"Dwight? It's Kolby Rae….Joshua and I have had a break-in. What do we do?"

"Kolby, I'll send a team. Are you in or out of the house?"

"We're out. Joshua and I are right outside."

"Kolby, get out. Get in your truck and go to town. Let me send the team in, and I'll call you when the house is secure."

Kolby turned to tell Joshua they were backing down and realized he was gone. "Dwight, Joshua just went inside."

"Kolby, are either of you armed?"

"Yes, we both are."

"Kolby, stop him. Go to your safe room, now. Lock down and stay there."

"Should I call 911?"

"Kolby, this is what we're here for. We'll handle it and investigate. We can file a police report when we're done if we need to. I can have a team there in one hundred and five minutes. You lock down, and you shoot anyone who tries to get in that safe room."

Kolby hung up, took a deep breath, and prepared for the worst.

She began peeking in the door, taking a wider and wider view, until the only part of the room she couldn't see was on the opposite side of the exterior wall. She blew out one long breath, brought her pistol up, moved quickly into the room, and then slumped down against the wall. Her hand touched Joshua as she stopped.

From where they were squatting, they could see the hallway that led to the safe room under the stairwell. Kolby whispered, "Safe room."

Both their eyes were adjusting to the dark. They listened for any sign of Fylgja. Joshua whispered, "Up and two-step, slowly." He stood up and then felt her press her back against his side. They moved, very slowly, across the kitchen and into the hall. Slow slow. Quick quick slow. When they reached the safe room door, Joshua turned and faced it with Kolby on the wall. Joshua motioned at the door. Kolby reached out, grasped the knob, and slowly turned it until the latch was free of the strike plate. She pulled it an inch open and listened, not releasing the knob.

Joshua held his flashlight in his left hand and his raised gun with his right, pointing it at the door opening. Joshua smelled Kolby's perfume mixed with the smell of the gun oil. He blinked in a moment of déjà vu, remembering Jessica Addison and the smells after the shooting. He nodded to Kolby. She pulled the door open, and Joshua lit up the room with the flashlight. They both looked inside: it was empty except for the supplies Dwight insisted they keep there. They quickly moved into the room, shut the door, and then locked the three deadbolts, top, middle, and bottom.

Joshua pulled the light string, and they both blinked as they adjusted their vision. Kolby returned her pistol to her holster, but Joshua kept his gun aligned with the door. She saw the sweat on his brow and a small drip running down the side of his neck. He was focused on what was in front of him.

"Joshua, how could this happen?"

"I don't know. Big house in the country? Maybe they didn't know who we were? This same thing happened to David Adams last year. What did Dwight say?"

"Get to the safe room and wait. He said he would have a team here in a hundred and five minutes."

"God, why does he always talk like that? How long is that?" Both Joshua and Kolby counted.

"Hour and forty five minutes," said Joshua.

"We should call 911" Kolby reached for her phone. There was no signal in the safe room. "No signal. Maybe we should have thought about that."

"What did Dwight say? Anything else?"

"Yes, if anyone comes in the safe room, shoot them."

Joshua didn't say anything back but kept his eyes focused on the door.

Kolby watched for his reply and then asked, "Joshua, this is real, isn't it?"

He nodded.

"Joshua, could you do it, for real?"

She looked at his intensity. She had been beside his every emotion. She had seen him shy, she had watched him be seductive, and she had seen him be protective. He was never comic, but he liked to laugh. He had been amorous, affectionate, and on rare occasion impulsive. She had never seen this side of him. This was focused rage. She had never felt so terrified and invincible in the same moment. She knew it was the wrong time to ask, but the question that had been on her mind since he had first told her about Grant's Hill and all through her reading of *Faith Shattered* came out of her mouth,

"Joshua? Is this what it was like?"

Again, he didn't answer.

"How long did you lie there in pain before that deputy came in and shot him?"

Joshua was breathing heavily, almost as loud as a snore, as if he didn't hear any of her words. She asked one more question.

"Was it the lady sheriff who saved you? Sergeant Jessica?"

Joshua nodded. "We did what we had to do."

Near the end of the hundred and five minutes, they heard footsteps in the hall. Joshua raised the gun level with a cold-focused stare.

"Is it them?" Kolby asked. "How will we know?"

"We don't." Joshua kept his pistol aimed at the door.

A voice from the other side of the door spoke the code names they both resisted and disliked from the New Year's concert and wedding. "Kingston, Jamaica. All clear. Dwight sent us."

Kolby and Joshua looked at each other. They both let out a sigh and then hugged. Kolby tried to hold back the tears until she realized she felt subtle sobs from Joshua as they both trembled in the safe room. When they let go, Joshua rubbed his eyes with his shirtsleeve, and Kolby dabbed the corner of her eye, trying not to smear her mascara further.

Joshua said, "I don't get it. When he says those code names, they sound cool. When I say them, they sound dorky."

Kolby snickered. With that, they opened the three deadbolts and were greeted by a bald man in a black suit holding a tactical rifle. They both recognized him from the New Year's party and the wedding.

"You came alone?" Joshua asked.

"Negative." The bald man turned and let the two walk toward the front of the house. At the front door stood a woman, also wearing a dark suit and also holding a rifle. Through the front door, Kolby saw the driveway: two vans' headlights illuminated the front of the house. As they walked out the front door, they saw men at each corner, and then as they turned around, four more men were walking down the stairs,

"The house is clear," reported one of the men descending the stairs.

Joshua turned to the man in the suit. "Did you find our dog?"

"Negative."

Joshua turned, and Kolby saw the shaking in his shoulders. It made her cry at the same time that they had lost Fylgja. Joshua turned around and looked at Kolby, then the Flanigan men, "Did you check the garage?"

"The house is clear. The grounds are clear. The dog is gone."

Joshua threw his hands in the air, walking past them all and out across the grass in the dark, calling Fylgja as he went. The security detail looked at Kolby.

"We're fine," she said. "Get Dwight Evans here."

CHAPTER FORTY-FOUR

DETAILS

JOSHUA CRACKED A BOURBON BOTTLE, the same brand as they drank the night of their engagement, and looked at Kolby with a sheepish smirk. Kolby glared back with a half smile as if to say, "Joshua Stone, you don't say one word."

He understood the look and began to pour two very small, very neat glasses and handed one to her. She tossed the shot back and handed him the empty glass. There was a knock at the front door before both Dwight Evans and Sarah walked in.

Sarah quickly crossed the hardwood floor, her boot heels tapping the entire distance. Dwight gestured with some fingers to his team leader, the tall bald man who had met Kolby and Joshua outside the safe room.

"Oh my God, are you okay?" asked Sarah. "What happened? Are you hurt? Is Joshua hurt?" She was embracing Kolby and turned to her right to look Joshua up and down.

"I'm fine. We're both fine," Joshua answered. "Fylgja is missing."

"No, no way. She'll be back. She couldn't have gone far."

Kolby began to loosen her hug when Sarah hugged her tighter one more time, then stepped back.

Behind Sarah, two college-age women in dressy pants and blouses were talking on cell phones. "Who are they?" Joshua asked.

Sarah nodded. "They're with me. We've ramped up the media team. Don't worry; none of this is going on the web. We were in a meeting when Dwight called."

Dwight came closer and suggested they all sit down. The group arranged a few chairs and then he began speaking.

"Here's what I know, and then you tell me what you know." He paused and made eye contact with each of them as they sat in the chairs. "We've had forced entry through the rear slider door. We want to get that fixed and change out the way it locks. The kitchen looks like there was a scuffle. You'll want to tell me if anything is missing. The upstairs bedrooms are fine. The bedroom in the east wing has been tossed pretty good. The laptop is disconnected from all the cables, and there is blood on the floor. It looks like whoever was there was interrupted and hurt."

Joshua turned to Kolby. "This isn't my place to say, but I'm not sure we want the whole team here for this part of the conversation."

Sarah and Kolby exchanged looks, and Sarah agreed. "Can you two work out of my truck for a bit? We need to talk some business here." The women left.

Joshua turned to Dwight. "Is it human or dog blood?"

"I don't know. There's a bit of the blood trail down the stairs and out the back door. Not a lot. One or both of them were bleeding."

"So she could be out there, hurt?"

"Could be. It's too tough to search in the dark. We'll do it if you ask us."

Joshua looked at Kolby. She nodded, and he turned back to Dwight. "No, I looked for her. Not tonight. We'll look in the morning. If she's hurt, she'll hunker down or come back here. Do you think I should look around upstairs?"

"If you'd like. If you have a big financial loss, the insurance company will want a police report. If we can avoid that, it's better."

Sarah nodded in agreement.

Joshua walked up the stairs. Kolby's music room was undisturbed, the door unopened. He peeked in and then shut the door again. He continued down the hall to the bedroom office. His office had been tossed. Papers were everywhere, drawers were open, and his laptop was partly open, upside down, on the floor. His collection of bobbleheads was scattered across the shelves and the floor.

Joshua thought back to his conversation with David Adams and David's concern about losing the pink envelope. David had said, "I could never excuse myself if someone else, this Toomey character or some petty thief, ended up with it."

Joshua went to the desk drawer and looked for the envelope. When he didn't find it, he opened another drawer and then another. He felt the panic rising in his throat, and he turned and looked at the books on the shelf. He found *One Good Bread Pudding* and opened it; the envelope was not at the back pages. He looked through the other books, dumping them on the floor and then looked at the next shelf. There was a stack of journals and notebooks. He began opening them one by one.

Nothing.

Nothing.

Nothing.

Joshua saw his desk calendar still on last month, and near the back page, he found the pink envelope. "Enough," he said and quickly turned it to rip open the side. Then he stopped himself. His heart pounding, he hesitated, then walked across the hall and into his and Kolby's bedroom. Joshua opened the top drawer of the dresser and pushed his underwear and socks aside, slid the envelope underneath, and closed the drawer. He walked back downstairs.

"I don't see anything missing. Just a big mess to clean up." Joshua faced Kolby. "They didn't go into your music room."

He stood at her side. She reached up, took his hand, and lightly kissed the scar on the back of his left hand.

"Fylgja must have heard the noise in my office and interrupted them," said Joshua.

Dwight began speaking. "Kolby, you and Joshua are the client. We respond to your requests, but Sarah and I feel we need to make some changes."

Kolby looked at Sarah, then Dwight, then back to Sarah, and then up at Joshua. Joshua was pacing, looking out the window and then back up the stairs.

"Joshua, please sit. We need to do this together," Kolby said.

Sarah began speaking. "Kolby, we're bigger now than we've ever been. I think we need to think about some options."

"What kind of options? I am not going to have bodyguards hanging around me all day and all night."

Dwight interjected, "We don't want to interfere in your life. We're not going to give you a full detail all the time. Sarah and I have discussed a low-profile team here at the house, at the gate. Out of your way, out of your life. But they keep the curious and the unwanted out and can be here in seconds if you have a problem in the house.

"Next, public appearances. When the two of you appear in public, we want a detail with you on the way in and to get you out."

Joshua interrupted. "What? Like going to dinner? Movies? Eating at my restaurant?"

"No, not yet, but if you go to a public event, like a concert together, or you go to an awards show, we do a plan. We're with you; we escort you in, and we escort you out."

"And every performance," Sarah interjected.

Kolby considered the options and then told Dwight, "Okay, you win. One bodyguard can hang out with me."

Dwight looked at Sarah and back at Kolby. "Kolby, Joshua, if I gave you one man, I would be putting you at more risk and risking my man. We don't work that way. You need a detail, and a trained detail. My teams are the very best there is."

Dwight moved to the sofa next to Sarah and sat down.

"Let me just tell you about one of my clients. We have a certain Nashville star who is a lovely lady, well mannered, enjoyable at parties. She posted an offhand comment on social media about not being able to sit at the same table with people who didn't eat meat. Well, someone took it the wrong way, and as she was on her way into a restaurant, this nut job jumps from the parking lot and tosses a mason jar full of cow's blood at her."

Sarah, Kolby, and Joshua all cringed. Sarah asked, "How long ago was this?"

Dwight turned to look at her. "Let's just say within the last six months."

"We haven't been out of the loop that much. We would have heard about it," Kolby said.

"Yes, you would have if she had been alone or had only had one bodyguard." Evans's voice inflection showed his dislike of the word *bodyguard*. "She had our detail with her. One of my people was covered in blood. Two of my people took down the attacker and got him out of sight. The star got a tiny bit of blood on her outfit. Because we had a plan, my client had a change of clothes and was able to switch shirts before she entered the restaurant. You didn't hear about it because we didn't want anyone to hear about it. That's what my team does."

Kolby spoke. "Wait, I know who you mean. You're talking about Sherrie Elliot. Sherrie said that thing as a joke. I remember laughing at it when I read it on my phone." Kolby paused. "No, wait a minute. It can't be Sherrie. I've seen too many photos of her to know that if she had a bunch of your guys around her, I would have seen them."

Sarah pulled out her tablet and did a web search for Sherrie Elliot photos. The search results displayed some preconcert shots, some CMA Awards shots, some ACM Awards shots. Sarah looked at some of the wider views, ones that included other people from her entourage.

Sarah handed the tablet to Kolby. Kolby looked at three photos and then looked up at Flanigan's detail in her living room. Two of the Flanigan team in her home were in the photos with Sherrie Elliot.

Kolby giggled. "Oh my God." She looked at the woman holding a rifle discreetly at her side. "And I thought you were her makeup artist."

The woman cocked her head, then nodded.

"Only a few of our celebrity clients are at high risk. There are some very, very disturbed people who want to kill someone famous. But most celebrities truly underestimate the number of people who want to use them or harm them to promote their own cause. We don't want you covered in blood or feces or hurtful words or a pie in the face."

"Seriously, a pie in the face?" Joshua asked.

"Yep. Two CEOs within months of each other." Dwight paused again and looked around the room, making eye contact with all. "One more thing. When you are part of our detail, I need to ask both of you not to carry your firearms."

Joshua became defensive. "Dwight, what happened to every day?"

"Rule change: when you are on your own, if you feel the need, carry. But when you are in our charge, an extra firearm is a risk to my team and to you."

One of the men from the back of the house came forward and whispered into Dwight's ear. "Will you excuse me?" asked Dwight. "I need to take a call. Why don't the three of you talk about this, and I'll be back in a bit?"

Kolby said, "My fans will hate this. I'll hate this."

Sarah clicked her pen cap and set it on the low table in front of them. "Kolby, your fans already think you have bodyguards. They expect it. Until we announced you were marrying Joshua, most of them thought he was your bodyguard. It's not just you. Joshua, too, has his own following, good and bad. He's more of a public figure every day. There are lots of people who are still curious about Grant's Hill and what went on there."

Kolby looked at Joshua and said, "Yes, there are."

Dwight returned with a confident expression. "The county sheriff is investigating a report of a dog bite, worried they had a victim, and wouldn't you know it? Their victim had three outstanding warrants for breaking and entering and burglary. They impounded his van in the hospital parking lot with a virtual used electronics shop in the back. It looks like the dog who bit him had a pretty good time based on what they told me on the phone."

Joshua beamed for a moment; then his eyes searched the room and down again. Kolby touched his hand, and he nodded.

Evans continued. "This is my job, what I do for a living. I provide advice. I don't tell you to change your life. Here's what the guy with the dog bites told the police. When he's not breaking into houses, he likes country music. He follows Kolby on social media. She posted a photo of your new house a while back. He searched public records online for Joshua's name in real estate transactions and got the address, and tonight, you posted you were going out to dinner. He figured it was a quick score. He said to be sure to tell you nothing personal; he's a huge fan."

Joshua, Kolby, and Sarah each exchanged looks.

"The stakes are higher now. You need to consider that as you make your decisions," said Dwight.

It was like a silent auction, a secret vote. Kolby and Joshua looked at Sarah, and she nodded. The two women looked at Joshua, and Joshua shook his head. Then Joshua and Sarah looked at Kolby. Kolby wanted nothing like this in her life, and she hated that Sarah and Joshua disagreed.

Kolby felt a burn in the skin on her chest. Her mind raced back to the feeling of falling from the bumper of her daddy's truck. Even though he was so close, Daddy couldn't protect her then. And she thought about Joshua, so strong yet gunned down at the college. And Sherrie Elliot, the least of the three but still terrifying.

"Mr. Evans, you are hired," said Kolby. "We'll accept having a team here at the gate and with us for public appearances."

"My team is already at your gate. We have a full profile and plan in place. Sarah has given us your schedule of appearances. You both did the right thing tonight. You handled the break-in well, and we'll start a search for your dog in the morning."

They shook hands. Sarah hugged Kolby, then Joshua. Sarah turned as she walked to the door, extending her pinkie finger in the air. Kolby raised her hand and extended her pinkie finger, too, and then Sarah closed the front door behind herself. The house fell silent.

Joshua poured another shot in both of their glasses, and they sat on the deck chairs, looking out over the future garden. "I still want to make you a garden," he said.

Kolby turned and looked at Joshua. "That's fine, but I want you to tell me what's on your mind. Fylgja will come home. She just got scared, I bet. She thinks she's in trouble for biting."

Joshua replied with a hollow-sounding, "Don't worry. It's just a silly dog."

Kolby knew the tone in his voice. She felt his pain. She knew it wasn't just Fylgja but his whole past. He was rubbing his arm, and his tongue was moving across his teeth.

"Will you ever tell me about it?" she asked.

"About what?"

"About Grant's Hill that day…when you got this…and this?" She touched his cheek first and then his hand.

Joshua rolled his head down and back and forth. "I can't talk about it. But this"—he pointed at his cheek—"happened long before this," and he pointed at his hand.

Joshua shifted his body as if he were about to tell her a story when the sound of dog paws on the back deck alerted them. Fylgja, her mouth covered in blood, came to them, holding a piece of fabric with the pride of a retriever.

"Fylgja, *aus*," commanded Joshua, and the dog dropped a piece of denim.

Kolby rushed to the kitchen and grabbed a pan, then filled it with water and got a dishtowel. She came back out. Joshua was stroking Fylgja. The two of them took turns petting the dog and wiping her face clean, taking the mud from her fur and pulling the cockleburs from her hair.

They left the office and kitchen cleanup until morning and walked to their bedroom. Kolby was surprised that Joshua fell asleep so quickly after they made love. She lay there in the dark, listening to him breathe and then hearing Fylgja breathe, too. Joshua twitched. Kolby anticipated what was next. She wanted to hold him but knew that sometimes he startled and sat straight up. She resisted every urge in her body to cuddle him close and inched away.

"No."

That was the first thing he said.

"No, get down. Everyone down."

She expected the scream would come next, and instead, he said a woman's name.

"Jessica? Jessica."

Then he sat up and yelled it. "Jessica!"

"Joshua, it's okay. It's me," Kolby said.

Joshua opened his eyes and appeared to look straight through Kolby. He wiped his mouth, lay back down, and in moments was breathing in a deep sleep.

CHAPTER FORTY-FIVE

VOICE FROM THE PAST

JOSHUA ALMOST LET THE CALL from an unfamiliar number go to voice mail, but he recognized the area code from Grant's Hill. He didn't identify the familiar woman's voice on the other end of the call.

"Is this Joshua Stone?"

"Who's calling, please?"

"Doc? Hi, it's Jessica."

There was a long silence.

The woman continued, "Jessica Addison? Sergeant Addison?"

Joshua's memory connected the voice. "Sergeant — Jessica. Yes, hi. Wow, how did you get this number?"

"It hasn't been easy finding you. I had to ask around. No one seemed willing to share, but since I met that Dr. David Adams when he interviewed me for his book, I figured he owed me a favor."

"Ah, David. Did you read the book?"

"Yeah. He's kinda full of himself, isn't he?"

Joshua almost spilled the coffee cup in his hand. "Wow, that wasn't the review I expected."

"Well, you know me…" A beeping alarm sounded through the phone. "Doc, I need to go. Can I call you back?"

"Sure, sure, Jessica. Please do. Good to hear from you."

Joshua set the phone down on the kitchen table. It rang again about an hour later.

"Hi, it's Jessica again. Sorry about that. They have us running speed traps."

Joshua grinned. "Speed traps in Grant's Hill? A crime wave?"

Addison replied in her straightforward way, "Ever since the shooting, we've had a steady stream of looky-loos and curious tourists. We've had to double our daytime patrol deputies, and we have no budget, so we set up a speed trap. But the overtime is awesome. I was able to help get Larry that new truck he wanted. We think of it as the admission price to the circus. We only tag the out-of-towners."

Joshua reflected on the advantages of being a local.

"Well, what do you know?" he asked, trying to make conversation and find out why she had called him.

"I know that somebody got married."

Joshua smiled with a pride she couldn't see but heard in his voice. "Yes, I did. Can you believe it? How did you hear?"

"Doc, are you still a college boy? We have newspapers and magazines in Grant's Hill, and there's this thing called the Internet. You should check it out sometime."

"Okay, okay. I'm just not used to all this celebrity stuff. I hoped after, well, you know, I figured we would all go back to the way it was."

There was a short silence.

"Doc, I was wondering."

"What is this?" Joshua replied. "I get married and suddenly I'm back to 'Doc'? Eh, Sergeant?"

"Josh. I need a huge favor. It's asking a lot, but I have to ask."

"Jessica, what do you need?"

"I want you to come back to Grant's Hill."

The words hit Joshua like the slap from a jilted lover.

"Come back?"

"Josh, things have changed here. Guess who's on the board of the college? JB."

Joshua had met Sheriff JB Jardine once, following the shooting. He was a prominent and well-liked sheriff-politician.

"I'm not surprised."

"The town, the school, everyone is ready to move on. Have you seen what they want to do with the campus chapel?"

"No."

"The school wants to tear it down and rebuild it as a Center for Nonviolence. Sort of a modern glass and stone kind of thing. So they want to have a combination memorial for the shooting victims and fund-raiser event for alumni and donors and to show we're moving on."

Joshua nodded, then remembered he was on the phone. "Uh-huh, go on."

"Joshua, there is something that would really help bring the college and town together, and you're the one who can do it."

Joshua felt a slight rush of embarrassment. "Jessica, thanks for the vote of confidence, but I've seen my book sales. I'm not sure I'm the speaker you're looking for."

Addison laughed. "You've grown a sense of humor. I like that. Not you. Kolby Rae. Joshua, I want you to come talk to the board, tell them that Kolby Rae will perform, that she'll headline the night."

Joshua was half disappointed and half relieved. "Jessica, you know, I'm not really in that part of Kolby's life. She has a manager and this whole team. I mean, she has"—he paused with a stark realization—"she has people."

"Joshua, you're newlyweds. She'll do anything you ask her to do. Trust me, ask Larry…who, by the way, is her biggest fan ever."

"Can I think about this? Can I call you back?"

"Sure. But Joshua, the meeting is Tuesday. Don't think too long. How's Fylgja?"

"She's great. She's kind of adopted Kolby over me."

"Good. So call me. I can tell you the details."

Joshua set the phone back down.

He went upstairs to his office. After the break-in, they had repainted and put in new carpet. Kolby had bought him a leather chair, nicer than he would have ever bought himself. He had told her it was too much, but every time he sat in it, he admitted it felt really good. He flipped open the laptop and waited for the machine to boot. While he waited, he flipped the cap on one of the closest bobbleheads to him. He smirked, thinking not every wife would tolerate them.

When the screen came to life, the computer web browser defaulted to the Grant's Hill College webpage. "Old habits," he said out loud. The front page displayed an architect's rendering of a new Eastford Chapel with an inset photo of President Matthew Rose. Joshua clicked the link to the press release and skimmed the contents and a quotation from President Rose. "Now that the rest of the world has forgotten, it's time for us to remember." He skimmed the rest of the page and came to a yearbook photo of Liv Olsson.

Joshua slammed the screen closed. He stood up and walked to the window. Kolby was outside, digging in the garden. He banged on the windowpane.

Kolby, wiping some sweat from her brow, turned, looked up, and waved at him. He waved back and then walked to the desk drawer and fished through the contents. He didn't find the envelope and then remembered he had hidden it again. He crossed the hall into their bedroom. Joshua opened his drawer, moved the socks and under-wear, and at the bottom found the pink envelope. He sat on the edge of the bed, stuck his finger underneath the flap, and then stopped. He turned the envelope back over, looked at his own name, and then set it back in the drawer. He closed it most of the way shut. The tip of a sock blocked the drawer from closing completely.

Joshua walked back to the computer, opened it, closed the browser, and switched to his e-mail. The counter raced through dozens of num-bers until it stopped counting at 143 new messages. Joshua skimmed the list. Toomey had e-mailed several times. Several Nigerian bankers needed his help returning $90,000,000 to their rightful heir. The rest were copies of follow and friend requests from complete strangers on social media, most after news of his wedding to Kolby. He sighed, shut off the computer, and walked down and out to the garden.

"I'm going into Crossings," he said to Kolby. "I thought I'd stop and see Drew, see how the plans are for the new church."

"Hey, that's great. What about my kiss?"

Joshua wrapped his arms around her, his hands placed lightly on her hips. After their kiss, he gave her a huge hug.

"Wow, that was nice. What did I do?"

"Nothing. Just want you to know how I feel."

Kolby watched him walk to the drive, climb in the Rover, and drive toward the gate. She heard him tap his horn at the Flanigan team parked at the end of the drive. She took it as a sign he was getting used to them being there.

Kolby looked at the row of plants in the garden. "Oh my Lord, if this stuff all grows, who's gonna cook all this food?"

She looked back at the driveway and walked into the house to take a shower. As she crossed the bedroom, Kolby saw Joshua's drawer open and blocked by the sock. She shook her head. She opened the drawer, tucked in the errant sock, and felt the envelope with her fingers. She stopped, pulled it out, and flipped it over to the face. Another pink envelope with his name on it, written in the same woman's handwriting.

Kolby's heart fell. She flipped it over, slid her finger in the flap, and then stopped herself. She sat on the bed in the same wrinkles in the bedspread Joshua had made as he looked at the envelope. She couldn't bring herself to open it and instead put the envelope back in the drawer and closed it firmly.

Kolby walked into the shower, turned on the water, got undressed, and began to sob. The water sprayed on her back, and she slowly let herself slink to the shower floor. She lay there sobbing until the hot water was gone and the chill of the spray matched the chill around her heart. She got out, dried herself off, and called to Fylgja. The two of them loaded into KRAEZY and drove off. She honked and waved at the Flanigan team and then punched the accelerator. As she blew past the *Watch Your Speed* sign with the built-in speed sensor, the LEDs lit up and blinked 99.

Joshua came back just before 6:00 and began making dinner for the two of them. He looked over at the phone and then looked at the pasta boiling in the pot. He had sliced the veggies and made a white garlic and cream sauce. He looked at the timer and his watch. Seven minutes.

He picked up the phone and pressed redial. The phone rang twice; then a woman answered.

"Jessica Addison."

"Jessica, hi. It's Joshua."

"Hi, Josh. Hey, say hello to Larry."

Joshua heard a "Hey, Josh" from a distance. "We're in his truck. We're goin' to the movies. What are you doing?"

"Don't laugh. I'm making dinner."

"God, she has you trained good. Larry, he's cooking dinner for the two of them."

Joshua heard Larry say something about dessert and then laugh.

"Larry Addison, you cut that out," said Jessica. "You didn't hear that, did you?"

Joshua said, "No, not really," and then drew a breath. "Okay, I'm in. When and where is the meeting?"

"Really? Great, well done, good decision. Okay, it's during their board retreat. It's out at the president's compound. They meet at eleven o'clock and then have a lunch. Can you be there at eleven?"

Joshua made a mental note. "I'm there. Eleven o'clock in Grant's Hill on Tuesday. I'll come in the day before, probably late in the afternoon."

"Are you still on that bicycle? You may want to leave soon."

"No, no, I learned to drive. Wait until you see my truck. It's an old Range Rover with right-hand drive. David Adams let me use it. Hey, have a nice time at the movies."

"Thanks, Josh."

He hung up and set the phone down. He turned around just as Fylgja and Kolby came through the door.

"Dinner smells good. How was Pastor Drew?"

"He's good."

Joshua served up two plates and asked Kolby to get the salad from the refrigerator. "Just think," he said. "In a few weeks, everything in this salad will come from your garden."

"I'm so excited," Kolby replied.

He nodded at her and began to eat. She stared at him until he looked up. "What? Is something wrong? Too much garlic?"

"No, it's fine. Joshua, do you think we should pray?"

"We do."

"No, I mean at meals, when we're together. Did your mom and dad say grace?"

Joshua set down his fork. "Yeah, I guess we did. I haven't thought about it."

"Every meal, or just like holidays and stuff?"

"I guess my dad did at every dinner, not as much at breakfast or lunch, but my dad always said the prayer at dinner."

"What was it? Will you say it for our dinner?"

"What, now? I mean, yes, I know now we're eating, but now? On the spot?"

She looked at him.

Joshua reached his hand across the table and took her hand in his. He winked at her. "Lord, thank You for this meal. While we're reminded these gifts ease our hunger, let us not lose sight of our larger hunger and the reasons we love each other and You. We give thanks in Your name. Amen."

"I like your father's prayer."

The candle flickered, and they talked and laughed into the night. When the taper was no more than a puddle of wax on the small plate, Joshua and Kolby washed the dishes and then went up to their bedroom.

Joshua was brushing his teeth when she called to him from the bed. "Hey, isn't it that time of the month?"

Joshua laughed. "Oh yeah, it is. I've got a new number."

"What is it?

Joshua wiped his mouth. "I don't remember. The phone's downstairs. Hit the menu. You can see what the number is."

Kolby walked down, flipped on the light in the kitchen, and crossed the cool floor. She was smiling and began singing.

:: You could have slapped me with the truth ::

:: But you kissed me with a lie ::

:: You could have been a real man ::

:: But instead you gave that smile ::

:: You could have slapped me with the truth ::

:: But you kissed me ::

:: You kissed me with a lie ::

Kolby picked up the phone and tapped the screen. She hunted for the menu to display the phone's number and instead displayed the call history. Three calls, two incoming and one outgoing. The last one was right before dinner. The same number. She felt the same chill as when she had picked up the pink envelope. She sat down and tried to remember Joshua across the table from her. He was sincere, so open. She didn't want to believe Toomey. She shook it off and walked back up the stairs to bed.

Chapter Forty-Six

Reunions

JOSHUA CHECKED HIS SPEED AS he came over the crest of the hill before entering Grant's Hill. He was driving thirty-seven, and the speed limit was forty-five. He looked up at the road ahead and heard the abbreviated whoop of a police siren. Fylgja raised her head and turned. *Whoop-whoop.* And a buzz. Joshua looked in the side-view mirror to see the Ford with blue and red lights. He pulled over to let the sheriff pass by, and the deputy's Ford pulled in close behind him. Joshua put the truck in neutral and set the brake. He watched in the mirror as the deputy got out of the Ford and walked to the back of the Rover. The deputy placed his hand on the taillight, and then he walked to the right side where Joshua was seated. Joshua looked up and recognized Deputy Bill Simmons.

"Simmons, hi. It's me, Joshua Stone. What do you think of this truck?"

Simmons did not acknowledge or change his demeanor. "Do you know your license plates are expired?"

Joshua suddenly realized he'd never asked David Adams about license plates or registration. Joshua said, "Simmons, sorry, this isn't my truck. It belongs to one of the professors at Grant's Hill. I had no idea the plates were expired. Can you give me a warning, and I can get them taken care of when I get back to Tennessee?"

"What about the dog? Can I see the dog license?"

"What? Dog license?" Joshua thought, *No kidding, things have changed in Grant's Hill.*

"Doctor Stone, I am not here to play around today. We've had some complaints in town about dogs. But we've got it from the top—check every dog; get 'em licensed or write a citation and impound the dog."

Joshua was partially stunned and partially amused by the absurdity of the rule. "Simmons, look, I'm leaving town tomorrow. I'm not moving back. I'll register Fylgja if I do move back, I promise. But seriously, impound the dog?"

"Doc, look, everyone has a job to do, and I don't feel like second guessing. Just do us both a favor—do as I say, and we can both get back to our lives."

Joshua tossed his hands in the air. "Fine. What do I need to do?"

Simmons pointed at the car. "I can't give you the license. You need to do it at the office. Since your plates are expired, I can't let you drive in town. You need to leave it here. Rules are rules."

Joshua shook his head and called, "Fylgja, car." The dog got up and out of the Rover and walked to the door of Simmons's patrol unit. Simmons unlocked the electric locks, and Joshua opened the back door. Fylgja jumped in.

"Doc, you can ride up front with me."

Seeing Simmons and being in Grant's Hill brought Joshua back to his past. He thought about his victim's group and how they worked on deep breathing to manage stress. He took two deep breaths and then opened the passenger door of the black and white Ford. As they turned down the street toward the sheriff's office, Simmons didn't stop and passed by the parking slots in front of the building reserved for patrol cars.

"Doc, I need to take care of a deal up here at Mike's Pale Blue Moon Tavern. It will take just a second."

Joshua drew two more breaths. *Slow, deep, cleansing breaths*, he repeated in his head.

Simmons stopped the car. As he got out, he turned to Joshua. "Hey, do you mind giving me a hand? This way I won't have to make two trips."

Joshua got out, wondering if they were picking up beer for a stag party and if he could be charged with contributing to the delinquency of a sheriff's officer. Simmons held the door open, and Joshua walked inside.

"One, two, three, surprise!" came the shouts from a small group of people in the barroom. Joshua's eyes adjusted from the sunlight to the neon glow of Mike's Pale Blue Moon.

Standing at the bar were Mike Moon, Laura Hampton, Tina Rogers, and Sergeant Jessica Addison, all of them reunited from the tactical pistol class Joshua had taken with Dwight Evans. All of them had proud, happy smiles on their faces. Joshua put his left hand to his chest and then pulled it down. He hid the bullet wound scar by putting the hand in his jacket pocket.

Mike Moon popped a beer bottle under the opener stuck to the back wall of the bar. The beer fizzed to a head as he handed the bottle to Addison, who handed it to Joshua. The others had their own drinks, and Mike spoke first.

"Josh, I ain't much at making speeches, but now that you're not a teacher, I guess it don't matter." They all laughed. "Josh, er, ah, Doc, well, Josh. We just want to say thank you for what you did, warning those kids and all made a hell of a difference that day." Joshua looked directly at Addison, and she just looked back with an unchanged expression. "And congratulations on your wedding. That is so great."

Laura Hampton looked over at Tina before she spoke. "Josh, we all chipped in and got you a little something," Laura said. Tina reached behind her and pulled out a brightly decorated box.

Joshua looked around. Simmons was grinning with a smug face. "So I guess I don't need a license for my dog?"

Everyone laughed. Addison piped up. "Is that what you told him?"

Joshua took the box and set it on the table. When he opened it, there were two champagne glasses, engraved with JOSHUA AND KOLBY RAE STONE.

"Wow. I don't know what to say."

"You don't have to say anything, Doc. We're here to say it for you. Congratulations."

"So are you staying at your house?"

"No, I rented it to a temporary faculty member at the college. I'm hoping she buys the place, but so far, she's strictly semester to semester."

"So you need a place to crash?" Mike asked.

"No, I've got a room over at the motel."

"What time is your meeting tomorrow?"

Joshua looked at Addison and said, "Eleven o'clock? Out at the president's compound?"

Addison nodded.

"Hey, I ran into an old friend of ours," Joshua told them.

"Really? So did we," Mike replied. "You go first."

"I ran into Dwight Evans."

"Dwight Evans? The tactical firearms instructor? Okay, did you take another class?" Jessica asked.

Joshua suddenly became self-conscious about what he was going to say. "I, uh, okay, this is really, really odd, but…his company, remember he told us about what they do?"

The others nodded. Tina said, "Security or protection or something?"

"Yeah, well, he talked us into a protective detail for Kolby and me — well, Kolby mostly. But yeah."

Laura turned her head. "What's that like?"

"Well, they're good, really good, at what they do. So we have a detail at the gate to our house, and then when Kolby does appearances and shows, there's a detail with her…well, us."

Joshua turned. "So who's the other old friend?"

"That writer guy, did he ever get in touch with you?" Mike asked,

"Who, David Adams?"

"No, that other one, Jeffrey Toomey."

Joshua bristled and then exhaled. "No. He tries, but I don't take his calls."

Mike laughed. "He's a decent tipper."

"What do you mean?"

"The first time was last summer. He came in. He was clearly out of place, and he asked if I knew you."

"What did you tell him?"

"I said, 'Sure, he comes in every night.'"

Joshua looked at Mike. "Mike, no offense — I never meant anything by this, but I've never been in your bar until today. I guess I owe you an apology. I'm really sorry."

"Doc, don't worry. It's not your thing. Even though I know you haven't been in here, this guy Toomey didn't know. So I kept him here for four nights, saying you were coming in. I think he drank about two hundred dollars' worth of booze."

The others laughed.

"Toomey called me," Jessica began. "I returned his call, and he asked about me and you and the shooting, and I told him I would talk to my lawyer and the union rep, and they would call his lawyer and see what we could work out. I never heard from him again." Jessica looked at Joshua. Simmons's very odd smirk returned to his face. Jessica looked at Simmons and then at Joshua. "Simmons, tell him."

"No, I'd better not."

"C'mon, you don't have anything to be ashamed of. Tell him," said Jessica.

"Doc, I was running radar, and this guy Toomey blew through at forty-six mph."

"And the speed limit is?"

Simmons whispered, "Forty-five." Mike laughed loudly. "So I start writing his ticket, and he sees my name tag and starts asking me questions. So clearly, I become suspicious that he's under the influence, so I ask him to step out and comply with my lawful order for a field sobriety test."

Tina was smirking behind her raised glass.

"That took forty-five minutes, and then I performed a vehicle road-worthiness inspection. That took another thirty minutes. Did you know his license plate was crooked? Then I thought I smelled something suspicious, so I called for a state patrol drug dog, and that took almost an hour."

Joshua snickered as Simmons told the story. Toomey wasn't getting the chamber of commerce introduction to Grant's Hill.

The group of them talked for nearly an hour before the party wound down and Mike's regular night crowd began coming in, eyeing the two deputies sipping colas at the bar. Simmons offered to drive Joshua back to his Rover.

"What about the license plates?" asked Joshua.

"Don't worry. Just get it figured out before some other agency stops you."

Simmons dropped Joshua and Fylgja at the Rover, waved, and

drove off. Joshua looked around and drove to the Grant's Hill Motel.

The next morning, Joshua showered and ate breakfast in the motel restaurant. He sent a text to Kolby.

<Joshua> Good morning. How's Austin?

<KolbyRae> OMG, Joshua Stone, who gets up this early? These people never stop. I'll send you pictures from the photo shoot.

Before Kolby, Sarah, and the Flanigan team flew to Austin, Kolby told Joshua about Austin's murals and the idea to pose in front of as many as possible. His phone lit up again, and the photo she sent had her standing into front of the Austin Postcard mural, her arms outstretched above her head pointing to the words *Greetings From*.

Joshua looked again. Her denim dress was pulled high on her legs. It made him smile and filled his mind with ideas of what they should be doing together in his motel room rather than 419 miles apart.

Joshua left Fylgja in the motel and drove out of Grant's Hill north toward the president's compound. He passed the spot on the side of the road where he had found Rex, his black dog, and thought back to the night he rescued him. He turned toward the house and parked the Rover alongside the other cars in the circle lane.

Joshua walked up the steps, remembering the times he had attended parties and functions as a guest of President Matthew Rose. Mrs. Rose greeted Joshua at the door and then led him to the formal dining room where Joshua opened the door. The assembled board of trustees and a few faculty members were seated around the table. There were no smiles, no congratulatory welcomes, no visible reaction at all except a warm smile from President Rose.

"Dr. Stone, welcome home to Grant's Hill. I hope you had a pleasant trip."

Joshua looked around the room. Everyone made eye contact, nodded, and then looked down at their agenda.

Sheriff JB Jardine began after being given the nod by President Rose. "I want to thank the members of the board for allowing me to move this agenda item early in our meeting. I know we've often had this conversation about finding a way to close the gown and town gap here at Grant's Hill. I think I've got an idea that might help us do that and do a couple of other things. President Rose has given us a challenge to raise the money to make a Center for Nonviolence and to rebuild Eastman Chapel."

"Eastford, Sheriff."

"What? Yes, East*ford* Chapel. Yes. Well, everyone likes their own kind of music, but it occurs to me that country music might be one way to bring the town over to the college. As most of you know there's a little lady who wore a Grant's Hill varsity jacket this fall on the Heartland Benefit Concert, and let me tell you what, that has truly helped our image."

Joshua looked with surprise as several of the oldest board members nodded in agreement. The murmurs included the names of a couple of Kolby's songs. JB turned on his political charm and rested a hand on Joshua's shoulder.

"This man is our hero, Dr. Joshua Stone. What he did that day before my deputies came and put an end to the shooting is the truest definition of heroic."

JB double-checked the room to be sure they were still with him before he continued. When he saw they were looking his way and nodding, he went for the close.

"Dr. Stone is a newlywed, and if you don't know, his wife is none other than Kolby Rae."

There was a pause and then a spontaneous burst of applause and grins from the board.

"I've invited Dr. Stone here so that we could ask him in person if he would be so kind as to invite his wife to perform at our scholarship fund-raising kickoff this spring. And if the board would approve, I'd like us to ask him to do that today."

The board, even with the spontaneous applause, was still reserved. Joshua found himself imagining Nils, Roberto, and Kim sitting at the table with them all, coaxing them into shots of Linie balanced on the backs of their hands. He tried to imagine introducing them all to Kolby Rae. He imagined the smiles on the men's faces and the frowns on their wives' when they saw what she wore onstage. But Joshua Stone knew the town would turn out for her show.

Matthew Rose turned to Joshua. "Dr. Stone, as always, we welcome you to our campus and this meeting. Would you like to share any words with us?"

"Thank you, President Rose, members of the Board of Trustees, fellow faculty, Sheriff Jardine. I was moved when I read President Rose's comment that now that the rest of the world has forgotten, it's time for Grant's Hill to remember. I would be honored to accept your invitation on behalf of my wife, and I will gladly work with your board and Kolby's management team to make the necessary arrangements."

"Dr. Stone, thank you, and if you will excuse us, we will discuss and vote on the matter."

Joshua got up, shook Jardine's hand, and walked out of the room and into the large great room in the center of the mansion's first floor. The memories of galas and promotional soirees came flooding back. Once or twice, he imagined Liv Olsson in a black dress. He turned to see it was a drapery rustling in the wind. He felt his jacket pocket. The pink envelope was there, right where he had put it when he packed yesterday. It didn't feel any easier to open here than it had anywhere else. He heard a woman's footsteps, turned, and then looked down when he realized it was not Liv but Mrs. Rose approaching him and asking if he was staying for lunch.

"Thank you, but I need to return to Crossings tonight."

Mrs. Rose smiled. "Dr. Stone, you have a very pretty wife. Congratulations to you both."

The door to the room opened, and Sheriff Jardine stepped outside. "Joshua, congratulations, you did it. The board has voted to have Kolby Rae be our performer for the fund-raising kickoff. Now, who do we talk to about the money?"

Joshua gave Sarah Miles's contact information to Jardine, and they shook hands.

"Thank you for coming, Joshua. Have a safe trip home." And with that, Jardine returned to the board meeting.

Joshua walked out to the Rover and drove back to the motel to take Fylgja for a walk before their drive back to Crossings.

CHAPTER FORTY-SEVEN

STONE HOUSE

JESSICA ADDISON WAS PULLING AN overtime shift with one eye on speeders and the other on her cell phone, hoping to hear from Joshua about the outcome of the trustees' meeting. Her attention drifted to the radio console when a priority call displayed: a home invasion in progress. When Jessica Addison heard the address for the dispatch, she keyed her microphone.

"Dispatch, 6-70, I'm nearby. I can head that way, too"; 6-70 was the designation for her patrol shift sergeant's car. The other two on-duty deputies in Grant's Hill responded as well. She turned down a side street and crossed town.

The dispatcher added more information about the call: "6-70 and deputies responding, this is a neighbor calling. She is saying there is no home invasion but now is telling me an unknown man is sitting on the front steps of the house. He appears to have an aggressive dog with him."

As Addison turned on the street, she saw a row of neatly trimmed lawns and well-kept houses, and one yard that was overgrown with a for-sale sign slightly askew. As she got closer, she recognized the man sitting on the front steps with his elbows on his knees, staring down the sidewalk.

Addison keyed her microphone. "Dispatch, 6-70. I'm on scene. You can advise all other deputies to disregard. I'll be out with a male subject. We're code four." She stepped out of her car; the man didn't react to her presence.

"Hi. Nice house. What do you think? Should Larry and I sell ours and move into town?"

Joshua startled, looked up, and then looked back in the opposite direction. Jessica kept walking up the driveway and then the walk, then sat down on the steps next to him.

"I told my dispatcher I didn't need backup. But you look like you could use some. How'd the meeting go?"

"Great. The trustees want Kolby to do the show. I'll tell her people on the way home. It will be a great show."

Addison nodded, looked at him, and looked up and down the street and back at Joshua. "So what's on your mind?"

Joshua looked all around his former front yard, across the street, and then at her patrol car. He asked his question quietly. "Do you ever talk about it? That day in the chapel. The shooting, I mean. You and Larry or anyone?"

"No." She shook her head and looked up to the sky. "I can't. They wouldn't understand. How about you? Did you tell your new wife?"

"No, I can't tell her." They sat there. Fylgja was sleeping on the sidewalk between them. "I'm not sure if I can ever tell her. You and I have our secrets. At least until this guy Toomey's book comes out."

"Do you think he knows? Toomey? About us?" Addison's voice lacked concern. She was probing.

"How would he know, Jessica?" They looked at each other and nodded. After a moment of silence, Joshua asked, "Do you know much about her? About Liv Olsson?"

"She worked with you. That's about it. The other stuff I know is all forensics. Height, weight, wound pattern, next of kin."

Joshua pulled the pink envelope from his jacket and held it out for Addison to see. "Can you believe I've had this for over a year, and I can't open it?"

"What is it? A love letter?"

"Worse. It's a voice from beyond the grave."

"Whose?

"Liv's."

Jessica Addison turned and cocked her head to the side. "Liv Olsson from the chapel?"

Joshua nodded and continued. "Yeah. I met Liv the year I found Rex on the side of the road. She was the psychologist in our student counseling center. We were…I don't know. She was always there, always pretty, and every time we started something, it never started.

"But then one day I was an ass." He stopped and looked up at Addison. "I said so many hurtful things to her. I thought it over for a few days, cooled down, and I went to apologize. And you know what day that was? The day she died. That was the day I went to tell her 'I'm sorry.'"

Addison turned toward him. "I still don't understand the envelope."

Joshua drew a breath. "Neither do I. I worked it all through. I said my goodbyes. I let her go. I went to therapy. I closed up my house, boxed up my stuff, took a nice long vacation. I was healed…I thought."

Addison listened and watched him.

"And then David Adams came to visit after I got settled in Tennessee. David's book had just come out, *Faith Shattered.*" Addison nodded her head. "On the last day he was in Tennessee, David and I talked about Liv. It felt amazing because I felt like I was free. I felt like I could say her name and not see the memory of that day. And then, he dropped this on me." Joshua let the envelope fall to the ground, and the two of the looked at it. "David told me that when you guys— the sheriff's office—left Liv's office, the college let him go in and look around. He said he found this under her desk blotter."

Addison interrupted. "Wait, under the desk blotter and our people missed it?" Addison shook her head.

"And so David Adams came to Tennessee nearly a year later and hands me this envelope. After I've put it all behind me, he opens the old wounds." Joshua rubbed the back of his left hand. "I recognized Liv's handwriting, and he told me it came from her office. It's from her."

Joshua took a deep breath and changed his voice to a rhetorical style. "So, what's the big deal, right? She's dead. It's been over a year. I can just read it…someday…and so I looked at this damn envelope every day from the time he gave it to me until the day I met Kolby. And then I started hiding it away. Every time I found it, I hid it again. I remembered it again the day you called me. After we talked, I looked online at the college website. I saw Liv's photo." He looked at the letter. "Can I tell you a story?"

Addison gave him the look she reserved for speeders offering excuses. "You're the writer. I should've seen this coming, right?"

"After the shooting, I finally followed your advice and got counseling. I went to group therapy sessions. You know all the wisecracks about group therapy? Let me tell you something—it works." He stretched each leg out one at a time and then rested them on the next step down. "I was...wow. I was lost. And there were these three other women there. Alycia had been raped and beaten up. Patti, she's the one who suggested I start writing in a journal. Her husband had thrown her down a flight of stairs."

Addison nodded.

"And until today, I hadn't thought about the third woman. Tina. She was in group because..." Joshua took a deep breath, looked away, and then looked back into Jessica's face. "She was in group...because her live-in boyfriend...shot himself on their deck. Killed himself."

Addison shook her head. "Yeah, I heard about that call. I was off duty that day."

"Well, I think I was blocking her memory because the second week I was in group, she didn't come. Our counselor, Diane, told us, that... Tina went home to their trailer, sat on the deck where her boyfriend shot himself, and she...she killed herself."

Addison nodded. "I was on that one. It was really sad."

"Diane said that many people who are desperate and depressed and feel like they've lost their life go back to the last place they felt alive before they kill themselves."

Addison sat back, crossing her ankles.

Joshua took another deep breath. "I never understood what she meant by that. It seemed like psychobabble. But today, all of a sudden, when I was in the president's house, I thought about Liv and I remembered Tina, and I think I get it. I know what it feels like to have a place where your life ended. I had that place, that moment. Here. On these front steps. With Liv Olsson."

Joshua waited a few moments, and then half-boasting, half-embarrassed, said, "We almost kissed."

"Whoa, Joshua, TMI. I don't want to hear about your sex life."

"No, it wasn't like that. It was..."

Addison waited for him to finish. When he didn't, she said, "Joshua, I'm sorry she died."

Joshua turned to face her. "Do you ever feel like you weren't fast enough?"

Jessica looked down at Joshua's hand with the bullet wound. She stared, then nodded. "Yeah. I think about it every day."

"I wasn't fast enough, either. I didn't get there fast enough. I just wanted a chance to tell Liv 'I'm sorry.' Just to tell her I didn't mean the things I said to her. I mean, really, other people pray for fame, for fortune, for transplants, for whole new lives. I prayed every day to just have thirty seconds to say, 'Liv, I was wrong, and I am sorry.'"

Addison looked out across the grass. This was when she was supposed to cry, she thought, but she felt nothing but cold, stoic strength. It made her good at her job, and at times like this, she hated it.

Joshua shrugged and then nodded. "I get it. She died. Just like Rex, just like my parents. They died. It really doesn't matter what killed them in the end. There was nothing else I could do. Everything I did, I—" He stopped, unwilling to continue the story. They both sat in silence. "I just couldn't face what she had to say to me. But now, being back, being here…I think I'm ready now." He leaned forward and picked up the pink envelope from the sidewalk.

"I understand," said Jessica. "Do you want me to leave you alone?"

Joshua stared at the envelope, not moving, holding it out for both of them to see. "No. Will you stay here with me while I read it?"

Addison nodded. Joshua slipped his finger under the flap and tore open the envelope that had been sealed for nearly two years.

The letter inside was dated the day before Joshua said his hurtful words to Liv.

My dear, dear friend, Joshua,

It has been so hard for me to watch you in pain these last few months. You mean so much to so many people, and you touch the lives of so many students. I have long tried to find the words to say to you to help you heal. I am so sorry for your loss. Rex was so special to you, but I know you are a strong and courageous man.

We have a tradition in Sweden. On New Year's Eve, a famous actor recites a Swedish poem as the countdown to the new year. It's actually a translation of

Tennyson, and I hope it gives you the permission to let go of the past and some hope for your future.

Your friend,

Olivia Olsson

Addison shook her head. "I wonder if she knew how much those words would come to mean to you."

Joshua looked at the second sheet and began to sound out the Swedish-language words handwritten on the pink paper.

"*Ring klocka ring I bistra nars-natten,*" he said out loud.

Addison suppressed a laugh, leaned in, and read over his shoulder. "Geez, Doc, is there anyone at the college who writes like normal people?"

Addison looked at the page, the words were hard to say and harder to understand:

> *Ring, klocka, ring i bistra nyårsnatten*
> *mot rymdens norrskenssky och markens snö;*
> *det gamla* året *lägger sig att dö...*
> *Ring själaringning* öfver *land och vatten!*

There was a handful of Swedish stanzas below the first, each as difficult to read. As Joshua turned the page over, they both saw the English version:

> Ring out, wild bells, to the wild sky,
> The flying cloud, the frosty light;
> The year is dying in the night;
> Ring out, wild bells, and let him die.
> Ring out the old, ring in the new,
> Ring, happy bells, across the snow:
> The year is going, let him go;
> Ring out the false, ring in the true.
> Ring out the grief that saps the mind,
> For those that here we see no more,

Joshua's eyes filled with tears, and Addison took the page from him. "Here, let me. You just listen." She read aloud the final words written by Liv to Joshua:

> Ring in the valiant man and free,
> The larger heart the kindlier hand;

Ring out the darkness of the land,
Ring in the Christ that is to be.

She turned to look at Joshua and saw that he was closing his eyes. She let him sit in the quiet moment. She didn't move. She breathed softly and slowly. She watched as first his body tensed and his chest moved quicker, and then she saw the tension leave his face and leave his body. He was calm. Joshua opened his eyes.

"I was…I was somewhere else."

"Tell me."

"I was in another place and time. I could feel Liv near me. Jessica, it was like she was smiling, nodding, telling me it was okay to let go. When I closed my eyes, I was in this large grassy field in Sweden. And it was like a movie, like I was in the movie and watching the movie at the same time. And I could see her. I could see Liv Olsson walking in a summer dress, and Rex, my beautiful dog, Rex, was walking at her side. And then the damnedest thing: I waved goodbye to her."

"See?" She nudged him. "I tell Larry the same thing. You always have to wave goodbye. And he won't do it."

"That's what Kolby says, too. She says, 'It makes the hurt go away.'"

Joshua dried his eyes and stood up. "Wow, I guess I just kinda wussed out like a college boy, huh? What would Mike and everybody think now?"

Addison stood up, arched her back, and surveyed the neighborhood. "Doc, you didn't wuss out. Someday I'll do the same. It just hasn't happened yet." She fiddled with her dark glasses and flipped them up to the top of her head. "You know that bit about Tina and going back to where her life ended?"

"Yeah."

"Doc, your life didn't end here. It's just beginning. Go home. Kiss your wife. Remind her why you married her. And then tell her that she has to meet Larry before the show and let him take a picture with her. He's her biggest fan ever."

Joshua looked at Fylgja.

"One more thing?"

Joshua turned toward her. Addison flipped her dark glasses back down. "Gear check?"

Joshua smirked. "Every day."

Addison flipped her chin and pressed the microphone on her uniform shirt epaulet. "Dispatch from 6-70, we're code four here. This is the property owner checking on his tenant and reading some old mail. No report taken. I'll be back in service."

Joshua picked up Fylgja's leash and walked back to the motel.

Chapter Forty-Eight

Toomey

KOLBY WAS RUNNING LATE AS she pulled on the stiletto shoes with the leopard print that matched the tight belt wrapped around her black dress. The charity breakfast began in an hour and fifteen minutes, and if they had valet parking, she would be there for the opening remarks. It would not be easy to slip into the head table after it began.

She spilled the contents of her purse across the counter next to Joshua's pocket dump from the night before. His pocket dumps were always the same. He arranged each item he carried in his pockets in a neat row as if it were some form of still-life art. His pistol was always in the safe, his holster, wallet, cell phone, keys, and flashlight all arranged on the table.

Kolby found her keys at the bottom of the pile from her purse, tossed in the cell phone, and headed out to KRAEZY. She stopped and chatted with the men from Flanigan for a few seconds, then took off down the road.

When she got to the hotel, the valet, a young, pimply-faced teen, opened her car door and immediately blushed as Kolby's leg extended from the seat, her dress scooting up near her hip. She nodded and said, "Thank you." He murmured as she walked in just before the breakfast began.

At the end of the breakfast and presentations, they asked the board members to pose for a grip-and-grin photo with the president and then a group shot of them all together. Kolby had avoided Toomey all during the breakfast, but now with the group photo of the board members, he managed to stand next to her. She felt his hand, first around her waist and then sliding lower across her body.

Through her tooth-filled smile, she whispered, "Get your hand offa my ass."

Toomey replied through his own toothy grin. "How's the song go? Just a piece of this—sass?"

Kolby raised the heel of the leopard print stiletto and brought it down on top of the sport sandal on his right foot. "I'm a short but mighty girl, Toomey. If I shift my weight, you'll spend the next twelve hours in the ER and the next six weeks in a cast. I'll give you a piece of my—"

She felt his hand drop away.

"I owe you, Kolby Rae, so I want you to be the first to know. I've got the proof."

"So do Jim Beam and Jack Daniels."

"The proof about Joshua and the lady cop."

Kolby pretended to not understand. "What lady cop?"

"You know which lady cop. Sergeant Jessica Addison. And Joshua Stone."

"Toomey, f- you." She turned and walked away and Toomey walked after her.

"I would like that, but then there would be two philanderers in the Stone house." He slid the folder into her hand, and she began to open it. "The photos are in the back."

Kolby pushed the folder back at him.

"Okay, suit yourself. But ask yourself this—is Joshua going with you to Grant's Hill?"

"No, he's staying at the restaurant."

"Is that what he told you?"

"Yes."

"Why do you suppose he would go all the way back to Grant's Hill to spend the night and see his lady cop friend—who is kinda hot, now that you mention it—and yet he won't go back with his wife?"

"What are you saying? Joshua hasn't been back to Grant's Hill since the shooting, Toomey. His house is for sale. He's built a new life in Crossings."

Toomey's face lost the twinkle of lust. For a moment, Kolby thought he looked almost sincere and genuine.

"Kolby, sometimes you and I play games, but I'm not playing games. Don't like me. Don't speak to me. Do what you must. But you have to ask yourself why he won't go back there with you. What is he hiding?"

She began to turn, and he touched her arm, turning her back toward him.

"If I'm wrong, if you ask and he's all 'Sure, lovey dovey, I'll go with you,' then I will take back everything I've said. But if not, if he won't go back with you, there is something going on. Either he's still gettin' frisky with the cop or they're hiding something about that shooting. It makes no sense. He tells stories for a living. Why the hell won't he talk about it?"

Toomey's words echoed Kolby's own curiosity.

He shrugged and slid the file folder back into his black messenger bag. "Either way, my book is gold. It won't cause your divorce, but your fans won't tolerate him for hurting you. They won't take kindly to her, either. If you ask for old Toom's advice, you need to dump him quick before the story breaks, Kolby. Little sister Sarah would tell you the same thing. I'll be there at Grant's Hill with a photographer. If you need to dump him, let me help. I can spin the story. It won't be your fault."

Kolby pulled away, and Toomey pulled her back one more time. "Kolby, I'm on your side. You are almost there. Don't repeat the past. Don't get it right just to get it all wrong again."

The photo session ended. Kolby quickly left and ran to the SUV. She got in, started the engine, and opened her purse, searching for her phone. She pulled it out.

"Oh Lord Jesus, could my day get any worse?"

She was holding Joshua's phone. She had left hers behind on the counter when she grabbed the wrong one. She scrolled through the phone screen and found the call history. She was going to dial her own phone number from the directory to ask Joshua to meet her for dinner. It would be a nice night out, just the two of them. When the screen scrolled to the calls in the history list, the first numbers listed were the three matching numbers she saw the day she found the last pink envelope, the one in his underwear drawer.

She knew it was a mistake the moment she did it. She didn't know what she would say. It wasn't smart, but she highlighted the number and pressed CALL. The phone rang twice, and then Kolby heard a woman's voice answer. "Jessica Addison."

Kolby froze, holding the phone away from her face. Her finger hovered over the END button, unable to move.

"Joshua, is this you?"

Kolby's hand began to shake as the woman's voice became whimsical.

"Hey, Doc, I think you pocket-dialed me. Helloooooooooooo."

Kolby hung up the call. Still trembling, she pushed the power window control, and the glass opened in time as she threw up most of what she had eaten for breakfast. She leaned back in the seat and saw her reflection in the mirror: she was pale and perspiring, and her eyes were red from the beginning of tears. She couldn't stop the shaking enough to control the phone display screen.

In a few minutes, she opened her eyes, focused on Joshua's phone, and found her own phone number in the directory. Still shaking, she pressed CALL. It rang, and then she heard her own voice mail greeting. "You know what to do."

She hung up. Next, she sent a text message. It was odd, sending messages as <Joshua> and waiting to see if <KolbyRae> would reply.

<Joshua> Hey, it's me. Well, it's me pretending to be you. I took your phone.

She waited. He didn't reply for several minutes.

<KolbyRae> Hey, I just got this. Where are you?

<Joshua> Nashville. Where are u?

<KolbyRae> The Pizza Stone.

<Joshua> This is weird, texting myself.

Kolby typed a question. <Joshua> Will u take me to dinner?

<KolbyRae> Sure, what about the Roadhouse?

<Joshua> I would like that.

<KolbyRae> See you at home about 6?

Kolby laid the phone on the passenger seat and slumped back into the black leather of the driver's side. She put the truck in gear and took off. She hit the interstate and revved the truck speed higher. At sixty miles per hour, she was telling herself Joshua would have told her if had gone to Grant's Hill. At seventy miles per hour, she told herself that Joshua loved her. At eighty miles per hour, she was nodding in the mirror, deciding that Toomey was a publicity-seeking leech. At ninety, she confessed Joshua wouldn't even acknowledge her questions about Grant's Hill, the shooting, and what happened to him. At one hundred, she admitted she really didn't know anything about Joshua at all. By one hundred ten, her eyes were filled with tears to the point she took her foot off the gas and coasted into a rest area, parked the truck, and sat there.

Her imagination was going wild. She pictured Joshua lying helpless on the floor in the smoke of the Grant's Hill chapel and a strong, beautiful policewoman coming in with her guns blazing. She was probably busty with a half-unbuttoned uniform shirt. She had perfect teeth and nails. The bad guy was down, the pretty heroine taking Joshua in her arms, lifting him and dragging him to safety where they embraced and kissed. The narrative in her mind was a kind of first-time romance writer drivel. The image made her laugh. She knew it had been nothing like that.

But it was possible. The white knight syndrome. The breakfast speaker had asked Kolby and the board to approve funding for more psychological support for burn patients, especially pediatric burn patients. The speaker said that sometimes, patients experienced the white knight syndrome, falling in love with their doctors. A policewoman who saved your life would be the ultimate white knight.

Kolby remembered her own fear and exhilaration the night of their break-in. How terrified she had been at the thought of losing Fylgja. The evil of someone trying to hurt her or Joshua. And that after it was all over and everyone had gone home, the passionate and powerful lovemaking with Joshua, so over the top. The same emotions that drew her to Joshua that night could have caused Sgt. Jessica to seduce him, too.

Kolby placed her hand on her chest, able to feel the rough, scarred skin through the light fabric. She wondered how the feel of her own scarred body compared to his memory of his fling with the sergeant. The white knight's memory was more than enough to draw Joshua back to Grant's Hill again.

Kolby drove home to Crossings in time to shower and change into her rhinestone pocket jeans before Joshua picked her up and they rode together to the Roadhouse. She waited in the passenger seat of her truck as Joshua walked around the front and opened her door. She noticed that he was still a gentleman, still attentive, still opening her car door. Once inside, they sat, by coincidence, at the table from their first date.

"So other than grabbing the wrong phone, how was your thing? The charity breakfast?" Joshua asked.

Kolby looked up from her menu, surprised and encouraged at his interest. "Oh, you know, I saw all the Nashville people. I sat with Sherrie Elliot. She still looks so great."

Joshua nodded. "None of my business, but why didn't you two ever tour together?"

"We were going to right before the *Garden Party* article came out, right before we met Sean." She thought about telling him about Toomey.

"You were in *Garden Party*? I didn't know that. When? I'd love to read it. See, this is what I like about us; every day we discover something new about each other. It's great, isn't it?"

He was reaching across the table as he set his menu back in the slot behind the napkin holder on the table, looking at her and smiling. Kolby remembered throwing up out the window of the SUV after hanging up the call she had dialed to Jessica Addison. She drew a breath, ready to ask him about Grant's Hill, when Jackie Gower interrupted her thoughts.

"Joshua, Kolby, how are you two? You all ready for your big show at that college tomorrow, Kolby?"

Kolby smiled. "Yes ma'am. I have to fit into my skinny jeans, too, so I think I'll just have a salad."

"I hear you. Just wait until you two have kids. I need to lose this baby fat. And my baby is gonna be a senior this year."

Kolby looked at Joshua. "How about the chicken-fried steak?"

Jackie nodded and returned to the kitchen. Joshua picked her phone out of his pocket. He looked at the display and began talking to Kolby. "I tried to take good messages for you. It started ringing at eight o'clock. I am so amazed by all you do."

He drew a deep breath and began. "Okay. Sarah called multiple times, but as near as I can tell, the Grant's Hill show is set. Then you have five days off. Then you go off on a sixteen-day radio station tour to promote *Crossroads*. She says already your older albums have doubled their sales in the time since the Heartland Benefit Concert. *Right-Hand Rover* is at six hundred twenty-three thousand." Joshua looked up. "Six hundred twenty-three thousand—that's good, right?"

Kolby nodded. Joshua looked back at his notes. "She thinks you need to double the web and social media team. Candace called. She works for Ashley, who works for Sarah." Joshua shook his head. "How do you keep them all straight?"

Kolby shrugged. "I don't. Sarah does."

Joshua continued. "Dwight from Flanigan has the operation plan for Grant's Hill. They will go over it with you on the bus tomorrow." He looked at his notes. "And some guy called. He wasn't sure if you would remember him or not." Kolby looked up, but Joshua was staring at the notes on his notepad. "But he says he used to hang out with you."

Kolby cocked her head. None of her exes would even think of calling her.

Joshua continued, speaking slower and softer. "And he knows you're busy, but that…" He looked up and took her hand. "He's totally crazy in love with you, and he thinks you are very pretty, and he wondered if…when you come back from your trips…if maybe the two of you could go out on a date?"

Kolby forgot about Jeffrey Toomey, Jessica Addison, her exes, and throwing up. The spark was hot, and his eyes and voice stole her heart. The flippy-flop thing was all she felt.

Joshua continued, "Sarah said she's booking dates for summer and fall. She wants to meet with the band and the production manager to talk about staging and crew."

Kolby took the phone from his hand and laid it in her purse. Then she took the notepad, set it on the table, and took both of his hands.

"Sarah who?"

Neither of them saw Jackie Gower begin to move toward them with their food and then quickly turn and go back to the kitchen. Joshua and Kolby continued looking into each other's eyes for several minutes, and then Jackie picked up the plates and walked out to the table a second time.

Chapter Forty-Nine

Glass House

Joshua and Kolby drove back to the new house, holding hands. When they stopped at the gate, Joshua rolled down the window and nodded at the two men sitting in the SUV parked just inside.

"Kingston and Jamaica reporting for duty. Roger, ten-four, over and out." Kolby slugged him, snickered, and peered through the open window at the men from Flanigan.

"We're just doing our job, sir."

Kolby asked, "Did you eat?"

"No ma'am," the second man said from the passenger side of the Flanigan SUV.

"Good," Kolby replied and then reached behind Joshua to the backseat. "We brought you a couple of sandwiches from the Roadhouse. And they sent along a cooler with some water and pop."

Joshua interrupted. "She means soda."

Together, they handed the bags and cooler through the SUV windows, and then Joshua drove on to the house. Before he got out of the truck, Kolby turned to him. "Wait, kiss me?"

Joshua leaned over, kissed her cheek, then her mouth. She heard him draw a breath, and when she opened her eyes, he was smiling at her.

"Joshua, if I asked you to come to Grant's Hill with me, would you come?"

"I have a big banquet for the basketball team and their families. It's all set to go," he told her.

"I know," she said. "I'm just asking, if I asked, would you come?"

"Yes."

She looked at him. "What do you mean, yes? Yes, you would come?"

"Yes. I'll call, and I can have the crew cover the night. They're ready. They can handle the banquet. I'll come with you."

Kolby began fumbling for her purse and then her phone. "Seriously? You mean it, Joshua Stone?" She gave him a quick kiss on the cheek. "Okay, I have to tell Sarah. This changes everything."

She sent a text to Sarah, who replied they were on their way to pick up Sean at the Adams farm and then would stop for the two of them.

Joshua unlocked the door to the house, and Kolby walked upstairs. She stopped and turned around as he asked, "I'm going to walk with Fylgja. Are you going up to change before the bus comes and gets us?"

She looked back at him. "Joshua Stone? I want you to know that as much as I want you to be with me, I believe in you and what you want to do for the kids here and your restaurant. We knew when we got married that our life would get crazy. I just want you to know I believe in you."

"Kolby Ruth, I believe in you, too."

He opened the front hall closet, and she watched as he pulled out a moving box filled with jackets, pawed through it, and pulled out the Grant's Hill jacket.

"I haven't seen that since the benefit," said Kolby. "You look good in it."

As he got to the door, Joshua looked back. "I forgot where it was. Thanks for a great date, Kolby Ruth Stone."

Kolby winked.

She walked up to the bedroom and flipped on the light, then flipped it off again and looked out the window, watching Joshua and Fylgja standing in the grass, looking around. "I'm crazy to marry into this two-dog pack," she said. "I'm crazy about this guy. I just have to remind him with nights like tonight." She had forgotten about Toomey. She and Joshua were just as close as ever at dinner.

Kolby thought about her parents and tried to imagine her mother marrying a coal miner and then both of them packing up and moving to Mississippi. She wished her daddy had been alive and could have walked her down the aisle. She sighed a deep sigh, thinking about him, his shop, his big red toolbox, and the sound of his voice.

:: Dance with me, Daddy, let me dance on your shoes ::

She tossed back her hair and then playfully admitted she was happy neither Momma nor Daddy would see what she did next.

She unzipped her jeans and slid them off her legs. She unfastened the snaps of her shirt and then left all of her clothes in an impulsive, erotic pile on their bedroom floor. She opened a drawer and found one of Joshua's T-shirts, a light-colored one. She put it on and looked in the mirror.

"Not really sexy. I have dresses shorter than this," she said and flipped out the lights.

When she heard the front door open, wearing only the T-shirt, Kolby walked down the stairs. Joshua came inside with Fylgja at his side, and then Fylgja ran up the stairs and to their bedroom. Kolby looked at Joshua and with a coy tilt of her head lifted her T-shirt, revealing her naked body underneath. "I can't seem to find anything to wear."

"I suppose you could wear this?" Joshua lifted the Grant's Hill jacket.

Kolby pointed over at the long, slender table in the entryway where her purse, car keys, and cell phone were piled next to the mail.

"Do me a favor first. Will you grab my phone? Let's be sure we have enough time before they get here."

Joshua picked the phone up and handed it to Kolby, turned, and began to hang up the jacket in the entry closet.

She scrolled through her messages. The first was from Toomey. She was about to delete it when the photo attached popped up on the screen. It was two new covers of *Garden Party* promoting the future release of *Stone Unturned: An Unauthorized Biography of Joshua Stone*. The first magazine cover had his photo and also a photo of Kolby. They were back to back, and using digital imaging, it looked as if they were in the same photo, and, through photo effects, the photo was torn in half. A sunburst on the cover had the words "Spoiler Alert: Unhappy Endings."

The second magazine cover was new. It had a photo of Joshua and the ID photo of Sgt. Jessica Addison that Toomey had shown Kolby when they met at Skip's. The sunburst on that cover read, "The Truth About Grant's Hill."

There was another message from Toomey.

<Toomey> Look now, so you know.

Kolby felt she should delete it, but she opened it. As she did, her heart fell. She spoke the first words that came to her. "What the hell? What is this?"

Kolby felt the weeks of subtle doubt turn her desire into the back edge of love's knife. The cut of jealousy sliced deep. On the phone display was a social media post from Toomey with a photo link. In the photo, Joshua and a woman in a police uniform were sitting on the steps of a house she had never seen, with Fylgja. The caption read, "Puppy Love. Kolby Rae's husband, Joshua Stone, and his police friend enjoy walking the dog together. Read a preview of *Stone Unturned* in *Garden Party* April 1."

Kolby sat down on the last stair staring at Joshua, then the phone, then back at him.

"Joshua Stone, what the hell is this?" Kolby threw the phone.

He managed to stop it with the back of the jacket and grab it before it fell to the wood floor. He looked at the display, dumbfounded, whispering, "Where did this come from? How did you...?" He looked up at her. "Kolby, it's not what you think."

"You're the damn writer, and that's the best you can do?" She mocked his voice, surprising both of them with how much it sounded like him. "'It's not what you think.'" She watched Joshua turn away, refusing eye contact. "I don't need your fancy Ph.D. to think. I am not stupid. I know about Sergeant Jessica."

Joshua stopped and turned quickly. "No. You don't know anything about Jessica."

"Toomey warned me about you and her."

"Toomey?" Joshua looked at her. "Jeffrey Toomey? How do you know Jeffrey Toomey? I've never told you about him. When did you talk with Toomey? No, *why* did you talk to Toomey?"

"Jeffrey Toomey wrote about me long before you and I ever met. He wrote the article in *Garden Party*. He called me after the Heartland Benefit Concert, asked me to meet him. He told me about his book about you. He said there was something between you and the lady cop."

Kolby waited for some reaction in Joshua's eyes. "Why can't you let her go? Whatever you two shared, you had your fling with your little badge-wearing hottie. Her time with you is over. This is my time to be with you. Damn, Joshua, I get it. I can see she's cute, but why?"

Joshua looked blankly at her. "Who's cute? Jessica? She is? I guess I never really noticed."

"You can't even lie like a man." Kolby ran up the stairs and slammed the door behind her. Through the door, she heard Joshua coach himself, "Deep breath. Breathe…" After the third breath, she heard him climb the stairs two at a time and stop at the door. He knocked.

"Kolby, I'm sorry. I shouldn't have yelled at you. If you let me in, I'll tell you everything."

Kolby stood on the bedroom side of the door and made him wait in silence. Black rivers flowed from the eyes that at dinner were hanging on his every word. Through her sobs, she heard the sincerity in his voice and opened the door. Joshua said to her, "If you will listen, I will tell you the truth."

"I always expect the truth." She turned around and walked back to the bed. He stayed in the doorway. "Joshua Stone, don't lie to me. Not now. Not if I mean anything to you. Why did you let her do this to us?"

"Don't blame Jessica. It's not her fault."

Kolby glared at him. Toomey was right. Joshua had a secret. She was unsure if Joshua was admitting an affair or if Toomey's other theory was right. For the first time, Kolby felt the truth she always expected would end them.

She spoke with a curt staccato. "Wait. Stop. I won't do this here with you. I am not going to sit here in our bedroom and have this conversation. You walk outside. I will talk to you there."

Joshua looked at Fylgja, who was standing next to the bed. The man turned and walked slowly down the stairs, through the hall, and out the sliding doors that separated the kitchen from the deck. Kolby turned around, walked to the closet, pulled on sweatpants and a sweatshirt and came back into the room. She scratched Fylgja's ear and sat on the edge of the bed.

"Momma, what do I do?" she whispered. She sat there petting Fylgja and then stood up and walked down and out to the deck. Just before she passed through the doors, she stopped. She looked at the shape of Joshua's body in the moonlight, the way his hair fell against his neck. Even when she hated him, she felt attracted to him.

"Oh Lord, give me strength."

Kolby stepped onto the deck. Joshua turned and began to speak.

"Kolby, I swear, with God as my witness, this is the truth. The whole story. Yes…it's true."

She felt her knees buckle, but she managed to stand straight.

"I met Jessica when I went back to Grant's Hill. I had some unfinished business, and I went back to my old house. That must be when they took that picture. Jessica found me there. All we did was have a long talk."

"All you did was talk? That's what you think this is about? You still don't get it, do you? Joshua, I saw your phone." Her voice was direct and emotionless. "Sergeant Jessica called you. And you called her. That's bad enough. But it's when you did it that's killing me. You switch phones every month, and you called and talked with Jessica before you even gave me your new number. You talked to her from our home. Where? Were you standing here? Were you in our kitchen?" Kolby made a panicked expression as she looked over her shoulder toward the stairs. "Tell me you were not in our bedroom." She waited, and he didn't acknowledge her. "And this picture. This is you and her, isn't it? And Fylgja? Where is this? Is this your house? The house you said I wouldn't like? Well, you were right. I hate it already. I hate what she did with you there."

"But all we did was talk."

"Joshua Stone." Kolby's voice shifted from anger to a whine as she folded her body in half and held her fists to her forehead.

Joshua stammered, "Yes, yes, yes. She called me out of the blue and asked me to come to Grant's Hill. She wanted me to talk to them about you. I should have told you."

"What does she have that I can't give you? Aren't I enough of a woman to love? How can you let this woman do this to us?" Kolby drew her arms to her chest and covered her breasts.

Joshua looked at her. "You are so much woman. It's not about Jessic—"

Kolby felt the snap. Like one of Roberto's guitar strings during "Tequila Temptress," the weeks of suspicion snapped inside her, and she yelled back, "The hell it isn't, Joshua Stone!" Fylgja scampered back into the kitchen and hid under the table. "Shame on you. You lie when you pretend to tell the truth. Don't tell me it's not about Jessica." Kolby waved her arm in an arc. "You try and hide everything about her. You think I never noticed all the pink envelopes from her lying around? In your book, in the cabin, even in your underwear drawer in our bedroom?"

"Pink envelopes? You saw it? Kolby, there weren't pink envelopes. There was one. One envelope, okay? One stupid pink envelope. And it wasn't from Jessica. It was from another woman. It has nothing to do with Jessica."

Kolby felt her knees buckle again. She hadn't wanted to hear him admit one affair; now he was admitting two. "And you said you were awkward with women."

"Damn!" he yelled loudly.

Kolby tensed up and pulled her arms to her body to protect herself. Fylgja cowered farther under the table.

"Oh my God, is this what this is all about?" said Joshua. "The pink envelope was from Liv — Liv Olsson, the woman who died at Grant's Hill. Not from Jessica Addison." He smiled with relief as if the argument was over. "Kolby, I love your music, but my life is not one of your cheatin' and drinkin' country songs." He held up his hand and began ticking off his fingers as he made each point. "I'm not going to prison. I don't drive a damn pickup truck. I'm not drunk." He paused. "And I'm not cheatin'. This has nothing to do with Jessica Addison."

He brought his scarred left hand to his forehead, wavering his head side to side in small movements. "The stupid pink envelope. Okay, Liv wrote me that note to help me get over Rex's death. But I didn't get it until after Liv was long dead, and then…"

Joshua shook his head more and then looked at Kolby. His expression seemed as confused as she felt listening to his story. "Like a fool, I carried it around until I was able to find the nerve to read it. I'm forty-three years old, and I was afraid of what it might say."

He looked away, down to the deck behind him, and then back up. His face was filled with remorse. "Kolby, if I had known you found it…I would've opened it on the spot. I wasn't hiding it from you. I was hiding it from me. Jessica didn't send any pink envelopes."

They both were silent. Then Joshua added, "Please forgive me. I should never have hidden it from you…or me. But please don't think I was sleeping with Jessica."

"Damnit, Joshua, this isn't about you sleeping with her. I'm not talking about you sleeping with her. Don't you get it? It's not just the phone calls or notes.…It's all of it. Sergeant Jessica was there in Grant's Hill with you."

"Of course she was. She lives there. I saw her when I went back."

Kolby drew a breath in disbelief. "Oh my word, don't you beat all? Not then. She was with you…before. She was with you in that chapel when you almost died. She saved your life. She shares the one secret you won't share with me. How can I ever compete with her?" Kolby tossed her hands in the air, turned halfway around, and then turned to face him. "Joshua, you dream about her…you…you call her name with me just inches away from you in our bed…and you won't talk to me about it. I don't even know who you are. No man who loves me could keep a secret he shares with another woman from his wife."

Joshua squared his shoulders. "You don't know who I am?" He shoved his hand out for her to shake. "I'm Joshua Stone. I used to be a college professor, and I wrote a few books and had a damned good life. It was quiet compared to yours, but I had real friends. Not followers. I met this wonderful woman named Kolby Ruth Miles, and I fell in love with her, the kind of love I never knew existed."

Joshua walked around the deck and stopped, looking out at the garden in their backyard. "You're blaming me for another woman? Let me tell you about the real other woman in my life. That other woman's name is Kolby Rae. Everything she does turns my world upside down. If we're going to break up this marriage because of another woman, you'd better at least make damn sure you know which other woman is the problem here. This Stone is tired of being thrown around your glass house."

Kolby slapped the deck railing with the palm of her hand. "You are right. You know that, Joshua Stone? You are right, right, right. This is not about Jessica. This is about you. You, you, you."

He stopped looking around and brought his focus to her eyes. She saw his neck veins throbbing, his face red with anger. For a moment, she was afraid. And then he closed his eyes, and she watched his lips move ever so slightly. His voice was calmer when he began again.

"If this is all about me, then you sit down and listen to what I have to say. But you listen. You think it's easy to be Kolby Rae's husband? K-R-A-E-Z-Y. It fits. All I wanted to do was to put Grant's Hill behind me, and now you've put it and me back on page one."

The bus horn blared from their circle drive.

"And look at what you've become. Kolby Rae, when did you stop trusting? Now you believe lies about me and hate me for something I didn't and wouldn't do because you listen to someone like Toomey more than you trust me. Really? Toomey? Look around us. There are guards at our front gate. You have people. Sarah has people. Sarah's people have people. How the hell did this happen?"

Joshua was seething. From the driveway, the bus honked a second time.

"Your ride is here. Go do what Kolby Rae does best. I've got a restaurant to run. It won't make the Internet, and I won't post pictures of the food all over social media, and I won't be beholden to assholes like Toomey. I'll stand and talk to my face-to-face friends and neighbors and help some kids grow up to be adults."

Joshua paced back and forth and then stopped and looked at the phone he had been crushing during their argument. He stared at the photos. He wasn't embarrassed or ashamed, and then he spoke with confidence.

"I had Toomey handled. He had nothing. Now his book—that I had nothing to do with, by the way—is gonna be a best seller? He talks to you. He finds out about Jessica and invents some crazy story. Either she and I are doing the hanky-panky in bed, or there is some big mysterious secret about the Grant's Hill shooting. Do you see what he's done? He's turned my life into the fable of the lady or the tiger. And guess what? Toomey's become the barbaric king. You're the princess I'm in love with." He shook his head. "And so point me to the door, princess. What is the sentence you choose me to serve? Is it gonna be the lady or the tiger? Jessica Addison or Grant's Hill? And which one is which? I'll be damned if I know."

Kolby paused, drew in a big breath, and started to walk off the deck and into the kitchen. She turned back around and looked at him, saying, "Joshua, Toomey is going to run one of those stories."

They looked at each other. Their loud, long, painful exchange had reduced them to standing ten feet apart in silence. The front door rattled, and Sarah's voice broke the silence. "Are you guys ready? Hello?"

Fylgja barked and moved to the entry and in a moment led Sarah into the kitchen, the dog grinning and wagging her tail. Sarah sensed the mood and hesitated at the open patio doors leading to the deck, then said, "So are we done here?"

Kolby looked at Joshua. "Are we?"

Joshua looked at Sarah and then at Kolby. "I don't know what to tell you, Kolby." He paused. Sarah shifted her weight uncomfortably, looking at the two of them. Joshua continued, "Sarah, last-minute change, I am—I'm not going with you to Grant's Hill."

"Oh?"

Kolby dropped her shoulders and turned to Sarah. "He's not coming, Sarah. He's done enough in Grant's Hill, don't you think?"

Kolby walked inside past Sarah with Fylgja at her heels. Sarah and Joshua heard the front door open and felt it slam behind her.

"Joshua? What?"

Joshua slid Kolby's phone across the patio table, and when it stopped spinning, the display faced Sarah. She picked it up and looked at the photo of Joshua and a lady cop.

"Joshua," she said in a partial scold, partial whine. "Never alone with another woman, remember? Kolby may forgive you, but her fans won't."

"Sarah, don't. Okay? Just…don't."

PART NINE
GRANT'S HILL

Chapter Fifty

Load In

It was a fluke of weather, but the forecast for Grant's Hill, ordinarily in the forties this time of year, was looking at five straight days of seventy-eight-degree high temperatures. The representative of the Grant's Hill College Board of Trustees was on the phone daily with Sarah Miles. Once confident the weather would hold, they moved the concert from the auditorium to open air. Kolby and the band would play under the stars on the north side of the campus. The grass field was historically important to Grant's Hill. During the fog of 1931, a lost postal service pilot landed his out-of-fuel airplane there, to the shock and cheers of students. Ever since, the college president declared a random spring holiday each year called Pilot's Day. The president decided the concert day would also be Pilot's Day on campus.

Kolby spent a sleepless night on the bus and then fell asleep mid-morning, secluded from the others in her bed in the room at the back of the bus. Sarah opened the small door, stuck in her head, and then came the rest of the way into the space.

"I've got your phone and the day sheet. Wanna go over it?"

Kolby rolled over, looked at the time: 2:00 p.m. She pointed to the sofa bed, and Sarah sat down, handing the day sheet to Kolby. Before she looked at it, Kolby hung her head and then lifted it up. "Sarah, we had this awful fight."

"And?" Sarah asked

"And what do you think? Did I make a mistake marrying him?"

Sarah gave a sympathetic, "Ouch," and then followed with, "You two did have a fight."

"Sarah, I think Toomey is right. I think we're over."

"Kolby, this is Toomey. He's a blowhard. I saw the picture. I could kick Joshua for being there, but he's outside, in public, in broad daylight, and Fylgja is with him."

"What does everyone think?"

"Who cares? Kolby, what do you think?"

Kolby shook her head.

Sarah sighed. "Kolby, I've seen you with him. You love him, girl. He made a mistake. I don't know; maybe he slept with her before, but I don't think so. I mean, I just don't see that in his way."

"Sarah, I think we're through. You should have heard us. You should have seen us." Kolby turned away and then looked at Sarah in the mirror. "What were we thinking? We don't even know each other. Why did I think we should get married? He's been single his whole life. I've been single. We don't have a clue how to be married, and this woman is gonna destroy us. I think we're through, Sarah. We have to figure out what to do and what to say."

They looked at the day sheet.

DAY SHEET — KOLBY RAE
Grant's Hill College, Grant's Hill
OUTDOOR SHOW

Crew Lobby Call @BUSES	1:00 PM
Load In	1:30
Kolby and Joshua PRESS CONFERENCE	2:45–3:05
BAND Lobby Call @BUSES	3:30
SOUND CHECK	4:00
DINNER CATERING	
GRANT'S HILL FACULTY CLUB	5:30
KOLBY Meet & Greet	7:00
Alumni and Donors (200 ppl)	
DOORS:	7:30
KOLBY RAE:	8:30–10:00
CURFEW:	11:00
BUS CALL	1:00 AM

GRANT'S HILL to CROSSINGS 242 miles 3 hours

"Sarah, " Kolby began, "I need you to sell this. Now that we've told them Joshua is coming, I need you to convince them that Joshua is here. Somehow. We can let it all blow up tomorrow. I don't care who finds out tomorrow. They deserve the truth. Just let these fans have this night. I just want to sing our songs."

Sarah looked at the paper and then took a marker. "I can sell it. Can you?"

"I can sell it." She added, "Pinkie swear?"

Sarah looked over and extended her left hand. "Pinkie swear."

Sarah began writing and talking at the same time. "Press conference, that's out. New rules, fifteen-minute window for photo and video, and we'll schedule a new press event after the show. There will be an embargo; absolutely no photos until the show is done. Toomey is here. There's only so much I can do." Sarah drew a line through the words PRESS CONFERENCE on the day sheet. "At the end of the show, we'll tell the press we canceled the press event. We'll tell them the night was too emotional. I can sell it."

At the end of the sound check, Kolby and Sarah walked with three members of the Flanigan detail to the dinner, looking at the buildings on campus and the lawns and gardens. It was an oasis.

"Sarah, do you understand how odd this feels to me?" asked Kolby. "I mean, I don't even know him, really. I can't picture Joshua here on this campus. You know, he won't even talk to me about what happened here."

"Which time?"

"The shooting on campus." Kolby stopped Sarah at the door to the bus. "Why? Which time did you think I meant? You know something, don't you?"

"Nothing. Kolby, I know nothing, I know what you know. Joshua set this all up. Joshua came here to Grant's Hill and talked to them and worked out most of this deal on his own by himself. He called me and told me about it on his drive back. Joshua wanted you to have this moment, to really have a chance to shine. He asked me to do the contract stuff, but this was all him."

Sarah stopped cold with a look of realization. "Kolby, that must be when the photos were taken. That's it exactly. But let's think about it for a minute. This is the best Toomey has? The two of them sitting on a porch? If Joshua even leaned over to smell her perfume, Toomey would have a much more intimate photo. I don't think he and the cop are an item."

Kolby thought for a moment. "I wonder what kind of perfume she likes?"

"God, Kolby, let it go."

They walked into the Grant's Hill College Faculty Club. The club, a small bungalow on the edge of campus, was formerly the rectory of the Eastford Chapel. Inside was a buffet of appetizers and assorted drinks, and the crew was mingling and mixing. Midway through their meal, the door to the club opened. Everyone turned, and one by one the conversations stopped. Joshua Stone was standing in the doorway. One of the student servers recognized Joshua and called him by name. "Hi, Dr. Stone. Welcome home."

Kolby Rae looked up from the table, and Sarah and Kim both turned to look over their shoulders. The silence was obvious and tense before Nils said, "Joshua, you should try this pizza."

Roberto said, "Joshua, glad you're here, man."

Kim and Sarah both looked at Kolby and mouthed, "Good luck," and picked up their plates and moved to another table.

Joshua moved through the buffet line, picked up a bottle of water, and walked over to Kolby Rae. He stood there and then said, "I looked all over the buffet, but I didn't seem to find my helping of chicken-fried crow."

"That's because I ate enough for both of us."

"May I sit down?"

Kolby Rae nodded, and he sat down opposite her.

Joshua offered the first apology. "I said and did a lot of things wrong."

She spoke from her broken heart faster than her mind could interrupt. "Yes, you did..." She stopped, closed her eyes, and opened them. "But I did, too."

"We've made a mess of things. Our lives, Larry and Jessica's." Joshua folded his hands in front of his face, looking over the top at Kolby.

"Why are you here?" asked Kolby. "What made you come? Don't

you have a restaurant to run?"

"I'm here because...you might want this jacket for the show." He pointed to the Grant's Hill jacket.

Sean, Nils, Kim, Skeeter, and Sarah were huddled at a table, their backs to the couple, except Sean and Nils, who were giving a play-by-play commentary on their actions. Roberto was standing behind them listening to Nils.

"They are looking at each other. But no smiles."

Kim asked, "The hair thing? Is she doing the hair thing? She always does the hair thing when she's not happy."

Sean looked and shook his head.

"Where is Joshua's hand? He always puts his hand in his pocket when he's nervous."

Nils looked. "I can't see it."

Roberto chimed in. "I see it. It's on the table."

"Yes!" cheered Kim.

"What's the set list tonight?" Joshua asked Kolby.

"Open with 'Right-Hand Rover'—that ought to be good for some giggles. 'Stay Here and Drink.' 'Candlelight and Chaos.' 'One Bar at a Time.' Skeeter's got something figured out with the Grant's Hill fight song so I can do my wardrobe change. Then we'll do 'I Don't Make My Bed That Way.' 'Tequila Temptress.'" Kolby looked at Sarah across the room and then back at Joshua. "And then we'll finish with 'Light a Candle for Rose.'"

She saw a flicker of pride in his eyes. "Is Sean ready?" he asked.

"We're all ready, Joshua," she retorted. "What about you, Joshua Stone? Where are you?"

Joshua slid his hand into his pocket. "I'm here to ask you a favor. I guess a final favor. I want you do a meet and greet with Jessica and Larry."

"Joshua Stone, you want me to meet with Sergeant Jessica? She's been your secret for our entire relationship, and today of all days you want me to make friends?"

Nils reported to the table, "Shit, she's doing the hair thing."

Joshua shook his head. "I don't know what you will have to say to each other. She may hate you just as much as you hate her. But I'm not asking you as Kolby Ruth; I'm asking you as Kolby Rae. Please do this for two fans who've been with you since Kolby Rae first came to Nashville."

They looked at each other.

Across the room, Nils shook his head. "They are not the happiest couple I've ever seen."

Kolby sighed. Her head and shoulders drooped. "Joshua, I'm angry. I'm jealous. I'm hurt. You have to go. I can't be with you now. I can't talk about us…and I can't meet Sergeant Jessica. I can't live with you keeping a secret, and you won't live with having your secret known. Whatever it is."

She held her hand to her chest, feeling the phantom pain and then the itching from her scar. "Joshua, someone else has made every bad decision in my life. I was right about the recording 'Landslide,' but we were late. I was right about hitching my star to Trent, but he died. I was right to wait until I found you, Joshua Stone, and now look what you've let this woman do to us."

Joshua got up from the table and whispered, "Okay, have it your way." He turned to the door. Each member of the band gave him a sincere nod, and Joshua walked out.

CHAPTER FIFTY-ONE

MEET AND GREET

THE ALUMNI AND CONTEST WINNERS filled the room reserved for the meet and greet. There were two hundred guests milling about, talking and laughing as they waited for the star to come into the room. Sarah Miles walked up and greeted Jessica Addison. Jessica motioned for her husband, Larry, to come join them. Sarah looked at the two of them, both a bit giddy from the backstage preconcert excitement and celebrity status.

Larry spoke first. "I don't know how to thank you. Jess and I listened to Kolby Rae ever since she first came out. I mean, we're almost her biggest fans."

Sarah smiled. "I'm glad that you can visit backstage, and I'm really sorry about the last-minute mix-up."

The Addisons looked at each other and then back to Sarah. Jessica asked, "Mix-up? Why, did something happen?"

Sarah looked at them both. "Well, you know how it is. I'm sure Joshua explained it to you."

Larry's facial expression fell; he could tell bad news was coming. Jessica looked at Sarah. Her jawline became visible, and she clenched her teeth.

"I am really sorry, but you can't be back here for the meet and greet. It's all people picked by the college and the radio station contest winners. We could get you back for this early part, but...." Sarah's voice trailed off. She shrugged. "You know how it is."

Sarah looked at both of them. Larry turned to Jessica and for the first time saw disappointment in his normally stoic and in-command wife. He reached over and took his wife's hand. Sarah continued, "So, look, I am truly sorry, but the three of us need to leave now. We can just slip out this door."

Larry whispered to Jessica, "It's okay. We still get to sit in the front row."

Sarah held open the door, and they walked from the greeting room into the open parking lot. "Why don't you come with me? We can get you a signed T-shirt." She stopped next to a tour bus and pressed the door-open button. "I left something on the bus. It'll just be a second. I need to get something." She paused and then looked back at them. "Hey, have you ever seen the inside of one of these things? I'm sure they won't mind if I let you take a peek."

The lights inside the bus were on, and Larry and Jessica put part of their disappointment aside with the idea they could actually be on a tour bus used by Kolby's band. When they got to the top of the few stairs and turned, they found a sitting room, and seated in the back chair smiling at them was Kolby Rae. Jessica's hand flew to her mouth as her eyes opened widely,

Larry Addison said, "Jesus, it's her."

Kolby Rae looked first at Jessica. She was a pretty woman, in civilian clothes, wearing a short jean skirt and tight tank top with a thin sweater layered over it. Kolby thought her haircut was cute, thinking back to the photo on the cover of *Four-Wheel Girl* when she wore her hair the same way. She swallowed her pride and gave the sheriff's sergeant an air hug. Then she turned to Larry, gave him a hug, and kissed him on the side of his face. A light hint of her red lipstick left her mark on his cheek. Jessica noticed it right away and beamed.

"This is a very special night," Jessica began. "Thank you for coming to Grant's Hill."

Larry continued, "We've, uh…" He stammered a bit. "See, I thought if I practiced what I wanted to say, I wouldn't act like a farm boy on his first drive to town, but I have to say, you are even prettier in person."

"Oh, why, thank you. That is so sweet. Your wife is very pretty, and Joshua told me about both of you." Kolby forced a smile as she looked at Jessica, then both Addisons. Larry and Jessica shared a mutual blush as they held each other's hand. "So how long have you known each other?"

"High school." Jessica replied. Kolby noticed the sparkle in Jessica's eyes and how Jessica kept looking over at her husband.

"I asked her out on a date freshman year."

Kolby whistled. "You've been together since freshman year in high school?"

"No, 'cuz I turned him down and didn't go out with him until my senior year."

"Her daddy," Larry began. Kolby watched as Jessica slightly rubbed Larry's thigh as he spoke.

Jessica interrupted. "My daddy wouldn't let me date until then. I was his baby, the third daughter."

"So how did you and Joshua meet?" Kolby asked, trying to camouflage the snarkiness in her voice by smiling more broadly at Larry.

Jessica looked at Larry. "What was it you said about him that one time?"

Larry grinned. "I told Jess he was all right for a college boy."

The two laughed and tilted their heads toward each other, lightly touching. They both lingered there a moment. Kolby felt as if she were at the third stool in the malt shop on a date with a couple of teenagers.

"For the longest time, he called me 'Sergeant Addison.'" As Jessica said "Sergeant Addison," she lowered her voice to sound like Joshua. Kolby giggled. "Okay, true story. I never expected to meet him. I figured the closest I'd get would be a next-of-kin identification in the morgue."

Kolby's eyes widened, and Larry gently nudged Jessica.

"Oh, sorry, cop humor."

Larry interjected, "It's how she copes with the stuff she sees. You get used to it after a while."

Jessica began again. "You know about the first assault, right?"

Kolby just nodded, with no idea what Jessica was talking about.

"That first assault in the parking lot, my deputy and I both thought Joshua was going to die. Kolby, I've seen…" She paused. "To this day, I don't know how or why he survived. And what that guy did to his dog was beyond words."

Kolby asked, "Rex?"

"Yes. So I met Joshua right after he regained consciousness in the hospital. He was out cold for three days." Jessica nodded and looked at Larry out of the corner of her eye. "He was just a nice guy, you know, the kind of guy you'd want to date your sister."

Larry teased her. "Not *your* sister."

Jessica replied, "No, you're right, not Justine."

Kolby noticed Jessica's body posture change as she began to speak again. The lighthearted, fun woman became more automated, professional, and less soft. She sounded rehearsed.

"He came out to the farm a couple of times, did some training with us, and worked with our teams. He was just a nice guy." Jessica paused and then added in a perfunctory manner, "And then on that day, when it happened..."

Kolby noticed her voice hesitate when she said "it."

"My dispatcher told me it was Joshua on the 911 call. I was prepared for the worst. I mean, hardly anyone survives the beating Joshua did the first time. And then to be staring down death a second time?"

Kolby was trying to process the words Jessica Addison was saying. Joshua had hinted that his scars had come from two assaults. Kolby tried to focus back on Jessica as she continued the story.

"And I kept hoping he would just stay out. But he ran in the chapel and told those kids to get down."

Kolby heard Addison became even more stoic.

"So when I got to the door, I knew those kids were in there with Joshua, and so..." She stopped. Her face was locked in a cool, calm expression, and she looked at both Larry and Kolby. Larry squeezed her hand. She nodded dismissively. "Well, we all know what happened."

Kolby's mind reeled. She understood that Jessica would be concerned about someone she knew in harm's way. But why was she so focused on Joshua? If she had fallen in love with Joshua, was she over him now? She tried to understand what "the kind of guy you'd want to date your sister" meant.

Sarah stepped up into the bus. "Kolby, we need to do the meet and greet. Can you be ready in five?"

Kolby replied, "Sure. Let me check my makeup." Then she turned to Jessica. "C'mon back. We can share some girl talk."

Sarah turned to Larry. "Hey, I'll show you the engine on this thing. You probably know a lot about diesel motors." The two stepped down and off the bus to explore. Jessica turned and followed Kolby to the rear of the bus, to the bedroom–dressing room. Kolby sat down, and Jessica made eye contact with her reflection in the mirror.

"This is a big night for the town," Jessica said. "We've had a hard time healing."

Kolby spoke as she added some eyebrow liner to her face. "Joshua won't talk to me about it."

Kolby noticed that Addison was moving and looking more like a cop than a fan. The protective and skeptical nature of her badge filled her mannerisms. Addison and Kolby looked at each other in the reflection.

"It was hard on everyone," the sergeant said. "I only did my part. What exactly did Josh tell you?"

Kolby had moved to lip liner, followed by a gloss coat. "Well, he didn't tell me much. I had to read it in that book, *Faith Shattered*."

Kolby glanced at a photo of Joshua, Fylgja, and herself at the cabin taped to the mirror. Addison's eyes followed her look.

"Nice photo. You two look very happy together."

Kolby whispered "thank you" and continued. "The book said he called 911 while running all across campus to find the class, and then, when the shooting started, Joshua was shot, and you came in and saved everyone's life. You are an American hero."

Addison stared at Kolby, then at the photo taped to her mirror. "Okay," Addison began, "this may be too in your face, but I don't know any other way but to be direct."

Kolby felt the tone of the conversation changing, set down the make-up, and turned around to look Jessica in the eye. "All right, shoot."

"Okay. I don't know what to think of this. I read the tabloids about people like you, and I don't know what's true and what isn't. I thought you were different, but I saw this today." Addison slipped her phone out of her purse and showed Kolby the link previewing *Garden Party* and Jeffrey Toomey's book. "I don't know what you said to Toomey, but you should never have talked with him. This jerk Toomey came around asking questions about a year ago, and I have no idea how he got this picture. At least Larry hasn't seen this yet."

Addison flipped the screen of the phone off and returned it to her purse. She followed with another interrogatory. "So what does this say about you? I know what it implies, and it makes me ask, what's your role in all this? Was I wrong about you? Does Toomey work for you or some publicity company you hire?" Addison raised both hands palm up as she asked the question. "Really, it's none of my business. I respect Josh. What you two do with your lives—well, that's between the two of you."

"Yes, it is," Kolby said with a slight defensiveness in her tone, then softened it with, "but that's not what you want to say, is it?"

"No, it isn't."

The two women squared off at each other. Kolby watched as Addison clenched her jaw.

"This is weird," said Addison. "Am I naive? I thought you were someone real. Is this some gimmick to sell records? You just make up a fake affair so you get on a bunch of magazine covers, and then what? Do you and Joshua just kiss and make up? Or what? Are you gonna say that Joshua has a problem and needs to be in rehab? Fans feel sorry for you, so they flock to your concerts? You may think this is a game, but real people with real families live here. Do you think it's fun to play in other people's lives?"

"Other people's lives? Look who's talking. I'm not gonna do this with you. I'm not gonna play pretend nice. I get it. You saved my husband's life. You came in with your guns blasting and killed the bad guy. Yes ma'am, for that, I am grateful. If not for you, I never would have met him."

Jessica set her jaw.

"But just because you saved his life does not give you the right to crawl into our marriage bed. You and Joshua share a secret, and neither of you will tell me what it is. So shame on you. Shame on your cheating heart."

"Shame on me? What are you saying? You think that I would leave Larry? For Joshua? He's your husband, and I have my own, thank you. Don't tell me you believe this crap Toomey sells."

The instinctive sheriff looked at the wedding ring on Kolby's left hand. Addison unfolded her arms from her chest and continued her interrogation without the rough edges in her voice. "I want you to tell me something." Addison looked down and gently turned her own wedding band and then looked at Kolby's left hand again. "Tell me, what were you thinking? I want to know what that ring on your hand meant when he gave it to you. Where is your faith?"

"This ring?" Kolby mirrored Addison's movement. Kolby wanted to lash out at Jessica's continued invasion into her life with Joshua. Instead, she imagined her mother scolding her, telling her to hold her tongue and resist the urge to tell Jessica Addison what she really felt and why she resented being accused.

Kolby looked at her ring. She looked at Jessica Addison. She remembered asking Joshua to marry her. Ruth 3:9. The world would see one of two *Garden Party* covers and would know that she and Joshua had split, that she made a mistake, that he had made a mistake. Then it hit her that in their separation, they had made the mistake. Even breaking apart, they were together. If Toomey was right, if she needed to leave Joshua before the magazine debuted, her time was limited. She turned the question back at Addison.

"I don't have to tell people like you and Larry what it meant. You know what it meant. Joshua tells me you two live it every day. Is that true? Do you still live what it means?" Kolby searched for guilt in the woman's face, but there was no guilt.

Jessica said, "For Larry and me, it meant no matter what, we stay together and work things through. Larry is the one for me. He is the half that makes me whole. He won't understand what all the attention is about over this photo. That's why I love him." Jessica Addison looked over her shoulder as if he were still in the front of the bus. "Do you love Joshua? Do you have any...idea ...what he would do for someone? What he would do for you?"

Kolby looked over at the photo on the mirror, peeled it from the tape, and held it in her lap. "I thought I did. I knew he was out there, and I refused to settle for anyone until I met him. And when I met him, I knew he was the one. And we got married." Kolby's voice changed as if she were trying to talk herself into it being a good idea. "Not wasting any time..." She laughed a nervous laugh. "Jumped right in... after only five months."

Jessica stood firm. This was her no-nonsense, law enforcement face. Then she opened her eyes wider in recognition. "You don't know, do you?" Addison put her hand to her mouth. "Joshua still hasn't told you, has he?"

"No, he hasn't. He won't. You are his secret, Jessica Addison. You. You are the secret my husband keeps." With her index finger, she pushed Jessica Addison on the shoulder. "Every day, I compete with his memory of what you did together, and I don't even know what that is. Jeffrey Toomey says either you two are sleeping together or that you're not telling us what happened in that chapel. Joshua says that I have to choose between the lady or the tiger. Shame on you."

"Kolby, Joshua and I are like blood brothers. How do I protect him and the people he loves? To do one betrays the other." Jessica Addison looked down, then at the photo Kolby held in her hand, and then back to the front of the bus. "Woman to woman, wife to wife, you deserve to know the truth."

"I always expect the truth, Jessica."

She faced Kolby, swallowed, and then extended her arms and took Kolby's hands in hers. "Kolby Rae, I have every one of your CDs. I've listened to every word in every song you ever wrote. I've listened when I was happy, when I was sad, when I was sober, and when I wasn't. I feel like I know you. Like I know your heart. Am I right about you?" She looked at Kolby, paused, and nodded her head. "If I know you…you know the truth already. You don't need me to tell you what you already know." The sheriff's sergeant nodded and ended with, "And you've known it since you married Joshua."

From the front of the bus, Sarah called out, "Hey, Kolby! C'mon, the crowd is getting edgy."

It was a few moments before the women walked out of the back. As they walked forward, Sarah could tell Kolby had retouched her makeup. "Everything okay?"

"Sure," Kolby said.

"Just girl talk," answered Jessica.

Jessica stepped down the stairs. Kolby turned one more time to Sarah, kissed her cheek, and whispered, "Sarah?" She drew a breath and looked up into the starry night through the open bus door. "I've been speeding into the dark of night, chasing the stars, running from my pain since I was seventeen years old. We can't run from this, Sarah. We've got to face it. Don't cancel the press event. Just let me have this show first, okay?"

The Grant's Hill hosts began showing visitors to the door, and when they had left, Kolby and the band made their way into the room. It was time for their private warm-up. By tradition, whoever began singing "Hallelujah" started with the "secret chord" verse, and after that, each musician was free to choose the verse he or she felt was most fitting.

Kolby nodded at Nils, who was standing on her left, and he began a quiet first "secret chord" verse. The singing went around the circle, and between each verse, they sang the hallelujahs. Kim sang the "baby, I've been here before" verse; Roberto sang about "moving in you and the holy dove."

After the hallelujahs, Kolby began to sing. With her verse, the band nodded with consensus:

:: Now maybe there's a God above ::

:: But all you ever learned from love ::

:: Is how to shoot at someone who outdrew you ::

:: And it's no complaint you hear tonight ::

:: And it's not some pilgrim who seen the light ::

:: It's a cold and it's a broken hallelujah ::

:: Hallelujah ::

Kolby began the preshow prayer. "Lord Jesus, please let us into your heavenly presence…" And then they all screamed very loudly, "As we all raise a little hell tonight!" The moment hung, and then they let go and walked out the door.

Sarah nodded at Kolby. "Sean is all set. The house is full." Sarah gave a forced smile and then continued, "Toomey is here. He brought a photographer. The pit in front of the stage is filled with cameras. It's everyone. They know there's an embargo until the end of the last song." Sarah pointed to her belt, two walkie-talkies dangling, along with her All Access laminate. "I can talk directly to Flanigan's team. Just in case." Sarah bit her lip and then asked, "Are you sure this is what you want to do? Do you want to talk to Joshua first?"

Kolby fought back a tear and held up her little finger. "I'm gonna sing you proud, baby sister. Pinkie swear."

Sarah stared, raised her hand, extended her pinkie, and said, "Pinkie swear."

Kolby Rae and the band took the stage set up in the large open field where the lost postal pilot, Arlen Rooney, landed his plane in 1931.

CHAPTER FIFTY-TWO

LIGHT A CANDLE FOR ROSE

FROM THE DARK STAGE MICROPHONE, Nils announced, "Ladies and gentlemen, please give a warm Grant's Hill welcome to Nashville recording artist Kolby Rae."

Roberto's rhythm guitar filled the impromptu amphitheater with a loud, driving Western swing rhythm as Kolby and the band kicked off with "Right-Hand Rover." She broke for just a moment before starting "I Think I'll Just Stay Here and Drink," the classic Merle Haggard song they sang during their midsummer's party. On the third chorus, Kolby stopped and pointed her microphone at the crowd, who all chanted the song's title. She finished the song, and the crowd gave themselves a powerful round of applause.

"Wow! Oh my goodness. You all came here to have fun tonight. Where's my GRITS at?"

The crowd cheered. Even in Grant's Hill, the GRITS screams overpowered the crowd. This was part of the Kolby Rae magic. They were here for a very solemn night, a time that President Matthew Rose called "a time to remember now that the rest of the world has forgotten."

But Kolby knew they needed to get the rowdy out of their system before she took the show slow.

"I love you, Kolby!" came a shout from a male freshman near the back of the audience.

"Oh, sugar, we love you, too."

Kim blew a kiss. Roberto wiggled his dark, bushy eyebrows and gestured with his right hand in the shape of a phone near his ear as he mouthed the words, "Call me," and pointed to the back row.

Kolby looked out and around the stage and crowd. Joshua stood to stage right with two Flanigan men. In the front row, stage left, stood Jessica and Larry Addison. Kolby and the band jacked up Grant's Hill for nearly an hour with a rowdy country twang.

Realizing she was there to bring them all together, she tossed out a one-liner. "You know what? When I look at everyone tonight, you all are the best-dressed crowd we've ever played for. Tweed and blue jeans always belong together." And that tipped the town and gown crowd into a roaring, self-congratulatory ovation.

Most of the faculty had brought lawn chairs but quickly learned they wouldn't be using them because everyone spent the concert on their feet. Sean had told Ellen and David Adams to be as close to the soundboard as possible to get the best audio mix along with an unobstructed view of the stage.

Sean seemed nonchalant, and David Adams looked questioningly at Ellen several times throughout the show. Graham and Rob at the other control boards moved sliders, adjusted knobs, and stared intently at their monitors while Sean sipped from a large fountain drink and checked his smartphone, tapping replies to messages during much of the performance.

"This is what we invested in?" David asked Ellen.

"Sh-h-h-h" was all Ellen replied.

David was about to say something to Sean when the tall younger Adams looked up, switched off his phone, slid it into his jacket pocket, and began to pace, ever so slightly, back and forth. Ellen looked over, recognizing the like-father-like-son habit. Then, for a reason unclear to his father, Sean walked up to the soundboard and reached into each ear, took out foam earplugs, and then placed a pair of headphones on his head. He stood focused on the board, adjusting a few sliders and pushing a few buttons, and a computer monitor began displaying multiple waveforms of recording channels. The waveforms continued even as Kolby left the stage.

An impressed David Adams turned to Ellen. "I guess it's showtime."

President Matthew Rose and his wife were standing with several of the trustees near the back of the crowd, nodding and waving to students, parents, and faculty.

Kolby had used the left side of the stage for all her entrances and exits, but following "Tequila Temptress," she stepped off to stage right. She searched for Joshua. There were thirty-two bars of instrumental but enough time to find him. He wasn't there. She turned around and looked a second and third time. Then she saw him in the Grant's Hill varsity jacket and an All Access laminate walking toward her. It reminded her of the Heartland Benefit Concert.

There were eight bars left. Roberto looked right and then raised his guitar head, cuing the band so that at the end of the thirty-two-bar break, they replayed an extra eight-bar refrain.

Joshua looked at Kolby, dressed in what she called her skinny jeans and a short-cropped top that exposed her belly button. The jeans showed so much of her hips, Joshua wondered if they would stay on.

"You look great," he said.

"Joshua, I did what you asked me to do for you. I met Larry and Jessica. They're nice people."

Joshua sighed, then unsnapped the front of his varsity jacket and held it out for her to take and put on for the band's closing number. She shook her head. "No." She pushed the jacket back at him.

They studied each other's faces for a clue to the other's feelings. Seeing none in his, Kolby turned around and said, "Do it this way."

He lifted the jacket, draped it around her shoulders, and touched her cheek.

"And what will you say to Toomey?"

The band ended, the crowd applauded, and Kolby didn't answer. Instead, she blew him a kiss and took the stage. The crowd erupted seeing their own school colors on the star. Kolby sat with her twelve-string guitar on her lap, the microphone nearly touching her lips, and the crowd quieted.

"This next song..." She looked up and out. "This next song was brought to me by my sister, Sarah Miles. She had most of it written, and she asked me for my help. We drove out to our momma and daddy's grave and sat there all afternoon talking about life and drinking wine, and we wrote this together. I want to share this with you tonight as we remember."

Kolby began strumming the guitar, and Kim's cello played a mournful melody.

Kolby closed her eyes and sang:

:: I lay some flowers on my daddy's grave, ::

:: When I saw her, two stones down. ::

:: She shared a smile and a friendly wave ::

:: And said, "Girl, I've seen you around." ::

:: She said, "I come here every day ::

:: You see it's…just my way, ::

:: Not a day goes by, ::

:: I don't miss her eyes, ::

:: So I come here to sit and pray." ::

:: (and I) ::

:: Light a candle for Rose ::

:: Let it light up the night ::

:: Let it burn true and bright ::

:: Light a candle for Rose ::

:: The woman's hair was silver grey ::

:: Her wrinkles, clearly earned. ::

:: Her voice was soft; her patient eyes ::

:: Shined as bright as the candle burned. ::

:: She said, "You should have heard Rose play guitar ::

:: You should have watched Rose dance. ::

:: And she'd always cook a meal for you ::

:: If you gave her half a chance." ::

:: (So I) ::

F.R. "Fritz" Nordengren

:: Light a candle for Rose ::

:: Let it light up the night ::

:: Let it burn true and bright ::

:: Light a candle for Rose ::

:: "The winter of eighty-three was cruel ::

:: Cancer came to visit Rose that year ::

:: Her hair was gone, her breast was too ::

:: She so inspired me, living life without fear. ::

:: We ate our dinners by a candle's glow ::

:: We made angels in the snow ::

:: She played me every song she knew… ::

(SPOKEN – The Kolby Rae Whisper)

:: And the end came all too soon… ::

(SILENCE)

:: The doctors told me that I couldn't come in ::

:: I lost her hand at the hospital door ::

:: They told me, "Only family and next of kin." ::

:: And I cried and said, "I'm so much more." ::

:: See in those days, they shunned us away ::

:: Nobody saw us as we were ::

:: Two young women so in love ::

:: To us, married in every way ::

:: (So I) ::

:: Light a candle for Rose ::

:: Let it light up the night ::

:: Let it burn true and bright ::

:: Light a candle for Rose ::

When they came to the final chorus, Kolby, Kim, and Nils sang:

:: Light a candle for Rose ::

:: Let it light up the night ::

:: Let it burn true and bright ::

:: Light a candle for Rose ::

The song faded out, leaving Kolby alone, center stage, finger-picking the guitar and leaning into the trademark Kolby Rae whisper. Sean Adams had every breath, every note, every subtle moment captured.

As Kolby sang and played, Kim, Sarah, Roberto, and Skeeter walked to the stage wings, picked up baskets of vigil candles, walked down the stage steps past the men in EVENT SECURITY T-shirts, and moved through the crowd handing the candles to the concertgoers.

They had reworked the arrangement. Kolby made a four-bar pause at the end of each chorus, and during the pause, Nils spoke a name, the name of each of the victims of the Grant's Hill Eastford Chapel shooting. And after each name, Kolby repeated the "Light a Candle for Rose" chorus.

"Shelly Parmar," Nils announced.

:: Light a candle for Rose ::

:: Let it light up the night ::

:: Let it burn true and bright ::

:: Light a candle for Rose ::

"Connor Westwood."

:: Light a candle for Rose ::

:: Let it light up the night ::

:: Let it burn true and bright ::

:: Light a candle for Rose ::

"Tamara Banner."

:: Light a candle for Rose ::

:: Let it light up the night ::

:: Let it burn true and bright ::

:: Light a candle for Rose ::

After the three student names, Kolby set the twelve-string aside and sang an a cappella chorus. Len "Over" Kiff, the backline tech, came from stage left and stood close to Kolby to block any breeze as he lit the candle she was holding. The yellow flame brightened her face, and the stage lights dimmed even lower.

:: Light a candle for Rose ::

:: Let it light up the night ::

:: Let it burn true and bright ::

:: Light a candle for Rose ::

As Kolby walked to the far stage left, Nils read the final name. "Olivia Olsson."

Kolby knelt down and lit the candle in Jessica Addison's hand. Jessica turned and lit Larry's candle. Larry in turn passed the flame, and one by one, a single ribbon of new flames wove through the rows, each candle illuminating another face.

The line of candles reached the back of the audience where a single-file line of student volunteers and alumni had gathered to pass the flame from one to another until they reached the base of the new Eastford Chapel spire. At the base of the scaffolding, the flame was passed from student to student, higher and higher, until it reached the unlit eternal flame. The final candle touched the base, and the flame came to life.

The silent crowd turned back to the front of the stage as Kolby made a large circle with her candle and blew it out, and as if they had rehearsed, everyone in the crowd blew out his or her candle, too. The space they shared was dark and quiet as new light shined over Grant's

Hill and glowed above the crowd.

Kolby touched two fingers to her lips, made a fist, touched her heart, and then extended her palm and pointed to the sky.

Larry Addison was gently holding Jessica as she sobbed for the first time about the shooting. After two years, it finally came out. She sobbed in his arms, shaking. Tears fell from his own eyes as well, and he whispered, "I love you," over and over.

President Matthew Rose stood with a respectful expression, wholly unaware that he clutched his wife's hand with such a forceful grip, the diamond of her wedding ring cut into the skin of his palm.

Joshua stood stage right. He was standing strong and very courageous, just as his mother had told him to do many years ago. He knew it wouldn't last. Kolby, too, was strong. She walked offstage in silence. There was no applause, no cheering, just a reverent quiet.

Kolby held it all in until she reached the privacy behind the stack of equipment next to the stage, and they both began to tremble. They touched, first with both hands, as timidly as the first time they had undressed each other. Joshua stepped closer, and they both began to sob. She pressed herself to him and felt safe in his embrace. Both their chests were pounding together.

And then it began. A deafening and thunderous applause from the crowd—a holy hallelujah. It went on for a minute. And then another. And then the two thousand invited guests of Grant's Hill College—students, townies, and alumni—began to chant, "Kolby! Kolby! Kolby!"

Kolby stood there, unable to move. They called her name fourteen times before she finally took the stage. A follow spot picked her up stage right and kept a tight focus as she crossed the stage and stopped in front of the microphone. She stood there, wearing the black and white Grant's Hill varsity jacket. And then crowd cheered even louder, standing on their feet. Kolby stood humbly in the spotlight glow, trying not to worry about the mascara running down her cheeks.

When the roar began to soften, she slowly wrapped her left hand around the microphone and looked out at the standing ovation.

"Ladies and gentlemen, thank you so much." The applause built again and then quieted. "It has been our pleasure to perform here for you on this very special night." As she said the word "our," the band stepped together behind her in a line, their arms wrapped around each other, with Sarah Miles in the middle, fighting back tears.

"There is someone I want to introduce to you, and there are so many words I could say to tell you about him." Kolby looked out into the crowd, smiling and making eye contact with as many of the fans as she could. "But the three words that say it all...the three words that I'm proud to say to you tonight...I'm his wife....Please welcome my husband and your friend...Joshua Stone."

And the crowd exploded a second time.

Kolby looked to the wing, and he stood, shaking his head no. She gestured, pointing at herself, then forming the fingers of her hand to make the now-familiar three and nine.

Joshua stepped onstage, and the crowd's cheers grew louder. He walked toward her, seeing only her outline in the glow, lost in the awesome sound. As Kolby took Joshua's hand, he leaned in and kissed her cheek.

CHAPTER FIFTY-THREE

HOUSE LIGHTS UP

DOWN IN THE PIT AT the front of the stage, Jeffrey Toomey was next to his photographer, who had broken Sarah's press embargo and was shooting photos. A Flanigan team was moving across the row of fans when Sarah waved them off, shaking her head from the stage.

Through her tears, all the while holding Joshua's hand, Kolby said, "Ladies and gentlemen, I need to make another introduction. Please join me in welcoming to the stage a pair of American heroes. He grows the food we eat, and she saves lives. Please welcome my friends and heroes, Larry and Jessica Addison."

The Flanigan team cleared a path to the stage as the spotlights lit up the Addisons holding hands and climbing the stairs. They paused at the top as Kolby and Joshua extended their arms. Then Larry and Jessica crossed the stage, and the two couples embraced, the two men slapping each other on the back, the women kissing cheeks and holding hands.

Kolby turned one more time to the audience. "Please forgive us. We're about to turn our backs to you and pose for a photo. We don't mean to be rude because we want each and every one of you to be in our photo with us."

The audience cheered. The freshman men started chanting, "Grant's Hill! Grant's Hill! Grant's Hill! Grant's Hill!"

Sarah looked at her watch. The photo embargo was officially lifted, and the press began moving in the pits, turning on cameras, taking pictures and video.

Kolby turned back to the microphone. She quieted the crowd. Sarah looked at her with   puzzled concern. Joshua watched out of the corner of his eye.

"I'm going to get in huge trouble for doing this because I shouldn't tell his secret."

Jessica quickly snapped her head and looked at Joshua. Joshua stepped back, unsure what to do or say. Larry Addison, still caught up in the excitement, grinned and looked out at the crowd.

"But this man is just so special to me, and he's done what no one knows, and it's not right that tonight of all nights..." Kolby's voice caught on the edge of a tear. "It's not right that we don't let the world know what he did."

Toomey was tapping his photographer on the shoulder, urging him to keep shooting.

"You all deserve to know the truth." Kolby looked out into the crowd. She waited as they quieted, taking deep, slow breaths. She felt her chest pounding. In the quiet after singing her song, the single spotlight reminded her of the trouble light hanging from the hood of the truck her daddy was fixing the night she fell, the night she was burned. The light was just out of her reach. She felt a twinge of phantom pain. She heard Toomey's warning, "You are almost there. Don't repeat the past. Don't get it right just to get it all wrong again."

The audience quieted. Kolby made her final decision and looked to Sarah and Joshua. Recreating the silent auction vote they had done the night the house in Crossings was robbed, Kolby first looked to Sarah. Sarah paused, then nodded.

Kolby turned next to Joshua. He pursed his lips and nodded, too.

"Before tonight, there was never a chance for me to meet this woman, Sergeant Jessica Addison, and thank her for saving the lives of the students and saving the life of my husband. She's a strong woman." Kolby took Jessica's hand and raised it above both of their heads. "Loyal, faithful, and, oh my God, the fact that we all are here tonight is all because of her."

Kolby lowered their hands and clasped the microphone. "But also because of the actions of one man." Kolby looked around the stage, pausing at Joshua, and then around the fans on the grass. "One man who would prefer we don't know all the truth of what he did."

She timed the pause just right. "That man is Jeffrey Toomey. You know him as the journalist, but what you don't know is…how hard he worked to reunite my husband with the woman who saved his life. They've not seen each other for nearly two years. And then how hard he worked to be sure that their reunion and this new Grant's Hill chapel was featured in *Garden Party*."

The audience cheered.

"Tooms will hate me for telling you all this, but he deserves to be seen by each of you as the man he truly is. Jeffrey Toomey is donating one hundred percent of the proceeds of his book *Stone Unturned* to the Grant's Hill scholarship fund, creating a scholarship in the English program in my husband's name, the Joshua Stone American Story Scholarship. So please help us thank him. Stand with us and be a part of our photo because you all are gonna be on the cover of *Garden Party* next month."

The freshmen men began their chant again. "Grant's Hill! Grant's Hill! Grant's Hill! Grant's Hill!" A beach ball bounced across the audience and onto the stage. Joshua looked as if he was starstruck and blind. Toomey's face looked as if he felt the weight of the short but mighty girl's shoe heel on his foot. He winced as she said the phrase "donating one hundred percent of the proceeds."

"So thank him, won't you? Tooms, I know you're out there. Come on up and join us onstage right now. We want you to pose with the Addisons and the Stones. We are all one big Grant's Hill family tonight."

Toomey was reaching for his phone when his hands were grasped by two of Flanigan's men. "Mr. Toomey, play nice. We're going onstage." The balding member of the Flanigan team took Toomey's phone and slid it into his own jacket pocket. "I'm sorry you misplaced your phone, sir. Perhaps it will be in the lost and found tomorrow."

They turned to Toomey's photographer. "Make sure you get plenty of photos. Your boss will be mad if you don't have these on the wire before those guys over there. You don't want to be scooped on your own cover story."

They pointed at the other photographers, who were busy shooting images and transmitting photos to the wire services via their laptops.

Sarah Miles counted at least three cameras live-streaming the video to the Internet.

Jessica and Joshua stared at each other, still dazed by the crowd sounds and blinded by the lights.

Toomey was escorted to the stage, looking the part of the celebrity surrounded by the Flanigan security detail. He stood between Kolby and Jessica. Kolby's arm reached around his waist.

Sarah Miles stepped up with her finger crooked in an imaginary pinkie swear. She looked at Kolby. Kolby raised her pinkie as well. Sarah took a photo from Nils's riser and then nodded. The Flanigan detail allowed the press also to come up to Nils's riser and take their photos. In a few minutes, the digital world had a truth: that Jeffrey Toomey made it possible to reunite long-separated heroes, that Kolby Rae was proud to be Joshua's wife, and the Addisons, Stones, and Jeffery Toomey were all one big, happy family giving money to support Grant's Hill students.

Later that year, the world learned the final truth of that night: the live recording of "Light a Candle for Rose" would be the first Grammy nomination for Kolby Rae and Sarah Miles as songwriters and Sean Adams as engineer.

PART TEN
THE ROAD HOME

Chapter Fifty-Four

Home

THEY WERE DRIVING IN A convoy, the bus with the trailer and the right-hand Rover behind, when Joshua's phone lit up and began to ring. The caller ID displayed FORREST.

Joshua answered. "Hey, Forrest. How's life, and why are you calling me at four in the morning?"

"Doc-tor Stone, how are you on this fine, fine morning?"

"Well, I guess I'm pretty good." Joshua thought about the last two nights, the last year, and the last two years and then looked over at Kolby sleeping. "You know what, Forrest? I'm great. I'm really, really great."

"Well then, you are about to be doubly lucky, my friend. Guess what Rooster and I found? Your thing. You know, the top-secret thing, from the place? The memorabilia? We found it, just like you described."

Joshua sat forward in the seat. "No way. You found it?"

"Yep, color, size, even the markings. It's the real deal."

"Forrest, really? Where is it? When can I drive down and see it?"

"Well, I'm sitting in your garage right now looking at it."

"What? You're in my garage? At four in the morning?"

"Yeah. You know, those cheap remote controls don't offer much security. Rooster is here with me."

Rooster's muffled voice shouted, "Hi Joshua!"

"Where is our security detail?"

"Oh, they're here right now. They have us on your special list. They let us right in. One of 'em's playing with the scoop on the skid steer — city guy, you know. Said he never drove one before."

Joshua looked again at Kolby. He lowered his voice. "Look, you guys gotta help me out. Can you cover it with something, a tarp or a blanket? Kolby and I are about an hour away."

"Oh, no worries, Doc-tor Stone. I know how women are. She is not going to be happy when she hears I spent your whole budget on this one piece. Don't you worry. We'll cover it up."

Joshua hung up, and as he did, Kolby opened her eyes and looked at him. "Do you know how handsome you are to me, Joshua Stone?"

He smiled.

"Who was on the phone?"

"Forrest and Rooster. They wanted to know when we were coming back."

"Where are we?"

"Maybe an hour from home."

Kolby raised her head from the pillow she had propped against the Rover door. "You said 'home.' I like the way it sounds when you say it."

"You want to sleep more?"

She sat up, yawned, and reached back and scratched Fylgja's ears. "No, I'm awake." She stared out the side window and then at the bus and trailer ahead of them. "You know, I thought when you didn't come with us that we were over."

Joshua sighed. "When I saw the look in your face, I thought so, too. So how did you decide what to do? How did you decide to bring Jessica and Larry onstage and then Toomey?"

"I told Jessica about what you said, the lady or the tiger. Jessica told me I already knew the truth. She said you were the kind of guy she'd want to date her sister."

"I don't know her sister, and I don't know if that's a compliment. But Jessica and I never…"

"Joshua, I know. Once I met her and Larry, I knew. So I figured maybe if I let the tiger out of his cage, he might just eat himself instead of you."

They were both quiet; then Kolby continued. "But Joshua…she was with you at the single most important moment of your life. How do I compete with that? I'm just Kolby Ruth Miles from Tremont, Mississippi."

"You're teasing me, right? Now you're making fun of me. You're Kolby Rae. Hello? Kolby Rae?

"So you'd never heard of me when we met?"

"You'd never heard of me."

"I didn't know your name, Joshua Stone, but I'd heard of you. And Sergeant Jessica." She noticed Joshua look over and smirk. "What?"

He shook his head. "Nothing," he said and then started laughing.

"What are you laughing at?" She reached over and flipped his rearview mirror toward her to see if there was something on her face or if her makeup had smeared.

"Nothing. It's just that you're kinda funny when you're pissed at me."

"I am not," she protested.

"Yes, you are."

They both smirked.

Joshua tried to imitate her. "When you said, 'Little badge-wearing hottie'…I mean, c'mon, it was kinda funny." He laughed even louder.

When he began laughing harder, Kolby began double-slapping him. He put his arm up in mock defense, and Fylgja barked twice.

"But okay, I'm trying to be serious. I've never been anything to anyone," she whispered.

"Are you kidding? You're TheRealKolbyRae. Think about Deena, that woman you gave front row seats to. Think about that little boy with the hearing aids. Think about that whole lawn full of people tonight. Oh my. What you can do just by being you."

"But that's just it. Kolby Rae is something to those people. I've been a daughter, and I've been Kolby Rae."

Joshua listened and then asked, "What about me? I've been a son and Professor Stone, and now I'm your husband."

Kolby stretched and then sat taller in the seat, turning her body to face Joshua. "What does that mean?"

"I don't know. I have no idea. I'm hoping you'll show me what that means to you." He reached over and took her hand in his.

"I will, Joshua Stone. I will. Know what else? I told all those people tonight the truth, that I'm your wife. Will you show me what that means to you?"

"I will. We'll take this road together. We'll find our way."

As they drove through the gate and rolled up the driveway, the bus turned on the circle loop and slowed to a stop. Joshua stopped on the bend instead of driving to the garage. Kolby raised up from the seat and said, "Are you going to park out here?"

"I thought maybe we'd invite the band in. You know, for a night-cap?"

She looked at her watch. "Joshua Stone, it's five in the morning."

"Okay then, an eye-opener."

One by one, the sleepy band and crew stepped off the bus and grouped near the Rover. Joshua invited them in.

Nils spoke first. "Hey, how about an old-school garage party? We'll grab some drinks, make a little breakfast."

Kim nudged Skeeter as Joshua wrapped his arm around Kolby's waist.

They all walked across the driveway to the garage. Joshua entered the code on the door-opening keypad. The light came on. The door raised and came to a stop. The band started through the space to move into the kitchen when Kolby stopped them all.

"Wait, this is not how I left the garage." She pointed at the shape covered by a mover's tarp in the back corner. "That's new. What is that?"

The band gathered closer, and Joshua stepped in front of them. "I guess you're all wondering why I've called you here today," began Joshua.

"You promised drinks," Roberto said with a yawn.

"And breakfast," Nils added.

"Well, yes, I did. But first, I want to say to each of you that what you did for Grant's Hill means a lot to me." The group nodded. "I want you to know how great it is to be a part of this…" Joshua looked at Sarah, then Kolby, then each of them. "This family."

"Joshua, please. You're going to make Roberto cry."

"Okay, but, okay. I know you all know about Kolby. Hell, you've known her forever."

Roberto grinned. "Yeah, Joshua, and for the right amount of money, we can tell you all about her."

Sarah slugged Roberto.

"Roberto, thanks but there's no rush," said Joshua. "We've got a whole lifetime together for me to learn about her." As he said that, he looked down and twisted the wedding band on his hand. Out of the corner of his eye, he watched Kolby do the same thing.

"So. This." Joshua pointed to the moving tarp. "This is a gift for Kolby. When we got married, I never found the right gift for my new wife."

"That's not true. You gave me your mother's pearls."

"Yes, I did, but this is something more, a little more rare. So, well, Kolby, this is for you."

Joshua reached for the tarp and gave it a pull. The tarp fell to the floor, revealing an old red metal, standing tool chest. It had twenty-one drawers. The band paused, then giggled until they saw Kolby's hand cover her mouth. She began to shake, looking at Joshua, then Sarah, then back at the tool chest.

In a quivering whisper, she said, "Daddy's tools?" Joshua stood silently next to the red box, and she slowly stepped forward and ran her hand over the smooth surface. She counted down three drawers, pulled it open, and counted over three wrenches. "Three-eighths inch," she said.

Joshua knelt down, gently pulled the rolling chest away from the wall, and turned the back to face Kolby. Etched in the paint in a young girl's handwriting were the words *Miles, 1991*. Sarah began pressing her lips together tightly to fight back the tears.

"Joshua, how did you find it?"

Forrest stepped out of the house and into the garage. "Well, he had some help, little lady." Forrest was holding a twelve-pack of beer and began passing out bottles. Rooster, behind him, had an open bottle of bourbon and a stack of paper cups. Sarah began taking pictures with her phone.

Kolby wrapped her arms around Joshua. "I can't believe you…you did this. For me?"

Joshua pulled her closer. "I knew I had to do it. I got the idea the first night you told me the story. I wanted to find it and give it back to you. It belongs to you."

Kim chimed in. "Joshua, seriously, this is the coolest thing ever. But still, you don't give your wife tools on her wedding day."

Kolby laughed as she wiped away a tear, mascara running across her cheek. "Well, he always told me he was awkward with women."

Joshua wrapped his arms around Kolby, swaying, and then in a loud whisper loud enough for everyone to hear, he began to recite a lyric:

"And in good times and sad times, we'll find a way
But that doesn't mean I won't call you just to say"

Kim joined his speaking voice on the chorus, harmonizing:

:: Dance with me, Daddy, let me dance on your shoes ::

:: Twirl me around and chase away my blues ::

Nils, Roberto, and Skeeter joined in:

:: I'm your angel, your princess, your daughter, your light ::

:: Dance with me, Daddy....dance with me tonight. ::

ACKNOWLEDGEMENTS

This book is a work of fiction but does make fair use reference to public celebrities, places, and events to enhance the sense of realism. The characters are fictional and any similarities to real persons, living or dead, is coincidence.

Except from *Death in the Baltic: the sinking of the Wilhelm Gustloff* Copyright © 2013 Cathryn J. Prince used by permission of the author.

HALLELUJAH Written by: Leonard Cohen © 1985 Sony/ATV Music Publishing LLC. All rights administered by Sony/ATV Music Publishing LLC, 8 Music Square West, Nashville, TN 37203. All rights reserved. Used by permission.

Excerpt of Ernest Hemingway's Nobel prize acceptance speech. Copyright © 1954 The Nobel Foundation. The text is published in its entirety on:
http://www.nobelprize.org/nobel_prizes/literature/laureates/1954/hemingway-speech.html
As the Laureate was unable to be present at the Nobel Banquet at the City Hall in Stockholm, December 10, 1954, the speech was read by John C. Cabot, United States Ambassador to Sweden.

Chapter 22, "Steam" is inspired by the short story of the same title, Copyright © 2013 F.R. "Fritz" Nordengren, first published in ABATON, Des Moines University, Fall 2013.

Ring Out, Wild Bells. Published in 1850. By Alfred Tennyson The work is in the public domain.

Special thanks for Russ Kendall of Gusto Wood Fire Pizza for his inspiration and use of his company name in the text.

If you are interest in staying at Two Mile Ranch Iowa Writer's Retreat, visit www.twomileranch.com

A special note of thanks to the members of the RoadieJobs.com event production network forum for their insight and help into the backline world of touring musicians. Without them, this book and the music tours we love as fans would not be possible.

Finally thank you to Courtney Tompkins, PR and marketing guru, and Eve Flanigan, my editor, friend, and confidant. Both of whom make my publishing life easier. They do the behind the scenes work that brings the characters and books to your bookstores.

CONCEALED

The Book of Joshua

A NOVEL

F. R. "Fritz"Nordengren

FIRST CHAPTER EXCERPT FROM

CONCEALED

THE BOOK OF JOSHUA

The original story of Joshua Stone

Available online and in bookstores.

CHAPTER 1

THE ATTACK

THREE FLOORS ABOVE THE NORTHWEST parking lot at Grant's Hill College, Professor Joshua Stone glanced around his office and skimmed over the papers on his desk before turning off the lights. It was a few minutes after 6 p.m. and he had just finished teaching his last class of the week. On his way out the door, he flipped the brim of a bobble head doll near his computer and then closed the door behind him. The other offices in the building were dark, as typical for a November Friday on campus.

Just as the faculty offices in the Quad were known for their predictably quiet Friday nights, Professor Stone was known around campus for his predictably classic, if not cliché, wardrobe. His common uniform included a simple knit tie with a blue oxford weave shirt and a muted tone corduroy jacket. He dressed the part of a college professor. While his students' clothes would go out of style, along with their music, a college yearbook photograph of Professor Stone from 1998 and 2008 and today would look remarkably similar and yet, never unfashionable.

Even though his wardrobe was predictable, there were changes this term. He had struggled that morning as he fastened the grey flannel trousers in his bedroom. He had difficulty making the button meet in the center. He drew in a breath and tried a second time, and buttoned them around his waist. As he wrapped the belt through the loops, he realized it fastened one notch farther out to the end than last season. With a look in the mirror he had sighed, hoping the rest of the clothes in the winter garment bag would be more forgiving.

As Joshua continued down the stairs, he paused on the second floor. Liv Olsson's office was on this floor. She was the Director of Academic Counseling. Just last week, she had been taking a walk and told him it was only coincidence that she walked by his house. Neither of them believed it was just that, but he made them both some fresh coffee and they sat on his front steps.

That day was the closest they had come to a kiss. As awkward moments go, neither of them felt awkward; it was just a kiss that didn't happen. One in a continuing series of missed moments.

As he reached the first floor, and made his way outside, he passed the Skeppshult Swedish touring bicycle he rode to campus each day. He began to cross the mostly vacant parking lot to the West.

Then he noticed the smell. At first, just a whiff and then a powerful, disgusting, strange odor. He had never smelled anything like it. He walked towards the source, the space between the parking lot and the church next door to campus. That was when he saw the smoldering pile at the end of the median along the edge of the parking lot. It didn't look like much of a fire; it seemed more like the remnants of a Halloween prank.

Halfway across the parking lot, he passed the emergency beacon. The automatic alarm was one of a series of solar-powered call boxes placed around the campus. Each had a distinctive bright blue pole with a small canopy light and stenciled word EMERGENCY. The idea was like a fire alarm: breaking the glass in the alarm box, and then pressing a button the size of a silver dollar generated an emergency alarm in the Grant's Hill Sheriff's dispatch center.

As he approached a car parked on the church side of the parking lot, he felt as if he was wholly surrounded by evil and fear. It wasn't a ghost-stories-around-the-summer-campfire fear. It wasn't the kind of fictional fear he had shared with his students as they explored the novels of the twentieth century. This was an overpowering, guttural, end-of-life fear. The air turned to ice; he was unable to catch his breath. The hair stood on the back of his neck. The professor had written that phrase in a few of his novels, but had never experienced the feeling first hand. Then his head pounded as if he had smacked it into an overhead beam and in his last conscious thought, he realized that something big had hit him.

His beating was severe. After the initial incapacitating blow, his face was slammed twice into the trunk lid of the parked car. He hit with enough force to dent and deform the sheet steel. As his body slumped to the ground, he was repeatedly kicked in the chest, kicked in the head and kicked in the back and pelvis.

Joshua, unconscious, dreaming. He was falling, faster and farther, deeper and darker. In his unconsciousness, he didn't feel his wallet being taken from his jacket pocket. He didn't feel his feet slip out of his shoes. He didn't see the face of his attacker.

In between the skull linings protecting Joshua's brain, a very tiny blood vessel was leaking. His body's initial response was to get more oxygen to his brain and other organs. His heart rate sped up, his breathing sped up. His heart and lungs could only do so much, the trauma was too severe. He would not recover without help.

He wasn't conscious to see his attacker turn the red can over his fetal-positioned body. The tiny bit of gasoline in the can dribbled onto his blood stained jacket. He wasn't able to watch him strike a match, smile and toss it onto the jacket where it slowly burned itself out before it had a chance to ignite the fabric.

Professor Joshua Stone was left there to die. Given the time of night and the day of week, it would be hours before he would be discovered...

CONCEALED IS AVAILABLE ONLINE AND IN BOOK STORES.

About the Author

F.R. "Fritz" Nordengren writes at Two Mile Ranch. This is is second novel. His first book, *Concealed: The Book of Joshua* was an Amazon and Nook best seller. When he isn't writing or tending to animals at the ranch, he's traveling. He's visited 19 countries and recently walked the Camino de Santiago trail in Spain.

About Two Mile Ranch

If you enjoyed this book, we would appreciate your willingness to mention it to friends who might also enjoy it. If you are active on-line at Facebook, Goodreads, Amazon, Library Thing, Shelfari, and similar sites, we ask that you share your thoughts with other readers about this book. Your reviews help readers and all indie authors.

Two Mile Ranch is home to the Iowa Writer's Retreat. For more information, about staying at Two Mile to work on your own creative projects look for us at www.TwoMileRanch.com, as well as our Facebook page:

www.Facebook.com/TwoMileRanch

www.ingramcontent.com/pod-product-compliance
Lightning Source LLC
Chambersburg PA
CBHW071152020726
47502CB00002B/379